DOG PEOPLE

DOG PEOPLE

A NOVEL BY CRIS MAZZA

COFFEE HOUSE PRESS | MINNEAPOLIS

Acknowledgments are made to the following publications, in which por-
tions of this novel first appeared: *Notre Dame Review, 13th Moon, Nebraska
Review, Western Humanities Review, Disturbed Guillotine, Rockhurst Review, Crab Orchard Review, Third Word, Cups, Another Chicago Magazine,*
and *spelunker flophouse.*

Note: This is a work of fiction. Any resemblance to actual persons, living
or dead, is purely coincidental.

Coffee House Press is supported in part by a grant provided by the
Minnesota State Arts Board, through an appropriation by the Minnesota
State Legislature, and by a grant from the National Endowment for the
Arts, a federal agency. Additional support has been provided by the Lila
Wallace-Reader's Digest Fund; The McKnight Foundation; Lannan Foun-
dation; Butler Family Foundation; Target Stores, Dayton's, and Mervyn's
by the Dayton Hudson Foundation; General Mills Foundation; St. Paul
Companies; Honeywell Foundation; Star Tribune/Cowles Media
Company; The James R. Thorpe Foundation; Dain Bosworth Founda-
tion; Schwegman, Lundberg, Woessner & Kluth, P.A.; Beverly J. and John
A. Rollwagen Fund of The Minneapolis Foundation; and The Andrew W.
Mellon Foundation.

Coffee House Press books are available to the trade through our primary
distributor, Consortium Book Sales & Distribution, 1045 Westgate Drive,
St. Paul, MN 55114. For personal orders, catalogs, or other information,
write to: Coffee House Press, 27 North Fourth Street, Suite 400,
Minneapolis, MN 55401.

Library of Congess CIP Data
Mazza, Cris.
  Dog people : a novel / by Cris Mazza.
      p.   cm.
  ISBN 1-56689-055-1 (alk. paper)
  I. Title
PS3563.A988D64   1997
813'.54—dc21   96-54051 CIP

10   9   8   7   6   5   4   3   2   1

Table of Contents

with love and admiration for

Tara
Arcwood Scarlett O'Tara UD

Bizzy
Lobo Dell The Seduction O'Tara UD

Vixen
O.T.Ch O'Tara Strike Up The Band UDX

———————————

Thanks, Diane, for your heartfelt support of Fanny,
our imaginary friend.

———————————

and a note to all my friends, acquaintances, and
fellow dog sports enthusiasts:

Yes, I know no one would attempt to create a hybrid or any new breed
—with or without a wolf—
and then expect to show it in Schutzhund or any
other organized kennel club dog sport.
This is fiction!

Before getting into bed, after walking across the hardwood floor in her bare feet, Fanny paused on the mattress on hands and knees, brushing the soles of her feet together to remove dust and dog hair. One time Morgan stood in the bedroom doorway with his toothbrush in his mouth and said, "I'm going to bed with a cricket." In his underwear, with his thin legs and slightly rounded stomach, he didn't look much like a dancer.

He was over thirty-five, contracted by the Lorenz Studio Dance Company, never more than background—the *corps*—and he freelanced in the ensembles of musical theater. So far he hadn't even considered teaching or choreography or direction.

They'd met in college: Fanny, studying interior design, and Morgan, a graduate student in dance. Since the days of her school design projects, she had only completed one limited-budget job—she'd done over the interior of the little house they rented. She could dimly recall the vigor of that single miraculous day of endless energy. But then she'd stopped designing, except on paper, and at that hadn't even used a page in a sketchbook or tablet for . . . how long? She'd lost track. She'd waitressed through college and still worked for any one of five or six restaurants and caterers when they had someone out sick. She called waitressing the habit she got paid for.

Her husky slept outside, locked in a run along the side of the house, beside the bedroom. It was an early summer night, about 2:30 A.M., and the dog was going crazy, not only barking and growling, but tearing at the wire of the dog run with her front feet, spewing gravel as she ran back and forth, then she stopped for a long howl. "Maybe we'd better check," Fanny mumbled.

Morgan didn't respond. The dog was berserk.

"Come on, Morgan."

"Okay."

Morgan stayed in the kitchen doorway while Fanny went across the dark patio and opened the door of the dog run. The husky immediately charged across the lawn toward the darkest spot in the yard, under the tangerine tree. Fanny ran back toward the kitchen door, heard the brief spurt of a growling ruckus under the tree, then the dog flew past into the house. A second later, the wall of skunk odor arrived.

"Shut the door!" she screamed.

"Oh god, the dog."

Fanny found the dog rubbing herself on the sofa in the living room, held her still, and burrowed her nose into the dog's fur. Just dog smell. "She managed to avoid it!" Only a little scent lingered in the kitchen. "Look!" Fanny cupped her eyes against the window in the kitchen door. Then she opened the door softly. "Come on, Morgan."

They stood on the porch hugging their arms and watched the skunk amble across the lawn. His hair glistened, blew slightly in the breeze. Everything was quiet and cool. The odor had drifted off, leaving a musky scent of pollen from the petunias and the acrid smell of citrus. Sometimes the yard smelled of steer manure, which Fanny worked into the soil, but Morgan had complained about the stink and didn't want her using it while they'd had their house guest, Renee, who'd just moved to town after being contracted as a principal by the dance company. The garden hadn't been mulched for a month and a half. Renee had stayed for three weeks before finding her own apartment but still called daily and dropped by several times a week.

Fanny wanted to hold the skunk, to push her hands into the long, silky black-and-white hair and feel the cool pointed snout exploring her neck. She'd sat out here with Renee two or three nights ago, while Morgan was at rehearsal for a summer musical. She'd stared at Renee's huge oblique eyes while Renee looked at the dark flower beds, and she'd been astonished but not surprised when Renee took her hand and held it for a second. Hugging a man was like patting a dog, substantial and firm, not breakable. But a woman felt fragile, not secure, too delicate to be much comfort.

"I'm going back to bed," Morgan said softly. Fanny followed him inside. The dog was already lying on the floor, half under the bed.

"Morgan?"

"What."

"Have you ever hugged a woman?"

He sat down on the mattress. Then they looked at each other and laughed. Maybe everything that was or wasn't happening, everything that had been disintegrating while they pretended not to notice, was clear as ice for one second.

They slept as usual, not neatly cupped together, but more like squids, tangled in the sheets. And, as usual, didn't dare try to touch each other any other way.

After finding a rattlesnake in his living room, a coyote standing next to his mailbox, nothing else would surprise him. But Scott still said his springer spaniel, Sadie, must be barking at ghosts when she would bolt upright in bed somewhere between midnight and five and growl at the sliding glass window. He thought if he got up and took her outside, she'd find there was nothing and go back to sleep. It didn't work. She paced back and forth beside the hedge, sticking her nose in, snuffling, then woofing. She scattered leaves all over and tore little pieces of the branches off. Suzanne would kill Sadie if she tore up the landscaping.

"It's rats," Suzanne said. "Call an exterminator." She hadn't moved, but he knew she was a light sleeper. The dog growled low in her throat. "Do something, Scott, I've got to get some sleep."

Scott pulled on a pair of pants and slipped his bare feet into tennis shoes. He went to get a sweatshirt out of the closet, then came back for the dog.

"I heard the closet," Suzanne said, without opening her eyes. "Did you shut it?"

"Go back to sleep. I'm taking Sadie to the park to run her."

"Now?"

"Why *not* now? Why should I do the same thing at the same time every day?"

"What's that supposed to mean?"

"Just go back to sleep."

The park was three blocks away. Streetlights marked the perimeter, mostly lighting the sidewalk that meandered around the edge, but toward the middle it was so dark, all he could see was the white parts of the dog—her four feet, her neck, and the patches on her sides. She ran with her head low to the ground, disappearing into bushes, then bursting out again. She came back periodically to jump against him, leaving large wet paw prints on his sweatshirt. He sat on the swing set and watched his dog weaving in and out among the eucalyptus trees. He should've been tired—like Suzanne, he had to get up at five, his catering business didn't run by itself—but he suddenly felt a weird exuberance, a vague superiority, and a bizarre sense of belonging to something new, even if it only turned out to be an ability to join the chitchat conversations of his temporary employees. One of the waitresses he sometimes hired had been talking to another waitress as they set up tables before guests arrived for a party, hoarsely describing how she'd taken her dog to the beach and how it had disappeared chasing birds, charged right into the water even though it was a husky, not a water dog, then came back twenty minutes later with a piece of someone's boogie board in its mouth. Another time, the girl said, she'd been making Mexican food at 10:00 P.M. when she heard something banging on the wall of the house outside, so she went to see what the dog was doing, and it had been digging in some bushes, gotten into a sleeping wasp nest, and had been stung all over, making its whole head swell up, eyes shut, lips puffed out and hanging like a hound dog's. "But by one in the morning she felt well enough to eat soggy tacos and watch MTV with us," the girl said. By the time she'd finished her stories, she'd been telling them to him rather than the other waitress. He hadn't wanted to believe he was envious, but he'd felt odd and said something stupid: that he supposed he'd been missing something, never having eaten tacos after midnight. He'd never heard anyone talk so fast except his busboys. He'd never heard anyone talk so fast to *him*.

If she were with him, right now, she wouldn't be talking fast. He'd only hired her a few times recently, but he easily pictured her face in the dark, her eyes sharp and her nostrils flared slightly, her chin up, as though she could hear and smell what dogs sensed.

The chain on the swing set rattled when he got up. He whistled for his dog and she came quickly, her tongue flapping out the side of her mouth. For some reason, he didn't say anything to her. He dried her carefully in the garage, then took her quietly back into the bedroom.

Suzanne was snoring softly, stopped when the dog jumped onto the bed, then began again after Scott held the dog still for a few moments. The three of them lay and slept as they had for over five years, the dog in the middle. Scott and Suzanne never once, even by accident, touched each other.

I saw the husky bitch for the first time that afternoon. So it wasn't just the coyotes keeping me awake. Every time I closed my eyes, I saw the husky hit the chain-link fence, climb six feet, and dislodge her tennis ball that had stuck in the wire.

The coyotes that night were like an omen.

There must've been eight or ten, anywhere from right outside my bedroom window to a block away. Perhaps trotting en masse down the pavement like a street gang claiming turf. Coyotes in the city weren't unusual, but not an every-night thing, far from it. My old German Shepherd, Bruno, didn't so much as stir on his rug beside me. Maybe his hearing was slipping. But mine wasn't. I'd been keen as radar all afternoon, unable to shut it off. I got out of bed and pulled on the first pair of shorts and T-shirt I found on the floor. Bruno lifted his head, then got up and walked behind me through the kitchen and out the back door. The moon wasn't full. Almost every house had some sort of bright porch light. The coyotes sang louder and faster, perhaps at the moment of a kill, *Yi-yi-yi-yi-yi-yooowwww*. Bruno didn't care, just sniffed a spot on the lawn, it was *me* getting all stimulated. Chills crackled on my spine and tears stung my eyes. More than jazzed, though, I think I still had the same goose bumps I'd had in the park while watching the husky hit the fence . . . prickling me all over again that night in my own yard.

I'd been in the park almost exactly twelve hours ago, about 1:00 P.M., Bruno's regular training session. He had no interest in the other dog, had immediately taken advantage of the break in my attention, lay down with his chin on his tracking dummy, closed his eyes. So I left him there and followed the husky toward the girl throwing the tennis ball. She'd already thrown it again, far up an embankment of ice plant, and her dog was up there frantically scenting in circles, locating the ball, returning with not only the ball but a stringer of ice plant in her mouth.

"Sorry, am I bothering your training?" the girl said, grabbing for her husky's collar. She practically had to throw herself on top of the dog to get her to lie down.

I guess I forgot propriety, no introduction, just: "Is this a bitch? Is she intact?"

"Are you from animal control?" she asked.

I couldn't remember if I'd been smiling or talking too forcefully or simply staring at the bitch, who lay panting on the ground, her ice blue eyes fastened on her ball. "Sorry, no. Doreen Connor. Trainer. I've been looking all over for a bitch like this."

The girl glanced at Bruno. "Why?"

"Don't you realize what you've got here?"

"She's an unholy terror. If I don't exercise her, she tears up the yard."

Exactly! "Do you show her?"

The girl smiled and her face relaxed. "Oh, you're a dog person. I thought maybe that was a police dog you were training."

"Schutzhund."

"I've heard of that. Yeah, she's been shown. The breeder I got her from wanted to show her, but I decided not to keep sending her out."

"Why?"

"Too aggressive, too wild. Unpredictable. She was excused once for knocking the judge over when he tried to bait her."

"That's *perfect.*" My voice leapt a pitch every time my heart sped up. "What you call unpredictable are probably her natural drives. Ever consider showing her in Schutzhund?"

"The AKC doesn't recognize Schutzhund."

God. "The AKC doesn't care what being a dog *means,*" I pointed out. These attitudes *kill* me, but I can be patient. "Didn't they penalize your dog just for showing true canine behavior? Have they ever seen the chase instinct she's got, her *prey drive?* They don't care about that. Does the Miss America contest care if *you* . . . I don't know, what's some sort of *human* instinct they would count against you?" Hypothetical question, of course. But she answered:

"Craving sex?" The girl had a nervous laugh.

Who cares. I was just staring at the husky. "I want this bitch."

"Well . . ."

"I mean for breeding. I want one of her puppies."

"Well . . . um . . . with a German shepherd?"

"No, not him." I knelt beside the husky. The dog's blue eyes still never left her tennis ball. "Bruno's only average, at best. Got all his titles, but he's not exceptional. I know what I need to create the perfect Schutzhund dog—the perfect breed of dog, *period.* I need your bitch."

"And what stud?"

I touched the tennis ball between the husky's feet with a single finger. The bitch closed her mouth, flattened her ears, growled almost inaudibly until I removed my finger. "A wolf," I said softly.

The coyotes had been silent for several minutes. Their cries had cut off abruptly. Bruno went back into the house through his dog door. But I went farther into the yard, off the patio, and out where the grass was not directly hit by an electric light. Two eyes glowed through the backyard fence. God, I could hear my heart beat. My armpits were wet. The hair on my neck felt brittle. I blinked tears from my eyes. The coyote glanced at me, then turned his back, walked away, turned again and sat, stared at me, then walked slowly between some tumbleweeds. No need for hostility because he wasn't afraid. Bold yet aloof toward anyone outside his pack; confident always; able to use aggression when necessary for his own benefit or protection, but not out of fear or nervousness; devoted to his pack; full of spirit and power, always alert, courageous, and keen. Why shouldn't *I* be the one to put those desirable canine qualities back into the domestic dog? Add those things to the good-natured loyalty of a family pet. Sure, people bred wolves, but not with any informed mission to *accomplish* anything. Why shouldn't I be known as the one who finally created the perfect breed? I had gotten the girl's phone number on a piece of paper, with the name "Fanny." At that point, I couldn't remember if it was the girl's name or the dog's. It didn't matter much.

She'd finished three squares for her new afghan: yellow, orange, and red. Scott's only comment had been, "Who's going to get *that* one?"

The afghans collected dog hair and you could never get it out. She'd had to give three to the Salvation Army. Two were so bad she'd thrown them away. Now she donated most of them to the rest home where she was the receptionist. That's what Scott's question meant, but she actually never knew who got which afghan. She never went into the patients' rooms. Her desk was by the front door. She came in the front door and went out the front door.

At first she'd been able to sleep when Scott began taking the dog out for midnight walks. But then she'd found it more and more difficult, the second, third, fourth times. When Scott and the dog came back, the dog would be panting hard enough to fill the room with dog breath, and Scott would probably be coated with a thin film of sweat, like a glaze of oil on water. She would feel him sit on his side of the bed and take off his pants and shoes and socks, but not the damp underwear and undershirt. Then he would get under the covers and instantly lie still, and soon after that begin to breathe deeply, hoarsely. The sweat would soak into the sheets or dry on his skin and get sticky. Maybe that was one reason she couldn't sleep. Suzanne couldn't get comfortable if her skin touched any other skin, even her own. It felt gluey. Before bed, she powdered her underarms, the backs of her knees, the insides of her elbows, and the insides of her thighs.

She slipped out of bed and straightened the covers. It was two-thirty. He'd left about four minutes ago. She filled the tub with hot water, turned on the whirlpool jets, hung her nightie on a hook, stepped out of her slippers and straight into the bath. Before sitting down in the swirling water, she took her cap off a hook and eased it gently over her hair.

She used to use the shower exclusively—hadn't ever, even once, sat down in a bathtub for over thirty years, from the time she was ten until three years ago, when Scott had the whirlpool tub installed. Taking a regular bath was like sitting in a stagnant pool of her own dirt. Before using the whirlpool, she usually took a shower, but it was okay now because she'd showered at eight before going to bed.

Maybe next time she would go with him. Put on jeans and a cozy turtleneck sweater, her leather walking shoes, tuck a handkerchief in her pocket so he could wipe the sweat from his neck before they sat on a bench under a shadowy streetlight, and she could lay her head on his shoulder. If she shivered just slightly, he might put his arm around her, knowing her that well. She would close her eyes, then open them again when she heard the footsteps—but neither she nor Scott would move when whoever it was he might have been meeting in the park after midnight twice a week would come into the circle of light and stare in hurt surprise, seeing that Scott and Suzanne had been together for over twenty years and had the kind of love only time can ripen. Her scrubbed, pale little face would fall, her shining eyes would understand everything instantly, and she would turn and run back into the darkness until her footsteps and breathing were lost in the sounds of the dog rustling in the bushes, digging for mice and chasing rabbits.

The dog barely acknowledged Morgan when he got home. But if he went outside and threw a ball, the dog went nuts, couldn't get enough of him. Fanny once said, "If you want her to be excited when you come home, bring a live grasshopper and drop it on the floor when you come through the door."

He'd asked, "Would a cockroach do?"

Fanny was already in bed, maybe asleep. He closed the bedroom door softly without looking at the bed, held the door firmly against the doorjamb until he heard the click. Otherwise the door would slowly swing back open and bang against the wall and Fanny would cry out, "What?"

It was close to 2:00 A.M. He used to have to call if he was going to be home later than ten-thirty because Fanny might be planning supper. She also said if he was late she immediately assumed he'd been squashed in the street like a stray cat. But after the scene the day Renee found her own place, they'd set new ground rules: Fanny wouldn't expect to always go with him every time he went out after a gig, and he wouldn't have to call home if he was going out. He wouldn't have to tell her what every phone call was about. The same went for her, of course.

He got a glass of milk and a bag of chips, squatted in front of the TV and began flipping through the channels. Too late for any sports roundup; the news was long finished. He found an obscure Clark Gable film. Clark Gable didn't even have a mustache. He kept the sound low so Fanny wouldn't wake up. Even though the characters were very excited about something, it seemed as if they were whispering because it was so quiet everywhere, except for the swishy sounds outside—branches against the house, leaves in the gutter, and a sound like his mother used to make through an empty cardboard paper towel tube, *hoo-hoo.* The dog barked in the run, which was right next to the bedroom, so he got up and went out to get her or she'd wake Fanny. But Fanny was standing in the bedroom doorway when he came back in. She was wearing one of his old shirts, the tips of the tails touching her knees. "Didja hear the owl?" she said. "Pretty neat, huh?"

"Yeah. You can go back to bed, she won't bark anymore."

Fanny yawned and stretched, bracing herself in the doorway and contorting her body. "Okay. I made pudding. It's pretty horrible, but it's in there if you want it."

When she turned back toward the bed, he closed the door, almost catching the dog's nose. The owl called and the dog growled in her chest. Morgan rapped her muzzle.

Morgan returned to the flickering blue light in front of the TV. He inserted his hand carefully into the bag of chips to keep the cellophane from rattling. Clark Gable came through a front door. A woman in a frilly, off-the-shoulder gown stood up from the sofa to take his overcoat, then they sat down together and she poured him tea. No one could accuse Morgan of wanting *that* when he got home. But he *could* imagine other ways to come home. He and Fanny could arrive at the same time, but in different vehicles. Maybe she would've been doing last-minute set adjustments at the Broadway Playhouse and he would've had a dress rehearsal at the Civic Theater. She would sit on the sofa with a beer and he'd show her a move the choreographer had changed in the finale at the last minute. Behind her huge dark eyes, focused intently on him, he'd know ideas were forming, growing, taking shape, until she leapt up and cleared away some furniture and . . . No, that wasn't Fanny. That was Renee. Several times while Renee had been staying with them, she'd come out from her evening exercises and had ended up brainstorming a routine with him. Fanny would make soggy cinnamon popcorn or melt down chocolate chips as dip for overripe strawberries. She'd suck on a wine cooler and watch MTV. Renee kept turning the sound down because she was dancing to a different melody in her head, humming it even though she couldn't carry a tune. But Morgan knew Fanny was also watching them as he and Renee worked. Once she'd said she was going to bed and Renee said, "No, stay and help, we need your input."

"Be our mirror," Morgan had said, followed by a moment of weird silence, until, thankfully, Renee started humming tunelessly again. That had been just a day or two after the outburst.

The whole thing had come dangerously close to not happening at all, until Fanny finally decided not to go along when he and Renee went to look at an apartment Renee was considering. After seeing the apartment, they'd run a few errands, so it was later than expected when they returned. As they pulled up in front of the house, Renee was telling Morgan about a woman who'd answered her personal ad, but she was sure it was a straight woman who either wanted to prove her own hipness or satisfy some buried curiosity or get someone else's goat by playing in taboo territory without really going in all the way. She was comparing for him the woman who'd answered her ad to first meetings with *other* women who eventually became lovers. "I can practically smell the difference," Renee had said, which Morgan asked her to explain, but she said it was an instinct that couldn't be articulated because words were a rational language, not intuitive. They'd stayed in the car by the curb to finish this conversation, rather than interrupt it—probably never to be resumed—by getting out, gathering their packages, and going inside. The sun was just down. He could tell the light was on in his living-room window. Periodically as they sat there and talked, he had seen the mini blinds pulled apart, creating a wider band of light. He couldn't see into the room but knew Fanny was there, checking, probably wondering why they didn't come in. The band of light appeared more and more often, and stayed longer, but it didn't make him restless or want to go in quicker. He imagined that Fanny could see the intensity of their conversation—maybe she counted the seconds in the long pauses when Renee sat looking out the windshield before turning to him urgently again. He'd been hungry and getting a little chilly but, buzzed with adrenaline, he'd also wished the conversation could go on all night. He'd felt ignited over and over by the band of light, the shape of a long slanted eye, as Fanny parted the mini blinds to watch them. When they finally decided to go inside, Morgan discovered he had an erection.

Fanny had been grim and quiet for an hour, then moments after Renee went out again, she'd said, "Don't ever do that in front of me again."

His whole body had trembled almost violently. Then the heated, even tearful discussion resulting in new ground rules.

But they hadn't actually discussed him and Renee. Obviously Fanny hadn't known that he'd seen her watching them.

Now he had another erection. Staring at the TV without knowing what he was seeing, he drained the rest of the milk from his glass while his other hand went to his zipper. The owl called again, farther away.

For her nighttime routines, Renee used continuous New Age music. The volume never tipped over mezzo forte, the tempo never faster than allegro moderato, and that not often. The best parts were a shimmering smear of blending tones, the proper mood for the full, fluid use of her body. There was a time when she would've used these late hours of the day to make love, possibly with the same music but adding candles in beer bottles, bowls of tangerine segments and red grapes within easy reach, and chocolate kisses—only a few—to be sucked from her partner's body slowly, the small chocolate point barely showing, like a second clitoris, sipped and nipped at languidly, to make it last. That had been Kay's idea. But Renee had been alone for three years now, since she'd turned twenty-one. Without a lover, without the chocolate kisses, but not without herself, so she hadn't lost anything important, she didn't need a therapist to tell her so—and how many times had she said that to weeping friends who were unable to find meaning in their lives without a lover to show them their value? Renee had told Fanny, when they went out for a late-night supper the other night, that she'd conquered The Beast—being alone. After all, the hours spent alone are the most important to a dancer's life, time that was hers, no one else's. Time to enjoy, not just an obligation. That's why she'd been able to leave her teachers and immediately dance lead parts in companies all over the country. That's why she'd won international contests. That's why she had her position as a principal in the Lorenz Studio Dance Company.

Sweat ran down her temples, down her neck, between her breasts. Her leotard grew dark patches.

A cat fight outside rose over the music, then dipped behind again. Listening closely, Renee could hear the moaning growls of the cats, a prelude to the next screaming flurry of claws and teeth. Dogs all over the neighborhood began to bark.

It was a relief to be in her own place now, without Fanny's dog always tearing around, chasing something: birds rustling in the trees at night, lizards that had scuttled under a planter hours before, a cat sitting tantalizingly on the other side of the fence. But it had been good to live with them for a while, to feel other lives and rhythms weaving in and out around hers. Fanny would often come home from a waitressing job during Renee's nighttime routine, so when Renee came out of the spare room in her wet leotard, a towel around her neck, Fanny and Morgan might be frying donuts or making Chinese food or smoking a bong and watching a stand-up comic on TV. Morgan usually lay on the floor, Fanny in an old armchair with her legs hanging over one arm. Renee often sat on the sofa where she could glance at the TV occasionally but also see the TV reflected in the dark window behind Fanny's chair, letting her eyes slide over Fanny's pert profile, the scattering of freckles across her nose, her almost pointed ears, her hair the color of straw but the texture of downy feathers, her large mouth with small teeth that flashed when she laughed. Fanny could draw her brows down and make her mouth a straight line and look almost scary, despite the freckles and fly-away hair that looked as if it was cut with a bowl. And she could also suddenly seem abnormally shy, her greenish eyes darting around, her cheeks slightly flushed, her nostrils seemingly becoming translucent.

The feline moaning began to grow again, a dissonant, clashing wail. Renee continued her mixture of ballet, yoga, and gymnast's stretches. When the cats lashed back into their screaming rage, the audience of dogs resumed barking. The spitting screech sounded like skin and hair flying, eyes slashed out of sockets, soft kittens being cut to bloody pieces. Renee shut her eyes and felt the muscles of her thigh contract and relax against her cheek as she flexed her pointed toe forward then back.

A few times, because it was cooler, Renee had used Fanny's studio, working on a mat on the floor between three desks. During the stand-up part of her routine with her heel on one of the desks, she'd paused to look through a sketchbook and found room plans and furniture designs, although she hadn't noticed Fanny spending any time in the studio. When she asked about it, Fanny said she hadn't done anything new for a long time, she wasn't sure why, that the drive had left her. Some of the rooms in the drawings were all shades of blues and grays, some earth tones, some surreal and garish with tall purple palm trees in the corners, a yellow lounge chair shaped like a v so a person sitting there would have her feet over her head, windows shaped as triangles or lopsided rectangles.

At dinner the other night, Renee had told Fanny that she should stop waitressing and work more on her furniture and room designs. Fanny shrugged. "We need the money."

Renee had ordered meatball soup. Fanny said the one huge meatball looked like a bull testicle. Renee ignored that remark. She tried to remember everything they'd talked about, from Fanny's description of being let go from a waitressing job because she didn't smile enough . . . to Renee's anger at her brother for giving her a nightgown for Christmas last year. From the college drama director who had rejected Fanny's set designs because everything had to be a primary color . . . to Renee's early attempts to persuade the artistic director to feature her as prima soloist in every number for a series of divertissements. They shared a chocolate mousse for dessert. While Fanny talked, she'd carefully shaved the pudding with her spoon in an upward motion until her side looked like Half Dome, then she suddenly plunged in and ate several whole spoonfuls. The waiter kept filling their coffee cups. Fanny's fingers were trembling. The next time the waiter came back, Fanny switched to decaf. They sat quietly looking around for a while. Suddenly Fanny said a strange thing. "I wish," she'd said, "that I would stop handling everything so well. I wish I would just go ahead and fall to the floor, twitching and foaming at the mouth."

Suddenly Renee was holding Fanny's hand and saying she felt very close to her, but Fanny seemed barely able to meet her eyes.

The cat fight snapped off abruptly, creating silence like an echo slapping down the street, but the dogs in the background continued barking a few moments longer. Renee lay flat on the floor until they stopped, then got up to peel off her soaked leotard.

Traffic in his residential neighborhood was still just a whisper when Scott left at five forty-five in the morning, but at six, at his catering business downtown, taxi horns, jackhammers, buses, trash trucks, police loudspeakers, and boom boxes were revving up. He parked in the alley behind one of his trucks and went up to the second floor, where his offices and kitchen were located above a bakery. Already the sweet smell of breads was thick like dust. It was Wednesday. Midweek parties weren't often fancy, didn't usually require waiters and waitresses or bartenders. But Wednesday was also the day that advance preparation started for weekend bashes, especially weddings. They made the cakes on Wednesday, prepared and packed the table settings, double-checked with the liquor wholesaler, and made sure all the supplementary waitresses and busboys were still free and knew where to go. Scott had two full-time cooks, two full-time drivers for deliveries and errands, his secretary, and a general assistant who did a little of everything. The two cooks had overlapping shifts, and one was already clanging pots in the kitchen.

He had three hours in the morning to get organized and think clearly before Mexican music started in the bakery downstairs, the smell of meatballs simmered in the air, the phone screamed, and both cooks began slamming and clattering and clanking every metal utensil in the kitchen. Mornings were quiet enough, despite the street noise, that he could hear the rats and mice that—despite exterminators—preyed on any food supply not locked in refrigerator or freezer.

Scott propped his head up with his hands and closed his eyes. He tried to concentrate on hearing himself breathe, imagining the cool breezes that spring up then die a minute later in the predawn park. He'd gone out with Sadie again last night. He knew the dog was forming a bad habit, but something made him willing—almost eager—to be awakened after half a night's sleep to swish through the dewy grass in canvas shoes, sit on top of a slide, and even let the dog chase him in the dark from one side of the park to the other. By the time he got home, he only had an hour or two before he would have to get up again, but he slept better in that time than in the hours before the dog woke him. Throughout the day he found himself thinking of simple details—the delicate sound of twigs snapping; the crunch of the play area's damp sand under his feet; the pounding of his heart, ringing in his ears, and trembling in his legs after he'd loped across the grass several times; the surreal feeling that he could probably run forever without dropping. As though he once again had a twenty-year-old's one-track mind, except that instead of sex, he was daydreaming of visiting the park after midnight. When he imagined someone else there with him, it wasn't for a tumble on the grass or a blow job on the swingset. It was her hushed laughter that answered his like a dialogue. It was a vague wisdom in her smile, and a clear look of admiration in her eyes.

He had to call waitresses today, and he'd put her name first on the list but knew he would call two or three others before calling her.

He got up to check the rat traps. All six were full, four of the rats still alive. He used sticky traps because he didn't want to catch one of the resident stray cats. Scott watched a rat weakly try to eat the bait even as it lay mired in the glue. He had to kill the living rats with a shovel, appalled every time at how many times a man had to pound a wounded rat with all his strength before it died.

After he washed his hands, he went to the big calendar on the wall with all the jobs color coded for type of service. He checked, calculating quickly to make sure he'd planned enough extra help. The jobs were listed in more detail in his ledger calendar. Five years ago, when he'd had to hire the second cook and buy another truck, he'd decided to stop expanding the business. "No more building," he'd told Suzanne. "From now on, we glide under our momentum." Scott could not recall anything particularly exciting that had occurred since that decision.

But this was exactly the business he'd planned when he was seventeen, the only taxi driver in Big Elm, Nebraska. The dispatcher—the cab's owner—also owned the laundromat and took calls for the taxi there. Rather than a luxury, the taxi was mostly used by poor people outside of town who had no vehicle and needed to get to work or to buy groceries. Every day he picked up a hot dinner from the diner on Main Street and brought it two blocks down and one over on Apple Street to a weathered two-story house with paint peeling from its gingerbread trim. He took the food to the front door, rang the bell, then went on inside. The rooms were dim and musty; years of dust choking the colorless, overstuffed Depression-era furniture; the windows too clouded to let in much light, even if the heavy rotting draperies had been pulled aside; the carpet worn shiny in the middle. At a large, darkly varnished, scratched up table, one place setting was always laid out. White china with a barely visible blue pattern of flowers that had been fading away under years of hot water and scrubbing. Tarnished silverware and clouded, cut crystal water glass. Scott would arrange the food he'd brought onto the plate—a piece of meatloaf, mashed potato and peas, or two pieces of roasted chicken, stuffing, and green beans. Then carefully covered everything with the linen napkin that was folded at the side of the plate. Before leaving he took his tip, always a quarter, from under the place mat.

As soon as he'd saved a thousand dollars from his taxi job, Scott left for California to start his own business. He'd planned on enough money to live in refined style and to travel abroad to unusual places, but not so much he would have to kill himself to get it. And he'd felt lucky to find a wife who wanted the same things. It wasn't even the grandest of dreams, he admitted. But it had plateaued five years ago, before he'd reached forty.

He shook his head and muttered, "What's next?" looking at his desktop: last week's invoices needing to be entered, phone messages to be answered, bills to be paid, collections to be made . . . and the list of waitresses.

The morning light was shadowy brown. It would be cool blue if the bedspread and curtains were blue, liquid green if they were green. Right now the plants, crowded together on the old trunk in the corner and hanging from the ceiling, were black. The philodendron had thin arms and large hands, partially covering the black-and-white still life photos Fanny had done in college. The plywood chest of drawers had been given to them by Fanny's mother, who had used it for thirty years in her own home. It had been painted green once, then black, then antiqued in reddish brown and light tan to look like wood. The bookcase headboard had been left behind by the former tenant. It didn't attach to the bed frame and rattled against the wall if either Fanny or Morgan turned over in bed too heavily.

She'd loved the room the day she'd arranged it, called it her ground-floor attic garret. It had seemed a place of cool, rumpled, sensual comfort. But, for too long now—maybe since the morning after doing it—it had just looked like junk. Fanny, lying in bed at this early hour, had repainted the bedroom in her head a hundred times, moved the jungle of dusty plants outside to the patio, reframed the pictures in thin silver metal, replaced the musty curtains with white or light gray vertical blinds, junked the mismatched furniture and arranged new white, red, or gray pieces of her own clean, simple, yet asymmetrical design. But the gutted and refurbished room in her head still had the same two people lying in the bed. What was the use?

She closed her eyes and remembered when Renee had first arrived: a pillow under one arm, duffel bag slung around her shoulder, she'd looked around the crowded house—the other rooms furnished similarly, with wooden crates and plants and bricks-n-boards—and said, "So you're an interior decorator."

"Interior *designer.*" Fanny answered. She had not smiled. It had not been her idea to have Renee as a guest. They'd bought an air mattress for Renee to sleep on, put it in the extra room where, years ago, Fanny had mounted barres on one wall. But any dance-related activity Morgan had done at home since the year-of-no-work had been in the living room with the TV on. That year was two years ago now. They'd spent an evening telling Renee about it, how the dance company claimed insolvency, let all the dancers' contracts expire, then proceeded to bring in Martha Graham, the Dance Troop of Harlem, and the Moscow Ballet for one-time performances. Renee was mostly interested in the negotiations, the Chapter Eleven threat, the grievances filed, the arbitrators, the press conferences. Morgan spoke sardonically about picketing in leotards, how the Harlem dancers picketed with them for an hour before their show, the programs that the locked-out dancers had attempted to produce on their own. Fanny slipped in details about picking up weekly boxes of government surplus food—five-pound blocks of processed cheese, a pound of rice, five pounds of flour—the committees for helping other dance families with yard work, fixing plumbing, electrical repair, and giving each other haircuts; doubling her waitressing to pay the rent and utilities; the emergency fund dipped into by greedy soloists who then found work in other companies and never paid it back; the mistrust if someone showed up to picket in new Reeboks; the phone tree calling to inform them of any new rumor of a development; coming home after midnight and sitting for an hour in her studio—not too tired to hold a pencil, but eventually not picking one up anyway.

"Is that when you stopped designing?" Renee had asked. Fanny had not answered. She didn't tell Renee how she had sat beside Morgan watching TV without seeing anything, thinking over and over, *No one's going to take care of us, no one will take care of us, we're on our own,* not daring to say "How can they do this?" one more time because Morgan had begged: *Please,* can we not talk about it for one evening, just one?

"It's not as though we were out on the street or wearing rags and down to our last dollar," she finally said to Renee, "but it was the cold hard fact that they could win. They could squeeze us and win."

"No," Renee had said. "Not if you fight. They can dissolve the company, lock you out, terminate all future series, but they *can't* take away what you are, they can't prevent you from being what you *are.* And it was certainly no excuse for *you* to quit."

Fanny had looked at Renee, her huge oval eyes and small cheekbones, her dark serious mouth, her black hair practically standing on end like a fire, and a light behind her face that always made anyone uncomfortable or on edge or hyperactive or ready to pounce—the type of girl who everyone falls in love with, one way or another.

"You weren't there," Fanny had said dully. "You wouldn't understand."

Morgan was slouched back on the sofa, smiling weirdly, his eyes moving from Fanny to Renee and back again.

"I understand the choice we make when we decide to be dancers," Renee said. "We *choose* to struggle. We choose to work our bodies raw for the art, and work the rest of ourselves raw *not* just to *survive* but for the respect and recognition we deserve."

"She's so young," Morgan had said, with the same smile. Renee shot him a zinger of a look.

"Morgan and I were robbed," Fanny had said. "It wasn't very long after we'd moved in. Before we got Lacy. We were sleeping, and there was all this noise in the living room. When I got up to check, I opened the bedroom door and heard huge footsteps run away through the kitchen. Someone had been there taking our house apart, stacking our stuff in the middle of the floor, packing it up to take it away. Like that was just their job, to undo other people's houses and pack up their stuff and take it for themselves."

"Our crummy stuff," Morgan said.

"But *ours*—what made them think they could just see someone else's stuff and decide to move everything around, rip everything apart, and then just *take* it?"

Renee was staring at the television, a news teaser showing a brush fire. She was sitting on the coffee table.

"Morgan and I," Fanny continued, "couldn't sleep the rest of the night, of course, but we couldn't do anything else either. We couldn't even put our stuff away. In fact, it might've taken weeks, maybe months, before everything got picked up and put back. But that night, especially, everything just sat there on the floor and we sat on the couch staring at it . . . and listening listening listening. We could probably hear each other's hearts going like rabbits. Not because we were too tired. Oh, we were *mad* too. But how could we fight back? We couldn't. We were totally helpless." She was still talking to the back of Renee's head. There was a moment of silence, except the television, music, and credits rolling, then Renee turned her fierce soft eyes back to Fanny.

"Anyway," Fanny had continued, "I just realized *that's* what the lock-out felt like, like sitting there the night we were robbed, only it took longer, lasted a whole year."

"I'd be more mad at *myself* for *ever* thinking I was helpless," Renee said.

"Maybe I was," Fanny had said softly.

"I was only scared because I can't *do* anything else," Morgan said.

"What would *ever* make you think you should do anything *else?*" Renee shot at him. "With an attitude like that, you *deserve* to lose your right to be a dancer."

Morgan exhaled with a little laugh. "What made me deserve to be a dancer in the first place?"

Renee swiveled around on the coffee table so she was facing Morgan, knee to knee. "Look, Morgan, you overcame all the odds. You went to that dumpy state school, had teachers who were barely more than weekend square dancers, and you rose above them, you went farther than anyone with your training could be expected to go. Something drove you, you must've had *something.*"

Morgan hadn't answered. He'd just stared back at Renee's face as though hypnotized.

Fanny rolled over carefully so she wouldn't rattle the headboard. She stared into her open closet, where all her clothes looked dark brown. She could almost smell the thick damp odor of the pile of dirty clothes on the floor, almost see the colors of her shirts hanging in a row, almost taste the clouds of dust behind her tennis shoes and sandals. She had a vague notion of what Morgan wanted, but wasn't sure what *she* was missing . . . and she didn't know if it had once been there and then something had taken it away—the robbery? the lock-out?—or had it just slowly bled dry all by itself? Or had she never had it in the first place? What did she have in herself to fight for?

She rolled the rest of the way to her stomach, her face halfway off the mattress, one eye staring at the dull hardwood floor, badly in need of wax and varnish. She didn't remember how that evening with Renee managed to slip back into a lower gear before they'd parted and went to sleep that night. But she had held back the last thing she might've said about the lock-out; maybe that's why she still remembered it. She knew that if she'd tipped her head over the back of the chair, stared at the ceiling, and said, "It's not what made me stop designing, but I guess the lock-out made me realize that I don't really have the gumption to fight for *anything,*" too scared to look Renee in the eye . . . if she'd said that, Renee would've written her off as worthless and had nothing more to do with her. So she'd remained silent. Now all of a sudden Morgan was practicing two or three hours a day, ordering videotapes of productions to study, talking about going to some auditions in bigger cities. The rest of the time he lamented years of his life wasted, moaned about all the time he'd allowed himself to float along without any goals. He lay curled motionless on the bed or crumpled contortedly on the sofa . . . unless Renee was around. Had she brought the end or a new beginning? Whose end and whose new beginning?

The same thing happened every morning at seven-thirty. From down the street, louder and louder, came the screams and chirps of kids on their way to school. They shrieked and ran with loud footsteps on the sidewalks, dropped books, stopped to babble at the top of their voices in the middle of the street. In the kennel, the dog rushed toward the gate with a spray of gravel, barking at the kids, who probably stood taunting, barking back, screaming, "Shut your fucking mouth, dumb dog," throwing rocks.

Morgan grunted, then said, "The dog's barking."

"I know. She hates kids."

"So do I. Either bring her in or let her go ahead and kill one."

Fanny laughed and got up to call the dog in. She fed her and locked her in the studio, knowing a piece of rug or a decade-old book on floor design might be eaten before she returned.

There always seemed to be a film of grease on the surface of the stove. Even if Fanny hadn't cooked for a week, the stove, the burner knobs, the wall, and anything else close to the stove grew a sticky skin that then caught dust and dog hair like flypaper. Fanny had absently wandered into the kitchen from her studio, where she'd managed to organize her colored pencils and take some old business cards off the bulletin board. She picked up a grayish sponge that used to be yellow, wet it and rung it out, then just stood holding it, looking at the translucent grime around the stove's burners. She glanced at Morgan, in the living room draped like upholstery fabric samples across the arms of the chair, reading dance programs Renee had picked up in Europe right before she'd come to town.

"I don't wanna clean the stove again," Fanny said.

"Then don't."

"It's so gross."

"Then don't look at it."

"You wanna do some of those exercises the doctor suggested?"

"Not now."

Fanny put the sponge down and went into the living room. She sat on the sofa, looked at Morgan's bare foot, which was propped on the coffee table in front of her, then held his big toe in two fingers. "This little piggy went to market."

"Don't tickle my feet," he said, smiling. "I'm warning you, if you tickle me I won't be responsible for my actions. I might kick you in the head."

Fanny laughed. Then she yelled "Shut up!" at the dog, who was barking in the yard, running around the tree, staring at a branch where a jay had been a half hour ago.

"Your yelling is worse than the barking," Morgan said. "And it doesn't work."

Fanny got up to let the dog in. The husky was panting hard, stopped to drink for several minutes in the kitchen, then came into the living room with her tongue dripping. "Time to be flipped over so Mommy can check you," Fanny said. She pressed on the dog's shoulders to get her to lie down, but when she tried to roll her to her back, the dog began to kick and twist. "Help me, Morgan. Hold her back legs."

"How would you like to have two people hold you down so someone could check between your legs, spread you open, and look inside?" He knelt on the floor and held the dog's ankles.

Fanny looked up at him, then went back to what she was doing. "I have to make sure she doesn't go into season without me knowing."

"You're still going ahead with this breeding . . . to a wolf?"

"Doreen knows what she's doing. Okay." Simultaneously they released the dog. "Nothing happening yet."

They returned to their places on the chair and sofa. Morgan picked up the dance program, then flipped it to the coffee table. "They don't print the dancers' ages."

"They're all fifteen and on drugs to stay that way."

Morgan went to the kitchen and came back with a glass of milk.

"Is there any left?" Fanny asked.

"Three drops." He drank half the milk in the glass. "Anyway," he wiped his mouth, ". . . he wasn't a real doctor."

"I know."

"He's a cretin."

Fanny laughed with relief, but felt herself start to sweat. "God, he's repulsive. The way he smacks his lips when he talks, the way he crosses his legs, the way he pulls his pants up too far. Can you imagine, someone probably has sex with him."

"Someone probably has sex with everyone."

Fanny wiped sweat from her upper lip. August, but not late enough in the day to be unbearably hot. The doctor, or whatever he was, had said it was normal for couples to not want to do much lovemaking in hot weather. "But there *are* fans," the creep had said, smiling, long yellowish teeth showing, his thick lips getting thicker, "and air conditioners." He had a white mustache that he would feel with two fingers every so often.

"Do you think Renee knows we're seeing him?" Fanny asked.

"How would she know?" Morgan finished his milk. "We shouldn't tell her, though . . . should we?"

"I was wondering the same thing." Fanny invited the dog onto the sofa. "But why do I wonder if I should tell her? Why *would* I tell her?" The dog was stretched out lengthwise on the sofa, across Fanny's legs. She lifted the dog's lips to create a snarl.

The guy's office was in a building called Family Therapy Services. One waiting room was jam-packed, standing room only, but the sign said Adolescent Group and Individual Sessions, and they'd passed it, smiling at each other. "Thank god for segregated waiting rooms," Morgan had said.

They'd filled out forms, mostly asking about their families' mental health records. But after the receptionist had taken the forms, Fanny remembered she had an aunt she'd never met who'd been institutionalized since 1932 as a chronic schizophrenic. "I hope I haven't left out an important clue in his investigation," she'd whispered to Morgan.

"I don't think it'll have anything to do with this, Sibyl."

But he'd stopped seeming so at ease when the session started. Mr. Foss had pulled up his polyester pants and sat down, crossing his legs, showing off his thin, light brown socks and a strip of white leg with frizzy white hair. Fanny had glanced at Morgan, saw that he also had his legs crossed, although none of his skin showed. She put her purse on her lap, then put it at her feet on the floor, then picked it up and returned it to her lap. Meanwhile, Mr. Foss, after finding out that Morgan was a dancer, was casually commenting on a musical revue he'd seen. "Those fellows could really move," Mr. Foss said.

"I wasn't in that one," Morgan said.

Thank god, Fanny had thought, imagining Mr. Foss watching Morgan dance and whispering to his wife, who probably had a basketball-sized hairdo, "That fellow can really move."

Then he'd asked them what they thought their problem was. Fanny had watched Morgan's foot bounce up and down. She traced a plaid pattern in the sofa with one finger. "It's like," Morgan said, "like . . . like it's too much trouble."

"Is that how you feel as well, Frances?" Mr. Foss said. Her stomach turned over, hearing her full name come from his white mustache.

"Yeah. The same. I never knew it was so . . . difficult."

"Difficult in what way?"

She looked down. Morgan's foot was still bouncing frantically, so she reached out and held his ankle to stop him. He jerked his foot out of her grasp, shifted so his legs were pointing away from her. "It hurts," she said without looking up. "And he can't get in . . . and then his erection goes away."

"Don't you get lubricated enough?" Mr. Foss asked, a sparkle of moisture on his mustache. She closed her eyes and let a thin quick dizzy spell pass. "Do you take your time with foreplay?"

It seemed a long time before she heard herself answering. "He has to get me ready. I take too long. Then it still hurts. Or else he's not hard enough to try anymore."

"Morgan," Mr. Foss said, "are you telling yourself that once your erection goes away, you can't get it back?"

"I don't know." It didn't sound like Morgan's voice. "Maybe."

"Are you telling yourself there's something wrong with you?"

Mr. Foss was wearing light brown leather wingtips. "There *is* something wrong with us," Fanny said. "We don't want to do it anymore. It seems like neither of us can even get turned on enough to be *able* to do it."

"Morgan, can you think about Frances and become aroused?"

Fanny leaned her forehead on her hand, her elbow on the arm of the sofa. She could feel Morgan shift and cross his legs again. He didn't answer.

"Do you ever have sexual feelings at *other* times?" Mr. Foss said. "While driving, at a party . . . or during a rehearsal?"

Fanny suddenly wished she had not worn jeans and tennis shoes. She was about to say something when Morgan said, "I don't know."

"Have you thought about discussing your problem with any close friends at work?"

"I don't think I could do that," Morgan said.

"Do you ever feel being with your coworkers . . . your, uh, buddies . . . is preferable to being with Frances? More comfortable? Fewer . . . expectations or . . . no role to play?"

Morgan didn't answer. Fanny peeked up from under her hand and saw his throat move up and down as he swallowed.

A long, silent moment passed. Fanny didn't stop Morgan from bouncing his foot up and down. His shoelace ticked against his shoe on every bounce. Her own tennis shoes were fastened with velcro, and she had an urge to bend down and open her shoes, to make the harsh ripping sound.

"What you're thinking," Morgan finally said to Mr. Foss, "it's not the answer. Not even close."

"Do you know what the answer is?" The gentleness of Mr. Foss's voice made Fanny squirm.

"What do you mean?"

"Do you *want* to make love to Frances?"

Again, a breathing silence. Fanny could hear Mr. Foss rub his mustache. Very slowly, Fanny sat up, then leaned back on the sofa. It was so soft, she almost felt she was lying down. Morgan was leaning forward. His back was in front of her.

"There's no simple answer," Morgan said. "Maybe it's gotten to be so much trouble to try . . . it's like, maybe I don't *want* to try anymore."

"Do you feel a responsibility to help Frances to relax and enjoy sex? Do you feel pressured by this responsibility?"

Morgan sighed, as though giving up or giving in. "Maybe."

Mr. Foss uncrossed his legs, then crossed them the other way. "I'd like you to think about something, Morgan," Mr. Foss said. "Don't try to answer now. Maybe you could tell Frances the answer when you're alone together. Forgetting what you've been going through, does the idea of good sex with Frances interest and arouse you?" Mr. Foss stood, went behind his chair, and opened the blinds. The room brightened considerably. Fanny sat up. She was reaching for her purse, but Mr. Foss sat back in his chair, pulled his pants up, and crossed his legs again. This time his toe was pointing at her. "Frances, had you any sexual experiences before Morgan?"

"No."

"You were a virgin when you got married?" Mr. Foss's white eyebrows went up. The sun coming through the window was hot on her cheek.

"No, I was with Morgan before we got married," she said.

"Have you always had this problem *getting ready*, as you called it?"

She shielded her face from the window with one hand. "Not as bad at first. It got worse instead of better. Right Morgan?"

Morgan turned, but not all the way toward her. "I don't remember. I guess so, if that's what you think."

Fanny took a quick breath, but Mr. Foss was already saying, "What was your parents' attitude about sex, Frances?"

"I don't know."

"Did your parents somehow teach you that sex is bad or dirty?"

"No, they—"

"Did they talk to you about sex?"

"No, but—"

"Didn't that give you the idea that sex was something to hide and be ashamed of?"

"No, it just never came up in conversation—"

"Do you think maybe deep inside you think you shouldn't be having sex with Morgan, that it's a dirty thing to do, that it's nasty or immoral?"

Fanny groaned inside. *Oh, god,* she thought wearily, *guess again, quack.*

The exercises he gave them all involved touching each other without having sex, trying to find simple pleasure in a finger run along the inside of an elbow, a hand caressing a shoulder, a back rub, a feathery tickle. Fanny knew if they tried it, they'd both crack up laughing. She'd end up wiggling his kneecap back and forth, he'd fold her ears down to see how she'd look as a puppy. The session had been two weeks ago. They had another appointment in a few days.

———————

There wasn't a real reason to worry. Fanny hadn't written down her husky's last season, that's all, so we had no way of knowing if she was late coming in. She thought the dog had been in season somewhere around Christmas, or some holiday, maybe Easter. God, I had to check my urge to say, *You have a valuable animal here, but you don't monitor her health very well.* The husky *was* in excellent condition, though. Clean teeth, thick, shiny coat, lean but well muscled, free of both internal and external parasites, well sprung rib cage, perfect angulation, very bright eye. I provided Fanny with a new diet for the dog, a lamb-based kibble, and daily supplements of fish meal, powdered eggs, and cottage cheese. And I wanted the dog road-worked every day, but Fanny wasn't sure she had time.

"Why?" I asked. "You don't work until night, right? What do you do all day?"

"I'm supposed to be building a portfolio of furniture designs."

"For who?" Reasonable question, right?

"For myself."

"Who says you're supposed to, who asked for it?"

"No one. I should've been doing it for years now and haven't. I should *start.*"

"And I should be exercising my fat butt off, but I wouldn't put it ahead of preparing my bitch for a healthy litter." Did she get it? Who knows.

She was a funny girl. And a funny name. Who went by *Fanny* when you could be Fran or . . . *something* else. The other choices weren't great either, but I'd have changed my name if I found myself one day in my thirties with a name like Fanny. Of course what did you expect from a girl who watched reruns of *I Love Lucy*, had a husband who always looked like a pile of laundry thrown into a chair, and could be alpha-rolled by her own dog? I had found them that way in the park, Fanny on the ground on her back and the dog standing over her, her forefeet on Fanny's chest, staring down at Fanny's face. Fanny was laughing and tickling the dog's stomach.

"How can you let her do this to you, don't you know what it means?" I said as I grabbed the husky's collar and pulled her off, ignoring the animal's low growl.

Fanny rolled over and sat up on her knees. "She's just playing with me. I get a big head start, then she chases me, and when she catches up, I fall. I *let* her win."

"Not as far as she's concerned. *You* lost."

There were a lot of reasons why a bitch would be late coming into season. Even if you rule out poor health and age, sometimes a bitch living alone wasn't very regular, needed other intact bitches around to induce her to come into season. Then there were emotional reasons. I asked Fanny if the dog was under any stress.

"Maybe she's upset that she hasn't caught any of the wild animals she's sure are prowling around the house at night."

"I'm serious," I said. *Duh.* "It could be a factor."

"What's going to cause *her* stress? She eats, she sleeps, she plays in the park just about every day."

"But is there any *other* stress?" I tried to be tactful. "I mean, you . . . are *you* nervous about something . . . is there any, like, tension around?"

She scratched an ant bite on her leg, inspected the spot closely, then looked up with a sappy expression, almost pleading. *I didn't want to hear it,* so I quickly started jabbering. "Maybe I'll use my experience in dental assisting to get a job working for a vet. Then maybe we can get big discounts, you know, for ultra sound to see if she's in whelp, the examinations, and for the pups, the dew claws, and all that stuff. I can do their shots and worming, so no problem there. I just wish one of us had ever whelped a litter before. I've only had male dogs."

Fanny stretched out on the grass, then rolled over and was poking a caterpillar with a stick. "Anyway," I slowed down, "maybe it doesn't matter why she's late, as long as that's what it is—late. I mean, it's better to be late than if she had a silent season and we missed it. God, then I'd have to wait another whole year to get started. I'd have a screaming fit, I swear."

Fanny let the caterpillar walk up her arm. The husky came loping back across the park with someone's grotesque old sock, then started rubbing her face on it, ground her shoulder against it, finally rolled to her back, twisting back and forth over the sock.

"She got some perfume," Fanny laughed. "Maybe she's getting close to coming in and wants the boys to start noticing her."

So I told her that some stud dogs will completely ignore a bitch in silent season. "They can't even tell. She probably ovulates, but nothing else."

God, she was weird. Abruptly she jumped up, shot me a peculiar look, then grabbed the hideous sock in her bare hands and started a violent tug-of-war game, growling as loud as her dog.

He was sitting on the edge of the tub, brushing his teeth and reading a travel magazine, the water running in the sink. He could hear Suzanne talking to the dog, stopped brushing to see if he could understand what she was saying, but by that time the dog was barking. Suzanne came into the bathroom and turned the water off. The dog was with her, still vocalizing, a combination whine and bark. Scott stood, turned the water back on, and began rinsing his mouth.

"It was like money going down the drain," she said.

"Maybe three cents," he tried to say, then spit a mouthful of water. The dog put her front paws on the sink shelf, looked at his face in the mirror, barked four or five times until he said, "What do you want, Sadie?" She ran out of the room, then started barking again.

"She wants to go out," Suzanne said, smiling.

"So put her out."

"No, I mean, I asked her if she wanted to go for a walk *now*, instead of later tonight. I thought if you took her now, maybe she'd let us sleep all night."

"You can sleep all night."

"You think I don't wake up when you go out?"

"You can go back to sleep."

"Well," Suzanne said, smiling again, "I don't see what's wrong with taking her now instead of later."

"Nothing's wrong with it. It's just not what I want to do."

"Why? She'd get her exercise, then you could sleep all night."

The dog was still barking. "Sadie," he called, "it's okay." She came bounding back to the bedroom, jumped onto the bed, and stood with her legs braced, ears cocked, eyes fixed on him. "Thanks," Scott said, "you used the word *walk*—she's not going to forget."

"So take her now. *Now's* when she wants to go. You always take her when *she* wants to go."

"She only wants to go now because you said the word to her."

Suzanne's mouth got tight and she left the bathroom but didn't go out of the bedroom. She straightened a picture on the wall, wiped a dog hair off the nightstand with one finger. "I just don't see what's so wrong with taking her now, Scott. You could both get

your exercise, then you could take a shower and sleep all night."
The dog barked again, just once, pricked her ears at Scott, then
began a rhythmic cadence of barking.

"Well, I guess I'll *have* to take her now, won't I," he said. He
jerked his pants off the hook on the bathroom door. "Okay, Sadie,
shut up already," he shouted. The dog lay on the bed with her chin
on her paws. "I'm sorry, girl." He zipped his pants and sat on the
mattress, stroking the dog's brow. "Dad's not mad at you."

"Dad's taking you on a *walk,*" Suzanne said, her smile resumed.
The dog darted off the bed and headed down the hall toward the
door.

Scott pulled his socks on without looking at Suzanne. He tucked
in his shirt and put his keys in his pocket, still not looking at her.
But he could hear her hand smoothing a place on the quilt bedspread she'd made a few years ago. Then he heard her flipping pages
of the magazine he'd put down. "Have you been reading about
Greenland to get ready for our trip?" she asked brightly.

"No."

"We've got to decide on the exact dates and make a deposit."

"Maybe." He reached under the bed where he kept his shoes at
night, then sat on the floor instead of on the mattress beside
Suzanne to put his shoes on.

"Why maybe? It's all decided."

"I don't know. It's a lot of money."

"It wasn't a lot of money when *you* decided that's where we would
go next."

Scott got up and headed toward the door. When he got the leash
out of the hall closet, the dog began barking again, jumping up and
thudding against the front door with her paws. *"Don't let her do
that, Scott,"* Suzanne screamed. Her voice sounded nasal and brittle.
The glass in the front door rattled.

They'd had a listless lunch. Renee watched Fanny drain the bottom
of her glass through the straw for the hundredth time. The glass was
right in front of Fanny, where her plate had been, so when she
drained whatever ice had melted in the thirty seconds since her last
suck, she tipped her face to the straw without lifting the glass. She

kept her hand on the glass, her palm over the top, the straw coming between her fingers. She was like a whale having to come up and breathe every so often, except Fanny's head kept going down. It wasn't much like sitting in a restaurant with Kay, who might find a dark corner or private nook behind beaded curtains and feed Renee with both hands, push sushi into Renee's mouth with two fingers while two fingers toyed with her under the table; either that, or Kay might see five or six other women she knew and turn the date into a party.

Renee had her back to a wall and could see all the other tables in the small café. Fanny would only be able to see Renee, the wall behind her, and whatever picture was on that wall. It wasn't as though Renee had planned it that way when she sat down, but somehow instinctively she must've known Fanny would be more comfortable not being able to see other pairs of women at other tables.

But it wasn't that Fanny's sensibilities were so delicate that Renee had to keep *all* her thoughts to herself. Just today as they were pulling up in front of the café, Renee had said, "Everyone will think I've got a cute date!" Despite the funk she'd been in for what seemed like weeks, Fanny had *laughed,* looking Renee right in the eye. It had *sounded* like a joke, especially with Fanny laughing—but *was* it? Renee hadn't taken Fanny's arm as she stepped inside. But, *as* a joke, couldn't she do that? Was it fun, even titillating, to play and pretend . . . or was she just pretending it was a game for Fanny's sake, for a while? Until . . . until *what?* Renee had the strange sensation, for the first time in her life, that she didn't know what she was going to say before she said it, and once something was said, she didn't know exactly what she meant.

"Hey," Renee said, picking up the check. "Let's go get that futon I've been wanting. I need help carrying it."

"Futon? Okay. I thought you had a bed." Fanny's voice was thin.

"The futon's for the living room. Does it fit my apartment's style?"

"What style? Your living room's still empty."

"I got those lithographs framed," Renee said. "You can help me put them up."

Renee watched Fanny as they left the café, but Fanny didn't peek at the other customers, even though there was a bull dyke at one table against the wall. A few of the women did glance up at them as they left. They might've merely been noticing Fanny's delightful haircut. Without a part, the hair all seemed to originate from the crown and spread out in every direction, some lying flat, some sticking up, the color of a natural field where dozens of different kinds of grasses grew and had been dried in the sun. When Renee got in the car, she said, "If I was a man, *you'd* be the one who was nervous."

Fanny looked up but didn't laugh this time. "Huh? Why?"

"'Cause it would look like you were having an affair."

Maybe Fanny started to laugh then, but checked it, turned and looked out the windshield as Renee pulled away from the curb. "So then why're *you* the one who's nervous?" she asked, too calmly. As though she wasn't really interested.

Renee used a slightly theatrical voice, "Maybe it looks like *I'm* having an affair . . . with a *married* woman."

"Ha!" Then Fanny groaned, "Oh, that's funny." But she was smiling.

Suddenly Renee said, "It's not that funny. It kind of does feel good, I mean in a weird intense way, you know, to realize *why* there's this sensation in my stomach when other people look at us."

Fanny stopped chuckling under her breath, continued looking out the windshield, a peculiar smile still barely tightening her lips. Renee had a difficult time navigating corners while trying to see if Fanny was shaking her head.

"I just thought of that," Renee said, hoping she was looking nonchalant as she checked the left lane for traffic. "I mean, just now, it just seemed weird when I suddenly thought it, you know what I mean?"

Renee stood back while Fanny studied the four walls of her tiny living room, then Fanny pointed toward a corner, and together they shoved the frame diagonally across the corner on the same wall as the door, so if the weather was hot and the door left open, no one outside would be able to see whoever was sitting or sleeping on the futon. They lugged in the futon itself, which smelled like dried wild weeds, and folded it into a sofa on the frame. Then simultaneously they flopped, panting, onto the seat.

"Well," Fanny said, "you can't invite very many people to a party."

Renee stretched, then put her hands behind her head, leaned back and looked at the opposite wall, still blank. "Maybe it would go better there."

"Maybe so," Fanny said.

Twisting her body, Renee let herself fall sideways, away from Fanny, her feet still on the floor. Arms dangling off the end of the futon, over her head, fingertips barely grazing the floor. "I wonder how it would feel to make out on this thing." She lifted one leg, pointed her toe toward the ceiling light fixture, then lowered the leg again but put it across Fanny's lap. "God, I'm tired, and I still have to do my routine tonight."

"Maybe I'd better go so you can do it," Fanny said. Her arms were stretched out on either side of her, across the back of the sofa.

"You could stay, listen to the music, then we could go out for ice cream."

Fanny seemed stiff, turning her head to look at Renee without moving her arms. "I never even sit around watching Morgan exercise, why would—" She stopped and laughed, then said, "Besides, I've got to exercise my dog." Her voice was still shaking with a silent laugh under the words. "Everyone's got exercises to do."

They sat without moving. Renee let her neck relax, tipped backwards off the edge of the futon, making it difficult to see Fanny. She felt Fanny touch the toe of her shoe, a thin black leather ankle-high boot, slightly resembling old-fashioned boxer's shoes. "Funky shoes," Fanny said. "Know where I can get a pair?"

Renee put her foot back on the floor, sat up, then stood. "Let's go shopping sometime, pick clothes for each other."

Fanny paused in the doorway. "You need an area rug, some small tables. Want me to do this room for you?"

"I've got some ideas for what I want," Renee said as she took off her shoes and tossed them through the bedroom doorway. "Then you can tell me what you think."

Fanny smiled, stepped outside, let the screen door shut behind her before she said, "See ya."

After cutting the grass, Scott left the mower in the middle of the front lawn and kneeled beside it, his back toward the house. He took the motor cover off and started removing some bolts that were easy to get to. Once Suzanne heard the mower go off, she would expect him to return to the house, but he continued to hold the bolts in his palm, shaking them like dice, staring at them. He thought of going to the garage for a screwdriver so he could poke it into the motor or tap it against metal parts, but Suzanne might be watching and she'd probably follow him, ask what's wrong with the mower, maybe return with him to watch him work on it. The dog had to be kept in the backyard when he mowed or she would try to kill the mower and probably get her ears sliced off. But she always started to yip, a shrill noise halfway between bark and howl, as soon as the motor went off.

At work there was always someone calling his name, the phone ringing, delivery people at the door, employees dumb as mud asking for their next instruction. Sometimes after a job like yesterday's—a large fund-raiser with tables for four set up across the big lawn behind the museum—he wished he could spend a day someplace like Montana, alone, or with someone who would talk about other things, lie in the middle of a glacier, climb a tree while discussing how sensitivity to color and shape is encouraged in girls but not in boys, or surmise the evolution of body language. The latter two *had* been actual conversations, but not yesterday, something he remembered from jobs a week or two ago, and had only been overhead—the girl had neither been talking to him nor up in a tree.

But yesterday . . . wouldn't any other employer have fired her, finding her in a tree like that? Ten years ago, five years, even two years ago, he might not have hired her again after the first time he used her, after seeing her palomino hair like a short horse's mane, and how she wore black sneakers with velcro fasteners and white ankle socks with her waitress skirt. Then yesterday she was in the tree during her break. When he asked what she was doing, she said she'd found quieter places six or eight feet *up* than twenty or thirty yards away. And besides, she'd added, people never look *up*. Her leg was swinging slightly, her black sneaker tapping against the tree trunk as she spoke. He'd said, "I don't know if my insurance will cover a fall from a tree."

"I won't fall." Then she'd said, "Does your insurance cover going crazy?"

"I thought this job was going smoothly, what's the problem?"

"No problem. I just thought I'd save my seething fit until I was covered."

For some reason he hadn't walked away, had put one hand on a low branch and said, "I'm sure glad a breeze came up," then shook his head at his own insipidity.

"Yeah," she said, "but it hasn't been hot enough to blame the heat for anything."

"Like what?"

"Well . . . like keeping my dog from coming into season."

"Oh, yeah?" He'd looked at her pale, slightly freckled face—fuzzy gray-green eyes, sand-colored brows and lashes, slightly high, prominent cheekbones, thin sharp jaw, wide straight mouth and nondescript nose that turned neither up nor down, and that messy hair—and suddenly, instead of being sarcastically patronizing, as he normally would be to a waitress complaining about her petty life, he'd said, "Is she okay? Did you take her to a vet?"

"Oh, she's fine. Just late." Then she'd smiled and her eyes had darkened or something. She was making eye contact with him for the first time. "I forgot, usually non-dog people don't know what I'm talking about, so I try to switch to common usage and call it *in heat*. Are you in dogs?"

Instantly he knew if he'd said no, whatever was happening would be over. "Sort of," he'd said, then added, "Talk about common usage, before we spayed our dog, my wife said she didn't want Sadie to have her *period*."

The girl laughed, and he'd joined her. But the break was over, the head waiter ringing a little bell to call the waitresses. Although he'd extended his hand to help her out of the tree, she'd jumped down without touching him, still laughing, dusting her little butt with her hands. He'd probably been blushing.

Crouching on the lawn, he put the bolts back into the motor and removed them again, probably five or six times. Sweat was trickling out of his hair, down his neck and temples, and ants were tickling his ankles. Suddenly the dog stopped whining in the backyard, and in a second she had her front feet over his shoulders, licking his ear, then jumping down to spin in circles on the lawn. It wouldn't take long for Suzanne to relatch the gate and follow the dog to the front lawn.

After an evening dress rehearsal, Morgan and Renee stopped at an Irish pub for a beer. Several of the musicians had mentioned they were going there, so Morgan suggested it to Renee, and she said, "I've been there, it's a cool place, very mixed."

He didn't ask what she meant, then saw, as they squeezed into places at a long table, that what she'd meant was obvious: the crowd consisted of red-necked toughs playing darts, a few men in kilts and women in Gaelic costumes, symphony musicians in tails who'd just played a concert, spike-haired lesbians, long-fingered queens, office girls giggling together, young men in suits with briefcases, and a few nondescript couples seated near a small stage where a long-haired trio nasally sang Irish folk songs.

The noise in the place made intimate conversation difficult, but Renee was talking about getting tapes of productions by a choreographer friend to convince management that a series of programs featuring her in pieces all choreographed by her friend would create a more meaningful continuity. She was directing her dialogue as much toward another woman across the table as she was at Morgan. He recognized the woman as a photographer who did stills of productions as well as portraits of the principals for posters and programs.

"This is who you should be talking to," the photographer said, indicating a woman seated beside her. "You probably already know each other? Renee Talbot—Dani Clark."

Morgan knew Dani. She worked in the management office and used to sometimes come to parties given by performers.

"Yes, I've seen you in the office," Renee said.

"Glad to finally meet you," Dani said. "Hi, Morgan, how's Fanny?"

He wasn't aware of what he said in answer because Renee turned quickly to him, for just a second, as though she'd forgotten he was there.

Then Renee picked up where she'd left off. Her clear, intense voice and rapid words, brightly enunciated, caught the attention of several others at the table. Morgan saw people glance toward Renee, then glance again, then let their own conversations dwindle away. They watched Renee's eyes burn while she described a program in Chicago by her choreographer friend: the featured soloist began the series of dances in total absolute white, then each costume shifted through a spectrum of grays until the last number. When the audience naturally expected black, she entered through a slit in the backdrop wearing neon red, the music a weird concoction of drum, oboe, viola, and trombone. Renee described how the dancer spent a primordial five minutes on the floor, raising each limb one at a time, the only action a series of intricate wrist or ankle movements. She went on to emphasize that management ought to realize that the public liked to follow a recognizable star, as they did in sports. If they promoted someone as a star, a following would grow.

Morgan listened, nodded each time Renee snapped her eyes from the other two women's faces to his, proving to everyone that he was included. From the corner of his eye he also continued to watch the others at the long table. They were all falling in love with her, all probably wishing that *they* could be the one she called when she needed to borrow a driveway so she could wash her car, or the one she conferred with when she was preparing her new résumé, or the one she turned to to share her feelings when a news editorial made her angry or a friend from college achieved something equal to or better than what she'd accomplished. He wondered if any of them knew that he—and Fanny—were the ones Renee had lived with while she got settled and looked for the right apartment. In fact, Renee was the one who had hinted broadly about staying with them.

He and Fanny had met her when she'd first won the position—she was in town for a week and there was a party at a board member's house. Since the year of the lock-out, most of the members of the company refused to socialize with management, so he'd been one of the few performers at the party. The artistic director kept stealing Renee for introductions to a rich patron or influential board member, until finally Renee had said, "Let's have lunch tomorrow so we can talk with some privacy." It seemed the three of them could talk as though they'd known each other their whole lives: Renee speaking in detail about former lovers without any careful preamble or reserve. And Fanny told the story about being at Girl Scout camp in junior high and pretending she was a boy—the cook's son who'd been forced to come along—flirting with a plump girl who'd gotten a crush on her, going so far with the joke as to write her a few love letters after camp. Once when Renee was staying with them, she'd come into their room in the morning, kneeled on the foot of the bed in her nightshirt, then laughed and leaned forward to rub her hand in Fanny's turbulent hair after he'd said that Fanny was difficult to sleep with because her hair tickled his face and woke him up. His heart had felt like a flopping fish when Renee actually said, "Maybe you need another body in bed to keep you apart." But Fanny's quick answer—"Yeah, we'll let the dog sleep there and see if *she* tickles him"—had changed the subject.

He had a sudden vision of describing that scene to Mr. Foss instead of the way they'd lied their way through their second session earlier that afternoon. It might've been even funnier, if that was possible. Neither he nor Fanny had spoken about the session until they were pulling into the parking lot, when he'd said, "What the hell are we going to say?"

"What does a kid tell his music teacher?" Fanny had replied. "You swear that you practiced all your scales. It's not as though we're going to have to demonstrate anything to *prove* it to him."

And so without any kind of collaboration, they'd described how they'd done the exercises and had found sensual pleasure in both giving and receiving a simple light caress because each touch was charged with feeling. They'd said they planned no other activities, didn't have a time deadline with some other obligation waiting, had turned the telephone off. Without so much as a sideways glance, Fanny added that they'd lit candles and played classical music and fed each other cool pieces of cantaloupe and honeydew from a fruit salad she'd made.

In the car afterwards, they'd looked at each other and laughed. Morgan even had to pull over and pound Fanny on the back because she started to choke, and he'd said, "Why didn't you go all out and tell him we read poetry to each other?"

"Don't make me laugh anymore," she'd gasped. "It hurts."

"It's too bad we can't tell anyone about it."

"But we *can't,*" she'd said, calmer, still leaning forward with her face buried in her arm on the dashboard.

He knew she was right, although every time there'd been a pause in conversation with Renee while driving to rehearsal that evening, he'd thought about telling her. But then, if she knew he was going to sex therapy, how could Renee say things backstage like, "Morgan and I are going girl-watching tonight"? And how could the three of them go to Seattle and share a motel room, as they'd idly discussed recently, if Renee knew about Mr. Foss and his instructions for erection exercises? What the *asshole* didn't know was that he had no trouble at *all* getting and keeping a hard-on, for hours, sometimes, and, yes, he *was* thinking about Fanny, although not imagining *himself* with Fanny, but Fanny with other men, and, recently, Fanny with Renee—nursing Fanny's troubled pussy back to life, and, since Fanny probably wouldn't yet be able to suck Renee's nipples or circle her clit with a finger, *he'd* be there to be sure Renee felt loved, showing her he was different from other men and could touch her the way she needed to be touched.

It still always seemed like the year started in September. Whenever Fanny had felt a vague hope that she might be on the verge of renewing her energies for building a portfolio or creating prototypes of new furniture designs or redoing the house or thatching the lawn or laying down a new sprinkler system, it was usually in September. Not that any hope of discovering a lost reserve of ambition ever panned out.

But this year, September was just another month. She was still working three or four nights a week, sometimes an afternoon shift. She still watered the yard. She still snipped off the dead roses but never cut fresh ones to bring inside. She still read the newspaper and watched the news. She still took the dog out every day, often to the park to meet Doreen. The dog still hadn't come into season.

Renee had said to do something nice for herself, give herself a treat. Morgan talked about going to Seattle.

Doreen said that probably the stress of waiting for the dog to come into season was keeping her from coming into season.

Fanny wandered into her study, picked up some junk mail from her desk, and threw it away. She went into the kitchen, moved a dirty glass from the shelf to the sink. Went outside, pulled a milkweed from the garden. She returned to the house, went into the bedroom, felt the plants to see if they were dry. On her way back to the kitchen to get water, she stopped in the living room and fished the Easy Living section out of the pile of newspapers. Morgan used the remote control to turn the sound down on the television and said, "Wouldn't that friend of yours take care of the dog when we go to Seattle?"

"She might think changing her environment like that right now would upset her system and set her back even further."

"Our lives can't revolve around that dog."

"*She's* never been the reason we have or haven't done anything."

Morgan turned the sound back up. He was watching an old Roman epic movie, a group of black natives with huge feather head-dresses entertaining Caesar. "Too bad the movies don't have much work for dancers anymore," Fanny said.

"Who'd want it? Like asking Renee to be a majorette in a circus parade," he said. Fanny watched the caesar take some grapes off a platter. He held the whole bunch in his hand and bit the grapes off the stems. A boy was rubbing his back. "Want to do something tonight, Morgan?"

"Like what?"

"Something different. Let's *do* something."

"Like what?"

"I don't know, something fast and fun. Let's go to a nightclub. We've never done anything like that before. Maybe it'll . . ." her voice trailed away, "help." She looked down, hoping Morgan wouldn't ask *Help what?* Neither had said a word about Mr. Foss's next step: continue the touching and caressing, but now include genitals, concentrate on the pleasure given and received without trying to go on to intercourse.

"What would we do there?" Morgan asked when the scene on the TV changed to an overview of gladiators marching into an arena.

"I don't know. Listen to music. Dance."

"I don't dance."

Fanny briefly watched the gladiators, then said, "Do you realize what you said?"

They laughed together for a moment. "You know what I mean," Morgan said. "That kind of dancing. I never did it."

"So why not start now? C'mon, Morgan, let's snap out of it."

They stood in front of a thumping dance club for several moments but didn't go inside. The music was canned and there was a ten-dollar cover charge and no alcohol was served. There was a mass of people gyrating to heavy bass and unintelligible lyrics, and Morgan said their average age was about twenty.

"Renee's only twenty-four," Fanny said.

"That's different."

"I think Doreen's about that age too. Maybe a little older."

"Well, *she'd* fit right in here."

The name of the nightclub was written in neon script above the roof. Fanny stood trying to read it while Morgan unlocked the car. The music from the club abruptly ended and in the sudden silence she could hear people screaming across the street where a plaza of shops and fast food and arcades had been built around a restored wooden roller coaster. The roller coaster was lit up with strings of white Christmas lights that outlined the track. She could hear the wheels making clickety sounds and the screams, which sounded half real and half scripted. Morgan was inside the car, leaning across to unlock her door, but Fanny didn't get in. She opened her door and said, "*That's* what we can do, the roller coaster."

The first part of the ride was fairly fast and in nearly complete darkness. Fanny heard herself laughing like a witch. She clutched the safety bar with both hands. Then the string of cars came out of the tunnels and began chugging up the steepest incline. After that there was only the hysterical speed and vicious vibrations, turns whipping her head back and forth, more inclines and explosive motion down steep corkscrew corners, both her arms clutching Morgan instead of the safety bar, and her voice shrieking "I'm scared," a strange shrill sound, "I'm scared, I'm scared." But apparently Morgan didn't hear her, or didn't believe her.

By the time Suzanne finished showering and dressing, Scott was already outside painting the post that held the mailbox. She fixed herself a cup of coffee and stood sipping it, watching him through the kitchen window. Then she poured most of it down the drain, splashed a little water in the sink to rinse it away, and put the cup into the dishwasher. From the crumbs on the counter, she knew Scott had eaten one of her oatmeal cookies.

She'd already made the bed, right after her shower, except she hadn't pulled the bedspread up over her handmade quilt. The quilt was plenty big enough to cover the bed, but the spread protected it from the dog. She balled the bedspread into her arms and took it to the washroom, started the machine. She washed the spread every Saturday.

Scott had gotten up first, but Suzanne had already been awake. She'd sat up against her pillows and waited for him to come out of the bathroom. "We should enjoy a lazy Saturday morning without rushing to get dressed," she'd said, smiling and stretching. "If it wasn't for the dog, we could have breakfast in bed."

He'd taken his old jeans from a hook in the closet. "Did *Sadie* say she forbids doing anything in the bed except sleeping?"

Scott was almost completely dressed before Suzanne answered, "I wish she'd let us do *that.*"

"So sleep now," he'd said. "Sadie's coming outside with me. You'll have peace and quiet."

But she hadn't stayed in bed. She left the washroom and went looking for Scott. He was rinsing paintbrushes in the gutter in front of the house, water gushing down the street. "Scott, honey . . . ," she started, picking up the hose and directing it onto the lawn. He took the hose from her and sprayed the water through the bristles of the brush he was holding. "I . . . ," she laughed lightly, "let's redo the bedroom today."

"Why?"

"Oh, you know," she laughed again, "I thought maybe we could try a homier look."

Scott shook the paintbrush, a motion like chopping wood with an ax. The water from the bristles splatted in a line along the sidewalk. "Go ahead, if you want to." He took the hose and walked up to the house where the faucet was, rinsed his hands, then turned the water off. It was as if she'd been shouting to him across the noise of a waterfall, and suddenly the waterfall was gone. Maybe everyone on the block could hear her now.

"I'd like to do it together."

"It's more your room than mine." He turned and looked at her. "We're not there together much. At least not when we're both conscious."

Suzanne watched the cloudy white water in the gutter clear up. She went back into the house, into the bedroom, into the bathroom, and shut the door.

About three weeks ago, a box of condoms had appeared under the sink. She checked it every day or so, but it still wasn't opened. The nights he got up, took the dog to the park, and came back breathing hard, she made sure she was dead asleep, or at least looked like it.

I'd been describing the Schutzhund exercises—because I wanted the husky to be titled so my pup would have more credibility, in addition to the heart and courage that would *genetically* be there—when Fanny said she wanted to see the protection training. And she said she wanted to feel what it was like to have a dog that weighs almost as much as she does go one-on-one with her. So, with the husky tethered to a tie-down stake, I helped Fanny put on the agitator's sleeve.

"I'm not taking any responsibility," I said after the sleeve was attached to Fanny's arm. "*You* wanted to do this."

"I know, go ahead."

The husky was watching, panting in a way that showed all her teeth, her eyes squinting. It was a devious expression, very keen. Beautiful. I was anxious to get Fanny to start training her dog in Schutzund but knew it wasn't a good idea now. A new routine, new stress, anything that upset the life that the dog was accustomed to might delay her season even further or make the season silent when it finally came. I'd been to visit the wolf twice already by then. He was an impressive creature, too high in leg to be a good working dog, but proud and powerful. The owner had made him howl, and I had almost passed out, it was so poignant and *audacious.*

An amateur as agitator . . . *stupidity* . . . but I could trust Bruno. "Okay, ready?" I said. "I'm going to tell him to hold you. That means barking. Count to ten, then try to escape. As you run away, shout at him, threaten him. That's when he'll use the bite. When you freeze, he'll let go and hold you again. It's noisy, so just remember, freeze, and he'll stop."

While Bruno held Fanny—bracing his forelegs, coiled on his back legs, ears flat back—I did notice that Fanny's dog had sat up, her head thrust forward almost level with her shoulders, no longer panting, her ears alert and quivering.

Bruno may not have been competitive, but he sounded good. Not the happy, repetitive vocalization of a dog playing ball, and not the hollow sound of a bored dog left in the backyard—his voice was harsh and low, the barks strung together with a gnashing growl. Yet he still wasn't quite enough for me. I wanted a dog who would actually spray saliva during the hold.

Fanny took off, shouting "Fuck you," laughing, and, as I should've predicted, she fell when Bruno hit the sleeve. But instead of the sound dying down to a teeth-clenched growl, as Bruno bit and held the sleeve, *another* roar was obliterating my commands. And I was screaming my head off! Instead of the frozen agitator and vigilant dog holding, everything blurred and accelerated, and the park reverberated with the thunder of a dog fight. The husky had ripped her tie-down stake from the ground and charged. The two dogs were locked together, upright, a tornado of bristling fur and furious bodies. It seemed like a whole crowd of people was also shouting, screaming, but it was just me and Fanny, trying to grab and hold anything, to smother the fight with our bodies as though putting out a fire. Like holding my breath, closing my eyes, and diving below rushing water, I plunged in. The scrambling feet clawed streaks down my chest, but I kept my head down and grabbed handfuls of Bruno's skin until I finally reached far enough and found his testicles. He screamed, and in the sudden split second of slack, I dug my knees into the grass and pushed him away from the husky.

So the noise subsided, except for the husky, still growling beneath each heaving breath. My head was on Bruno's ribs. I could hear the deep, rough rush of air going in and out, and his thudding heart, louder than my own rapid panting and thin ringing in my ears. I felt where toenails had raked my chest and arms, but no fresh sting, so I knew I'd avoided being bitten. I sat up and looked at Fanny, lying completely over her dog, who continued to growl in her throat. One of Fanny's arms was hidden somewhere underneath the dog, the other like a clunky flipper, still wearing the agitator's sleeve, sprawled out to the side.

"You okay?" I said, still breathless.

"Yeah." Fanny pulled her knees under herself, then yanked her arm out from under her dog. "Wow, that was . . . real!"

So we laughed, still not enough breath to make much sound, but I saw blood on Fanny's hand. "Oh, look, they got you."

"What?" Fanny looked at her hand. "No, it's not me."

"Then maybe *she's* hurt. Oh god—" I left Bruno and crawled over to the bitch. "Please don't be hurt." The husky fought while we held her head and lifted her lips, inspecting her teeth and gums, then started searching through the fur around her throat. Her hind legs were flailing around. "Stay *still.*" I was getting mad.

Then Fanny said, "Look!"

"Where? How bad is it?"

Fanny was holding one hind leg out and up, exposing the dog's underside. "She's not hurt, she's come into season!"

We knocked our heads together, each bending to look, still panting, still laughing, Fanny's hand still shaking, my joints suddenly weak and hot. God, to display such tremendous heart and strength the very day she comes into season . . . another omen!

If Fanny was right that the bitch had warned us, then she'd warned us every step of the way. Ten days after her season started, when she was in standing heat—flagging her tail and flirting with Fanny—we brought her to the wolf. He indicated that she was ready, becoming erect immediately and testing her rump with his nose to see if she'd let him mount. But the husky whirled around with a shriek, ears flat, teeth bared, hair bristling.

"No," Fanny screamed, "he'll kill her if they fight." Oh, yeah? The wolf just seemed bewildered for a moment and went to pee on a fence post.

So we had to muzzle the husky. That didn't stop the growling and bristling and spinning around to face the wolf every time he approached her rear. We tied and held her, one on each side, Fanny's hand on her belly to keep her standing, me holding her tail to the side. The wolf mounted, the husky rumbled and snarled and tried to twist away.

"Did he find the spot, is he in her?" I asked, trying to tip my head and see what was happening under the bitch's tail.

"No, I think he found my hand," Fanny laughed, pulling her hand away and releasing the dog. The wolf was left humping air, a stupid look on his face.

"What a pansy," I said. "I thought he had some pride." I was sweaty, dog hair sticking to me, scratch marks up and down my arms, my own hair getting in the way every time I bent my head to see what was going on. "Maybe I'll throw the two of them in the pound and go back to German shepherds." I swatted a fly with a towel, which made the husky start barking. The wolf was lying down, panting. "Oh, shut up," I snapped. "Jeez, I could kill the both of them."

But Fanny continued laughing. Why was she always laughing? Sort of a high-pitched, breathless giggle, even while she talked, making everything she said sound shaky and too fast. I sat watching the bitch lick under her leg. The wolf closed his eyes to slits like a stupefied animal in a zoo. Finally I said, "We're going to have to get an A-I kit."

"I thought you were giving up."

"I don't *ever* give up."

Silly girl with her silly mop of hair.

So we came back with the artificial insemination kit. It's a long funnel made of floppy rubber attached at the small end to a hard plastic test tube. Then there's also a syringe and a thin, hard plastic tube that goes into the bitch. The wolf's owner made us sign a waiver saying we wouldn't sue if the wolf hurt us in any way. We muzzled him, but he just stood there, his back and butt jerking while I made the collection, holding the rubber funnel over his penis, my fingers in a ring behind his knot. The little test tube filled with cloudy liquid. Then with the bitch on her back, her butt elevated on Fanny's lap, Fanny put the hard plastic tube into her dog while I kept the sperm warm between my hands. I had read exactly what to do. I drew the sperm into the syringe, attached the syringe to the thin tube, and slowly shot the liquid into the bitch. After that, we just had to hold her on her back for twenty minutes, the same amount of time the animals might normally be tied, allowing the sperm time to get to their destination. The wolf stood off to the side, his erection hanging out of him, unable to pull it in until the knot subsided. Fanny stared at him as she held her bitch on her lap. "I had no idea they were so big," she said, strangely. "And so . . . almost human shaped."

I wanted to laugh out loud but didn't. But I couldn't help it, later, when we let the bitch up and immediately there was a puddle of liquid on the ground. "Oh, puppies!" Fanny said, pretending to pick up microscopic dogs and put them in the palm of her hand. "All our puppies spilled out!"

"They're also all over the front of your pants," I said. The whole crotch area of Fanny's pants, where she'd held the bitch, was damp.

Fanny looked down at herself, touching the wet denim. A minute later she was laughing again, when the husky was pawing at my leg, then rushing to the gate and staring out. Likely she smelled a cat, but Fanny said, "She wants an abortion."

We inseminated the bitch three more times, and, as if that was the way dogs were supposed to get pregnant, she started changing shape three weeks later. I told Fanny to keep her inside during the last few weeks so she wouldn't hurt herself or the puppies charging around the yard, jumping at the fence, chasing airplanes that happened to be flying across.

When the time to whelp came, the husky told us once again that she had no intention of having puppies. The contractions started. We were ready with towels and rubber gloves and gauze and a heating pad, scissors and iodine and surgical soap. We shaved the bitch's underside, prepared the whelping box with blankets, charted her temperature. The dog kept asking to go outside, then standing in the yard trying to poop, squeezing out a shard, then coming back inside. "She thinks the contractions are the same thing as having to shit," Fanny said. "She's afraid of making a mess inside."

The dog was standing at the bedroom door, sniffing through the crack, then turning to look at us over her shoulder.

"Do you think this dog is *afraid* of anything?" I said.

But afraid or not, the bitch put a halt to her contractions. "She's *refusing* to have puppies!" Fanny laughed.

"It's been forty-five minutes, they could be dying inside her, call the vet!" I had to shout. It's like she didn't take *any*thing seriously.

So while Fanny held the dog on her lap, I drove, weaving in and out of traffic, bursting through red lights and stop signs, half hoping a police car would chase me so I could pull up at the animal hospital and scream *It's an emergency!* at someone who wouldn't *laugh*.

Then it was the dog screaming when the first pup came halfway out of her and stopped there, waiting for the next medically induced contraction. The little blind thing also opened its mouth and screamed, but silently. We were sitting on a blanket on the floor at the animal hospital. After the first puppy, which the vet took and cleaned up in another room, the pups came too quickly in succession for the bitch to see what they were. By the time she ate the placenta and gnawed through the cord, another contraction was coming, so she never had a chance for that important initial bonding with each pup.

"God, she's more keen on eating the afterbirth than taking care of the pup," I moaned.

"She has her priorities," Fanny said, holding a puppy onto a nipple. We had to do the bitch's job and make sure each pup got its first meal, took its first shit, and could breathe without bubbling.

But I have to admit, despite the laughing, Fanny seemed to sacrifice everything, at least for a few weeks, to ensure the survival of our eight wolves. Her sink was piled with dishes, dirty clothes thrown like pillows on the sofa and chair, her face pale but eye sockets dark and puffy, her house kept overly warm for people but just right for the pups, smelling damp and sour, the washing machine going twice a day to clean the towels and blankets that were quickly soiled by the litter. Half the time when I arrived in the afternoon, Fanny's hair was matted and dirty, and I would have to tell her to go take a shower, but even then Fanny might simply throw herself across the foot of the bed for an hour before she dragged herself into the bathroom.

So all the early problems were really *one* problem—it was all because of the one thing the husky bitch *didn't* have on her résumé, the one thing I hadn't had the foresight to suspect, the one thing that couldn't be verified in play or behavior tests: *The bitch had no maternal instinct.* There were eight black puppies, still blind, each sleeping curled in the shape of a kidney bean, five males and four females. Yet, for probably the only time in her life, when the bitch looked at them, there was no spark in her eye, no eagerness, not even curiosity, just sort of a dull glance when she was willing to look at them at all. Thankfully, she wasn't trying to kill them. But maybe if she had, at least they'd learn some sort of canine behavior or dignity from her.

The *physical* problems caused by the bitch's disinterest were easy to solve—Fanny had to put the bitch into the whelping box every hour or two, round the clock, and make her stay there until all the pups had eaten. She had to smear each pup with butter to make the bitch lick their little butts. But if pups and dam don't bond as they're supposed to, they won't look to her as their link to the world. If she doesn't interact with them, play with and discipline them, they'll not only have no pack experience, they won't learn behavior and attitude from her, they won't imitate, they *might* not gain her spirit and drive.

Before they were born, I went to the library almost every other day, ordered books out of dog magazines, rented videos on wolf pack studies. But no one seemed to know how much of the instinct, personality, energy, boldness, or other traits of the spirit were *genetically* passed to offspring and how much was *learned*. It shouldn't have even mattered: when you have a bitch with everything you want, physically *and* mentally, then if the genetic code doesn't carry the personality, the bitch herself will still be there as the center of the universe for the pups' first three months and they can *learn* the traits. For all I knew, the vigor of a bitch's tongue licking them would show the pups her intensity and keenness. But this bitch showed them nothing.

"She told us, from the start," Fanny laughed, despite looking haggard and not changing out of her sweatpants and T-shirt for two weeks because she was sleeping on the sofa, an alarm set to go off every ninety minutes so she could feed the pups. She dozed an hour or forty-five minutes at a stretch, day and night, her hand hanging off the sofa into the whelping box as a thermostat so she'd know if the heating pad was getting too hot or too cold. She was usually up in the afternoon when I came for several hours to sit beside the pups with a journal so I could note everything they did. "We should've listened to her," Fanny said, her dark-circled eyes staring at the pups with half-lowered lids, "when she didn't want to come into season. She was telling us. She told us all along."

The bitch would bring me a ball or an old sock tied into knots and drop it into my lap, then stand braced and staring at the toy, waiting for it to move so she could pounce and kill it. "You crazy thing," I said, unable to stop my smile, "take care of your damn puppies, will you?"

When they were two-and-a-half weeks old, the smallest male had his eyes half open, lifted his head, and rested his chin on the back of the sleeping body beside him. A sure sign of dominance, and so early. So the omens were *also* there each step of the way.

They had to plan their trip to Seattle for Christmas, but Renee and Morgan said they didn't want to plan too much, they wanted everything to be spontaneous. The only thing they'd decided so far was what day to leave. Morgan was sitting on the coffee table because Fanny was on the sofa and Renee in the chair, and the rest of the sofa was filled with newspapers and clothes. But then Renee got up, went to the whelping box, picked up a puppy, held it against her cheek for a moment, and put it back. Every time she'd ever touched the puppies, Renee had commented that they'd better not pee on her. Instead of going back to the chair, Renee pushed the newspapers over and sat beside Fanny, close enough that she pinned Fanny's arm to her side. Fanny pulled her arm free. Morgan remained on the coffee table. He was saying, "Let's make sure we travel light."

"So *we'll* bring the pajama tops and *you* bring the bottoms," Renee said. Her elbow nudged Fanny's side. Morgan was grinning. Fanny smiled and bent over the arm of the sofa, away from Renee, to look at the puppies. At three weeks, they all had their eyes open and crawled on their bellies.

"Doreen saw one of these guys humping another yesterday," she said.

"That's our kids," Morgan laughed, looking at Renee. "They start early."

"It's not sexual, it's their way of showing their position," Fanny said. She stopped. Morgan had told her he hated it when she started droning on about dog behavior.

"Positions are usually sexual," Morgan said.

"How about dance positions." Fanny's head was still hanging over the side of the sofa, her voice aimed at the whelping box, so she thought maybe no one would hear her.

"I had a teacher once," Renee said, "who said *Dance like your sex life*. He was German and didn't quite know how to express what he meant. A friend of mine used to say, *He's trying to tell me to quit, isn't he?*"

"Is that the guy who was always looking at you with love-forlorn eyes?" Fanny asked. She glanced at Morgan, then hung her head back down toward the puppies. The side of her leg was warm where

Renee was sitting against her, but her upper body was draped over the arm of the sofa.

"Yeah, poor Benjamin, my buddy."

"Did he not know that you . . . uh . . . weren't available?" Morgan asked.

"You mean that I'm a dyke?" Renee said. This time Fanny laughed too, and sat up, looking at Morgan, but he remained completely unabashed and joined the laughter. "Anyway," Renee continued, "I *was* available. I've been available for three years now."

Fanny stopped laughing, leaned back, and looked at the ceiling so she wouldn't be able to tell if anyone was looking at her—although she could feel it, she just didn't want to know which one it was.

"Flings aside," Renee added.

"We haven't gotten much accomplished," Fanny said. "I mean, do we need to make motel reservations, are we stopping in Sacramento?"

"Yeah, we'll stop and suck-a-tomato." After she spoke, Renee pushed the newspapers completely off the sofa, turned and stretched out on her back, lifted her legs, and put them across Fanny's lap. Fanny and Morgan stared at each other.

In a moment of silence, the dog scratched at the door. Not a gentle request—it sounded as if she'd dig her way through the door if no one responded. Fanny immediately started to get up to let the dog in, but Renee's legs were still across her lap, so all she did was flinch, then settle again. "Morgan, go get the dog, okay?"

Morgan had a weird grin, but he swiveled around on his butt on the coffee table, then headed toward the kitchen. Renee began talking about almost getting a serious injury the other day, stepping off a curb that was higher than she thought. She'd gotten the company to pay for a doctor who said it wasn't quite sprained but that she should massage the ankle and lower calf two or three times a day. The husky came trotting into the room, panting, and headed for Renee's face—the easiest face to reach—so Renee put her feet on the floor and pushed herself upright, and Morgan was coming back with a basket of grapes, saying, "Here she is, Miss Immaculate Conception."

As soon as Renee sat up, Fanny was off the sofa and grabbed the dog's collar, pulling her toward the whelping box. After she made the husky lie down in the box, Fanny pulled the dog's lower hind leg forward and up so that she was fully on her side, exposing her whole shaved belly. "Go get them nippies," Fanny said to the pups, who were already scrambling toward their mother.

"Really?" Renee said, stretching out alone on the sofa on her stomach, her hands folded on the armrest, her chin propped up, looking down into the box. "She didn't even mate with the father?"

Fanny looked up, laughing again. "She didn't wanna have nothing to do with that wolf and his wanger!"

"Fanny got her pregnant by herself," Morgan added.

"Believe me, it was Doreen too." Fanny was still squatting on the floor beside the box. She couldn't let go of the dog's hind leg or Lacy would abruptly stand up and the pups would fall from her like fruit from a tree. "You should have seen her, kneeling there jacking off a *wolf*, saying *Come on, baby, let me milk that sperm outta you!* She's got bona fide ironclad balls. I'm surprised she even needed the wolf at all. She gets what she wants, believe me."

"I'd like to meet her," Renee said.

"No, you wouldn't," Morgan said quickly. Fanny stared at him, but Renee was still looking at the pups, stroking one down its back with one finger. *"You* may be surprised Doreen needed the wolf," Morgan said, "but I'm surprised she needed *Lacy.* I'm surprised Doreen didn't try to get that wolf to fuck *her."*

The husky jerked her hind leg out of Fanny's fist, grunted, and heaved herself to a standing position. The pups dropping off made wet snapping sounds as their mouths came loose. "Now look what you did, Morgan," Fanny laughed, "you made her mad, that wolf was *her* husband."

"Maybe *husband* should be redefined."

"Then so should *wife.*"

"You two," Renee said, rolling to her back, cupping a puppy to her chest. "Should I leave the room?"

"Hell, no," Morgan grinned. Then added, "If we're redefining husband and wife, that means you should *stay.*"

Renee raised the puppy in the air. When Fanny took the pup from her, Renee swung her arms up behind her head and stretched her body, arching her back up from the sofa. "Oh," she groaned, "my leg needs massaging."

Holding the puppy under her chin with both hands, Fanny looked at Morgan, and he looked back at her, rolling a couple of grapes around in his cupped palm. The husky walked through the room with a rawhide bone cocked out of her mouth.

On the bathroom counter, Suzanne laid out her panty hose, earrings, necklace, bracelet, slip, bra, and underwear. She hung her pearl gray skirt and pink silk blouse on a hook on the wall, uncapped two or three lipsticks, and held them up against the clothes, then selected one and put the rest away. She did the same with eye shadow, then chose rouge powder. Earlier in the week she'd called some old friends—a couple they used to go out with at least once a month. Careers and buying new houses had gradually slowed the activity between them. During the past two years, they might've gotten together once or twice, but that was only because Scott and Suzanne had been invited to big parties at the other couple's house. So Suzanne had chatted on the phone with the wife, saying, every time a topic died down, "There's so much we have to catch up on," until the other woman had suggested they get together for dinner soon. The second time the woman mentioned getting together, Suzanne said, "I don't think Scott has a job this Saturday." So it was set.

When she'd told Scott, at first he just looked at her, then said, "Why?"

"What do you mean, *why?* We haven't seen them in so long."

"Why *now?* What made you all of a sudden decide to set something up?"

"It just came up, Scott. Did you have other plans?"

He hadn't even answered, had gone back to sanding a new doghouse he'd gotten because Sadie had chewed the doorway of her old one so badly that Scott said he was afraid she'd get splinters.

Just as she was about to turn the shower on, Suzanne heard Scott come in the back door. She tightened her robe and went out to the kitchen. He was eating crackers from a box and drinking a glass of orange juice, looking out the window into the front yard, the refrigerator door still open. She gently pushed the door shut with two fingers, then came up behind him and touched his back with the same two fingers. He moved, as though to turn and face her, but also moved sideways to the other end of the kitchen counter, looked out the window again as if there was something he could see from there that he hadn't been able to see from where he'd been.

"Don't eat too much," Suzanne said, "We want to be hungry tonight."

"It'll be hours before we eat," he said.

"What should I wear?" she smiled.

"Whatever you want."

"Come on, hon. My black dress with the low back? The flowered one with the pleats? Or how about evening pants, the white satin ones?"

"Wear whatever you want," he said. "Does this have to be a dressy thing?"

"It seems like we haven't dressed up in a while, don't you want to?"

He put his empty glass down in the sink. The clink of it seemed too loud. "Aren't you making this too much of a big deal?" He went past her, opened the refrigerator again, then closed it and left the kitchen.

Suzanne went back to the bedroom and into the bathroom. She went straight to the cabinet under the sink and checked the box of condoms. It was still unopened. She got into the shower and shut her eyes while she wet her hair. She always kept her eyes shut the entire time in the shower. She knew where the soap and washcloth and shampoo were by feel. She listened for Scott to come into the bathroom and notice the things she'd laid out on the counter. Maybe he'd say, "This'll look nice." But how likely *was* it—he hadn't seemed to notice what she was wearing for quite a while. After all, she knew what he liked, she'd figured it out long ago, that's what marriage was all about, wasn't it? Having the *same* taste, that's what marriage was. Weren't compliments, therefore, unnecessary?

There was only one suitcase and one garment bag. Morgan told her that he would use one and she could use the other, instead of mixing their clothes in both. Fanny spread the sheets and blankets semi-flat on the bed so she could lay her stuff out before packing it. Morgan and Renee were at the last Sunday matinee performance of the company's modern dance version of *The Nutcracker,* Fanny had a waitressing job that night, then they were all leaving for Seattle early the next morning, as soon as Doreen arrived to stay with the dog and her six-week-old pups.

The only trips she and Morgan had ever taken were to his mother's in Arizona for Christmas, and she would just pick up a handful of underwear from the drawer then throw it into the suitcase. Now she found herself examining each pair and discarding those with blood stains or frayed waistbands or worn-out elastic. She picked up the huge sweatshirt she usually slept in and imagined Morgan asking, *You sure you want Renee to see you in that?* She tossed the sweatshirt into the laundry basket and dug through a drawer of T-shirts, finally chose a gray one that had shrunk and was a little too small for her. Once, a long time ago, Morgan had circled his finger around her nipple while she was wearing this shirt, saying it was so tight that it made her look as if she had bigger breasts. She quickly wadded the shirt and threw it into the suitcase.

Yesterday, during an unusual evening watching TV without Renee there, Morgan had said, "I'm glad you and Renee have gotten to be such good friends."

"It's funny," she'd said, "considering the difference in our ages and . . . everything else."

"What do you talk about?" Morgan had turned the volume down. "I don't mean I'm entitled to know everything you say to each other, you can say and do whatever you want, I'm just . . . I don't know . . . maybe I'm being too nosy?"

"No, I don't mind telling you."

"Well . . . I think she likes you."

Fanny had concentrated on her arms, making sure they stayed relaxed along the back of the sofa. "Friends usually like each other."

"You know what I mean." He'd smiled, almost shyly, like the first time he'd told her he loved her.

"Oh, you mean *like?*" she'd said. "The way we meant in junior high?" She didn't tell him how Renee, at the reception following the first *Nutcracker* performance, had smiled strangely, looking at a bartender pouring champagne, and said she'd told an old friend over the phone *I think one of the male corps dancers likes me . . . and I like his wife!*

"Okay," Morgan said, "I think she's attracted to you."

"What makes you think so?"

"Well . . ." Morgan had turned back toward the TV but he didn't turn the volume up. "You're probably her type."

"What's that mean?" Fanny was acutely conscious that she hadn't moved her arms or legs during this whole conversation.

"You know," Morgan twirled a half-full glass of orange juice, swirling the juice around and around, watching it. "You've always, uh, felt different from other people. Don't you, you know, feel not *as* different with her?"

Fanny decided which jeans she would wear on the trip and which she should pack. She pulled out a crewneck gray wool sweater, paused, dug deeper, and gingerly picked up another sweater that she saved for special occasions, hadn't worn in years. It was black with a brightly colored, off-center design on the front, splashed with a few sequins, a low-cut back. It usually slid off one shoulder. She couldn't remember the last time she'd worn it, had almost worn it to the *Nutcracker* reception, usually pictured herself wearing it when she imagined someone putting a hand in her hair or kissing her neck.

Last night, after a moment of silence, Morgan had said, "I just want you to know, it's okay with me if you . . . you know . . . want to be with Renee. If you want to . . . see what happens . . ."

"I don't know that anything's going to happen," she answered slowly. She'd finally lowered her arms from the top of the sofa, folded her hands in her lap. Her armpits ached.

"Well, if it does, if things start to develop . . . you know . . . it could be . . . good for you. It could be what you need."

"What I need . . . ," she'd echoed. Paused, as though watching the nearly silent ad, which involved a Christmas party with people coming through the snow to a warmly lit cottage, long enough that when she spoke again, she obviously wasn't finishing the old sentence but starting over: "I was a disappointment from the beginning, in every way imaginable . . . wasn't I?"

Morgan hadn't answered.

After counting out enough socks for the trip, Fanny shut the drawer, then opened it again and felt under the folded socks until her hand found the smooth, round vibrator. It was Mr. Foss who had recommended it on their third visit, which turned out to be their last. They'd walked out past the reception desk without stopping to make another appointment. Outside, Morgan had breathed deeply and said "Free at last!" and they'd both laughed. But Fanny had gone ahead and bought the vibrator. When she'd showed it to Morgan a few days later, he tried it on the back of his neck, smiling and closing his eyes like the dog did when they scratched the right place behind her ear.

It was unusual to have a Sunday night catering job, and when he'd booked it, he'd been a little annoyed that he'd have to stay up late on Sunday, then return to his building early Monday morning. But after Saturday night's dinner date, Scott wished he had jobs scheduled all day Sunday and on into the night. As it was, he left three hours early Sunday afternoon for a six o'clock job.

He did some paperwork at his office, then, still an hour early, drove to the job site. It was on the opposite side of downtown from the theaters where matinees of the symphony, plays, and other performances would've attracted people and filled the weekend streets with parked vehicles. That's why he was able to notice her car, the only one parked on the block, a ten-year-old faded red economy car with a rusty fender, bent bumper, and red cellophane taped over a broken tail light. As he pulled up behind the old car, he saw she was still sitting inside. Getting out of his car, retrieving his briefcase from the backseat, putting on the alarm, and locking the club to the steering wheel, he moved more deliberately than usual, consciously slowing himself down, glancing over at her now and then, waiting for her to see him so he could wave hello, then maybe she'd unroll her window and he'd step over to have a few words. But she didn't turn. He locked his car door with the key, even though it had already automatically locked when he'd closed it. Then he put his briefcase on the hood, opened it, checked the contract inside, lifted the contract, and looked underneath it. He shuffled his foot on the ground to get rid of a large pebble he was standing on, making a loud scratchy noise in the vacant street, but still she didn't turn. She was looking down, as though reading something.

It wasn't as though he hadn't been talking to her fairly regularly for two or three months now. He'd continued to inquire about her

dog, then found out about the pregnancy and the arrival of the puppies. She seemed to enjoy giving him details about the progress of
the litter. He tried to ask both intelligent questions about the various behaviors she was noticing in individual puppies and silly questions like did she make a papier-mâché moon and hang it over the
puppies to teach them to howl? She'd laughed and said, "No, but
we've put up little framed pictures of rabbits and fawns on the sides
of the box so they'll get their prey instinct."

When he got close to her car door, she did look up. She wasn't
reading. Something was in her hands on her lap, but he couldn't see
what it was. She put it on the passenger seat and got out of the car,
smiling. He felt his muscles relax and his last breath ease away like
an inaudible sigh, then he was breathing normally again.

"Hi, boss."

"Don't call me that," he smiled. "I hate that."

She didn't say anything else, just stood there, leaning against her
car. She looked up the street as though expecting someone. It wasn't
the most awkward moment he'd ever had, but it was enough to use
the topic he'd been saving. His vet had recommended that he find
a behaviorist or experienced trainer and ask for advice about Sadie's
tremendous energy surges. He could hear Suzanne say, "He said a
professional trainer, Scott, not a *waitress*," but he'd already decided,
from the moment the vet had made the suggestion, that he would
talk to Fanny about it.

She listened to him with her eyes focused somewhere on the front
of his shirt. He described how Sadie had been chewing sheets and
pillowcases, ripping up throw rugs, digging holes in the lawn, even
gnawing on the edge of the wooden fence and the doorway of her
doghouse. He said he tried to allow her to run all she wanted, once
a day if he could, but sometimes, because of his schedule and wanting to make sure the park was empty, it was after midnight. "So, do
you know of anyone who specializes in problems like these . . . or
maybe you already know what I'm doing wrong?"

Her eyes came up to his face. "I've a friend you could ask, but I
already know what she'd say, since she already said it to me about
my crazy dog."

"What is it?"

"Dog sports."

"You mean like that Frisbee thing?"

"No. Not just that." Her voice was steady and lower, not choppy and breathless with an invisible laugh as it frequently was, nor the scary monosyllabic monotone she seemed to use just as often. "There're all kinds of things, like obedience competition or hurtle relays or Schutzhund—that's a competition for working dogs, not for sporting breeds like yours. What *I'd* do is agility."

"Tell me about it." He checked his watch. Still plenty early.

"The dogs climb things like A-frames and planks, and they jump different kinds of jumps and go through tunnels."

"What's the point to it? How will it solve my problem? How is it different than letting the dog run free in the park?"

She smiled. "A dog needs a purpose in life. Doreen said that's what *my* dog's problem is—although having puppies sure wasn't her idea of a *purpose!*"

A car was coming down the street, so Scott moved sideways and leaned against the back fender of her car. "What if a dog's purpose in life is digging and chewing?"

"Those are signs of boredom. Put your dog to work, and she won't need to look for something to do during her time off."

"Well, I can understand that a dog who herds sheep all day isn't going to hunt squirrels under the bed, but dogs don't have jobs like that anymore—"

"So we have to invent work. All of these things involve training, there are rules and right ways and wrong ways . . . the dog has to learn and then think and then keep thinking when you go to compete—"

"These are competitions? My dog could win ribbons?"

She laughed louder than he'd ever heard her. He knew he was blushing.

"I want to hear more about this," he said. "I think I'd like to do this with my dog. I'd like to get more information. Are there any books? Maybe . . . could we maybe have, uh, lunch sometime . . . so I could find out—"

"You should come out to the park with Doreen and me." She turned and reached into the car for a sweatshirt, then locked the car door. "But I don't have any equipment."

"I can help build some."

"You'd better wait and see before volunteering—this takes a lot of time."

"I can make time. I'm the boss, remember?"

"Right," she smiled, then lowered her eyes again. She stuffed her keys into a pocket in the sweatshirt, draped the sweatshirt over one arm, then crossed her arms over her chest. "We better go," she'd said. A car was coming. She ran across the street before it passed. He stayed staring after her, long after she'd turned and looked back at him with a quizzical expression, then disappeared into the building.

He couldn't remember ever saying *I'm the boss* to anyone in his life before this. Not even joking, as he had been, and surely Fanny would've known that. But Suzanne had found it easy enough to pull out and use last night. And how in the world had they ended up on the subject of going to Greenland from where they'd started, after that silent drive home, when Suzanne had said dryly, "I hope we got home fast enough for you"?

"What's that supposed to mean?" he'd said, reaching to loosen his tie but stopping. He left the tie on, and the coat. He wouldn't have been wearing either if he hadn't found them hanging on his closet door after he'd come out of the shower.

"Did you have to act so obviously *bored?* Yawning, checking your watch—"

"I'm tired, okay?"

"You hardly said a word all evening. They noticed, too. What do you think it looked like to them? You didn't even look at me. It was like three of us were out to dinner, having a conversation, and you were just . . . *eating.*"

"I was hungry. I didn't have lunch." He sat on the bed, then stretched out one leg so he could reach in his pocket and remove the money clip. He only used it when they went out; Suzanne always handed it to him at the door so he wouldn't have a wallet bulge in his rear pocket. He took the bills out of the clip, got his wallet out of the nightstand drawer, and put the money away. He'd long ago stopped asking her how he was supposed to drive without his license when they went out.

He *had* been tired, and extremely hungry, but it was also true he'd been bored, so all of this was not unexpected. But when Suzanne went into the bathroom and shut the door, he'd thought it was over.

He'd removed his coat and tie, changed into jeans and sweatshirt, was tying his tennis shoes and about to go get the dog from her run when Suzanne came out of the bathroom, smiling, talking about going shopping for the clothes they would need when they went to Greenland. He kept staring at his shoe, twisting the laces into a knot, then undoing them, as though he'd never successfully tied shoes before.

When Suzanne paused to pull her slip over her head, he'd said, "How can you bring this up now?"

"What?" Her voice came from inside her slip.

"A big trip like that, how can you even think of something like that now."

"It's coming sooner than you think, this summer—"

"How can you even think of going at all? It's not cast in stone."

"I made the deposit, Scott. I thought you heard me, yesterday." She was still in her bra and panty hose, looking around for something, then took her nightgown off a hook in the closet, put it over her head, and, with her arms loose inside the nightgown, finished taking off her undergarments. He'd never seen her undress like that. But he hadn't been in the same room when she dressed or undressed for a long time. She stood on one foot and then the other, putting on fuzzy slippers.

While she was washing her face, he thought of saying that losing the deposit was better than wasting the money on a trip when maybe what they needed was time away from each other. He considered saying business was a little slow and they shouldn't be spending that kind of money right now. He could've suggested she find a traveling companion and go without him. What he'd ended up saying was that he didn't have anyone he could trust to run the business while he was so far away for so long.

Suzanne turned toward him. Her face was paler, hard, the lines around her mouth seemed deep and rigid, her eyes lashless and staring. She held her robe closed with a hand that looked bony and stark. "That's some excuse, Scott," she'd said, resuming the flat voice she'd used as they'd walked in the door. "You didn't have a problem leaving when we went to Galapagos or Hong Kong. No," her voice moved from flat to icy, "back then you were the *boss.*"

Scott had gotten up and started to leave the room, one shoe still untied. The dog had heard them arrive home and was yipping in her pen. But he'd forgotten her leash and had to turn back to get it from the closet. It was just as he'd realized he didn't have the leash—when he'd pulled his hand away from the doorknob and started to turn back—that Suzanne suddenly blurted, "And don't you dare try to bring up sex."

"What?"

"I know what you've been thinking." Her voice was harsh and wild, like someone in an asylum. She hadn't moved since turning from the sink. "I'm not just a convenience for you to jump on and leave your slime behind when you jump off. Just forget it."

Then he couldn't find the leash. He had to go past her into the closet and look on every hook, her voice still reverberating like the shimmer of a gong, so when he finally said, "I guess I already have," he couldn't be sure she even heard him. He'd eventually found the leash draped across the inside doorknob under where he'd slung his coat.

Of course it had rained since their arrival in Seattle, but that's what Morgan had expected and even wanted, the shine of lights in wet streets, the freedom of being without an umbrella, wet to the skin; the invigorating energy of running into their warm hotel room and stripping off soaked clothing. But it was still just the first night. Renee had gone into the bathroom and now was in the shower. Fanny had waited until Renee's clothes splatted on the floor and the shower was splashing before she peeled off her jeans and sweatshirt and wrapped herself in the bedspread in a chair near the heater, reading a magazine. Morgan stretched out on his back on the bed, the only bed in the room, his hands under his head, letting his body shiver in his wet clothes, listening to his heart beat in his ears.

After actually looking at a map, they'd all agreed to fly to Seattle instead of drive. Renee had pointed out that it would cost as much for gas and motels as the airfare would be. He'd told Fanny it would be their Christmas presents, she'd nodded, and Renee had made the arrangements. It was late and they were lucky to get seats, she'd said, so the seats were split, two together and one five rows up, on the aisle. Fanny insisted she sit by the window, took two sleeping pills and puked during the takeoff, then curled up with her face against the window and didn't move for the entire flight. Renee had stopped by his seat once, on her way to the rest room, and asked if he wanted to switch. "What good would that do?" he'd asked. "Both of us would still have no one to talk to."

Again in the cab from the airport, Fanny insisted on sitting by a window. Renee sat in the middle of the backseat beside Fanny, who was collapsed sideways, leaning against the door with her forehead against the window glass. Morgan squeezed in beside Renee. "She's a baby when she's sick," he'd said. "She wants to be fussed over."

"I want my mommy," Fanny had groaned.

Renee laughed. "I know, some people want attention when they're sick, some people want to be left strictly alone."

"Usually when I'm nauseous," Fanny had said, fogging up the window, "someone has to lightly rub my stomach with one finger."

"Guess who gets that job," he'd said.

Renee had smiled again but didn't say anything.

Fanny would actually claim his finger running lightly up and down her stomach made her feel better, but if he moved his finger in a circle, it made her more dizzy. She would lift her shirt up to just below her breasts and push her underwear down past her hips, then sigh over and over as he moved his fingers on her skin. But other times, if she was on the sofa watching TV or reading in bed, if he ran his hand under her shirt and touched her breasts, she would stiffen, her body almost convulsed, like an anemone closing when it gets touched. She'd started that a couple of years after they'd been married, but of course it hadn't happened lately, not in the past several years—he didn't give it an opportunity to happen. She still wanted to be hugged when she was cold and stroked when she was sick, and she held his hand when they walked through crowded stores, but he didn't touch her in any way that would turn her body into a fist.

In the steamy cab, he'd watched Renee's hand move slowly up and down Fanny's back. He'd almost felt light-headed too, but it was different.

By the time they were trooping around the streets of downtown Seattle, Fanny had recovered. And when the sidewalks seemed a little crowded, she took hold of his hand. Renee was on his other side at that moment—a hot streak of adrenaline had made him weak for a second, but he'd done it anyway, reached out and took Renee's hand too. Only seconds later Fanny had broken free to press her face against the window of a gallery, and Renee's hand just sort of fell away from his.

Fanny said she didn't want to make any decisions, claimed she was always making decisions and she didn't want to make any more for three days. She said she was going to close her eyes and point to the menu and eat whatever her finger landed on, which just happened to be pork chops. But he suspected she'd been peeking. Renee had ordered scallops and he'd gotten an eggplant casserole. He'd asked her what was the drug she'd taken and Renee laughed, but when Fanny went to the restroom, Renee had said, "Do you think she's having a good time?"

The waiter had arrived with salads, so he didn't have to answer. When Fanny came back from the restroom, her hair damp and slightly slicked down, she'd said, "I miss the puppies. Five weeks is the cutest age, and I'm missing it. What if they bond to Doreen and forget who I am?"

"You're not going to keep one," he'd said. "You're not *considering* that, are you?"

"No, we've already got one uncontrollable beast in the house." As her hair dried, it started to stand up again.

"Which one of you would *that* be?" Renee said, grinning, huge dark eyes glinting.

"We take turns," Morgan had returned.

The shower went off. The pipes clunked and rattled the walls of the old hotel. Fanny looked up toward the bathroom door, then looked at Morgan. He smiled at her, but he wondered if it really looked like his regular smile.

After Scott had fallen asleep reading some kind of dog training book, Suzanne was still awake. The bed seemed to rock gently with the breathing rhythms of both Scott and the dog, like being in bed on a boat. Slightly dizzy, she sat up and got out of bed, not being especially careful to go easy, but neither man nor dog missed a breath. This might have been the night she joined them on a midnight walk, but it didn't look as if they would be going. She had planned on being more patient and serene when she accompanied him to the park. Try again, it would go better. It wasn't as though she had brought up things he'd never heard of—these were their plans, *his* plans—but he'd looked at her for a moment as if she'd walked into the wrong living room and spoken to the wrong husband.

He'd been on the floor watching a football game, his legs stretched out in front, his shoulders propped up against the couch, eating a microwave pizza off his stomach like a sea otter. She'd told him before that it was bad for his digestive system to eat that way but let it go this time. There were no crumbs on the rug. He'd certainly seemed himself when he first got home from work, had told her about an employee whom he suspected of petty stealing and how lazy everyone was. So later it seemed entirely natural for her to say, "So, isn't Fred working out?"

"Who?" He'd taken a huge bite of pizza.

"That guy who's supposed to be second-in-charge?"

"Fernando. He's okay."

"Do you think he'll be capable, or will you have to start looking for a manager?"

Scott hadn't faced her when her voice trailed away. He took another bite of pizza.

"You know, it's getting to be time to plan who's going to run things . . . you know, for when we live in Europe? . . ." She'd taken a breath, waited, then gone on. "I've been thinking . . . when we come home, you could let your secretary go and I'd take her place. I guess the only problem will be when we take trips to look for our retirement spot—"

That's when he'd looked at her. Hadn't stared or glared or questioned, just looked. Then he'd said, "I don't want to think about this right now."

"I know the word retirement is scary," she'd said with a gentle laugh, "but if you're going to retire early, five or six or seven years from now would be the time . . ."

Scott was picking the crumbs off his chest and putting them on his plate. Then he got up and left the room.

Almost from the day they had married, Scott had talked about having a whole year to live in Europe instead of pathetic tourist packages for two weeks at a time. He'd talked about selling his business, investing the money, renting out the house for a year. Later he'd decided he'd hire a trustworthy manager, let the business support them in Europe, then come home and work five more years and focus their vacations on exploratory trips to find the perfect spot to retire, reward themselves for the years of hard work by being completely free before they were old.

Scott hadn't come back to the football game. After waiting about ten minutes, she'd followed him and found him clipping the dog's nails on the bed. Not pausing, he'd said, "We can't go away for a year, what would happen to Sadie?"

The two of them were both still asleep. She wondered if Scott was faking. Then someone finally moved—the dog crept up toward the headboard and settled with a sigh against Suzanne's pillow.

It was still before midnight. They'd gone to bed early. But Fanny was up again, sitting at the window with the closed drapes pulled around the chair to make a private room. She put her heels on the seat of the chair, wrapped her arms around her legs, and propped her chin on top of her knees. It was raining, again or still, spattering against the window and running down the glass, so she couldn't see anything outside except blobs of lights, some standing still, others moving past with the hissing sound of tires on wet pavement.

Long before the trip, she'd told Morgan, "The only way I'm getting into a bed with the two of you is if I'm in the middle."

"Fine," he'd said mildly.

She was in bed first, dead in the middle. Then Morgan and Renee each got in and they'd all shifted into the only comfortable position: each on their left side, all facing the same direction, all with their knees cocked, Renee in front of Fanny, Morgan behind.

It had always been easy to determine when Morgan was asleep. His breathing got deeper and his body would twitch or jump. Tonight she hadn't noticed anything that obvious, but his breathing was slow and a little heavy, right against the back of her neck. He'd draped an arm around her, so his hand was wedged between her stomach and Renee's back. Fanny couldn't hear Renee breathing at all, but then she felt Renee start to push backwards. The back of Renee's head was right in front of Fanny's face, her shoulder and spine inches away from Fanny's breast and stomach. As Renee snuggled backwards, her butt pushed into Fanny's groin. Fanny didn't know whether she felt Renee wiggle, as though wagging an imaginary tail, or if it was her own pulse she felt pounding there. At the same time, Morgan began to edge closer on her other side, pushing his pelvis against Fanny's butt. *Like being in a womb as one member of triplets,* she thought, *our mother impregnated by three different men.* The bed might've been moving a little, she couldn't tell, it could've been her own breathing, it could've been everyone's breathing, but it also could've been Morgan and Renee rocking back and forth against her. She was afraid she might get nauseated again, wondered if she coughed, if they would jump away from her and lie like sticks on the edges of the mattress.

Morgan had a hard-on, a lump against the crack of her butt. She'd told Mr. Foss how Morgan sometimes got that way in his sleep and pushed against her like this, feeling her with his hand and nuzzling her neck, but so solidly asleep he didn't remember it in the morning. "Do you enjoy it?" Foss had asked, and she'd nodded, looking away from his white mustache. "Fine, just let yourself enjoy it," he'd said.

"Too bad *I* don't get to enjoy it," Morgan had said with a weak smile.

But she was pretty sure he wasn't asleep this time. He wasn't rubbing his hand over her chest, he wasn't grinding his face against her shoulder blade . . . but he might actually stick his cock in her if it was the shortest way to get to Renee.

So she'd eased herself out of bed. She sat up and moved down to the foot of the mattress, put her feet on the floor, and stood up. She'd heard rustling in the blankets behind her, and when she turned, they'd both adjusted to their stomachs, facing away from each other, still space enough between them for her to lie back down, but she hadn't.

Fanny dialed her home phone, then took the receiver back to the chair by the window behind the drapes. When Doreen answered, Fanny said, "Hi. I knew you wouldn't be asleep." Her voice was spooky low in the dark room.

"Having a good time?" Doreen said brightly.

"Yeah. But weird. Like a different world. I mean . . . because I was locked up with the puppies so long. How are they? Does she like them any better?"

"She still tries to eat their shit, but other than that . . ." Doreen laughed again. Fanny smiled. "They're great, though, every male shows signs of dominance, they all played tug-of-war with a towel today and in five minutes shredded it to pieces, no one gave up. I haven't seen *any* of them run into a corner with his tail tucked. I just don't know which one of these guys I'm gonna want."

"Well, I better go," Fanny whispered.

"You okay? You sound weird."

"I just don't want to wake . . . uh, Morgan up."

"Couldn't remember old what's'is name, huh? Boy, you *do* need a vacation. Okay, I'll see you in a few days."

Fanny stood looking at the bed where the two bodies lay on the outer sides of the mattress, heads tucked in so neither was any more than a bulge in the blankets. If she didn't get in bed, they would find her sleeping on the floor or in the bathtub when they woke. So she crawled back to her spot, lay down with her forehead against Morgan's spine. Almost immediately, Renee moved closer so their backs touched. Morgan whispered, "How're the puppies?"

It was still early enough that the sidewalks were virtually empty. Service trucks with screechy brakes and backfiring exhaust seemed louder than usual but they also added somehow to the overall quiet feeling of the wet streets, closed storefronts, gray light. Renee had gotten up at five and taken her clothes into the bathroom. When she came out, already showered and dressed, Morgan sat up, pulling the covers off Fanny, who then grunted and yanked the blankets all the way over her head. Renee had only gotten a peek at how Fanny's hair was barely different when she woke up than when she combed it, maybe a little more free to zing in every direction.

Morgan had asked, "Where're we going for breakfast?"

"You and Fanny go," Renee said. "I've got to go see a friend, she works in a bakery, they start real early, so we can meet back here at, say, ten?"

Morgan had pursed his lips to one side and looked away. "Maybe I'll take a walk."

"There's only one extra key," Renee had said, putting one key in her pocket.

The room was silent until Fanny's voice mumbled from under the blankets, "S'okay, I'll stay here."

Renee stopped to look in the window of a gallery shared by several artisans. Yesterday Fanny had stopped here, then slipped inside and bent over the glass cases displaying earrings and ear cuffs. She'd rested both arms on the glass and slid her upper body along the entire wall-long display case. She'd come back, over and over, to a silver cuff shaped like a hand that would grasp the rim of her ear. "That would look cool on you," Renee had said. Fanny continued moving along the counter, but came back again to the ear cuff. "Get it," Renee urged. She could've slipped ten bucks into Fanny's pocket. Instead, she'd called Morgan over from where he was examining men's shoulder bags. "Don't you think this one would look good on her?" Renee had said. Fanny was once again sliding away to a different part of the display case.

"Yeah," he'd said. "How much?"

"I don't want it," Fanny had said and left the store. Morgan and Renee had looked at each other. He'd shrugged and turned to follow Fanny to the street, but Renee hissed, "Get it for her. For Christmas." So he'd bought the ear cuff, but he still hadn't given it to her. As he was paying, he'd asked Renee, "You want anything here?"

The bakery Marsella worked in had a little pastry shop in front, but it wasn't open yet. Renee went in through the employee's entrance and found Marsella cutting donuts from a slab of dough. The yeasty smell of Marsella and the floury, dusty feel of her skin rushed back over Renee when Marsella stopped work, hugged her, and said, "My little honey." She'd known Marsella since high school, when Marsella, sixteen years older, had worked in the cafeteria. After the hug, Marsella slid her fingers down Renee's arms, grasped her hands, and didn't let go. They sat on stools facing each other. "Tell me everything," Marsella said. "Your new life, your new loves . . . everything."

Renee took a deep breath from air pungent with smells of baking, especially thick sourdough, which was the bakery's specialty. "It's okay," she began, "I shouldn't complain . . . *but* . . . I'm not a real prima yet."

"Is there an apprentice period? Do you have to understudy at first?"

"I've been sharing principal spots, but that's how it's done, you switch off, especially if there's a matinee and evening performance the same day. Or if you're doing school assemblies—which you only do to qualify for grants—we split the company to cover more schools. But it's such a waste to dance at schools and old folks homes when there'll never be an agent or choreographer there who might notice me. I'll try to get an exemption from the community enrichment shit."

Marsella used one hand to push a wisp of hair back, leaving a flour smudge on her forehead, then took Renee's hands again. "Go on, what irons do you have in the fire?" She laughed. "You always do!"

"Well, I want to sell them on my idea to feature one dancer in a series of programs, ideally using one choreographer. We could have a national search to pick the choreographer—a contest for women who haven't done a major production. It could probably get the company a grant. Then the public would start to get to know my range, like an actor, you know—they start to like the way certain actors play roles. They won't just follow dance, they'll start to follow *me* dancing. But I have to have people believing in the idea . . . for that, I think they have to know me, be close to me."

"You've never had trouble with that."

"But I don't want people to think I'm sucking up to management. So I can't start socializing with *them*. Not with the political climate in this company. It's like a dysfunctional family that needs therapy!"

Marsella laughed mildly. "If anyone can bring them together, you can."

Renee sighed. "I just have to be patient, even though it's eating at me all the time. I have to be patient and make friends naturally."

"Sweetheart," Marsella said, holding one of Renee's hands in each of hers, clapping Renee's palms together softly, "be careful. I know your art is your body, so for you, emotions and sensuality are so often the same thing. You've never had a friend who didn't turn into a lover. But look how many of them couldn't *stay* your friend—they want to devour you and then are mortally hurt that they can't have you, can't steal you away and keep you all for themselves in some secret place."

"I don't always do that," Renee said, looking away. Her arms were totally limp, and Marsella, still holding onto her wrists, was gently shaking them, the way a carriage driver slaps the reins over the horse's back. "*You* stayed my friend. You didn't regret it."

"Sweetest afternoon of my life. But I didn't *need* you, little monkey. I was happy to give *you* what you needed, but *I* haven't needed anything for years. Just to watch you blooming, to see you get up when you fall, overcome and cry and overcome again."

Someone somewhere dropped several pans. The clanging echoed and someone shouted, then someone laughed, the voices rounded and enlarged so neither anger nor humor was recognizable.

"Tell me about your new friends," Marsella said. "Do they believe in your vision?"

"They're too fucked up to be much help."

"Did little Renee explode on the scene like a fireball and burn up all the oxygen and leave them dizzy and gasping?" Marsella laughed, dropping Renee's wrists, putting her hands on her own lower spine, stretching, arching her back.

"I think they were fucked up before they met me." Renee pinched off a piece of dough and put it in her mouth. "But sometimes it seems I'm the one who can't breathe. I don't know why. They're not good for me, but I'm always with them."

"How can you afford that? Is this the married couple you spoke of?"

"Yes." Renee was reaching for the dough again, but Marsella caught her hand, threaded their fingers together.

"Little honey, don't let yourself be someone else's forbidden fruit."

Renee looked at the fans high up in the ceiling, moving slowly, like aimless flies in a band of sunlight.

"Let me get you some coffee and sourdough," Marsella said, patting Renee's cheek. A loud buzzing machine started somewhere in the building, and Renee was suddenly light-headed and famished.

———————

The last Christmas catering job was December 24, the first New Year's job was December 31, anything in between would've been too small to bother with, so Scott gave his employees five days off. He had found a book on dog agility that specified obstacles and gave sample plans plus rudiments of training. The day after Christmas, he started building equipment. He might've started Christmas day if the hardware stores had been open, would've at least provided new material for the customary back-slapping banter at the party— *a Santa's workshop for the dog? business must be good, eh, buddy?*

Maybe he hadn't managed a hearty laugh or returned the quips, but he *had* smiled at the usual ribbing from Suzanne's father and uncles about why didn't he put on an apron and serve them their Christmas dinner, wasn't he dying to go out there and whip those women into a first-rate catering staff, or why hadn't he hired a few of his cute waitresses to serve beer and snacks? Kept himself occupied with talk of new roofs, new secretaries, new problems with old plumbing; kept watch to make sure the kids kept their feet out of the garden and hands off the walls; remembered to replenish the wine decanters on the counter. He made his list for the hardware store in his head, tried to slip out to the garage to see if he had enough purple paint for the teeter-totter, but never made it. The women spent half the day in the kitchen, their words and laughter getting louder and looser. And while he didn't spend more than a passing few moments trying, he never picked Suzanne's voice out of the cacophony, although he was somewhat curious about what news she might be sharing.

So he got through it, then he'd had five days to begin building equipment and training his dog, to move from room to room in an empty and silent house while Suzanne was at work, and to try to find Fanny in the park.

At her last job before Christmas, Fanny had told him which park she used, that the time of day varied, and that she'd be out of town for a few days—all while she packed up some leftovers, which the employees were allowed to do. Generally only the busboys took anything—usually just nabbed something with one hand then ate as they pulled keys out of their pockets and left through the back door. She hadn't said when she'd be back. The first four days, he'd driven slowly past the park a few times a day. The fifth day, he'd pulled into the parking lot at ten-thirty and assembled his equipment, everything he'd finished so far—except the teeter-totter—had played ball with Sadie, taken her on a walk, started short training sessions, sat on a lawn chair while Sadie chewed rawhide bones. He was prepared to stay all day, but someone appeared a little after noon.

A tall woman with long, straight red hair tied a German shepherd to her truck's tailgate and began unloading an A-frame made from two doors.

She didn't merely glance curiously from the corner of her eye—as soon as she noticed Scott's jumps and obstacles, she came right over and asked what he was training for, reaching to pat Sadie as she spoke.

"Agility" he said, "I've just started. Do you know Fanny? She said she trains here."

"Yeah, we've done a litter together. She got home yesterday, and she's bringing the pups out today—their first trip to the park! You've got great jumps here. God, I love the catwalk, is this sand in the paint for traction? Bitchin', I mean, these're *great.*"

While she was talking, walking around his equipment, touching each jump, running her hand along the ramps, holding one arm out and letting Sadie tug on her sleeve, he noticed Fanny's old car waiting to turn left into the parking lot. Then when the light changed and the car entered the lot, the redhead looked over and grinned, "There they are, can't miss 'em, can you?" Not only did the car's body rattle and exhaust buzz like a lawn mower, it sounded like a dogcatcher with dozens of howling, barking, whining, growling voices inside. A husky rode in the passenger seat with head, upper body, and front legs out the window. The dog's front feet were standing on the outside door handle.

"By the time she sells them, they'll've finished totaling her car," the redhead said.

"I heard the father was a wolf."

"Yup, I'm starting a new line of working dogs to get some of the original canine drives back into these spoiled domesticated things. Looks like you've got a live wire here."

"That's one reason I'm getting into this."

Then Fanny was with them, her car still snarling and barking behind her in the lot.

"Where d'ya want them?" she said. She gave him a wan smile. The husky jumped out of the window and took off across the park. Fanny made a quick move as though to chase her, then stopped. "Oh, let her go, she's so sick of those puppies clamping onto her and sucking while she walks." She didn't seem to be talking to either one of them in particular. Then she looked at his jumps and smiled at him again. "You don't waste any time, do you?"

"Look at the catwalk, Fan, it's perfect," the redhead said. She had a loud, tactless voice, but at least he was able to just sit back down in his lawn chair while someone else exclaimed to Fanny about his equipment. Fanny stood there smiling, squinting and keeping one eye on her roaming dog. "I gotta try out this tire jump," the redhead continued. "Hey, let's set up a little course with my A-frame, okay?"

"Sorry I don't have my teeter-totter here too," he said. "It's almost finished. Well, it *was* finished . . ." But as his voice trailed away, no one asked him what had happened.

The third day of his vacation, he'd been painting the teeter-totter out on the patio when Suzanne arrived home from work. There hadn't been enough purple, so he'd painted the long board in alternating purple and yellow stripes, changing color every eight inches where black strips of wood had been nailed for better footing. Suzanne had stopped to watch him paint. He could see her feet if he turned his head slightly, but he didn't pause. He did say "Hi," but not right away. After he spoke, she said, "You must've gotten home early."

"Early? I'm not working this week. Not till the thirtieth, you knew that."

"No, I didn't, Scott. I could've taken time off too, if I'd known." Her voice was stiff and tight.

He'd taken a deep breath, looked at his hand carefully as he let paint drip off the brush into the can—it felt as if he might be trembling, but he couldn't see anything. There was a flutter everywhere inside him. "Well . . . it's not a *vacation*. All I'm intending is to get some things done around here."

"I see. I guess you've been wanting to be alone," she'd said. "I guess that's why you couldn't wait to get rid of everyone on Christmas, I guess that's why you were so uptight and withdrawn, I guess that's why my mother asked if you weren't feeling well."

"I wasn't uptight. I've had some things on my mind. You told me you wanted me to do something about how destructive Sadie is." He used his handkerchief to wipe some yellow paint off one of the black strips and heard Suzanne make a sound. When he was finished, she took the handkerchief out of his hand, went to the hose, and rinsed it out.

"Why do you use your dress handkerchiefs when you're working around the house?"

"I just took the top one." His voice snapped off and left the outdoor type of silence: children playing out in the street, a dog barking about a block away, a power tool somewhere whirring with a thin nasal pitch that rose and fell like a wavy line.

"This is cute," Suzanne eventually said, her voice unusually high but suddenly pleasant. "Like a little playground. I always thought it would be fun to build a little playground. That's why I never wanted a pool, you know, because we have room for a playground back here."

"Why would we want a playground?"

Suzanne went around the teeter-totter and sat on a patio chair, crossed her legs, put her purse on the patio beside her feet. "Why didn't we have children, Scott?"

He looked up, felt his jaw hanging open, shut it, opened it again to speak, then slowly closed his mouth, continued looking at her. Finally he'd said, "I don't know why you're asking that. We never wanted kids."

"How do you know, you never asked me."

"I thought it was an understanding between us."

"What made you think so?"

He'd begun painting over a yellow section that was already finished. "Well," he said after a moment, "you never brought it up. It was pretty obvious to me."

"You just assumed we both wanted what *you* wanted."

"I don't understand something, Suzanne," he'd said, putting the paintbrush in the can and leaving it, which was something he never did. "Do you all of a *sudden* want kids? Is this one of those biological clock things?"

"Don't you dare stereotype me. You could spray babies all over the world until the day you die, so you wouldn't understand any kind of feeling a woman has. Men never feel alone, you're like nomads, that's why you didn't even think to tell your wife you have five days off, you just think of yourself, that's how men are—"

"And *that's* not a stereotype?"

"That's right, just make me sound stupid so you can get your own way."

"What the hell's that supposed to mean?"

"*You* didn't want children, so we didn't have children. *It's stupid to want children, Suzanne,*" her voice a singsong chant. "Anything *you* don't like is stupid. For almost twenty years I've been scared to death of being stupid. Now *you're* out here building a stupid seesaw for a dog!"

"You're being totally irrational." He lifted the brush again and let it drip, watched the yellow paint stream into the can, then with his bare hand squeezed the bristles to wring out more paint. "I don't know what you're talking about. One minute you want to spend a year traveling around the world, a week later you're talking about having kids. First you want us to retire early and be free, then you're mad because we don't have kids to tie us down till we're sixty." His voice was getting louder, the words coming faster. Suzanne was looking steadily at the patio cement beside her chair. "Why're we talking about kids? Why're we talking about living in Europe or going to Greenland or becoming bohemians in Colorado or hippies in upstate New York or hip geezers in Los Angeles or millionaires in a dream house in dreamland USA when I don't even know what'll happen *tomorrow?*"

"What is this," she'd said acidly, "some sort of midlife crisis thing?"

He'd glared, cocked his arm that held the paintbrush, then shook the brush out as he said, "Now *that's* stupid." He'd forgotten that he hadn't washed the bristles with water yet. A splattered trail of yellow slapped the patio.

She'd stood. *"This's* what's stupid." She kicked the teeter-totter so the balanced board whacked the cement on one end, then bounced back and whacked the patio on the other end, yellow paint spattering onto the already dried purple.

Fanny was helping the redhead, Doreen, set up a circle with his jumps and catwalk and her A-frame. Then, after they'd set up a pen for the pups, the girls ran their dogs through the course. He sat in his beach chair and watched them, their high voices laughing praise and encouragement to the dogs. The pups in the pen yapped shrilly and threw themselves against the wire sides, growling and howling. Fanny's husky charged up the A-frame and leapt from the peak. Likewise, the husky flew off the catwalk instead of using all four feet on the downhill ramp. So when Fanny held her dog's collar and showed her how to walk down the ramps, the dog huffed and coughed, straining against the collar, while Fanny continued a soprano singsong of reassurance and persuasion. Then the two of them flew through his jumps, the dog taking only one step between, Fanny running on the outside, her arm high, holding the leash.

The girls stopped, and they laughed, panting, while their dogs shared the water dish. "Didja see them, Fan?" Doreen gasped. "Every single one've'em couldn't *wait* to get out and work. God. How'm I gonna choose one?" Doreen continued gazing at the pups.

Scott stretched his legs out, rested his head on the back of his chair with his baseball cap pulled over his eyes, but he could still see Fanny, the side of her face as she sat looking at his equipment. "Must be great," he said, "to be able to come to the park in the middle of the day whenever you want."

"But—" she started an answer.

"We could come up with a great course," Doreen said. "We could build a tunnel, Fan, d'you have a sewing machine?" Turning to Scott, "You say you have a teeter-totter too?"

Fanny was kneeling beside her dog, her arm across the dog's shoulders as the animal continued to drink. She was smiling at him.

"I'll have one soon," he said.

"Take notes, Fanny," Doreen said. "Let's see what they do out here."

Fanny swiveled so she was sitting on the ground beside Scott, facing the course. Doreen lowered the jumps to six inches, then she went to the pen and pulled out a puppy.

"Will you teach me to do this?" Scott asked softly.

After a moment—while Doreen crouched on one side of a jump, the pup on the other side, the little dog licking her nose over the board between their faces—Fanny said, "You won't need to be taught. Doing it will teach you. Just being out here with us . . ."

Doreen inched backwards, and the pup, still licking her, scrambled over the jump in order to stay with her. The rest of the pups continued to make their clamorous noise.

"They sound angry," he said.

"They've bonded to her."

"And not to you? Does that bother you?"

"No—I need to get rid of them now."

He picked a few blades of grass with the hand that was closest to her. "You don't sound too happy about that either."

"Oh, it's not that."

The puppy was chasing Doreen as she ran, bent double, back and forth under the A-frame. "Not a bit afraid of it," Doreen called over the racket. "But it's still too big for them to try it." She headed for the pen to switch puppies. "Keep track of who I've worked with, okay?"

"I'll make a smaller A-frame for you," Scott said.

"That's okay, they'll grow," Fanny answered. "They're *her* game."

"It's okay, I'd like to do it. I have one more day off, I could do the teeter-totter and A-frame tomorrow."

She looked up at him, smiling a whole smile, her eyes bright. "You're funny."

His ears burned, but his pulse didn't start its hot thick thundering until he was saying, "Want to come help me? I could also show you the doghouse I built. Maybe you could use one, I could build another . . ."

Doreen shrieked, lying on her back, the pup playing tug-of-war with the front of her sweatshirt.

"I'd really like to, but I have to stay home for phone calls," Fanny said. "My first ad might be in the paper tomorrow."

"Well . . . I'll do the teeter-totter tomorrow anyway." He picked a piece of grass from the back of her shoulder. "You should see what happened to my first one."

Doreen was switching pups again. "I'm doing all the boys first," she yelled. "I've got the big one now."

"So what happened?" Fanny said.

"My wife ran over it." He pulled the hat all the way over his face and listened to her soft laugh.

With Doreen finally finished with her daily visit, the pups asleep, and Fanny out of the house, Morgan could watch his new videotapes without earphones. Renee had suggested ordering the tapes, performances by various modern ensembles—the Denishawn School, recently remastered clips of Isadora Duncan and Loie Fuller, Kurt Jooss—some with unique and sometimes intimate camera angles, a view no audience could ever have. Renee said he should start visualizing the overall scope of the dance, read about various interpretations, listen to and learn the movement of musical scores instead of just learning a part, habitual moves, having basic control over his own muscles. "Don't be a typewriter typing a poem," she'd said, "be a poet."

"So what's T.S. Eliot supposed to do, be a dancer?" Fanny had said yesterday when he'd repeated Renee's advice.

"I'd expect that from someone who doesn't understand," he'd returned.

"You don't get jokes anymore?"

"I don't feel like joking about my career. I've been pissing away my time. I feel like I've just been taken off some drug. I should've been living like her. Maybe I'd be somewhere else now."

"She's not somewhere else," Fanny had said, making a face as she tried to mix kibble and canned dog food. Kibble spilled over the sides of the bowl onto the kitchen counter.

"Renee is a *principal* here," he'd said. "And she's just starting out."

"You mean it's too late for you?"

The dog was standing on her hind legs, front feet on the kitchen counter. She lay her face on the shelf and stuck her tongue out repeatedly, trying to reach the spilled food.

"I can be better," he'd said. He scraped some of the dog food from the shelf onto the floor, and the dog, as though starving, bolted the scraps and licked the linoleum. "Maybe even get a gig somewhere else. I'm not totally sucked under the quicksand here yet."

The back screen door had slammed at the end of his sentence when Fanny went out to put the food in the puppy pen. When she'd returned, he was in the living room with the biography of Twyla Tharp he'd borrowed from Renee.

"Do you think I am?" Fanny had said.

"What?"

"Sucked all the way into the quicksand."

He'd marked his place and looked up. She was holding her earlobe with one hand. Tempted to say, "Don't pull me under with you," instead he'd remembered Renee asking to see the silver hand ear cuff while Fanny was in the bathroom in the Seattle airport. "I sort of *made* you get this," Renee had said, "and I haven't gotten her anything for Christmas yet, so let me buy it from you." He hadn't seen Fanny wearing it in the three days since they'd been home, so he didn't know if or when Renee might've given it to her. On the jet on the way home, while Renee and Fanny slept, he'd closed his eyes and allowed himself to walk in on them: they would both be kneeling on a disheveled, unmade bed, sheets rumpled in a nest around them, trailing onto the floor, and they'd be naked, facing each other, Renee's skin rosy white, full breasted but taut, with a dancer's muscles showing in her shoulders and back; Fanny brown and less luminous, as though in shadows, ribs and collarbone showing, her head bent, leaning forward, her face hidden, as Renee held her chin and gently eased the ear cuff onto Fanny's ear.

Perhaps Fanny hadn't even expected an answer. She'd turned on the TV and switched to the Weather Channel.

"Maybe you should talk to someone who really has their shit together," he'd said. "When're you and Renee gonna have another girls' night out?"

"I don't know."

"You know," he looked back down at the book in his lap, "go cruise Hillcrest . . . get your mind off . . . you know, dogs and Doreen and puppies and cleaning up their shit."

"*Is* there any more to my life than puppy shit?"

She could've been smiling, but he didn't look up. "I'll bet it doesn't seem like it." Eight wolves did produce a lot of yellow shit.

"Yup. That's me. *Shit R Us.* Or is it, *We B Shit.*"

For a moment there was only the sound of a news report on a flood in Louisiana.

Morgan said, "I'm sick of moping. Like Renee says, you gotta face The Beast head on, realize it won't kill you, can actually be your friend . . . whatever your Beast is."

"You're my beast," Fanny said to the dog, "aren't you, Lace?"

Morgan could see half the television screen; the rest was blocked by Fanny sitting on the coffee table in front of him, her back to him. He could see the dog's feet in front of Fanny, between her legs. "Like," he'd said, "Renee's Beast is being alone. She had to live with it and outwill it, face it down, tame it."

"Doreen's been here too much, hasn't she?" Fanny said in a peculiar voice, as though she had her mouth full or was burping.

"I haven't complained." Every day when Doreen came to see the little wolves—the backyard a cacophony of party noisemakers, police sirens, toy machine guns, Doreen's shrieking voice—he'd had to lock himself in his room with a headset and do the new limbering exercises Renee had shown him.

"Well," Fanny said, "when I find out what my Beast is, I'll make it my friend. For now, I'll stick with puppy shit."

"Go out with her, though," he'd said. "Maybe on New Year's. You two could be . . . I don't know, I think it couldn't hurt, could only help . . . I mean . . ."

"I never said I *wouldn't.*" Fanny had turned off the TV. "Let's see, fifteen minutes, enough time for them to eat, poop, and walk through it." She'd left the room, the husky following, growling and nipping at her butt. Morgan had been looking at the page but not reading. He didn't want to hear Fanny come back in and resume wandering from room to room, looking out the windows as though waiting for something.

The equipment was set up before either Fanny or Doreen arrived. Scott tried teaching Sadie the catwalk, but she was too full of energy, attempting to jump directly from the ground to the eye-high level plank without using the ramp. When Fanny drove into the parking lot, Sadie was frantically scrambling, front legs on the ramp, rear legs over the side, Scott holding her lead with one hand, trying to keep her up on the ramp with the other. As Fanny's car door opened, Sadie succeeded in pushing herself away from the catwalk, knocking Scott to the ground, then she raced toward the nearest clump of bushes. Fanny was already out of her car, her husky joining Sadie in the shrubs. He'd wanted Sadie to be moving up and down the catwalk easily by the time Fanny arrived.

"I know I was doing that wrong," he said, approaching Fanny's car. Two crates in the backseat were rocking, full of scuffling claws and sharp, high-pitched voices.

"You have to teach her to go *down* the ramp first," Fanny smiled, opening the back door. Scott stepped forward to help her slide the first crate out.

The crate felt like the four pups would knock it to pieces in his arms as he carried it to the grass. Fanny was setting up the pen. When he brought the other crate out of the car, the first four pups were in the pen, sniffing, peeing, standing up against the wire with their feet and noses poking through. "When does Doreen pick hers?" he asked.

"Soon. Can't *be* too soon. Then the rest can go as fast as possible to whoever wants them."

"Well, I've got the course set up, we can run our crazy animals through."

"I want to, but I have my Schutzhund lesson now, can you stay and leave the stuff set up?"

Doreen pulled into the parking lot. Scott knew they had to talk fast. "I thought you were going to do agility."

"I am. I *will*. But Doreen wants Lacy to have a Schutzhund title."

"Why does she care what you do with your dog?"

"For her puppy." Fanny raised a hand to Doreen as she spoke. "So at least one of its parents is titled, 'cause, of course, the *wolf* isn't."

"Where's your dog?" Doreen shrieked. Scott turned his back so Fanny could see his wince but Doreen couldn't. But if Fanny noticed, he couldn't tell.

"Somewhere around here. *Lacy!*" Fanny walked toward the bushes where the dogs had last been seen, twirling her leash so that it wrapped around her arm, then reversing the motion and unwrapping it.

Doreen bent over the puppy pen. The pups all leapt toward her face like little fishes jumping out of water. "Okay, who wants me as their new mother?"

"Who's their mother now?" Scott asked, "Fanny or her dog?"

"Good question. Neither is up to it."

He was about to ask, "What do you mean?" but Doreen walked away, back to her car to get her A-frame. His own A-frame was almost finished, yellow and purple like the rest of his equipment.

He set up his lawn chair and sat down to watch Fanny's lesson. Sadie had come back, following Fanny and the husky from across the park. Panting hard, his dog lay under his chair where he could reach down with one hand and play with her silky ear while Fanny—kneeling in front of her dog, with Doreen kneeling beside her—held the husky's mouth closed over a dumbbell saying, "Hold it, *good* hold . . . hold it, good girl, hold it." The husky tried shaking her head, but Fanny was holding on, so the dog stood and tried to back away. Doreen forced her to return to a sit. He thought about Suzanne, yesterday, saying to Sadie, "Now don't you let our daddy force you into doing anything too hard for you." His stomach had sort of turned, but he'd managed a smile and said, "Sadie likes it. Jumping, climbing, running. Her favorite things."

Suzanne had been brushing Sadie after a Sunday afternoon bath. Usually Scott gave Sadie her baths, but he'd come home from the hardware store—he'd bought more supplies for his A-frame and a new flower jump he was building—to find Suzanne in the backyard lathering shampoo into Sadie's coat. "Turn the water on for us, okay, Scott?" she'd called out. "We're ready to rinse, aren't we, sweet girl?"

Scott had worked a late job Saturday night and slept as long as he could Sunday, which was only until eight o'clock. Suzanne had the newspaper spread on the dining room table when he went out after his shower for orange juice. She was looking at the movie listings.

After her bright "Good morning" but before she said anything else, he'd told her that he had to make a list for the hardware store, so if she needed anything, let him know.

"Want to see a movie today, Scott?"

"I've got a lot to get done." He'd hesitated. "Maybe later."

"Or we could have dinner at that lodge by Lake Henshaw. They have fireside dining. Sounds real cozy."

Scott had been drinking his orange juice while she spoke. He'd gulped the last half quickly, then said, slightly out of breath from drinking so fast, "Well, maybe a movie would be a good break later this afternoon."

He'd told her to pick one, then when she said, "Do you want comedy, drama, adventure, or science fiction?" he'd said science fiction, even though he hated science fiction. Suzanne had glanced up quickly but didn't say anything. He couldn't imagine sitting through a hot, physical scene with Suzanne sitting rigidly still in the dark beside him, the popcorn long finished.

Later, while she was brushing the dog, after he'd even loosened up and told Suzanne a little bit about agility, how the dogs can't wait to get on the course, seem to feel the thrill of competition, Suzanne had said to the dog, *"I'm* getting some fun today too, sweetie, our daddy's taking Mommy to the show!" He'd sucked in a breath quickly and turned to go to the garage, but hesitated again, turned back, and gave the dog a little pat before going to work on the A-frame.

Fanny's husky was lapping from the water bowl. Sadie bashed her back on the underside of his chair, getting up to ask Fanny for a pat. "All done?" he said, standing.

"Quick break."

He sat again, the top half of his dog in his lap, her hind feet standing on the ground. He held her ears gently, one in each fist. While Doreen heeled with the husky bound in close to her side, chirping *"Good* girl, atta girl!" Fanny reclined on half of Doreen's A-frame, her forearms lying flat along the peak, hands threaded, chin on her knuckles. Scott's hands slid slowly down Sadie's warm back.

Usually Morgan wound up beside or near her during her warm-up on the barre. Almost everyone used a favorite spot. People had their routines: Warm up twenty minutes, towel off, warm up ten more, leave ten minutes empty before rehearsal. Or warm up a half hour, practice routines, cool down, leave time to use the restroom. Renee liked at least five minutes with the glass bubble she'd invented around her head, muffling all the other noise of music and chatter and thudding bare feet on wooden stage floors. She would lean on the barre and stare at her pupils in the mirror, slowly look up above her head into the stage rafters and lights and ropes and old backdrops, then slide back down to meet her own gaze again, hearing the music for her routines, visualizing, becoming a part of the dance, making the whole dance a part of her. When this time came, she might turn her back on Morgan or slowly lower her eyes. As his voice grew fainter to her, he would turn and wander away or attempt his own version of her reverie.

Today Morgan was talking about how the new exercises she'd shown him were adding something-or-other to his overall comprehension or appreciation of something else. He spoke slowly, with long spaces between words and phrases, so when she thought he was finished, she said, "Who's the guy in a suit I've seen hanging around this week?"

Morgan grinned, his bony knee pushing into his cheek as he stretched on the barre. "Look close at his tie tack, it's a teensy ballerina."

"Who *is* he?"

"Maybe a board member or a lawyer or someone's husband."

"You mean you don't know? *Whose* lawyer, ours?"

"Theirs, of course. But he's not *that* lawyer, if he's a lawyer."

"Is he a management spy?"

"Well, he's doing a great job of disguising himself, isn't he!" Morgan laughed, showing all his teeth.

"What other kind of lawyer would there be?"

"Maybe someone to figure out what loophole in the contract could allow them to use canned music instead of live or turn off the heat during rehearsals."

"Who do you talk to in management?" Renee asked. "Who's okay?"

"I don't know. I don't need to talk to anyone in management."

"What about that girl, Dani, we met at the pub before Christmas? What's her job?"

"Not sure. I don't keep track of what they do."

"Does she work on the business or artistic side, maybe something with publicity?"

Morgan shrugged, still smiling his goofy grin.

"I think we should know," Renee said. "I mean, how they make policy for publicity or selecting and scheduling programs, we just ought to be aware of what goes on."

Morgan shrugged again. "They're figuring out ways to screw us, what else do I need to know?"

"Does Dani go out with you guys very often?"

"Occasionally. I haven't kept track. Sometimes she's there."

"Is she the only one? I mean, I noticed everyone treated her pretty friendly. Would *everyone* from management be treated like that?"

"Probably not. I don't know, but probably not."

"I feel at a disadvantage," Renee said, watching her foot on the barre as she flexed each of her toes individually, "because I don't know the behind-the-scenes things you've just naturally picked up on by being here so long."

"Being here so long has its disadvantages too."

Renee turned her back on Morgan, moved a few feet farther away from him on the barre. "How's Fanny?" She thought her voice suddenly sounded immature, less solid, less like a rising soloist in a dance troupe.

"Hasn't she told you," he said, "that her uncle offered her a job near Tahoe?"

"She can't *take* it, can she?"

"It's only for two months."

"Oh!" Renee's heart thudded in her ears and fingertips. The leg she had on the floor was hot and weak for a second, so she lowered her other foot from the barre. "Doing what?"

"Waitressing at this resorty-type thing for retarded kids and their parents."

"Waitressing? She'd leave town to do more of *that*? I'll have to give her a call."

"Yeah, do," Morgan said, smiling, "she's home today." He took his foot from the barre. His face was flushed, his hair dark and stuck together with sweat. "She needs—"

"I can't talk about this right now," Renee said, then wondered why she'd said it aloud. Morgan was still grinning at her, biting his lip, the lights making his eyes shiny and liquid. "I mean, you know, I need my time before we start . . ." But she couldn't hear the music or visualize her movements, could only see Fanny's pale smile as she'd walked past a townhouse window in Seattle, looking in and saying, "Hope someone gives them some *taste* for Christmas." Her ear had been poking through her hair. Renee still had the ear cuff in a box in her dresser drawer.

I would usually schedule Fanny's lessons at midday. I *did* like using the old guy's agility equipment, but early afternoon, with him not there, Fanny would spend more time on Schutzhund and then afterwards help with the puppies: take notes and provide the visual and aural stimulation necessary to test their sensitivity and fear responses and also to encourage boldness in unfamiliar environments. I wasn't sure how much Fanny was getting out of her lessons when *he* was there.

We hadn't even started the protection phase, drive and hold, which the husky obviously had an aptitude for—but still, there had to be *some* control. Instead, Fanny seemed more interested in teaching her dog how to balance midway on the teeter-totter and to tip-toe down the other side. Then one day Fanny left the dog free to forage in a eucalyptus grove while she sat straddling one end of the teeter-totter as though waiting for a playmate, and he ran his dog back and forth over jumps. Then when he approached her, seemingly to use the teeter-totter with his dog, he'd said something, Fanny had said something back, then he'd pushed the high end of the teeter-totter down with one hand, raising Fanny off the ground. Pumped her up and down three times. Fanny had laughed. I was working with the puppies and didn't mind the distraction created by Fanny's giggling on the agility course. But I still somehow felt annoyed.

Without him, lessons were just easier and cleaner, that's all. I remember Fanny standing beside the puppy pen, the husky lying near her, tied to the front fender of her car. The pen almost collapsed as I approached and our wolves leapt to meet me, some leaving the ground and beginning to climb the wire. Fanny was rolling her dumbbell between her palms.

I told her I had the temperament test set up for Thursday. "I want to start taking them for short rides in the car. Tonight okay?"

"No." Fanny's eyes were on the twirling end of the dumbbell between her hands. "I won't be home tonight."

"Oh. Working?"

"No."

Sometimes I wanted to pick Fanny up, drop her on a moving treadmill, and see if she'd run or just lose her legs in confusion, like when I had first thrown Bruno onto it. He'd soon learned: trot or fall backwards.

"Okay," I said, in my time-to-start-the-lesson voice. You know: *Don't tell me, then, I don't care.* I really didn't, as long as it didn't affect the dogs.

Fanny bent over her bitch, reaching to untie the leash. The dog, leaping to her feet, smacked Fanny under the chin with the top of her head, snapping Fanny's mouth shut. I could hear Fanny's teeth clack together; her head flew back, her hands held her jaw, she made a noise like she'd been punched in the gut, a squeezed sound that seemed to come out her ears. For a second, even the pups were silent. Then Fanny moved like bad animation, from holding her face in both hands, eyes shut, to a hard fist raised over her head, glaring down at the dog, "Damn you to fucking hell!" And the dog actually cowered, ears back, head down, shrinking body.

"Oh, my god." Fanny's legs folded, she collapsed beside her dog, holding her around the neck, burying her face in the husky's back. "I almost slugged her."

"I would've been proud of you," I said. *Not* that it was good *training* instinct. I picked up the dumbbell Fanny had dropped.

"Proud of me for slugging my dog—for something that wasn't her fault?" Fanny looked up, kneeling beside her dog, one arm across her shoulders. The husky was staring at a terrier being walked on the other side of the park.

"For finally getting mad and fighting back," I said.

"What do I have to get mad at?"

"Never mind." If *she* didn't know . . . I gave the dumbbell to Fanny. "As long as you're down there, let's do the dumbbell exercises."

"You didn't *want* to hurt me, *did* you?" Fanny said as she pried the dog's mouth open.

"Good hold," I said, reminding Fanny to *participate*. But she didn't take the hint, just held her dog's mouth closed over the dumbbell. The husky rolled her eyes, puffed her lips out, used one paw to try to scratch Fanny's hand away from her muzzle.

────────

She skipped her evening workout. Sitting on her front porch in the dark, Renee leaned her head against the wrought iron rail and closed her eyes, as though to let her body sleep, knowing her mind wouldn't. She couldn't stop seeing Fanny's face, the split second expression, only inches away. That might've been the last she saw of Fanny's face tonight, she couldn't remember, because after that they got into the car. Fanny said "Thanks, see ya," when Renee dropped her off. Renee had said, "I'll call tomorrow," and Fanny had said, "Uh, yeah, I'll be home in the morning." Fanny was outside but had turned and faced Renee as she spoke, leaned her arm on the car's roof, over the window, and lay her forehead on her wrist, so all Renee could see then was the tip of Fanny's nose.

The other cottages around Renee were dark. Someone's wind chimes tinkled.

It wasn't as though she'd come right out and said, *Hey, Fanny, let's go on a date.* It wasn't as though they hadn't been out together before.

Renee had suggested skating. Fanny said, "I haven't done this since grade school. I took lessons with my Girl Scout troop."

"See, full circle, back to skating with the girls," Renee had laughed.

Fanny had not joined the laughter. She'd stared solemnly at the lit neon skaters on the sides of the building—the girl figure in a little skirt like a ballerina's.

"I took lessons too," Renee said. "Only it was ice-skating. I was supposed to become an Olympic ice-skater."

"What happened?"

"I took acrobatics, gymnastics, and dance to enhance my skating, then just transferred everything over to dance."

They'd only touched once in the rink, as Fanny seemed about to fall and Renee grabbed her arm with both hands. But at the same time, Fanny had caught the safety rail with her other hand, so Renee had to let go or else rip Fanny's arm off. Fanny wasn't unco-ordinated, she glided easily, one foot then the other, used her arms for balance and speed going around corners, but never tried anything else, like skating backwards. When Renee skated backwards in front of Fanny, Fanny smiled and said if she were Renee, she would've stuck with *roller*-skating because you could be as serious about it as you wanted, and compete if you wanted to, but without having to rely on it to earn a living.

"Then I couldn't be serious *enough* about it," Renee had said. "Not if it was just a hobby or something."

Renee couldn't remember saying anything else—although they must've—until she'd suggested they go have drinks at The Flame. "You'll be a hit," Renee had said. "A new face for everyone to check out."

Fanny had laughed and said, "Yeah, sure."

Before getting out of the car, which she parked across the street from The Flame, Renee took her wallet from her backpack, slipped it into her jacket pocket, then pulled out the gift-wrapped book and held it out to Fanny. "Your Christmas present is a little late. Sorry," Renee had said casually, thinking of the ear cuff still hidden in her top dresser drawer, under her old workout leotards. Fanny had given Renee personalized stationery on pearl gray paper that she'd designed herself. "Don't open it now," Renee said. "Let's go." So Fanny had left the wrapped book on the car seat.

New Age music was still playing when they arrived. Rock music for dancing never started until nine. In the main room with the bar and dance floor, they sat at one of the small corner tables. This time neither had her back to the rest of the room. Since the dance music hadn't started yet, the bar was fairly empty. Pool balls were clacking in the game room. A waitress went into the reading room with a carafe of white wine. Renee told Fanny that the reading room was like a living room—sofas and chairs, pillows on the floor, bookcases and racks of magazines and newspapers, even a fireplace. Fanny said, "So that's where the famous flame is housed?"

"We could go in there if you want."

"This is fine," Fanny said.

"You okay?"

"Just tired. As usual, it seems."

"Glad the holidays are over?"

"Yes, but there's always something, isn't there?" Fanny said. "I've got to sell those pups. And every day I've got to decide what to make for dinner, and when. And Morgan's worried about the negotiations coming up this spring." She stopped as the waitress put their drinks on the table, Renee's beer and Irish coffee for Fanny.

"That's not for a while," Renee said.

"Soon enough. Is their goal putting on dance productions or just having a dance company in name and never spending any money?"

"Maybe a little of both." The smell of coffee and whipped cream was hot and sweet. "After I'm here a while, maybe I can help change things."

Fanny seemed to scowl a little. Or maybe she'd just been squinting. "How?"

"Well . . . by being part of the negotiations *now,* maybe someday we'll have more voice in how the company is run." She laughed. "That's like going backwards. Dance companies almost always start out run by a choreographer—*founded* by a choreographer—and everyone pitches in to produce. *Then* someday the company realizes its vision, gets an executive and board of directors, patrons, breaks into a civic series, and eventually grows into a public-backed institution. So they think they've got it made and turn into a *business* and start shafting the performers. Not unusual with the big classical companies, but I'm more than a little surprised to find it here. But don't worry. There's new blood here, dancers are more savvy nowadays."

The rock music started. The place was still mostly empty—wouldn't be crowded, Renee knew, until ten-thirty or later. She'd already decided to leave before it got really full, before the witching hour, before too many bulls showed up.

Fanny was turned sideways in her seat, as though watching a band perform, but the music was coming from speakers. She looked a little better than during the weeks she'd been up all night feeding her puppies—more color in her face, except that around her eyes she was still pale, probably from sunglasses. The dark circles under her eyes still seemed rather dramatic.

"I heard about your job," Renee finally said.

"Yeah." Fanny turned with a wry smile.

"Why would you even consider going so far away just to do more waitressing?"

"It's my uncle's place. He said I might be able to give him some ideas for designing the lobby and offices. So there's that too. If I feel like it."

"But—"

"In a way," Fanny interrupted, "this is a good time for me to get away from here. But in another way, it's not the best time to leave."

Renee had looked down at Fanny's arm on the table. Her thin brown arm had long, silky, straight light hair. Fanny's body was still turned sideways, facing the dance floor. But she was looking at Renee.

"I'll feel helpless," Fanny continued. "In a way relieved . . . but also . . . out of control."

"What will be out of control?" Renee brought her eyes up to Fanny's, but Fanny lowered her lids, took a sip of her coffee.

"Like, I'll go live a temporary life there, but when I come back, *this* one might be too far gone to save . . . I don't know. I'm just babbling."

"I know you felt you needed a shake-up. Not that I'm suggesting you *leave.*"

"Has Morgan talked to you much . . . about us?" Fanny stirred her coffee with one finger, then sucked the tip. "I mean, him and me."

"No."

"Well . . . you might already know . . . he's not real happy. Maybe if I weren't always so . . . lethargic . . . but I'm not lethargic when I'm out in the park with my dog . . . I'm babbling again. Sorry."

"It's okay. Say whatever you want. I think you need to say something."

"I've just been thinking about things lately."

"What things?"

"Like when we got robbed." Fanny leaned back from the table but kept both hands on the coffee cup.

"Wasn't that a long time ago?"

"Yeah, but . . . I can't stop thinking about how it felt to see the whole house trashed like that—at the time, *that's* what I thought was making me feel so . . . defeated."

"It was some dirtbags, it had nothing to do with defeating you." Renee tapped her foot to the bass rhythm.

"Well, that's something I've been thinking about . . . now I *don't* think it was just having the house trashed by some stranger that got to me. You know, I'd put a lot into that house, maybe I shot my whole wad there—the extent of my imagination or talent or whatever you want to call it. Then when someone trashed it, took it apart, neither of us even *felt* like putting it back together. Like: what was the use? It seems . . . symbolic."

"Of what?" Renee watched one couple dance a few steps on their way to a table.

Fanny licked whipped cream off her finger, looked at her hand, and touched her tongue to her palm, then spoke slowly, still looking at her hand, "Maybe . . . symbolic of why we got married in the first place. Maybe neither of us wanted to face our life alone. Not that we were like crazy recluses who might commit suicide if we had to be alone one more day. But just like we both wanted there to always be another person to look at and say, *We're in it together*—whatever *it* was anyway— and *that* would give us the motivation to make something of it."

"Sounds like you're at a real crossroad." Listening to her voice utter such a cliché, Renee wondered what was wrong with herself.

"Or have been for years and never knew it. Should've realized it during the lock-out. God, that year, every day, everything I did or said or thought was just for the sake of day-to-day maintenance, nothing more than that, no greater goal."

"Time to move on, isn't it?" Renee said softly, wincing again at her own banality.

A group of about five women had come in and Fanny glanced at them.

"Do you know her?" Renee asked when one of the women turned to look at Fanny two or three times.

"She looks familiar." The bar was dark. Most of the women had short hair or crew cut tops with shags in back. Fanny's was just Fanny's. "I think she's works for the dance company management, god, I never knew she was—"

The woman had disappeared into the small crowd near the dance floor. "Don't you recognize her?" Fanny whispered. "God, I *do* know her . . . Dani . . . something."

"I met her once, yeah, that's right." Renee scanned the crowd, a few of them starting to dance, but she didn't see Dani again. "Yeah, interesting."

As though suddenly remembering where she was or regretting the extent of what she'd just been saying, Fanny crossed her arms on her chest and leaned against the table, looking down into her coffee mug in silence. Renee got up. "Let's go."

After only half a beer, Renee hadn't understood why she'd felt a familiar surge of anticipation yet also of almost panic. Fanny ran across the street. Renee had to wait for a car, then ran after her, her heart in her throat, as though if Fanny got to the other side alone, it would be too late. *Too late for what?* Fanny was pulling up on the locked passenger door handle when Renee caught up, came right up close behind Fanny and reached past her as though to unlock the door. But instead of putting the key in the lock, Renee put her hand against the door, then put her other hand against the fender on Fanny's other side, pinning Fanny between herself and the car. She was breathing heavily, right on the back of Fanny's neck. Fanny froze. Then turned around.

Renee's arms were still braced against the car on either side of Fanny. Their eyes only inches apart, Fanny had looked directly at Renee, not as if she was scared at all, but as if there was a gun leveled at her head and she was determined not to blink. Maybe she should've backed off, Renee thought, but, in a way, maybe she *did* back off, because she didn't put her mouth on Fanny's, she didn't taste Fanny's coffee and cream with her tongue, she didn't even hover there with their lips brushing to see if Fanny was ready. Instead, she'd lowered her forehead against Fanny's, for only a second, perhaps longer, perhaps Fanny could feel her pulse throbbing, perhaps if she hadn't moved away, Fanny would've patted her back and told her not to worry.

No, not Fanny. All she would do was stand there and wait. Wait to be touched, told, led, pushed. Wait for someone else to do all the work and take all the risks.

Someone's cat came from beneath a parked car, froze on the sidewalk, and stared at Renee, still sitting on the steps. Bent suddenly and licked its flank, again stared at Renee, then stared past Renee. Its tail flicked once. Renee didn't move. The cat soundlessly disappeared down the sidewalk. No leaf rustled or twig snapped. She vowed never to skip another workout.

———————

Suzanne had read in magazines about extremely troubled women filling the kitchen, pantry, dining room, every available shelf and counter with uneaten cookies, bread, cakes, and pastries; hapless, depressed women digging up every available inch of ground, producing buckets of tomatoes no one would eat, bushels of squash and eggplant no one would cook; distressed women knitting miles of endless scarves no one would wear.

The backyard and patio were starting to fill up with jumps and tunnels, a teeter-totter, two different-sized A-frames, and other miscellaneous equipment. Every night Scott was out in the garage, sanding, painting, drilling screws. He was losing weight.

Bringing a cold can of soda, Suzanne went out the back door, across the patio, tapped on the garage door, then went in. Scott was leaning against his workbench, Sadie on her hind feet beside him, her front legs wrapped around his waist. A half-eaten deli sandwich lay on the workbench beside his elbow. He was sipping a beer.

Suzanne went to the extra refrigerator they kept in the garage and put the soda inside. "How's it going?"

"Fine."

"Scott . . ." She wanted her voice to sound strong, but concerned. A source of help, solace. "Are you okay?"

"Yeah. Fine. Why?"

"Well . . ." She looked around at the jumps stacked together against one wall, solid jumps, jumps with flowers instead of boards, jumps with white gates on either side. "Does building this stuff give you some kind of temporary happiness?"

"What?"

"So you'll have to go on building and building, just to feel good—"

"Suzanne," he said, "I'm building an agility *course*. I'm just about finished. I'm going to get a little trailer and fix it so all this stuff fits inside, in pieces, so I can take the course to any park to train or loan it to clubs for matches, so other people can use it too."

She smiled and came closer. "Like a dog show? What fun!"

He was chewing another bite of his sandwich. The dog, on tiptoe, was sniffing at his face, her nose just below his chin. "A club heard that I was building equipment and offered me a charter membership."

"I'd like to meet your new friends, Scott. I could bring a picnic and the beach chairs, I'd love to see Sadie do her tricks."

Scott pushed the dog down and told her to sit. "Please, let me do this alone. It's something I want to do."

"Can't I even cheer you on?"

"Suzanne . . ." He broke off a piece of the sandwich and gave it to the dog. "I know it seems unfair. I'm sorry, but please, let me do this alone."

"Is this that midlife crisis thing again, Scott?"

"You're the one who keeps using that phrase." He fed the rest of the sandwich to the dog, wiped his hands on his pants.

"I don't know what to say about a man who won't include his wife in his activities."

"I don't knit your blankets with you."

"*Afghans.* I crochet afghans."

In the silence, she could hear the dog sniffing for crumbs at Scott's feet. She looked at his hand, which was wrapped around the beer bottle on the workbench. "She's *our* dog, Scott," Suzanne said in a lower voice.

"I don't want to fight. I'm sorry you feel left out, I can't explain this." He turned his face away.

"I just want—" Then she saw him wipe his eye. He looked at her for only a second—she could see brimming tears, but he turned and left the garage. The dog also didn't look back at her, trotted quickly after Scott through the door he hadn't shut behind himself.

Suzanne followed. He wasn't in the kitchen or living room, nor in front of the TV in the family room. The bedroom door was shut. She stopped, didn't knock, turned and went back to the family room, picked up her latest afghan, and turned the TV on. The afghan was across her lap, but she wasn't crocheting. The show was a reenactment of an unsolved crime. She heard the bedroom door open, heard Sadie's toenails on the hardwood floor in the hall, then Scott's voice behind her. "I'm taking Sadie for her walk." Suzanne turned with a smile, but they were already gone.

At the short barre in his practice room, Morgan worked on his entrechat and sauté jumps, facing himself in the mirror, watching himself from the waist down. He'd started doing his jumps naked, as Renee said she did hers, but it hurt his nuts to snap up and down, so he'd put on a pair of tight bikini underwear.

Yesterday Renee had said, "Those pseudotryouts for those corny musicals won't be anything like a real open audition. Do you work on your jumps?"

She'd come over to do her laundry. The company was rehearsing for its only January production, then wouldn't do anything until May. In the meantime, Morgan was usually in the dance chorus of a local short-run musical. Likewise, all summer he did the musicals at the outdoor theater in the park. Before Christmas he'd asked Renee if she was going to pick up the same kind of work between the company's five productions a year, but she'd said she thought the company would have other plans for her, and she'd freelance, do recitals, go to some festivals—she was putting out feelers.

While Renee transferred her wet clothes into the dryer, Morgan had leaned in the washroom doorway and told her he'd decided to go to an audition for the Denver Dance Theater at the beginning of the February hiatus.

A familiar black sweatshirt missed the dryer door and smacked on the pavement floor of the washroom. The black leg of a leotard dangled over the side of the washer. But Renee didn't turn to face him. She picked up the sweatshirt and shook it violently. "Lost cause," she'd said, holding up the sweatshirt by the shoulders.

"Why?" His pulse had been hot in his ears. A thread of nausea in his gut.

"Too many dog hairs on your floor," she said, tossing the sweatshirt into the dryer.

"Oh!" He'd laughed. "Thought you were trying to tell me something, you know, about the audition."

"No," her voice airy and thin, "it'll be a good experience for you."

That night, when he'd mentioned to Fanny how he and Renee had discussed the audition, she'd sort of sniffed and said, "If I'd've said anything like that to you—like you were sixteen and had never performed—you'd bite my head off."

"You're not in a position to say anything like that," he'd returned levelly.

Fanny had left the room—as usual, on her way from one room to another, putzing around, looking busy. But she'd come back on her way back through the house, paused, and asked, without looking at him, if he'd told Renee that they were driving out together, at least part way.

"Yeah," he'd said, "she asked about you."

"She asked?" Fanny seemed to flush.

"Well, when she found out I was driving to Denver, she asked what you'd do without a car for a week, so I said that's when I'll be dropping you off at your uncle's place." He'd paused. "Didn't you tell her you took that job?"

"I haven't spoken to her for a few days."

"Yeah, she said she's been meaning to call you. Should I be your go-between?" He'd laughed, but Fanny had resumed her trip through the living room into the kitchen.

After a moment, Morgan had bolted out of his chair and followed her. "I did give her a good excuse, though," he'd said.

Fanny turned from looking at a wall calendar. "What do you mean?" He noticed she wasn't scanning the current month; she was holding up a few pages and looking ahead.

"I said you were busy getting rid of the pups 'cause they had to be gone by the time we leave."

"God. Or sooner."

Morgan stopped jumping, leaned his forehead against his mirror for a second, but backed off when the glass immediately fogged from his panting. Holding the barre, he sank into a squat, laid his cheek against one arm. Yesterday, when Renee's laundry had finally all been transferred to the dryer, she'd started the machine and turned toward where he was propped in the washroom doorway. He'd said, "Too bad they're not also looking for a prima in Denver." She'd smiled but hadn't answered.

It was a two-day drive to Denver. Renee probably wouldn't want to spend that much time without at least limbering. But they could stop at rest stops, let the blue-hairs in their Winnebagos stare as

Renee in a black leotard and he in white invented a spontaneously choreographed divertissement to one of Renee's spooky New Age music tapes. This trip, there'd be no husky in the backseat panting against the back of his neck. If it were Renee with him, there'd also be no mess of unfolded and refolded maps, which Fanny liked to read aloud—names of dry lakes, gullies, small towns. "I wonder what it's like to live in Lone Tree, why would a desert town be named White Peak, imagine having this ratty truck stop as your career . . ." Maybe Renee would sleep while he drove, her head against the door and her bare legs across his lap. Fanny wouldn't sleep on car trips. Once, she'd dozed off sitting upright, her head thrown back over the seat, but had snapped her head up and caught him slapping his cheek as he drove to stay awake. She said she couldn't let herself sleep because he might drive off the road and kill them both.

———————

I couldn't administer the temperament test myself because the pups were entirely comfortable with me. It had to be someome who was a stranger to them to get a good reading on their true fear responses as well as on the depth of their drives. The pup I was looking for had to show me that nothing was more important than chasing, stalking, pouncing. It had to be alert and perceptive but not frightened of distractions and new environments. It had to be able to take a correction without being cowed, come back after discipline with just as much spirit and confidence—the hierarchical distance between the human pack leader and the dog might be barely discernible. It had to be a dog who had what it takes to someday take over the pack.

So I asked a person who trained for standard obedience competition to do the test. I brought exercise pens to the tester's house and partitioned off a part of the lawn. I had new toys that the pups had never seen to be used for distraction and the fear tests. I sewed some of the ribbons Bruno had won onto a stuffed animal that would be dragged by a string to simulate prey for the pups to chase and pounce on. I duplicated the testing data sheets, put them on clipboards, and brought sharp pencils. I told Fanny to crate the pups all morning, put them in a dark room, and force them to sleep, so they'd be ready for action at one-thirty, leaving enough time afterwards to train in the park, early enough so the old man wouldn't be tagging along.

I could only hope the shade where Fanny and I sat was dark enough to canine eyes that the pups couldn't see us. I warned Fanny that we had to be quiet and not disturb the test. The tester brought the first pup from the utility room. "Red-collar male," I muttered, writing the pup's code name on my first test sheet, signaling Fanny to do the same.

The tester put the pup down, knelt ten feet away, and called, clapping her hands, singing "Here, puppy, puppy, puppy!" The little thing only hit the ground twice as it bounded toward the tester, then jumped at her face. The tester rolled back on her butt, lay flat on her back, giggling, while the pup licked her eyes and mouth, then began a tug-of-war game with her shirt collar.

"Passes that with flying colors," I whispered. While the pup was chewing on a stuffed animal three times its size, the tester banged a spoon against a fry pan. The pup braced all four feet, looked around, then went back to killing the pink elephant.

"What're we looking for?" Fanny whispered. I couldn't *believe* it!

"Have you been blind and deaf the past eight weeks?" I hissed.

The tester was walking around in a circle, the pup dodging in and out around her feet, growling and trying to catch her shoelaces. After a while, Fanny said, "No."

The tester suddenly kneeled, grabbed the pup, and flipped him to his back. The pup screamed and struggled. The tester shouted a sharp "No!" in his face, held him in the submissive position, then released him. The pup immediately jumped into the tester's lap, nipping at her hands, his tail up and wagging.

While I quickly scribbled on my test sheet, Fanny whispered, "I guess there've been a lot of other things to watch and listen for at the same time."

God. I put the first puppy's test sheet on the bottom of my stack, then looked at Fanny. She hadn't written anything. She was staring at me, her pupils huge from sitting in the shade, freckles standing out as though five minutes in the dark had faded any tan she'd gotten from spending five afternoons a week in the park. She was wearing a v-neck surgeon's shirt, showing skin stretched tight over her protruding collar bones. I wanted to say, *Get a grip, girl.* And I wanted to beg, *Please, don't tell me anything . . . everything's going well, everything's in place, there's no room for anything that doesn't contribute.*

"You don't handle distractions any better than your dog does," I managed to smile. "Except *she* doesn't keep thinking about them days or weeks afterwards."

"Do you really think about training sixteen hours a day?"

"Any other kind of thinking—that's what everyone's problem is."

The tester was carrying the first pup back into the utility room while he gnawed on a piece of rawhide she was holding. "Think about your dog's Schutzhund title," I said, "think about how famous her son's going to be. Think about who you'll breed your bitch to next, think about the puppy *you'll* start fresh with, think about a kennel name for our line of dogs."

Fanny looked away, tapping the eraser of her pencil against her clipboard. "You're lucky if you can really do that."

Another pup was out with the tester. "Look, shut up, okay? They can hear you. Let's concentrate on the test. We want to do this right." I wrote *Blue-collar male* on the top sheet. My fingers were almost trembling, but was I excited or just perturbed? She was *ruining* it for me.

Fanny sighed, whispered "Okay," leaned forward with her elbow on her chipboard, chin in her hand, and watched the next pup's tests. She didn't move, and after three more pups, she said, without taking her chin from her hand, "They're all exactly the same."

"Almost," I said. "We did a great job socializing them."

"They're little monsters!" the tester called, trying to wrestle the huge pink elephant away from a pup. "Hope you can tame them."

I laughed as the pup violently shook his head to kill the elephant, thrashing it from side to side. But I knew she probably meant *tame* it like crush it into a subservient slave. Some of these people who call themselves *trainers* . . . jeez. You don't break your dog's will, you don't crush it into second place. When we said these were *tame* wolves, we didn't mean we drained all the natural dog keenness and survival instinct and powerful forces out of them, like a cotton ball lapdog, afraid of its shadow. All it meant is we became partners, not enemies, so *what* he is and *who* he is gets channeled into the useful things we want him to *do*. That's what domestication is, not killing off millions of years of his developed abilities.

She'd rattled me, the so-called trainer doing the test, so I forced my attention back to the next pup. "Even the bitches have it," I whispered to Fanny. "But I don't want a bitch."

"Why?"

"If a bitch is any good, she has to divide her career between showing and having good pups who'll also win, so she can't win as much as the males, can't be ranked as high. Someday maybe I'll have a bitch *too,* but not now."

The tester came over to us, holding a wiggling pup under one arm, extending her other arm to show us red scrapes and scratches from elbow to wrist. She looked right at Fanny, not me, and said, "Are you sure you feel okay about selling these things to people? You sure they're not like wild animals? You sure they're not dangerous?"

Fanny looked at me.

"They're fine," I said, careful not to sound as angry as I was. "How many more are there?"

"Two or three. I'm curious, what do you want—I mean, none of these pups is afraid or overly sound-sensitive, they all chase, follow, and retrieve. I mean, what more do you hope to have in the one you choose?"

God, stupid *trainer.* This-is-a-recording: "He'll always want more. He'll get *mad* about losing. He'll always come back at you, never be beaten down. Never give up. I'll be the boss, but that won't mean he's a downtrodden peon."

After the tester went, shaking her head, to get another pup, Fanny said, "Sometimes when they're playing, it does look like they'll tear each other apart."

"Dogs don't do that to a healthy member of their own pack," I answered. "Let him pee first," I yelled to the tester as the next pup was placed on the lawn. Then I couldn't help it, I asked, without looking at Fanny, "If you had two dogs and one killed the other, would you kill the one that was left?"

"God. No. But I'd give it away, get rid of it. I'd never be able to look at it without remembering."

"That's how we're different."

"You'd kill it?"

"No. I'd keep it."

The tester was about to toss a squeaky toy for the chase-and-retrieve instinct test. She was sitting on the grass, the pup bouncing in circles around her. As she cocked her arm, the pup lunged for the toy in her hand. The tester yelled as the pup caught not only the toy in his teeth but her fingers as well. I stood as the tester snatched the pup up by the scruff of its neck and threw it. The pup hit the wire on the other side of the pen surrounding the testing area, landed on its feet running *back* toward the tester. The woman sort of threw the toy and held her hands up with obvious fear, but as soon as the toy began to bounce away on the grass, the pup went after *it* instead, then brought the toy back to the tester, tail curled up over his back, leapt up against the tester's leg, toy still in his mouth, jumping up and down on his hind feet. "Well, aren't you proud of yourself," the tester said. After she picked him up and wrestled the toy out of his mouth, he licked her face, at the same time struggling to be put back on the ground.

More than an omen, *that* was my dog.

———————

The back of the program for the production of short winter dances listed Dani Clark as an administrative assistant for the director of artistic development. Renee read it without surprise. Dani obviously wasn't someone who'd gotten a degree in business or finance and just happened to have a job with an arts organization. She'd probably majored in theater, then specialized in production when she was winnowed out as a performer.

Renee sipped Swiss mocha at a table outside the Kensington Coffee Company. She'd stopped here on her way home from the park. The day had warmed up to the high seventies and she'd decided, while she was out there sweating, seeing Fanny's shirt stuck to the middle of her back, that she'd stop for an ice tea. But after four, the temperature dropped quickly, and when the lamps along Adams Avenue began to glow, the twilight was cool.

If Morgan hosted a party, it would have to wait until after he got back from Denver. She'd suggested it to him the other day when she was doing her laundry, but she had let it drop when he told her about the audition. Getting to know Dani at a party might work better that way, anyway, with Fanny not home.

But Renee hadn't just burst right out and asked Morgan to have a party. She'd told him she'd seen Dani Clark at The Flame.

"Oh yeah?" he'd said, "I thought she was married. She used to be married."

"She was cruising," Renee said.

"Did you talk to her?"

"No, I was with someone else."

Morgan hadn't asked who. He had been making a milk shake out of yogurt and bananas while Renee waited for the washer to stop.

"I think she has a problem, though," Renee went on. "I mean, her work life and social life might be totally separate. Know what I mean? Some people still think they need to protect themselves. I don't mean she's closeted, but . . . you know, maybe she needs closer friends where she works. No wonder she sometimes comes to performers' parties." She stopped, noticing that Morgan was waiting to be able to turn the blender on. The nuts Morgan had thrown into the milkshake grated like rocks. Renee held her ears. "Maybe we could have a party," she'd said, as Morgan poured the concoction into two glasses. "My place is too small, but you could have a party *here.*"

The whipped cream had melted and was floating on the top of Renee's mocha. She stirred it in with the tiny plastic spoon. In retrospect, the park had been better than sitting in a car or in Fanny's house with Morgan in another room somewhere. The park had been bright and big, quiet in a way that made little noises, like the clink of the swing set chain, louder; but also noisy in a way that had made their voices—*her* voice, doing most of the talking—more muffled, without hard edges.

Renee skimmed some whipped cream foam from the surface of her drink and put the spoon into her mouth. It wasn't as though she expected to never see Fanny again—although probably not before she left for her temporary job. But maybe the park made it sound that way. The rattle of leaves in the gutter, distant dogs barking, kids on a school playground up the street. Maybe Renee wouldn't have been sure what she meant if she'd said it anywhere else. Although she'd known for several days what she was going to say.

She'd called Fanny and said, "Heard you've been busy. Designing?"

"No."

"How are the puppies?" Renee asked.

"Getting big."

"Ready to sell them?"

"Hell, yes. Doreen wants me to keep a bitch, but I can't. Not now. I've got enough interested people lined up from my newspaper ads."

"Um, listen," Renee said, hearing her voice go a little higher, "can we go on a drive somewhere, get some coffee? Is Morgan home?"

"Yeah, he's here. But I have to go out to the park." Fanny's voice was as close to monotone as Renee had ever heard it. Renee wasn't sure she'd heard Fanny be truly animated, except talking to or about the puppies, since the time she'd lived there.

"You could come out to the park before my lesson," Fanny said. "Or, no, how about after my lesson, at about three o'clock? I have to work tonight."

So Renee had found the park, left her car on the street, and waited at the sandbox. It couldn't be the same as when Kay left her, anyway, no matter where it happened. Not only were the tables turned, but with Kay it had actually happened in bed. Right after Kay's tongue had turned Renee into a quivering blob of liquid, her hands still cupping Renee's buttocks, Kay had lifted her head, their eyes had met, and Kay had announced she'd snagged a career-boosting job in New York assisting a literary agent and hoped Renee could find someone else to help her unwind after rehearsal. Maybe they'd meet again when Renee hit New York with the cyclone of excitement she was sure to cause wherever she went.

From where she sat on one of the swings, Renee could see Fanny's car in a parking lot across a large area of grass. Fanny and her dog had seemed to be marching around with a tall redhead sort of stalking them, circling, her loud voice coming across the park, but no words. After the other girl picked up her things and left, Fanny tied her dog to her car's bumper and began walking across the grass toward the sandbox. She walked the whole way watching her feet. Looked up and raised her hand in hello when she got to the edge of the sand, then climbed the slide and sat on top, her legs sticking out straight in front. Fanny didn't move, but Renee made the swing sway sideways, back and forth, keeping her toes on the ground.

"I've been thinking . . . ," Renee said. "Oh, by the way, sorry I didn't call sooner."

"That's okay."

"I mean, I was thinking about something that happened to me about two years ago. I knew this girl—she was an actress and she had a boyfriend who was in dance. So I would see her at some parties and shows, and around the theater at school where the drama people hung out . . . we all hung out together."

Fanny was tapping the toes of her tennis shoes together. Renee couldn't tell if she was watching her own toes or looking at her.

"Anyway, I remember once we were in a car together going somewhere. I was in the front passenger seat and this girl was in back, and she was leaning over the front seat with her arm around my shoulder, her hand on my arm. She wasn't one of my good friends, really, just an acquaintance. Anyway, I'd been alone for a while. It'd been over a year since Kay'd left me. I'd started to look forward to when I would see this girl. I would get, you know, that feeling in my stomach."

"Adrenaline," Fanny said.

"Yeah, and a day would seem pointless if I knew there wouldn't be a chance of seeing her—even if I had a lesson or rehearsal, it was almost a drag, like something getting in my way." She stopped and wiped grains of sand from her damp palms. "Then there was a party toward the end of the year, mostly people from the performing arts, and, you know . . . I just drank. Maybe I had a few hits. The host was a violist, and some singer took this guy's viola out and started playing it, so the guy started to give him a lesson. Then other people who played instruments started being actors, reciting Shakespeare badly, and everyone was doing what someone else was majoring in, the musicians called it *play my ax,* and this girl . . . we were in the bedroom, there were about five of us on a bed, including her boyfriend. She was giving him a massage, I think, and I was watching, and she knew I was watching, and I knew she knew, although I think he was actually asleep. Then she said she would play *my* ax, and I said, *My ax is my body,* which is what she'd meant, of course. She smiled and kept giving her boyfriend this massage, so I lay down across the foot of the bed and pretended to go to sleep. I think when she started on me she continued to rub her boyfriend with one hand and put her other hand on me. I said it felt good, and she commented on my muscles."

She noticed Fanny was no longer tapping the toes of her shoes together. She had leaned forward and was holding her feet, staring down at her knees. Renee pushed herself harder and started to swing with her feet off the ground, pumping a little to keep going.

"I, um, I don't even remember now if something happened that interrupted her, or if someone else came crashing in and plopped on the bed. Or maybe her boyfriend suddenly snored and people started laughing. But the next day, she acted like I was just *any*one, no different, sort of even avoided me, was too busy, always talking to other people, and I realized . . ." Renee took a deep breath. "I realized . . . why should *I* feel hot inside whenever I saw her if I was just . . . her experiment . . . I couldn't afford to waste emotions like that. Know what I mean?"

Fanny said, "Yeah." Then they'd raised their eyes and looked at each other. And Fanny slid down the slide.

Renee couldn't remember saying good-bye or wishing Fanny luck with her temporary job. She must've said *something* else after Fanny's feet hit the sand at the bottom of the slide, before Fanny turned to go back to the parking lot. She had watched Fanny walk all the way across the expanse of grass, this time with her head up. When Fanny got to her car, Renee saw the husky get up and stretch, then sit in front of Fanny, and Fanny kneeled to embrace the dog.

––––––––––

I knew it was going to be hard to say good-bye to the other pups. But I never thought Fanny would make it *harder*. I had carefully planned the best way to sell them. Fanny said she wanted to get it over with, and she had agreed: All the prospective buyers she'd lined up were coming to her house Friday afternoon, Friday evening, or Saturday morning. They would pick a pup from the pen in the living room, then take their pup out to the lawn to interact with it before their final decision.

When I arrived, Fanny had everything set up exactly as we'd discussed, the pups in the living-room pen, a photo album available showing the husky and a few pictures I'd gotten of the wolf, the husky herself locked in the bedroom, the lawn mowed and all the shit picked up, the toys put away in a big plastic bucket, shots stored in the refrigerator so each pup could be inoculated before going to its new home, the contracts all typed and xeroxed, stacked by the door next to the log book so we'd know the name and address of each pup's new family.

People started arriving almost immediately, so I didn't have a chance to review the contract itself until the first buyer was ready to take his pup. Fanny was in the kitchen preparing the shot, so I got the contract for the guy to sign. He was holding the struggling pup under one arm, the pup's feet slapping and bending the paper as he tried to read it, so I took the pup and let him loose in the room. If the guy had just signed, I never would've caught the change Fanny had made in the contract. Then I *would've* killed her.

"What's this mean," the guy said. "You want me to alter him. What's that?"

"What? Let me see that." I looked at the other contracts on the stack.

"What's it mean?" the guy said.

"Fanny!" I yelled, leaving the guy there.

Fanny was drawing the vaccination up into the syringe, carefully watching what she was doing. "Bring the pup in here," she said without looking up.

No holds barred: "Why did you put this shit about altering in these contracts? What's the idea? I spent a lot of time with this litter, they're *all* a part of my bloodline."

"The plan was you were only taking one." Fanny tapped on the side of the syringe to knock the air bubbles loose.

"But they're all part of my line, I plan to monitor their development and personalities, I want them *all* intact and available to me."

Fanny finally looked up, holding the syringe in front of her chest, the needle pointing out, her thumb poised on the plunger. "I want the rest of these bastards neutered. I don't want responsibility for these wolves, who knows what they'll be like with these inexperienced people?"

Bastards!

"No." I had to explain it to her all over again. "The bitches go with an agreement that they have to have a litter, with a stud of my choice. The males have to remain available. How do I know what'll happen? My pup may be dysplastic or have allergies."

"You can't just go take someone else's dog in a year or two."

"I won't take their dog, I want them *available*. If they're neutered, that's the end, it's back to square one. I don't know exactly what my next step is, it may involve your bitch and my pup, maybe my pup and a sister, it could be another brother and sister, but the options have to *be* there!"

Fanny looked out the window. There were two couples outside playing with the pups they'd chosen. The guy in the living room was talking to his. The doorbell rang. Fanny's head snapped back around, then she looked down at the shot. A clear pinkish drop was hanging from the end of the needle. "Get the door," I said, taking the syringe. The drop of liquid fell as the syringe changed hands. "Oh, wipe that up, I don't want any of them licking it and getting sick."

"There's the sponge," Fanny said, pointing to the sink as she went to get the door.

Holding the syringe with the needle toward the ceiling, I had to bend to wipe up the spilled drop but couldn't see where it had landed. "Excuse me." The guy with the pup was standing in the kitchen doorway. "She said you were ready to give my shot."

"Oh, yeah." In one quick movement, I lifted the skin on the back of the pup's neck, plunged the needle in and released the contents. "Keep rubbing here," I told him, and held the flap of skin until his hand took over. "You shouldn't feel anything wet, let me know if you do, I'll get your contract fixed."

The new arrivals went through the kitchen and out the back door with their puppy. Fanny was standing in the living room reading the contract. "We look terrible," I whispered. "We look like we don't know what we're doing."

"I know what *I'm* doing," Fanny muttered. Little *bitch*.

"No, you don't, this was never part of our agreement. Look, you get all the money from the sales, *I* get to decide what happens next, your part is done."

"You can have half the money."

"*No.*" I tried to take the contracts from Fanny, but she wouldn't let go. The papers crumpled in our fists. I was holding Fanny's wrist, trying to get her hand off the contracts. I said, "I know how to file a lawsuit. I swear I will."

"What for?"

"Breach of agreement."

"Try it."

"I will, you just wait and see, I'll do it!" My voice was high and shrill, fast and bristling. I didn't care. I couldn't breathe, each heartbeat an explosion. I had already decided long ago that the only intense emotion I ever wanted to have was elation for winning at a show, a national championship, an international title. But if I *had* to, if triggered, I knew I could get mad. It was better than crying, which *Fanny* started doing. The doorbell rang again. I suddenly succeeded in ripping Fanny's hand off the contracts. Fanny fell backwards against the wall, her head hit, her eyes shut, her face contorted.

I answered the door. "Fanny will tell you about the pups, then get your shots started and tell you what essential equipment you'll need."

It only took me ten minutes to go into Fanny's studio, flatten the contracts the best I could, black out the clause about altering them, then return to enter the names into the log book and pass out the contracts while Fanny gave the shots. I don't know if Fanny was talking to the people or not, telling them to rub where the shot went in, reminding them it was only the first in a series they would need. I brought the log book outside and stayed on the patio, had people sign their contracts there before they went in to get their shots from Fanny.

My voice was perfectly normal as I left with my own pup in a crate, reminding Fanny about her next Schutzhund lesson and that I was planning to take her husky home from the park afterward so I could take care of her while Fanny and Morgan were away.

"Morgan can call me when he gets home, unless you want me to keep her the whole time to keep her training going," I told her. I have no idea if Fanny answered me.

The night after we sold the pups, I played with mine in the living room for several hours with toys spread out all over the floor, calling *Jack, Jackie!* as I encouraged and praised, so he would learn his new name. God, what drive—he would chase and kill any moving object, no matter how far I threw it, then charge back to me with the toy for his tug-of-war game. But I also had to start teaching him to stay focused on what *I* was doing with him. I'd watched the pups playing together: when one wanted another's attention, it pounced and bit, so the attacked pup forgot anything else it was doing and focused on the game at hand. So every time his attention wandered—if he paused, eyed a toy I wasn't holding, or listened to a sound outside—I attacked him with a stuffed animal or squeaky toy. So refocusing on my game was not just part of his familiar pack behavior—it was voluntary and, better yet, instantly rewarded by another game of chase and tug.

I had a gate blocking the living room from the rest of the house, and Bruno lay just outside the barrier, his chin on his paws, not moving but watching us. I couldn't let the pup play with him. He had to bond to *me* and learn that I was the playmate he preferred.

After midnight it would only take Scott fifteen minutes to drive home from downtown, where he'd just catered a big party. As soon as he got home, he would take Sadie for a run. But he wished he had the dog with him now so he could stop at the park *before* getting home. He couldn't figure out what he was feeling—nothing like the crude intoxication after a high school party at which he'd gotten a hand into a girl's panties and had gone home with the smell still on his fingers. It was more like the adolescent sentiment that everything was perfect in the world because you'd danced every dance with the junior high queen. But not that either, because at the same time a dreariness hung around him, as though he would be alone for a while now, plodding through each meaningless day. He also knew he was feeling sorry for himself and that no one would find that attractive. Maybe, considering how she'd spoken with him tonight, it wouldn't have been inappropriate to suggest she could write to him while she was away. But then again, if he'd asked, she might've stopped talking and just stared at him with something going on behind those pale greenish eyes that he could neither read nor join.

He hadn't needed waitresses for this job—just a few busboys to keep the two long tables of food replenished, one person to slice and serve the large roast beef and ham kept under heat lights, and two bartenders, one for mixed drinks, the other serving only wine. He had hired her to do the wine. Ordinarily he wouldn't have had to stay at a job like this; his chief assistant oversaw most of it and carved the large meats.

At first he'd just passed by the wine bar occasionally. She'd said, "Maybe I should change careers. I like this."

He'd watched her serving wine to the guests, and she'd smiled, looked them in the eye, but never laughed out loud, didn't exchange banter, which was proper for this type of job, but not the way women usually handled the bar. In between guests, she rearranged the glasses, stacking and unstacking, making new patterns; wiped the counter top over and over, watching her hand move back and forth; made sure all the labels of the bottles faced out; and a few times she sat, completely disappearing behind the bar. He wanted to say, "I know how you feel." But he didn't know if he did.

Later—the party was thinning out but a stubborn core of people hung on—he'd gone to the wine bar and said, "I've finished my agility equipment." He took a stack of Polaroid shots from his jacket pocket, one shot of each individual piece, several shots of the whole course arranged in a park, which she probably would've recognized as the park she trained in. He hadn't seen her there the last few times he'd gone after work to set up.

"A whole course? Wow."

"Yeah. An agility club gave me a charter membership so they can use my stuff once a month, starting this Saturday. Could you come then?"

She wiped a few drops of wine from the counter with a rag. "I'm leaving town day after tomorrow."

"Going on vacation?"

"No." She'd looked up, smiling wryly. "Something you'll understand—work."

"You're moving?" He took a step back, as if he would've fallen if he hadn't caught himself.

"No, just a temporary job. Near Tahoe. My uncle runs a place up there."

"Oh. Taking your dog?"

"No. My training will have to wait."

"That's too bad." He noticed she was wringing the rag in both hands. "You'll miss her, won't you?"

"I guess."

He'd been standing at the open end of the portable bar, so when she suddenly sat down, he could still see her, but her face changed, she wiped her eyes, her nose was red. "Sorry," she said.

If a friend had been sitting like that in front of him, it would've been natural to ask what was wrong. But he didn't. He took a step forward. "It's okay, I'll take the bar."

"Thanks." Her voice was husky, but even. She took a deep breath, leaned her head back against the bar, looking vaguely up. Then she looked sideways at him. "You should've seen me when I sold the pups. Doreen threatened me. I *knew* she didn't have anything to back it up, complete bluff. Not that she wouldn't've *tried,* made everything a complete mess. Easier to just let her have her own way and get the hell out."

"What happened?"

"She wants those wolves to keep breeding. I don't. But I let her get signatures from every buyer promising to let her use them for studs or brood bitches."

"She threatened you?"

"Kind of," barely a whisper. "I just caved."

For a moment he could hear her breathing, then her voice came back, hard and harsh, "But I almost beat the crap outta my own dog!" Her eyes flashed up at him.

"What?" He'd moved a step closer. "After you sold the pups?"

"No, before. For no reason. Just because she— Like if someone stepped on my toes, so I stab them in the stomach. I don't know . . ." She'd looked away and swallowed. "Maybe I'm just running away."

Again, he'd almost said, "I know." Neither of them moved or said anything for a while. Then she turned her head even farther away, and her voice was half choked: "Everyone I know . . ." She wiped an eye. "Everyone I *used* to know . . . even my so-called husband . . . they're all, oh shit, I don't know what I'm saying." She faced him, her eyes red and swollen to slits, a weird sound that was probably supposed to be a laugh, "This friend—I guess that's what she is, or *was*—she gave me a book on *androgyny* for Christmas."

He'd been about to squat beside her, but a guest came to get a refill of wine. Scott took care of it, and when the person walked away, Fanny stood again. "Sorry," she'd said.

"I understand, it's okay, everyone has times they need to talk."

"Not bartenders," she'd laughed again, a short sound. "They're only supposed to listen, right?"

"Sure, bartenders aren't human . . . neither are bosses . . . right?"

She'd flipped one more small smile at him.

Five minutes before he got home, it started to rain, but that wouldn't stop him from taking Sadie out. She was supposed to be a water dog, and *he* hadn't gone out in the rain without an umbrella for too long. He accelerated to over eighty.

He was in and out of the house in minutes. The dog filled the car with her excited breath. He knew there was a pay phone in the park, standing alone off the meandering sidewalk. Scott could see a warped, murky reflection of himself in the Plexiglas as he approached, his hair plastered down over his forehead, making his nose look too large, his eyebrows too big and dark. He turned his back on the phone as he dialed her number. If the male voice answered, he would hang up . . . childish, he knew. But she picked it up herself, sounding quiet and mature. "Hello?"

"Hi, it's me."

"Still at the job? Did I forget to do something?"

"No, I'm in the park with my dog, she gets crazy being cooped up all that time."

"Yeah, I know what you mean."

There was a silence, but he wasn't afraid. He heard her waiting. "Look," he said, "I just want you to know . . . don't be scared of going away for a little while. You have friends here . . . your dog people friends will still be here. When you come back, we can train together, I won't be too far ahead of you."

"You can show me what you've learned," she said. "I'll be counting on you."

Sadie romped like a colt, splashing and kicking, play-bowing, lapping at every puddle. Scott darted across the lawn, calling for her to chase him. She leapt against him as he ran and they tumbled together, the dog growling, Scott laughing, covering each other with leaves and wet grass.

She drove the first two hours. Morgan didn't wake until she stopped for gas. When he got out, Fanny slid over, took an aspirin, leaned her head back, and shut her eyes. So he filled the tank, then went to the rest room to wash the gas smell off his fingers with rusty water.

"Sort of peaceful, without the dog," he said, adjusting the seat for his longer legs.

"Sort of strange," she answered. "She was always so excited to go anywhere."

Of course, as soon as you got out to where the speed limit went up to seventy, there was only cowboy music on the radio. He switched it off. "Find me one of those tapes I copied from Renee . . . please."

"Space music?" She fumbled around then put in a tape, synthesized flute and harp.

"Um . . ." He held the wheel with one hand and slid the other hand under one leg. "You don't have to tell me but whatever happened with you and Renee? I mean, I know you were confused about . . . I mean, did anything happen? Has it made you think . . . do you think you can ever be attracted to a woman, I mean, have you been thinking about . . ."

"She played around a long time," Fanny said slowly. "I guess I . . . I didn't stop her or anything. I was flattered, you know? And she made me feel . . ."

"Like you'd found out who you are?"

"I was going to say confused." Fanny was sitting like a crash test dummy, staring straight ahead. "But, yes, flattered, and . . . I don't know . . . I didn't ever tell her to forget it."

"You don't have to tell me if you don't want to, it's none of my business, I know." When he looked over at her for a second, she shrugged.

"I'm not hiding anything. At first I thought I was imagining things, and I didn't *want* to just be *imagining* feeling so . . . flattered . . . but I guess I wasn't imagining it. She almost kissed me. But what's an *almost* kiss? I don't know."

"Where? I mean when, where were you?"

"Standing around. I don't know."

"What happened? You don't have to tell me, but—"

"I've asked myself what happened—did I encourage her, give out signals? And *then* what happened? Was I just too much work, too much of a zombie? *She* crossed the line . . . then she tried to cross *back*. I guess she did cross back."

"Well . . ." He pushed his hand farther under his thigh. "I know you've been so . . . dissatisfied, unhappy, whatever, and I wondered if you thought you'd found something that could, you know, change things for you."

"Morgan, when I say confused, I do mean confused, but . . ." She turned toward him at the same time that he glanced at her. It seemed strange, as if they hadn't looked at each other for a while. Her face was thin, her eyes naked, as if without lashes, despite the dark patches still beneath each eye. "I knew I wasn't really feeling . . . that's what I mean by confused: why did it seem that I *wanted* her to want *me,* but I knew *I* wasn't particularly feeling . . . that way about her?" Fanny drew one leg up onto the seat, her body facing him, but turned her face toward the windshield. "Something about her makes people feel like she's got something they need, but I don't know what it could be."

"I know what you mean. Everyone falls in love with her. In various ways. Something about her . . ."

The cheap cassette deck was distorting the sound of the flute when it got anywhere close to forte. "But I also thought you may've found a more comfortable niche, something you may want to explore a little more, with or without Renee, so you can figure out . . . I don't know . . . who you are. That sounds corny, I know."

Fanny suddenly punched the eject button. The machine spit out the tape and switched to static from the untuned radio. "We do sound corny with this background music—two lost children of the seventies who never found a guru. How is this girl suddenly the answer to everything?" She turned the radio off.

"Well, something sure has happened to *me* since knowing her."

"But you know what bugs me? The closed-club attitude, like *you're not one of us.*"

"Your dog people are the same way."

"No, they're not."

"So if you're out training and some dweeb comes by with his mutt with about a dozen tags around his collar, and he asks what you're doing or can his dog jump over your jumps, what do you do, talk to him in your in-group lingo? You probably don't even take the time to grunt. Right?"

"That's not the same thing, Morgan. If an old fart in the grocery store tells you he learned the two-step in high school, do you go out for coffee and talk shop with him?"

"You're unbelievable." He pulled his numb hand from beneath his leg, gripped the steering wheel in both fists, made his arms rigid and straight for a second, stretching his back.

Fanny took a deep breath, let it out, then pushed the cassette back in. After the harp and flute faded and were replaced by a recorder with shimmering background instruments, Fanny said, "God, what're we gonna do with each other."

"What do you mean?"

"We're . . . are we too far gone? Is it too late?"

"I don't know." He glanced over again. She was kneeling on the seat facing him, her eyes darker because they were wet.

"Have we blown it?" she said.

"I don't know." He wondered if maybe he should touch her. "I wish I could say we haven't. I don't know."

Fanny's head dropped. She picked at the frayed edge of the seat belt. That morning when they'd left, her hair had been wet and slicked down with mousse. As it dried, it rose and stuck out in darkened points, like horns. When she brushed it later, it would spray around her head like a rock star's, but the pinched face underneath wouldn't match.

"How long has it been," he said, and with each word asked himself if he should stop, "since we said, you know . . . anything like *I love you* or . . . words to that effect?"

She didn't look up. "You're right. And this isn't a new thought to me. But . . . how can I say it when I don't really know what *it* is?"

"Love? Were you wondering what *it* was when we decided to get married?" He had a feeling her head was up now and she was staring at him, but he didn't take his eyes off the road to check.

"Don't think I haven't asked myself that same question," she said, "over and over. It's just that . . . *love*, or whatever . . . the thing you *think* is love keeps changing. So you wonder if it exists, or *ever* existed, or . . . I don't know. Don't you think it's scary that we might be needing something that might not exist?"

"I don't know about that." Morgan sighed. "Maybe, though, we should both have the, uh, freedom to look for . . . whatever it is we need or we're missing, however you want to say it. Someone else made up the rules for what *being married* means. We don't have to follow them if it's not what we want. We can make our own rules. We can have separate friends, different kinds of relationships with other people, not make limitations on the kinds of closeness we're allowed to have with other people."

Fanny's head didn't move. "Like an open marriage?"

"I guess. I don't like that term, it sounds like pop psychology, self-help books."

Fanny laughed. His stomach felt warm. He turned and smiled at her as she said, "Yeah, I'm-ok-you're-ok-my-dog's-ok-we're-all-ok, *okay?*"

Then, as her laugh died, he didn't know what to do with his smile. He rubbed the back of his neck with one hand.

Without Morgan around to whine and moan, Renee had time to think clearly about the developments in the upcoming contract negotiations. A committee had already been formed and had taken polls to find out the performers' most urgent concerns. She'd noticed Morgan writing at the bottom of his questionnaire, *Let's not go three steps backwards trying to go one forward. Status quo.* Then, if he hadn't been in Denver, he would've most certainly been on the phone to her the morning the paper ran management's press release explaining they were delaying any announcement of the fall dance season due to uncertainties of budget, possible sale of the theater to foreign investors who might want to renovate and make different use of the facilities, and a few vague quotations about "new directions" and "popular demand." At the first meeting yesterday, the committee reported that management wouldn't begin negotiations until the performers agreed to a gag rule. Rumor or suspicion buzzed that the first offer would include huge pay and personnel cuts, purposefully making the sides farther apart so negotiations would be difficult and lengthy.

Around lunchtime, after she'd used the empty stage for a morning workout, she climbed the stairs to the company offices. Towel around her shoulders, her white leotard darkened with large patches of sweat, her damp hair pushed back from her face with a wide, white headband, she stood by the vacant receptionist's desk, heard voices in another room, called in a low voice, "Hello, is everyone out to lunch?"

As she'd hoped, the familiar young woman came from the other room, dressed in a calf-length black skirt, black sweater with the sleeves pushed up to midforearm, white socks and white tennis shoes." Can I help you?"

"Hi, we've met, remember?" Renee said. "You're Dani, right?"

"Yes, I am," the woman said without much tone in her voice. She put one hand to the back of her short dark hair, then neatened a stack of papers on the receptionist's desk.

"I thought we could grab lunch together."

The woman stood still and stared. Renee dabbed her face with the ends of her towel, then moved the towel down to pat her throat while she laughed a little and said, "I'm just trying to get to know people. I figure, why wait around for chance meetings?"

"So obviously this isn't a chance meeting," Dani said.

The phone rang, an odd percolator sound, but stopped midway through the second ring. "What?" Renee tried the laugh again. Dani didn't answer. She moved a couple of bracelets up her arm, pushed them under the bunched sleeve of her sweater. "I just thought, um, you'd appreciate a . . . you know, friend," Renee said. "Hey, okay, I, uh, I won't be coy by trying to use codes or passwords or something. I've always hated that."

"Oh?" Dani looked directly at Renee, folded her arms across her chest.

"It's, um, juvenile, really. I like being direct. We could be friends. I've only been here about six months, I could still use someone to, you know, show me around."

"I think you get around pretty well."

"What's the problem?" Renee let her voice change key. "I'm just trying to be friendly, let you know there's a sisterly face around, someone on your side."

"I don't know whose side you're on," Dani said dryly.

"What?" Renee took a step backwards.

"I saw that note you sent my boss. You're a c-sucker. Well, mine isn't available."

"*What?*" Renee repeated. "What? I, um—if you read it, you'd know . . . maybe he misunderstood and told you wrong—"

"I read it myself. I understood."

"I just meant that being new here, I didn't feel I was *part* of the poisoned atmosphere or what might happen. You know, the preexisting rift, I don't feel part of it, and I don't want it affecting *my* relationship with management."

"Be *honest*—you meant you don't want to be associated with the concerns of your colleagues." Dani's bracelets rattled when she unfolded her arms and ran the fingers of both hands through her hair.

"How *can* I be associated? I don't know their complaints. I wasn't here then."

"How can you claim ignorance? You're pretty well associated with Morgan Nelson's wife, aren't you?"

"Hey, what is this, some sort of jealous snit?"

"You're a grease spot, you know that?" Dani turned to leave.

"Hey, yeah, I know Fanny. I know Morgan too. I know what they're, um, thinking and feeling. Maybe I, um, maybe I just wanted them—and *you*—to know we're not *all* scared and psyched-out like Morgan and some of the others."

Dani stopped and turned around again. Again she looked directly at Renee, her mouth small and tight, her cheeks flushed, her neck taut.

Renee felt her own breast rising and falling heavily. "Hey," Renee said levelly, "fear like Morgan's is palpable. Like a wounded animal near a bunch of wolves. Management will eat them alive."

"Them?"

Renee again touched the hollow in her throat with the end of her towel. "I won't go down with a sinking ship," she said quietly. She could feel her pulse in that soft spot.

Dani blinked slowly, twice. "I'll deliver your message. Anything else?"

"I'm sorry you feel this way."

Dani's nostrils flared, her eyes narrowed, but she silently left the room, closing the door behind her without a click. Renee wiped the new sweat from the back of her neck.

She smiled and realized for a vague moment that she was touching a man nearly the same way she fondled her dog's ear or rubbed her white belly. Her hand stroking his back; her fingers on his neck caressing under his hair; her lips on his throat, his shoulder, the inside of his elbow. Every time she touched him, he responded. He moaned. Or he sighed. He mumbled about how wonderful she was, how good she made him feel, how every day was a numb, dutiful blur he stumbled through while he waited to come back to her at night. Then he would suddenly roll over, erect and ardent, reach for her with his hands and mouth, moaning with a chuckle, and she would be incandescent for the next hour or more.

She was hungry, eager, something always boiling or fluttering in her gut. She was buzzed, flushed, hyped, keen, rapt, delirious, and completely unrecognizable, an exotic stranger. She moaned wistfully about wanting a mirror on the ceiling so she could see this miracle. He called her *Fancy.* Everything was delightfully corny, a tangible hallucination, she could say anything and it wouldn't be mushy, do anything and it would never be anything but voluptuous. He would finally climax with tremendous force at two or three in the morning, and they'd both sleep for three or four hours, seeming to need no more than that before the next day of work at the retreat and the next voracious night of sex.

He was a recreation therapist who ran crafts programs for the retarded kids. And Fanny was designing again, discovering exhilarating ideas for lobbies and foyers.

Why now? she'd wondered after her first intense session with her sketch pad, two hours that were gone in a breathless heartbeat, just like two hours spent with him. Did she really suddenly have some good reason to create rooms *now*, a reason she'd lost years ago after doing her own little house from end to end, top to bottom? It was almost like remembering a hallucination to think back to *that* impassioned day, and Morgan's reaction when he'd stepped through the door into the fresh, quirky room that'd been a pile of boxes when he'd left that morning: "Is the stereo all hooked up?" he'd asked before the door was even shut.

"Look around you."

"Oh, thanks for putting everything away. I hate unpacking."

"It's more than unpacking. Let me explain what I did today."

"I'm not really interested in a blow-by-blow description of you pushing a sofa around to different places."

"God . . ." She'd hardly been able to speak for a second. Maybe it would've been more merciful to rent a bulldozer and level the place right then and there. Instead, she'd lay on the bed in gruesome silence for three or four hours. He hadn't come in to apologize. She'd finally gotten up, slapped together some cheese sandwiches and chewed hers as if it was paper from her sketch book while she sat with him watching the eleven o'clock news. The break-in was only a few months later.

Fanny stood watching Roland running a finger-painting class after breakfast in the hour and a half she had free before preparing the dining room for lunch. The drooling, spastic kids were covered with shiny red, green, and blue, even tinting the strings of saliva that hung from their mouths. They laughed like lowing cattle, thick protruding tongues also colored with a sheen of paint.

Roland looked at her as he guided a child's stiff claw in circles through the oozing paint on the paper. With his other hand, he patted the boy's blond head. Fanny slipped her index finger into her mouth, sucked gently, then slipped the finger between two buttons of her blouse and touched her breast, watching Roland's knees go weak, his mouth open in a silent pant, his eyes blaze. Then she waved and left, stopping at the telephone in the foyer.

"Hello?" Morgan sounded sleepy or half-dead.

"Still in bed? It's almost eleven."

"So?"

"When did you get home?"

"Three days ago. No, four. What day is it?"

"How was the audition?"

"I don't want to talk about it."

"Oh." She paused. "Sorry. Did you get Lacy from Doreen?"

"Yeah."

"Does she miss me?"

"How should I know? She races around like usual."

"Uh, Morgan? . . . I, uh . . . you know that open marriage thing?"

"Yeah."

"Well . . . I guess it's happening."

"Oh, yeah?" His voice was still loggy and dull but came a little more alive. He sniffed, coughed. Fanny plugged one ear so she couldn't hear the classical music Roland was playing in the painting class. "Well?" Morgan finally said.

"Well what?"

"Well . . . who is she?"

"Not a *she,*" Fanny said solidly. She scowled, her forehead leaning against the top of the pay phone, eyes shut. "Morgan, I . . . I can't believe how . . . it's so . . . I'm so—"

"No details," he said, his voice wooden.

"Sorry. Okay. Sorry." She turned and leaned the back of her head against the edge of the phone booth, staring at a vacant wall. In one sketch, she'd opened that wall with a resplendent picture window. Or it could be a built-in aquarium. "It's just that you . . . we . . . never decided if we should tell each other . . . I didn't know. I thought you should know." Another one of those silences.

"Well . . . I guess it's sort of happening here too."

"Oh." She shut her eyes, suddenly wished she could see Roland from here, wanted to see him forget where he was and what he was doing as she ran her fingers lightly down her throat or wiped her wet hands on the inside thighs of her jeans, his hazy expression half satiated, still half-starving. "With Renee?"

"Yeah."

"Uh . . . okay."

"You wanna hear any more?"

"That's okay. You have my address here?"

"Yeah. Someone else called and asked for it too."

"Who? Doreen?"

"Some guy."

She smiled and thought of Scott's crooked-toothed smile, his embarrassed eyes, his dog stretched out and standing up against him, his hands cupping her ears and the back of her head, happily looking at each other. "Did you give it to him?"

"I didn't think you'd want me to."

"Why not? Go ahead."

"Isn't one at a time enough?"

"He's a *friend*, Morgan."

"Okay, hey, no rules."

"Are you okay, Morgan? You sound . . ."

"No, I'm not okay."

"Is it this?"

"No."

"Well . . . this is costing a lot, so we'll talk at a better time."

"Okay."

As she turned and hung up the phone, Roland's weight pressed in on her from behind, his paint-covered hands slid under her shirt and swirled the slime around her nipples. She had to hang onto the phone to keep from collapsing.

"See you later," he murmured in her ear, then returned to his class.

In her room, she peeled off the stained shirt to find her breasts blue and purple, as though bruised.

In Morgan's kitchen, Renee leaned on the stove, waiting for a kettle of water to boil. She could still go to New York to lay groundwork—she had a week of February and all of March to scout East Coast companies. But *here* she was already a principal—in a few years she could be the top prima. That gave her at least ten more years for the company to grow underneath her. Maybe she didn't need New York. She dipped a chamomile tea bag into a mug of hot water and carried it into the bedroom.

Morgan was still curled on his side facing the wall. He obviously hadn't showered or washed his hair that morning, he hadn't shaved, he was wearing sleep-rumpled sweatpants and a faded college T-shirt. Renee sat on the bed beside his curved spine. "Here's some tea, Morgan."

"Thanks." But he didn't roll to his back to reach for the cup. Renee took a sip, then put the mug on the bookcase headboard.

She regretted giving Morgan the Valium tablets two weeks ago, although she wasn't sure if he was using them or how often. He didn't seem to sleep *all* of the hours he lay curled on the bed, but he did spend a lot of time unconscious on the sofa, drooling on his arm, his bare legs and feet in slipper socks hanging off the other end.

"You ought to get back to working like you were before," she said calmly.

"No, I think I'll just lie here till I atrophy."

"You still have work."

"I suck."

He'd managed to drive home from his audition in Denver without killing himself. He'd stopped at her place when he got into town and spoken to her with his head hanging so all she could see was his lank hair, his words coming so slowly, "I'm a failure, I'm a clumsy old man, I'm a *joke* . . ."

Even though it seemed he'd been wearing the same sweatpants and t-shirt for two weeks, there were clothes all over the floor. One shirt, she knew, was Fanny's, one she used to sleep in. "Why're Fanny's clothes still all over?"

"The dog's been sleeping on it."

"Nice of you to leave it there for her."

"Know what it was like? Once, a long time ago, they had a call for extras for a big musical. For some reason, the newspaper printed it, just a little announcement, way back in the arts section, and some housewife showed up with her ten-year-old kid who was learning tumbling or something in school P.E. Like she had no *concept* that people do this professionally, like it was some cute club for her kid to be in after school. That's what they thought about me in Denver—some old fart who learned the jitterbug in charm school and thought he'd have a new hobby dancing on a stage."

"That's ridiculous, Morgan."

"Everyone was at least fifteen years younger." His words started to have that squeezed sound, so, as she had every time he'd cried the past two or three weeks, Renee lay down beside him and let him feel her there behind him as he silently shook for a few minutes, never any longer than that.

The dog started barking, running back and forth outside, digging at the bottom of the fence. Renee flinched almost violently as Morgan shouted, "Shut up, damn you to hell!" Then, nearly whimpering, "Please shut up, she won't stop, please shut her up."

"I could toss Fanny's shirt out to her," Renee said. She rolled to her back, put her hands under her head, and stared at cobwebs hanging from the blades of the ceiling fan.

He fumbled for a handkerchief that he kept in the waistband of his sweatpants, blew his nose, then said, "Fanny's got some guy."

"What do you mean?" Renee wrinkled her nose and squinted.

"She's fucking some guy."

"God," Renee grunted. "Why?"

"Why not, I guess." He wiped his nose. "Why not live a little. She's designing rooms too. I guess she's got free rein."

"She thinks she needs a *penis* to start working again?" The dog was no longer barking, but her nails were still scratching at both the bottom of the fence and the hard dirt. Renee sat up, put one leg on the floor, but kept one stretched flat on the bed. She picked up the mug of tea, then sat holding it in her lap. It was tepid. "Sorry. Didn't mean that like it sounded. You should do the same thing."

Morgan rolled to his stomach, flipped his head so he was facing her, half buried in the pillow, one eye open, shiny and wet. He was lying on both arms and she thought he started to pull the closer hand out from underneath himself. "I mean I know of someone for you," Renee said, then looked away. "She's probably just what you're looking for."

"I didn't know I was looking for anything." He turned his face away again.

"You're *wallowing*, Morgan, and people are going to get sick of it."

In a moment, Morgan sat up, rubbed his face, stood, and stumbled to the bathroom. Renee poured the tea into the dry dirt of a plant that still had two leaves.

While preparing for the litter, I had read that a coyote wouldn't eat a possum playing dead because in order to have an urge to eat, the coyote brain must receive a certain kind of excitement created by a particular enzyme only produced by the chase and kill, or at least by foraging, then claiming the cache. The food may be a *tangible* reward for the behavior of the hunt—necessary for survival—but the intensity of the stimulation was certainly enough by itself to drive the animal to repeat the desirable behavior.

So I knew *not only* would my puppy have to learn that the only things in life worth doing were those he did with *me*, but also that the exercises we would eventually do in competition would have to provide him the greatest stimulation and joy. Any canine could be *forced* to perform a behavior desired by a trainer, but even with a food reward, if doing the behavior wasn't *in itself* an excitement, if it was just perfunctory work, the dog wouldn't ever be a top winner.

Wild dog puppies play adult killing games and learn early the basic pleasure in survival behaviors that will occupy their mature years. But domestic dogs retain puppy characteristics all their lives, so even though all of the exercises in Schutzhund were behaviors performed by actual working dogs, all had to be introduced as— and always remain at heart—*games.*

Protection training started with a prey-biting response to a rolled burlap bag, which was actually a tug-of-war game, the wilder the better. Jackie, or *Bruno's Wolfman Jack,* at this point twenty-five pounds, had already shredded three bags, not by chewing or shaking them up but because his hold was so strong that the action of the tug-of-war contest eventually ripped the burlap. He would chase me as I ran, turned sideways, holding the bag with my hands about a foot apart, and as he overcame me with a well-timed leap, he traveled the last six feet in the air and grabbed the sack between my fists. He hit the ground with his jaw set and his feet braced for the game. I could even lift him off the ground and twirl him around as he hung onto the sack. He obeyed the *out* command promptly because Jack knew that meant the start of another exciting chase.

Playing on the agility equipment taught Jack the delight of extending his body in flight over the wall, the brush hurdle, and other barriers. Although he would never see the majority of the agility equipment at a Schutzhund trial, the variety of obstacles kept his interest level high. But with Fanny away, I wasn't seeing the old guy and his agility course in the park, even when I sometimes came out in the late afternoon to check.

Jackie had come to love the dumbbell and tracking dummies, as these had gradually become his only toys. If I was holding the dumbbell, Jack's eyes never moved from it, waiting for the moment I might either throw it, run away from him holding it out, tease him with it over his head, or drag it along the ground with a string like a wounded cat trying to escape.

Through all of play training, my laughing shrieks and Jack's happy barks echoed across the nearly empty park, sometimes misty before the early fog lifted, the grass sopping with dew, the tables and benches slick, the sandbox play area sodden and deserted.

While I had Fanny's dog for five days, I had begun training her in formal Schutzhund, but I had to come to the park twice, once with Jack and then again with the husky. I couldn't risk the pup forming a bond with *either* adult dog, especially the bitch, his mother, so the two had barely seen each other. Once, in a rush to answer the phone, I knocked over the gate separating the living room from the bedroom, and I came back to find the adolescent Jack on his back with the bitch standing over him licking his penis. I screamed *"NO,"* rattling the windows, scattering the dogs, and later wondered if the neighbors might've thought an ax murderer was breaking in.

The first night of the husky's stay, I set up a big crate in the living room and told the curious puppy, "No, no, we don't sleep in the same room as our mommy." *God* . . . yeah, so I was distracted for a while, even thinking about how it had been years before I allowed any dog to sleep on the bed with me. I didn't want to be bothered by scratching or stretching, didn't want to feel a body leaning against my back or sharing my pillow. It was maybe five or six years ago, Bruno had crept onto my waterbed and slept dead beside me until I found him there in the morning, and I hadn't kicked him off. Since then, watching television or listening to music, Bruno—and now also Jack—often shared the sofa with me, put a sleeping head heavily on my knee or draped half a torso across my lap.

But talk about *distracted*—I was even thinking about how before my mother finished dying of nothing, we each had a bedroom in Grandpa's house, even after Grandpa didn't know what was going on and went to live in a home. My uncle stayed the hell away, two thousand miles, and paid the bills out of Grandpa's money. At some point, I'd papered the walls of my room with pictures of champion horses, which remained long after I stopped reading the disintegrating paperback horse books. For two years, from the time I was thirteen till Mom died, I never slept the whole night in my room. I sat on my bed smoking in the dark till I heard her call. She couldn't sleep. So I lay down and held her hand, and she dozed.

I had come to appreciate the husky bitch even more while I kept her. True, the dog's keenness was as much a source of distracted attention as it was a working dog's strength—she was definitely disadvantaged without early play training, but the bitch had real promise. I adamantly wanted Fanny to put at least a Schutzhund 1 title on the husky, but I wondered if Fanny had the stomach to do what it takes to have an edge in competition, the air of absolute confidence the handler has to perform with, the suspension of emotion, the putting aside of hurt feelings or loneliness or any mushy crap that can lessen the effectiveness of a training session or weaken resolve on the day of a show.

The only thing that happened on a leash was lead training—getting from one place to another when there were crowds or traffic, the rudiments of heeling much later on, and eventually tracking on a harness. But in the park with my equipment, three hours every morning, Jack was free. I left him lying—panting hard, with his tracking dummy between his front legs—and, admiring his long scarlet tongue, dug a soda out of my ice chest. I'd been there all morning, the coastal overcast had lifted at least an hour ago. Tipping my head back while I drank, closing my eyes, everything was tranquil for a moment, even the tiny background noise of a toddler. Jack nailed him before I could move.

A boy, not over three, was screaming, had run four or five steps away and landed face down, muffling his screams in the grass. Jack was on his feet, looking at me. Also on the ground, a bulbous red plastic baseball bat. The fat parent, approaching across the grass, started to run as I was snapping my leash on Jack and telling him to lie down again.

"My god," the parent wheezed, "I just thought he fell or something." The screeching boy got up and hurled himself at his father's knees, red prune face with no eyes, only a gaping mouth. "What happened, oh, no, let me see it." The man seemed unsure whether to try to lower his huge body down to the boy's level or pick him up. I squatted behind the boy and turned him around. He struggled and batted at my head. But I handled everything with my composed day-of-show state of mind.

"It's not his face," I said. "I think it's his arm. I think he came running up, swinging the bat. This is a trained protection dog."

"He got out of my sight," the man blubbered. "Ronnie, I told you not to hit anything with your bat but a ball."

The boy continued to shriek in my ear. Holding his wrist, I pushed the sleeve of his sweater up while he thrashed and reached for his father's legs with the other hand. Two, three, maybe four puncture wounds on the boy's baby skin, black bruises already appearing around each. "We'll take him to a doctor," I said. "I'll pay the bill, he'll be okay, he's mostly scared." I released the boy, and he plastered himself to his father's shins. The man hauled him up by the armpits.

Jack was watching the scene, no longer panting, ears erect, nose working the air, taking in every sensation. One little mistake, but a champion's heart.

Nothing was simply watching television or sharing a snack in front of the fire or even just taking a shower. They never stopped reaching for each other. During a conversation over coffee in the deserted dining room, his arm would move across the table toward her like a branch reaching for sunlight, and she held his hand with both of hers, sliding two fingers up and down each of his, touching the soft spots in between, watching his hand writhe, watching his lips as he spoke, and she couldn't remember what they talked about. In the blue light of a black-and-white movie around midnight in the lobby she'd been sketching plans for, his pants unzipped, her shirt pulled up, their fingers brushed and grazed each other, mottled sounds coming from the TV blurred with his occasional groan. Later they would move, holding each other as though wounded, to her room, long after the movie was over or before it reached a peak. They sat together in the one chair, lay sideways on her narrow unmade bed, or right down on the carpeted floor, never even removing all of their clothes. He called the room their opium den and asked if she could get candles, lots of them, to put on the dresser, the nightstand, the windowsill, all over the floor.

She couldn't remember tasting the institutional meals she served to families of mother, father, and diapered teenager. Her stomach burned, there was the frail quavering of hunger, famished dizziness—especially if he paused in the doorway, slowly pushing a stick of gum into his mouth. The dishes on her tray chattered together like teeth.

That's where she'd first seen Roland—sitting at one of the tables with other therapists, a group of khaki clothes, canvas shoes or boots, knapsacks, sunburned arms and leathery necks. She hadn't noticed Roland in particular until she brought a pitcher of ice tea. He'd touched her arm and said, "You're not *really* a waitress, are you?" Instead of standing somewhere else the next time she came to the table, she continued to approach the corner where he was sitting for two days, until he returned after his group had left one evening, slid up behind her, and touched her back, three fingers between her shoulder blades, and said, "You're even sexier without a hundred morons in the room."

She tried to have the mind of an amnesia victim later that night on the floor in her room: *Who am I, where am I,* and his voice came suddenly, as though in answer, "The other day when I saw these remarkable little tits, I wanted to put you on the table and suckle you across my plate." After that, he'd fucked her slowly, richly, without pain, and her heaving pulse still hadn't slowed, four weeks later.

In the shower at 4:00 A.M., they'd already soaped each other five or six times. "Oh," he moaned, kneeling, his face pressed to her stomach, the shower pelting the top of his head, "I don't wanna go do ceramics today."

"Are you teaching them to make finger bowls?"

"Want me to practice on you?" he chuckled, still kneeling, gripped her around the waist with one arm, the other hand between her legs, a finger sliding into her. "If you don't get yourself outta my face, I won't be able to stop—we're like a couple of animals." He rose, sat her on the slick edge of the tub, then kneeled again, began fucking her with his feet braced against the other side of the tub, holding her butt, plunging urgently as if they hadn't just done it four hours earlier.

Face to face, they stared at each other, wide-eyed. She said, "This can't be me. Just two months ago . . . just a month ago, I was . . . frigid."

He picked her up, turned around, and sat on the edge of the tub with her on his lap, her legs around him. He still had one arm around her waist, one hand on the back of her head, her cheek against his, his breath in her ear, he whispered, "You were being kept on ice for me." The shower continued spattering, the drain gurgled, steam billowed like storm clouds. He said, "My girlfriend and I . . . it's sort of an understanding we developed when she moved out for a month or two . . . god, this was three years ago . . . so we have sort of an implied thing . . . that we need to get away from each other now and then."

Fanny tightened her legs around his waist. "Is this one of the separations you sometimes need?"

"Yeah. It's unspoken. It's just . . . a thing we have."

"I don't wanna think," Fanny moaned. But she did think: about how she'd told Roland about telling Morgan, the same day as her phone call. Roland had nodded, eyes shut, lying beside her on the bed, then nestled down under the blankets, pulled her close and sighed, the way a dog does before it goes to sleep, a transition into tranquility.

Chilly bumps rose on her wet back where his hands slowly moved. "Why," her voice deadened against his shoulder, "didn't you say this when I told you about Morgan?"

His hand moved quickly up her spine, into her hair, gathered a handful into a fist, brought her face to his, and kissed her vigorously.

She thought he might not answer, that maybe it was a foolish question, a distracting question, wished she hadn't said anything, but then he said, "I talked to her last night. She asked if I'd made any friends, so I told her about you. But I didn't tell her *everything*. I didn't want to . . . get into it right then . . . you know."

The shower had grown tepid. The few spatters that made it all the way to her back were cold. She shivered. She held onto him tighter with both arms and legs. Her toes curled. Her mouth was dry. She swallowed, looking at him—his eyes waiting, smiling. She said, "But what about your . . . arrangement?"

Her stomach knotted as he shut his eyes. He kissed her forehead, her nose, her chin, her neck. She felt hard and gnarled, uncomfortably alert, almost like the raw night so long ago when she'd surprised the burglars—when her heartbeat and the adrenaline had been anything but pleasant. But at least then, she'd acutely, innately *known* what she was afraid of.

———————

The suitcase Suzanne had bought a couple of weeks ago held almost all his shirts and pants, socks and underwear, and several extra pairs of shoes. He put the packed suitcase in the trunk of his car, threw some jackets in the backseat, plus a flight bag with his shaving gear, shampoo, aspirin, and other things from the medicine cabinet. He pulled the car into the driveway and hooked up the new little trailer that held his agility equipment.

It was around two-thirty in the afternoon. He'd left his business early, told his employees he'd be back for the evening job—a standard buffet reception. He mowed and fed the lawn, swept the clippings, trimmed a hedge, watered the citrus trees, then took Sadie on the grass with her Frisbee. Ordinarily he wouldn't want the dog on the lawn right after he'd spread fertilizer, afraid she'd pick it up on the fur between her toes, then lick her feet later. But he planned to rinse her off. He wanted her to be good and tired. Sadie was delighted with the unusual early afternoon romp, didn't seem to notice that Scott wasn't saying much, not cheering for her acrobatic leaps to pluck the Frisbee from its flight, not teasing her before he threw it, not laughing when she missed. When she voluntarily took a pause to go to her water dish and gulp noisily, messily, he ended the game, hosed down her legs and feet, then put her on the patio to dry.

When Suzanne arrived home from work, Scott was watching television, but he turned the set off as soon as he heard her key in the front door. "Scott? Did you already go out to the park with your dog things this afternoon?"

He looked at her for a moment. "No, I'm taking the trailer . . ." He was sitting on the floor, but got up and eased himself gingerly onto the end of the sofa as he motioned for her to join him. She smiled, put her purse on an end table, and sat. They were facing each other, at least a third of the sofa empty between them. He had his hands folded on his lap, one thumb pressing down on the other, nearly bending it backwards. She was already no longer smiling. "Suzanne, I'm . . . leaving. I'm not happy, and I've got to go."

A little over an hour later, he was in his suite at the Vacationland

Motel, Sadie rolling on her back on the king-sized bed. He hung his shirts in the closet on hangers that could not be removed from the pole.

March was not tourist season, so his car was one of only two parked in front of the wing of suites. The trailer stuck out pretty far, but he wasn't worried about it. He got his jackets and the grocery bag from the backseat. Suzanne had handed him the sack as he'd left. When he'd shut the front door, he'd heard her wail like a siren, cough, retch, wail again. It had felt as if he'd stood on the porch motionless, listening, with the front door closed behind him for ten minutes, but it had probably been ten seconds.

He went back into the suite and Sadie met him at the door, wagging her stump tail as though he'd been gone a week. The sack held peanut butter, a bag of cheese puffs, three cans of soda, and an opened box of donuts with four donuts remaining. He put the whole bag in the little refrigerator then went to shower and dress for the evening job.

The first thing Suzanne had done after he told her he was leaving was whisper "Why?" But before he could answer, she'd picked up the can of Coke he'd been sipping from and thrown it across the room, and while she'd screamed that he was a selfish coward who didn't care or understand what a woman's needs and feelings were, he'd watched two splotches of Coke stretch themselves down the wall from where the cola had spattered, and the remainder of the brown bubbly liquid burping out of the can into the rug.

"How can you do this to me," she'd shrieked, standing, mangling a dog magazine she'd snatched up from the coffee table. "It's not fair, go on, get outta here and take that messy mutt, it's not fair, you've always been so selfish, what'll I do, what'll happen to me?"

"Nothing will happen to you," he'd said slowly, his voice low and steady.

"We were supposed to get old together, I don't even have any children, you can't do this to me." Her voice was a raw screech. She hooked a foot under the glass-topped coffee table, flipped it to its side, an open-faced rock geode with luminous lavender crystal formations slid to the rug, then the table's heavy glass top fell out of its metal frame, cracking when it hit the rock. "What'm I supposed to do, I can't— You can't— How can you do this to me, you've changed, look what you're doing, you're destroying everything." She was still screaming, a raw sob in her voice.

"I'm sorry you feel this way," he said, "but I haven't been happy for a long time—"

"You're blaming *me* for that, you're punishing *me?*" Her face blotched, her nose red—it seemed to be longer, thinner, hooked— her eyes slits, Suzanne had been standing and Scott still sitting. He hadn't moved from the sofa. When the screaming stopped, he could barely understand her through the coarse sobbing. "We were working all these years for our future, you're going to throw it away, you're not giving me a chance to fix it, whatever it is, what about everything we've gone through together, is it all worthless?"

"Of course not," he murmured.

"Don't you want me to be happy? Doesn't it matter to you at all? How can you do this, just explain that to me, Scott, how can you do this to me, how can you?"

"How can you want me if you know I'm unhappy here?"

"You're unhappy, *you're* unhappy, that's all you think about." Her voice had echoed down the hall as she'd run for the bedroom. The door slammed, and still he hadn't moved. But she was back almost immediately with his dog training books from the nightstand, his photo album of Sadie's puppy pictures, a framed picture of Sadie from his dresser, his white ceramic pie plate clock with red hands, and three or four more magazines. "You'll need these," she'd said, like ice cracking, and dropped the armload. He hadn't taken any of it. It had all still been on the living room floor when he'd left.

The bedroom door had slammed again. This time she was gone longer. He watched a minute and a half tick past on the pie plate clock. When she'd come back, this time she had her robe on, her shoes off, her eyes puffy, almost swollen shut, her nose running, something in her fist. "What'll happen to me, Scott?" she whispered.

"We can still be friends," he'd said weakly.

She'd opened her hand and looked down at his money clip in her palm.

Later, after he'd finally gotten off the sofa, maybe after he'd stepped into the guest bathroom to rinse his face but before he actually had the dog leashed and in the car, Suzanne was looking at the pictures on the walls in the living room, his study, the bedroom, turning some around and hanging them precariously on the nail by the front edges of the frames. "These are yours, how can I look at them now," she cried, her voice harsh, yet watery. "You're ruining my life, you can't fix it now, you've ruined *everything.*"

"Suzanne, you're going to feel better someday," he'd said from down the hall. "We both will. I know it's hard to imagine right now."

"Speak for yourself, you're running away, you won't stay and work, you're throwing it all away. Is it another woman? Who is it? Are you afraid of getting old?"

"I'm just unhappy. I've been unhappy—"

"I don't want to hear about your unhappiness anymore, ever again, just go on, get out of here!" She was coming toward him, still wearing the robe over her work clothes, her hair awry and stringy from pushing her hands through it, her face slimy and contorted. He wasn't sure whether she was approaching to cling to him or to strike at him.

She went past him and sat on the sofa where they'd started. That's when he went outside to get the dog and put her in the car. He'd stood there for a moment, Sadie grinning at him through the glass. He had everything he was planning to take that night. But he went back into the house and stood behind the sofa, his hands on the back, not very near her head. "I won't leave until I know you'll be okay, I won't leave until . . ."

Her voice came thick and muffled: "I must've been awful to drive you away like this."

"It's not you, Suzanne, I'm . . . well, you don't need me to say it again."

Without looking at him, keeping her face averted, she got off the sofa and went into the kitchen, not really stumbling but scuffing her stockinged feet as she walked. He heard the refrigerator, heard packages rustling, she came back with the grocery bag. "I know you can get enough to eat at work. Here're some snacks . . . for tonight." He took the bag from her, not looking at it, trying to see her face, but her hair was all over. "I hope you figure out what you want," she'd whispered.

Scott wrapped a thin motel towel around his waist and looked at his shirts hanging in the half-opened closet. The entire sliding door of the closet was a mirror, steamed from his long shower. Sadie wanted to roughhouse, she met him with a play bow as he turned from the closet, so he let her pull the towel off him and played tug-of-war with her while he sat naked on the bed to use the phone.

"Hello?" It was six-thirty in the evening, but the voice was stupefied and groggy.

"Is Fanny home yet?"

"No."

"Oh. I had a job for her, a last-minute thing, but . . . I guess she can't take it. Thanks, anyway."

Scott was trembling and sweating as he hung up the phone. Sadie was whipping her head back and forth, shaking the towel, then she stood on one end and ripped it. She carried the ragged towel from room to room while he dressed.

———————

Fanny came home by bus. It had really been rather simple. Even though she'd known two weeks ago, their fucking had continued until the very last minute. Every possible opportunity. Sleep and food easily sacrificed. Jubilation or desperation. As though his fucking was meant to fill her, pack in enough to last a lifetime. But it was already gone.

She hadn't cried, didn't know when she would. She sat with her forehead against the cold glass window, straps from her luggage dangling out of the overhead rack and swinging over the empty seat beside her, where a portfolio sat upright against the cushion.

He'd used the word *fantasy*. But whose heedless delusion *was* it that she would go on that way forever? Hours of serving meals and clearing away garbage were never an intrusion on their pleasure but a time to build anticipation for the next stabbing touch. And in between touches . . . the inspired work she'd thought she'd been doing.

When she'd left her room that morning, the portfolio had contained three or four lethargic sketches for furnishing a generic lobby, a rec room, an office—done before she'd ever been with Roland. Then she'd eagerly embellished them, with pounding heart and shaking hand, while listening for his knock on her door, while waiting for him to finish a bingo marathon or jigsaw puzzle jamboree. The lobby, the rec room, the foyers, all became dreamscapes of thick padded furniture, sofas almost horizontal just off the floor, chairs with flattened arms like wings, jungles of vines hanging from shelves built in near the ceiling, thick candles, tall candles, mint green pillows furnishing a mauve-walled room, colors she'd never had the taste for before . . . for *who* to live in? Roland and Fanny? Who were *they*? He called her Fancy. He used the word *fantasy.* These weren't designs that—daily, through the smell of paint and sawdust, ringing hammers, echoing footsteps—would slowly materialize, never quite living up to the idealized drawing but at the same time ending up *better:* the wood floor adding depth, the books creating familiarity, the angle of the sun outside making movable patches of light and dark. Instead of the designs coming to life, *she'd* become animated, colored in acute shades and allowed to live in the wistful drawing, to sit in the colored pencil chairs, lean on the chalk-shaded walls, pick up the cat drawn curled on the bedspread. For a while.

Before boarding, she'd slid the sketches out of the folder. They were smeared and blurred from rubbing against each other. She left them on top of a hooded trash can and let the wind rip them away. What kind of designer was she? The only space she seemed to want to create was a place where she had someone with her. And had it *ever* worked? One time she'd created the space, and the love evaporated like steam. And *this* time—had it even been love at all, or just the flattering intoxication of someone wanting her? The passion for work had arrived, coupled with his desire for her, but had *it*—like the whole three weeks of sustaining intimacy—actually only existed in a wonderland mirage, and now was as flat, faded, and unalive as the sketches blowing somewhere against the soiled snow piled on the curb in front of the bus terminal?

All those hours stolen during the day, strung together through the night, yet she hadn't thought to mention that she wasn't really a waitress, she was a would-be interior designer who, until she came here, hadn't done any work in years, and that even her own house had disintegrated into a mishmash of castoffs and listless intentions. Conversation never included her tastes or ideas or her fear that she'd never be inspired to work again. She'd never talked about folding under Renee's almost kiss, cowering under Doreen's mandates, and she never told him about Lacy—how she admired her dog's undaunted self-esteem.

It had been one night two weeks ago, when a new snowfall had whitewashed the retreat and they were in the main lobby on pillows on the floor in front of the stone fireplace. It was a night after one batch of patients and parents had gone home and before another group arrived the next morning. Cocooned in a patchwork quilt taken from the burnt-wood sofa, which Fanny's sketches would've replaced with the bed-sized mint pillows and huge, sky blue beanbag chairs. Pulling her close against his chest, after more than an hour without words, he'd said, "We've been lucky." As though stoned, she'd heard the sound of the sentence floating in the room, repeated in a variety of tones—slower, faster, melodic, whispered, the beautiful sound of his private voice—without bothering to grasp what he'd said. Then when those words had finally died away into the hiss and crackle of the fire, he'd said, "I don't know when I'll ever have another lover like you." His hands stopped caressing her and just held on.

"You don't need another, you have me," she'd murmured.

"We're lucky," he'd repeated. "We lived a fantasy." This time the words hadn't sung poetry.

She'd scratched a thumb nail against her teeth. "Are we in the same conversation?"

He'd chuckled, stroking her ribs as if touching a delicate animal. "You're so wonderful . . . and strong."

The fire wasn't crackling, just breathing. "What makes you say that?"

Roland released her, rolled over, tightening the blanket around them, pushing his spine back against her. "I would love for things to be different." He paused to take a deep breath. "Gloria is so fragile, she's had bad experiences with men, she couldn't really take it if she knew. Our other separations weren't like this, and it's been a long time since we had one. This was an interesting job for me, that's why I took it. She didn't know . . . I knew I could never tell her. Her insecurities have been aroused. She's . . ."

"Fragile," Fanny had whispered.

They were both still for a moment, then Roland had sat up, struggled to push the quilt aside, pulled Fanny up by her forearms and kissed her, releasing her arms to hold her head in both his hands. "I knew you were strong enough to understand," he'd said, his lips still up against her mouth.

The bus had to wind slowly through mountain passes—her stomach roiled and she puked into a bag. Then, on the flat gray southbound freeway, staring at sparkling fields of winter produce, she thought about training in the park with Doreen and the dogs . . . and Scott.

She wrote hundreds of letters in her head—some piqued, some sad and quiet—in answer to the one she thought she would finally get in a week, two weeks, a month. But the mail wouldn't come and her phone wouldn't ring while she was home, so she took a cassette headset and went walking with Lacy, bush to tree to mailbox to telephone pole. The dog sniffed and drooled. Fanny watched from behind sunglasses, the bitch smiling up at her between gopher holes and sun-dried markers of dog shit. Each day the flicker of hope for a letter or message when she returned became fainter.

In her first week home, all the plants in her house died because she couldn't care about watering them. The dust that had settled on the furniture and books while she was away didn't get wiped up. The stacked-up newspapers, the pile of junk mail Morgan had saved . . . she didn't shovel them out the door. The backed-up bank statements waiting for her to balance her checkbook . . . she let them sit.

Morgan came home one day from a rehearsal or an errand, looked at her suitcase and boxes, still on the bedroom floor. "Aren't you ever going to unpack?"

"I'm not doing too well."

"I know. Neither am I."

She'd turned her teary face away from his watery voice. Then she loaded her boxes of winter accessories—scarves, gloves, sweaters, wool socks, and boots—into her car and drove them to the Salvation Army. The next day she emptied the suitcase into bags and made the trip again. On the way home, she stopped at a dime store and bought packs of men's undershirts to replace the blouses given away, boy's swim trunks that came almost to her knees, ten pair of underwear for a dollar, slip-on canvas shoes. When she climbed a ladder to put the suitcase back into the closet, she took down framed posters she'd been saving to put on the walls after repainting someday; box games of Monopoly, Uno, and Tile Rummy; and a briefcase she'd carried in college. She took them all to the Salvation Army. Then she went through the linen closet and removed fancy lace-edged pillowcases, a stadium blanket, place mats, a tablecloth, curtains, guest towels, and a box where they'd always put interesting articles clipped from the paper. As she woke each morning, she thought about that day's trip to the donation center and what she would take. Vases, platters, pitchers, trays, salt and pepper shakers. Books, records, knickknacks, dusty macramé wall art. An empty aquarium, baseball mitts, hanging plant pots. Then some of the smaller pieces of furniture started to go, bookcases and end tables, plant stands, a coatrack. On Sundays, when the collection center wasn't open, time crawled, she was restless and frustrated, tried to sleep late but couldn't, glancing often at the black garbage bag waiting by the front door to be taken out first thing Monday.

When there was no rehearsal and no other reason to get up, Morgan slept till ten or eleven. Those early hours of the morning were the time when Fanny tore through cupboards and closets, upper shelves and storage boxes. She worked so fast, sometimes she found herself breathing with her mouth open, making little sounds in her chest as though finishing a long-distance race. When she heard Morgan in the bathroom, she would stop, make a pot of coffee and pour two bowls of cereal, until the old coffeemaker was put into one of the plastic bags waiting by the door. One morning, she didn't hear Morgan get up. She was in her studio cleaning out her files, filling one of the outdoor trash cans with old school records; drawings; plans; fabric samples; designs for clothing, furniture, and rooms. At the sound of Morgan's voice she jumped, like a dead animal's spasmodic kick.

"Are you okay?" he said. He looked into the trash can.

"Say good-bye," she said, "I'm throwing away a lot of stupidness."

"I thought you've been preparing to start redoing the house."

"No. I'm a waitress. Hungry?"

Every other day in the afternoon, she met Doreen in the park, and she worked evenings or nights, almost exclusively for Scott now. He came out to the park too, whenever he could. At a job, his were the only eyes she would meet. They looked at each other often, silently, across a party or banquet room or foyer, as though he'd been her closest friend for years, as though everything had already been shared with him, instead of the two-line conversation they'd had during the first job after her return:

"A lot has happened," he'd said, his eyes glossy and dark.

"Yes," she'd replied, "a lot." And nothing more, until yesterday.

Yesterday the letters she'd been writing in her head to Roland had seemed, instead, to come out of her mouth, in fragments, a patchwork, which—on the warm grass at the park, with the thick turf scent from a morning mowing, the rustle of dogs digging through the shrubs, the spring sunshine genial on her face—suddenly made complete sense.

The first time she'd come to the park since her return home, Doreen had stared, then spoken to her as though she was a peevish invalid who had to be skillfully cajoled. After that, every time they met, Doreen asked, "How are you?" not as a toss-off greeting, but carefully. Yesterday after a tracking session, Fanny had reclined on her back with one arm across her eyes. The husky, free to roam after training, kept returning to poke her nose under Fanny's arm or paw at her ribs. "See," Doreen said, "training has made her more bonded to you. She doesn't want to go off by herself as much."

"She's worried about me," Fanny said. "She doesn't know what's wrong with me."

"So . . . something is wrong with you?"

Scott came back from picking up his dog's droppings with a baggie. He threw it in the trash, told his spaniel to go play, then sat cross-legged. Fanny peeked from under her arm—looked at Scott, not Doreen. "I don't know. Does it seem like it?"

"Yes," Doreen exclaimed. "The first time you came back out to train, I thought you were terminally ill or something. Then when you said you were taking stuff to the thrift store every day, I thought you were going to commit suicide."

"Huh?"

"You know, people clean up their affairs before they kill themselves."

"I don't think I can clean up my affair," Fanny said. Then she raised her head a little and looked out from under her arm once more, but again looked at Scott. "A man."

"I thought so," Doreen said snidely. "What happened?"

"Same old story: loved me, left me."

"And you let him turn you into a zombie. Is he really worth it?"

"No." She was still looking at Scott. She lowered her head, replaced her arm over her eyes. "I don't miss *him*. I miss *it*."

"You mean sex? Jeez, Fanny."

"Not just that. I'm afraid it'll sound stupid."

"Go ahead," Scott said softly. Doreen sort of grunted.

"I miss being . . . that alive."

In a moment of silence, Doreen called her puppy's name in a high singsong, and he answered, from his pen—a long, sweet howl.

"I know what you mean," Scott said, his voice still low.

"He was using me. I know that now," Fanny said. "But not in the usual way. He was using me to live out a fantasy. So he gave me another life to live. And I liked it."

"Did you actually think it would *last?*" Doreen asked.

"I didn't *think*. But I didn't think I'd wake up and be back . . . here . . . you know? I can't come back to what was here like nothing's changed. And I can't go back *there* either, because it doesn't exist. I found something I liked, and it doesn't exist. I liked the way I felt. But it wasn't *real*."

"Was he *married?*" Doreen hit the word hard.

"Something like engaged."

"You couldn't *pay* me to touch something like that."

"Looking back, some part of me was probably hoping he might like it enough . . . enough to want to keep it. But he didn't."

"But you're back with your dog now, isn't that better?" Doreen said, resuming the high cajoling voice.

"But it stands out so glaringly in my mind: I gave him a fantasy life, then *I* had to be understanding for the sake of some woman I don't even know or care about. I ended up being the *least* important person in the picture."

"Well, dogs won't bust your ego that way. Maybe they'll embarrass you at a trial," Doreen laughed. "Hey, guess what happened to me while you were gone. Jack bit a kid! He sure has the defense drives. With him, it's gonna be a matter of *corralling* all his instincts rather than trying to inspire what was buried by years of domestic breeding."

The spaniel and husky came back for a drink, sharing the water dish from opposite sides. Fanny sat up. The husky flung herself on the grass alongside Fanny's legs. The spaniel sat beside Scott; he put his arm around her. Doreen let her puppy out of his pen and held him between her legs, restraining him from leaning forward to sniff his mother. The husky curled her lip, then resumed panting. "I'll stick with dogs," Doreen said. "You only have to feel two things: winning and getting mad over not winning."

"It sure relaxes me to be out with the dogs," Scott said.

"That's not what I meant."

But Fanny looked at him again, looked at Doreen, then back to Scott. "Yeah, it's okay here. Out here I can feel okay."

She'd been in the bedroom when he first walked in with the suitcase. She'd smiled and put down the window cleaner, asked him if he was hungry, said she'd made cinnamon rolls and had saved some for him. He wasn't hungry, but said "Sounds good" while he put the suitcase on the bed and opened it. It was empty, he'd thought she'd known that, but she gasped, then sat on the bed, elbows tucked in her stomach, head down, rocking slightly forward and back.

"I found a tiny apartment that allows dogs," he'd said softly. "But I'll have to make sure she gets exercise every day."

"Do you expect me to feel sorry for how hard it is for you?" It didn't seem as if someone in that kind of miserable fetal position could have such a snotty voice.

It took four or five trips into the closet to get the rest of his clothes. The suitcase was full, with a stack of shirts and suits on hangers piled on top. "Maybe I don't need all these," he said. "I don't wear half of them. Do they take donations at the rest home?"

"They're patients, not derelicts."

"Okay, I'll just throw out whatever I don't want." He'd turned away, heard her make a broken noise, shrill and thin, yet wet and snuffed out at the same time. He'd gone to the den just long enough to get some things from his desk. When he came back to the bedroom, the closet door was shut.

She wasn't the type to lie down or even sit on the floor, but he couldn't imagine her just standing in there. He could hear some kind of soft rustling or swishing but didn't hear a whimper until he used the sink to fill the drinking glass. "Suzanne." He listened, waiting for an answer, then said, "Do you want to say anything?"

She didn't respond, but he heard sniffling, a light cough.

"I'm going out to mow the lawn," he said. "I'll come back in before I leave."

He took the suitcase and clothes to the car before getting the lawn mower out.

The conversation that he hoped to have with Suzanne hadn't taken place yet. He hoped to wait until Suzanne said *she* didn't want to be married *either*—that she was ready for an amicable good-bye. Or else she might lock him out, refuse to speak to him, get a lawyer. But she was nowhere close to either.

The thing he *had* planned to say that day was still drumming in his mind as he mowed the lawn. The engine drowned out random children's shouts or tapping hammers or faint tinkling phones, so he could clearly hear himself think. He was going to point out that you can't be happily married just because you *say* you are. But before he could say it, she'd have to *claim* they were happy together, and even then it was possible he'd *still* get that icy "Where'd you learn that—your *dog* friends?" which he'd already heard at least twice in previous attempts.

At the park one day this week, when Doreen was busy and out of range, Fanny had asked him for all the work he could give her. She'd said, "I can't be a designer by saying I am. But I can *not* be a designer by saying I'm *not*. At least I can do that."

He'd said, "I guess I can say the same thing about being married, can't I?"

She'd smiled. The only real advice Fanny had given him, though, was to hold out for an apartment that allowed pets—avoid having to get the dog back from Suzanne sometime down the road. Clothes and books, all that stuff's replaceable, if you even need it at all, she'd said, but hang onto the dog. The dog was part of him, the other stuff wasn't.

When he killed the mower's engine and turned to go back to the garage, Suzanne was standing there in the driveway. She was pale and her hair was damp, tied back in a kerchief. "Scott, I had to tell my parents. I thought maybe we could've told them together, but . . ." She followed him into the garage. "I said . . . I told them . . . they were real upset . . . so I said this could make everything better, some couples just can't live together, but we'll just adjust to it, we'll all adjust . . ."

He took the hedge clippers from a hook over the tool bench and examined the blade.

"Did I chip them?" she said. "I did the hedges yesterday."

"You did? I said I would take care of it for you." He rehung the clippers slowly, making sure they were straight, eyeing the rest of the tools, searching his mind for some other odd job to do until he could satisfactorily answer her, but the clear voice in his head was gone, everything jabbering on fast-forward, not even words anymore, just a Morse code heartbeat, so he didn't say anything.

"Scott, I did something stupid," Suzanne said, "I canceled our Greenland reservations. Then I tried to get them back, and the whole tour is booked. Should I put a deposit down for a place on the waiting list?"

"Why do you think it was stupid? I don't blame you for not wanting to go."

"But I do want to go. We planned it for such a long time. Don't *you* want to go?"

He wished he'd brought the dog. She would've been sniffing behind the trash cans for mice, jumping for her Frisbee, which still hung on a nail in the garage, or wrapping herself around his legs and drooling on his sneakers.

"Do you like doing this?" Her words were suddenly crisp. He looked out the garage window to the lawn, which should be watered after being cut. "Is it fun to keep taking things away from me? When did you become this way, Scott, when did you become the type of person who would selfishly ruin someone else's whole life?" Her voice rose to a near shriek. He wasn't close enough to the button to lower the garage door.

"I'm sorry it seems that way," he said.

"I'm over forty, Scott. I'm alone, I don't even have children to keep me company—what am I going to do? But do *you* ever stop to ask yourself that question?"

He put his hand on the lawn mower handle. "I'm sorry you feel so bad right now, Suzanne. But . . . nothing more has to change for a while. I'm still paying all the bills. Don't get ahead of yourself. Take it easy, okay? You're not being totally abandoned."

She was sobbing again. "What about our trip? We waited so long, and now . . . We had the money set aside, I already asked for those weeks off from work. Who else would I ever travel with?"

"Let's just leave it at that right now, okay? Let's just try to relax."

She nodded. The weather vane on the garage roof creaked. Suzanne said, "Oh, I'll get those cinnamon rolls for you."

While Suzanne was in the kitchen, Scott went back into the bedroom, feeling he'd overlooked something. In the closet, the side for his clothes was bare except for Suzanne's formal dresses, which hung at the end. He checked the dirty clothes, but everything there was Suzanne's. The shoes were kept on a set of shelves that pivoted like a Ferris wheel to bring the rear shelves to the front, a color spectrum of pumps. Fanny had told him that she knew she'd get more tips if she wore heels, but she had weak feet and needed athletic shoes. Sometimes she wore nylons with sneakers and sometimes she didn't, but the only way he could tell was that without nylons, the white hair on her legs sparkled in certain light. He'd reminded her she wasn't supposed to get tips at all during a catering job. "Then I *really* don't need the heels," she'd said. He remembered what he'd forgotten, but before he could get to the bathroom cabinet to get the condoms, Suzanne came back with the rolls.

At this time of year, she would've been planting petunias, Johnny-jump-ups, marigolds, snapdragons, and sweet alyssum. At one time, the little yard had sustained a bonfire of seasonal purples, reds, oranges, yellows, and deep violets. But Fanny was leveling the garden. Each time the shovel went in, the surface of the ground was flipped over, and whatever had been struggling to grow was thrown back, facedown. She stopped every three or four minutes, leaned on the shovel, and stared around. The dog was digging holes in the lawn. The only time the husky ever dug was while Fanny was gardening. Bending over the shovel, she could see dark droplets of her sweat peppering the hard ground in the garden.

She probably wouldn't be able to tell anyone about the other day with Morgan, but in her mind she kept hearing herself begin to tell it, as though rehearsing, testing to see how it would sound for her voice to describe it to Scott. Yet she wasn't getting much farther than a few sentences, could not picture what Scott's expression might be as he listened. Then she ran out of words when she ran up against the image of Morgan crushed against the pillows, shriveled and naked.

It was infinitely easier to rerun memories of conversations she and Scott had already actually had—while they were on a patch of grass surrounded by eucalyptus trees in the park with the dogs, cleaning up from a catering job in a festooned banquet room, having a late cup of coffee in a leatherette booth at Denny's. He sometimes wouldn't respond with words, but his eyes pointed down at the corners like a hound's, and his small serious mouth could and often did crack into a toothy grin.

In the park, after Doreen finished training and left, the husky and spaniel were free to run the length of the open grass, shoulder to shoulder, each holding the end of a tattered towel. Scott had a beach chair that he always offered to her. Usually neither of them used it. Fanny would lie on her back watching eucalyptus pollen drift toward her eyes, or on her stomach, chin on one fist. Scott sat with his arms around his knees. The dogs would come back to stand and play their growling game right over Scott and Fanny. Sometimes the husky stood on Fanny's back until someone, usually Scott, grabbed the towel and tossed it several yards away, sending the game off across the park again.

"Doreen only thinks about one thing, doesn't she," Scott had said once. "Winning."

"Not just winning. Being the founder of the modern-day Schutzhund dog. I used to be like that. I *thought* I was. Except not dogs—designing. And I'm talking *way* back, before I got married." With a blade of grass, she'd tried to keep a ladybug walking back and forth across a twig. "In college, I sketched rooms during history classes. I went to visit model homes and expensive furniture or wall covering stores or reupholsterers to take notes about new styles in color and fabrics. I was really into tweeds then, all-natural fibers. When Morgan and I first got married and hardly had any money, I reupholstered secondhand furniture with my mother's old Chinese red drapes and made throw pillows out of my earthtone skirts. Our house had plants and bricks-and-boards and fruit crates used for cabinets, lots of browns and tans and dusty greens, but underneath it all was that red furniture. Trouble is, it never turned out exactly how I imagined."

Scott had been holding out a long, thin branch with a few dead leaves at the tip, like a fishing pole over a pond. "So is that still where you live?"

"Yeah, same place. Some stuff got broken in the robbery and got pitched; we got furniture donations from relatives. There's still remnants of my design under the mess. I was planning a makeover, but . . . it didn't just die yesterday. It was long and slow."

"What do you think made it all go away?"

"I'm . . . not sure. Morgan was the same way—everything was dance. He studied how different performers moved. He practiced different walks. Now, he doesn't just sit around watching TV—he lies in a fetal position in the bedroom."

"What's wrong with him?"

The ladybug had finally figured out it could fly away. Fanny rolled over and closed her eyes against the sun. "I don't know. He's in love with a dyke, but that's not it."

"How does *that* make you feel?"

"It has nothing to do with me."

Then another day, leaning back in their regular booth at Denny's, "The one Morgan's in love with used to be a friend of mine," Fanny had said. "Hey, why isn't there a woman with a red beehive serving us? I think I missed my true calling. Where *are* all the waitresses with big hair?" Fanny had smiled, rolling her skull against the back of the booth, feeling the fat ribs of the upholstery. "Anyway, I tried to go out with her again when I got home. She'd been a close friend. I thought I could at least tell *her*, if anyone, about . . . what happened in Tahoe. But she didn't want to hear it."

"Maybe she was jealous."

Fanny had made her eyes into slits and looked at him. Her squinting eyes turned the amber lights into fuzzy blobs, Scott sinking into them. With everything blurry, she could smell coffee and eggs from the counter where breakfast was served twenty-four hours a day. She opened her eyes, and his face cleared. "I don't think so. When we first went into the restaurant, she saw someone she knew and said, *Oh no, look who's here.* It was this woman who works for the dance company—Renee said this woman hated her, and Renee didn't know why. I didn't care. Anyway, I guess there's no easy way for me to explain anything to Renee. The one thing I remember her saying is, *A man can't be THAT important.* She wasn't listening though—she was keeping her eye on this other woman who wasn't even paying any attention to us, but Renee was so sure she was. She kept saying, *I wonder what Dani thinks of us being here?* I stopped trying to talk and Renee said, *That woman's gotta have a dirty secret. She's not such hot shit.*"

"What was she talking about?"

"I don't know. I don't care. It hasn't anything to do with me."

"Did you talk to her about Morgan?"

Several plates crashed somewhere, causing a splat of silence. Fanny had waited until some noise returned. There were always at least six or seven tables occupied, even at midnight like this. More than once, someone had thrown up while they were there. "He . . . that's . . . something different. Anyway, Renee doesn't have anything to do with me anymore."

"You say that a lot, that things have nothing to do with you." Then the waitress came back. "Dessert?" Scott asked Fanny.

Two nights later, wearing a white apron over his tuxedo, surrounded by half-empty pots and pans and the aroma of southwestern-style chicken in salsa, Spanish rice, and frijoles, Scott had said, "I wish I could tell my wife that things have nothing to do with me. I wish she could *understand* that some things have nothing to do with me anymore."

"Maybe *you* don't feel it's true enough yet," Fanny had said, licking a spoon. "If you did, you wouldn't *care* if she understood. When things have nothing to do with you, you don't have to care about . . . anything."

"Is that how you feel?" He took the spoon from her and washed it in the sink full of soapy water.

"I don't know. I'm hungry."

"Do you still miss him?" Scott had said slowly. She barely heard him. She ate a couple of soda crackers.

"No. I thought I explained," she had said with her mouth full of dry crumbs.

"What?"

Fanny stood beside him at the sink, leaned over, and drank from the faucet. When she turned around, they were face to face. She felt a drop of water on her chin and felt it fall. "I don't think *he* has anything to do with it either. It's just that I found something I liked, but I had absolutely no choice about whether or not I got to *keep* it. It was all well and good for him to live a fantasy with me, but when it came to the long haul, someone *else* was best for that. What someone *else* felt and wanted were most important. Hey, you don't have to tell *me* twice. God, but maybe he *did.*"

"I'm sorry that happened to you," he'd said.

"I'd better freshen the drinks out there."

Back at the park, eyes shut, dodging his dog's tongue, feeling for the ball she'd dropped at his feet, Scott had said, "She's not getting enough exercise in that apartment."

Fanny got up from where she was lying, crawled to the ball that had rolled behind his chair. "You don't get to *have* a yard—but you still have to take care of one?" She kneeled beside his chair, playing with the frayed hole in the knee of her jeans.

"No, I finally hired a gardener to mow and trim over there once a week. But that caused another big . . . you know, *thing.*"

"Oh, god, a *thing.*"

"Yeah." He had slouched in his chair, head back, arm protecting his eyes from the sun glinting through the eucalyptus branches. "When I told her, she got all . . . she's got this particular body language when she's trying to act cold and proud, you know, like she's coated in a thin layer of glass and has to move around without cracking it. She said, *While you're at it, you might as well find another caterer for my family's summer picnic.*"

"Can't they cook their own hot dogs?"

"We . . . they always get something like a whole pig on a rotisserie. Anyway, she starts giving me the number of people and the date and the menu, all in this really snotty voice, and said, *Then we'll use the same caterer for the Christmas party so you won't have to bother again.* I think she expected me to say that I'd go ahead and do the picnic as usual. I had come over to pick up some sheets and towels, then she stopped getting them out and said, *You can get these yourself, you know what you want, you don't need me,* and her voice started wavering, but a real brittle type of wobble."

"The glass was breaking."

"I guess. But she came back in a second and said, *Maybe you can hire someone to go to the movies with me on Saturday night, or talk to me about my day at work, maybe you can pay some kid five dollars an hour to go on a picnic with me, since it would be too horrible for you to consider taking me to lunch or roller-skating or horseback riding.*"

"Roller-skating! Did you used to roller-skate?" Fanny had scooted backward and rested her shoulders against the tree trunk.

"No, I don't know where that came from, I even said, *You never do those things,* and she said, *No,* YOU *didn't do them, Scott, so because* YOU *didn't do them,* WE *didn't do them. I'm not asking too much, am I? Just hire someone to buy me a present for my birthday and tell jokes to me and send me roses now and then. Why not? You could hire someone ten times better than* YOU *ever were.*"

"Wow," Fanny had whispered. Scott was looking at her, his hands clutching the arms of his chair, his lips and nose swollen and darker, his eyes very glossy. He looked away, used a quick flick of his wrist to wipe at his eyes. When he turned back toward her, a tear crept around the corner of his nose. Then he had gotten out of the chair and lay on his stomach, most of his face hidden, but she could still see one eye and part of one cheek. The tears kept coming, squeezed through his lashes, across the bridge of his nose, and dampened his shirt sleeve.

She might've touched his wet cheek, but he opened his eye. "Here come the dogs," she'd said. "Does crying make your dog worry?"

"I don't know. Maybe."

"It makes mine crazy. I have to hide from her. She tries so hard to get me to stop. She tries everything she can think of."

This time the dogs came back and drank, then flopped to the cool grass on their stomachs with their legs extended behind them, heads up, eyes slits, tongues red and dripping, like flags flapping from the corners of their mouths. "You better watch out, Lacy, we'll make sandwiches," Fanny had said, trying to catch the husky's tongue between two fingers. "Can I ask you something?"

"Of course."

"How come she didn't say you could hire someone to have sex with her too?"

"She wouldn't think of that in a million years."

"Oh?" Fanny had kept her eyes on the bobbing tip of the dog's tongue.

That's when she probably could've told him about Morgan, but she couldn't because it hadn't happened yet. It happened two days later.

"I don't even know *why* it happened," she could've told Scott. "What was I *thinking?*"

Thinking was not what she'd been doing. She'd been ripping up the rug in her studio, all the furniture pushed to the middle of the room so she could go around the edges and pry up the nails. Then she was going to roll the rug toward the center, lift the furniture over the roll onto the bare floor until she had a roll of rug in the center of the room and could push it out the window. After the first five nails, she could tell that the floor underneath was cement, not hardwood. The rug was held down on strips of wood. But she kept ripping anyway.

The weather was warm and she was sweating, so the dust flying up from the rug stuck to her. Then the head of a nail abruptly broke and the hammer flew into her face, cracking against her nose. *"No,"* she'd shrieked, pounding the floor with the hammer. *"God fucking dammit to cocksucking hell!"* The dog scratched on the back door as Fanny lay huddled in a pile on the floor, holding her nose in both hands. Her face throbbed, her eyes swelled, she cried silently, her skin crawled with damp dust. It couldn't have been the same body, *her* body, two months ago, silky and graceful, keen and tinged with excitability, limitless in energy, then profound in relaxation.

Then Morgan had come home from a rehearsal. She heard the front door, heard the bedroom door. The dog jumped against the back screen. Fanny got up and went to the bathroom, washed her face, brushed her hair. Took off the damp dusty man's undershirt and boy's swim trunks, put on Morgan's bathrobe, and went into the bedroom. He was curled up, under the covers. "Kind of hot for the blanket, isn't it?"

"Just leave it."

"How was rehearsal?"

"Fucked."

"Hey, Morgan, I don't see why we can't . . . this seems so stupid to say out loud . . . but . . . well, I don't have a sexual problem anymore, so why couldn't we . . . it doesn't hurt me anymore, so why not . . . why shouldn't we . . . let's make love, it can't hurt, it can only help, right? Maybe it's what we need to do. We need to do *some*thing." She sat on the edge of the bed. He was clutching the blanket up near his cheek. She could practically see the outline of his fist through the material.

For some reason, they hadn't just sat like that, him balled in the comforter and her sitting there in his robe, for hours, as the warm afternoon passed, until dusk deadened the already dim light in the room. Instead, he'd rolled to his back, and she had shed the robe, slid into the bed beside him, run her hand down his chest and fondled his penis, which did start to stiffen. Her body knew how to feel good now, she told herself, it knew how to be wanted, knew how to purr and stretch and luxuriate and tingle and be euphoric. It didn't matter whose hand, whose lips, whose cock . . . if she could have it back, that buoyant serenity . . . then maybe each day wouldn't be so pointless, each coming week not so devoid, the rest of the year wouldn't seem so desolate, the years after that—the whole damn future wouldn't seem so frighteningly useless.

Tugging on him a little, she lay back and he rolled over her. She'd curled her toes, closed her eyes as he tweaked her nipple a few times, fingered her, then he'd stopped and said, "What d'you want me to be doing?"

"Do what you want to do," she had said softly. "Anything's okay, believe me."

"But what do you want?"

"I'm not going to give you a list."

He had slid his finger in and out a few more times, stopped, said, "What do you want next?" He was wiping his hand in the sheet.

"Don't *ask* me what I want. I'm not gonna lie here and give you instructions." She felt cold, clammy, and stark. Her stomach turned. "It's supposed to just happen," she murmured, hoping not to sound panicked.

Morgan didn't move. He was crouched beside her, one hand on either side of her torso. "But what do you want me to be doing?"

"It's making love, Morgan, not following orders."

"But I don't know what *you* want. Just tell me and I'll do it."

"I'm not going to *tell* you." Her voice had become sharp and thin. She clenched her fists, told herself to relax. "C'mon, it's okay, we can do this, just lie down, okay?" She got up and they changed positions. She cupped both hands around his genitals, bent and licked the tip like a kitten. "C'mon, Morgan." As she began to suck him, she could see down his legs to his long, white feet, rigid and crossed, the tendons sticking out, almost transparent. "We can do this, c'mon, we can." She pulled more and more of it into her mouth, moved her head faster, sucked harder, held on with her lips and ran her tongue around the end, then again brusquely, vigorously, pumping with her head. "C'mon," she muttered thickly, "c'mon, c'mon," but the penis was flaccid, being stretched by her movement like a rubber hose, completely bloodless, and when she paused to rest her sore cheeks, it flopped to one side against his thigh, shriveled. Aghast, she had backed up, staring, swallowing, as he slowly moved one inert hand from the mattress and covered himself. His face looked withered, his eyes closed so tightly that they looked as if they'd drained out of the sockets, his mouth a horrible puckered shape, like a frozen cry of terror.

Now, two days later, at least the flower bed was finished, a patch of upside-down shovelfulls of dirt.

It was the third time Renee had gone back to the Thai restaurant, each time alone, but Dani hadn't reappeared. Renee knew *she* would've returned to face her adversary in the place they'd so obviously filled with silent tension. But Dani, as though unaware of the challenge, the vow to return hanging between them, didn't show. To Renee, the pledge had been a neon thunderbolt zinging between their tables. She hadn't been able to hear the conversation going on between the two heads bent over steaming bowls of food at the table across the room. Was Dani's voice part of the steam, whispering to her companion about the ominous presence of Renee disturbing her quiet dinner? Or was Dani trying to act casual and normal, as though nothing was happening—discussing a movie, politics, an upcoming rally or speaker or Pride Parade? But Dani wouldn't be marching—she was hiding her orientation. The skirts and flats Dani wore to work; the purse she kept in her desk and brought with her to lunch but never took home; the absence of any friend when, on rare occasions, she'd joined a group of dancers after a performance. It was obvious. Renee had barely been able to see any movement at Dani's table, no laughter that might've changed the position of the heads, no hand gestures, no looking around the room. Was Dani trying to keep Renee from noticing her while asking her friend, *Do you think she's spotted me?* Were her legs aching with a jellied weakness? Was her stomach burning, making her unable to swallow? Could she taste the food?

As Renee drank her soup, the heat of the liquid crept up her neck. Had *she* been the *only* one with the burning stomach, the weak knees? Had Dani merely eaten her meal and talked quietly with her friend, the same as any other evening in any other restaurant, whether or not Renee was in the same room? Renee glared around at other people eating. Her pulse crashed in her ears. She broke her chopsticks under the table. So, if Dani hadn't sweated into her tea . . . yet . . . Renee knew she could make her *cry* into her tea. How *dare* she waltz around with her nose in the air in her flunky clerical job? She needed a warning—she needed to remember who Renee was. Renee bit into an egg roll and burned the inside of her mouth, but she didn't spit the piece out or desperately gulp ice water. She smiled—Dani was going to cave and *think* she was helping Renee get exactly what she deserved. Dani didn't have the power to *do* anything, but she was going to back down anyway. It was the principle. She had it coming.

The general manager and artistic director had already agreed to continue to pay Renee through any work stoppage that might occur—a likely possibility, considering that management was stalling on scheduling a meeting with the dancers' attorney and no new season was even being planned. Her negotiations had taken place over dinner at the director's home. "Rest assured there'll be no lock-out," the manager had said with an obvious mask of blandness. The director's wife rose to clear the dishes away. "No one will be getting any unemployment," the manager had added. Renee had laughed: "You mean because *striking* employees are ineligible for unemployment?" He'd shrugged with a smile: "Perhaps you'll *encourage* that particular course of action?" That was his offer in order to guarantee that her salary would continue. He hadn't known she could counter with much more: "There'll have to be some incentive to keep me from auditioning elsewhere." Director looked at manager with raised eyebrows.

But Dani wouldn't know anything about that. She might not have any power, and Renee didn't even *need* her, but that didn't mean she couldn't be brought down. Renee slipped a bill under her plate and rose, feeling every glorious muscle she'd used in an intense session alone at the theater that afternoon reminding her that she'd better take care of her business with Dani before the audition in Baltimore in August. Breaking the bitch might be her last great performance here.

The sofa they sat on, side by side in the counselor's office, was so old and soft that Morgan felt immediately immobilized. Leaning back made his eyes virtually level with his knees. Weighted down, almost powerless to get up—and Fanny the same beside him—practically falling toward each other. Probably planned, he wouldn't doubt. Why not just shoot each couple with a stun gun as they came in the door? Then commence with the brainwashing.

The lady would probably ask if they were comfortable, and he would say, *Why not*, it's not so much different than his chair in the living room at home, with its faded, threadbare upholstery made from some old bedspread or something almost ten years ago. *I'm surrounded*, he would tell the counselor, *I'm living in a haunted house.*

"Where'd you find this one," Fanny had asked him, after he'd agreed to go.

"I told them anyone was okay except that dick we had before."

They hadn't spoken about the upcoming appointment at all since then, except last night as they lay in the dark, the bed moving slightly because Fanny, as usual lately, had the dog in the house, lying on the floor beside the bed, and she was reaching down to stroke the dog's stomach. The husky panted for at least a half hour before finally sighing like a signal to all three of them that now they could go to sleep. The dog was still panting last night when Morgan had said, "Will you be talking about what's-his-name from Tahoe?"

Fanny hadn't answered right away. Then said, "Will you be talking about Renee?"

"What's she got to do with it? You were in a funk years before we knew her."

"I know . . . but didn't it all suddenly become, somehow, *worse,* more obvious . . . when she came?"

"I just don't think we need to bring up any of that shit."

She hadn't answered, and minutes later the dog had licked her lips, swallowed, sighed, and lain quietly.

Driving in today, Fanny had clutched her purse on her lap like some old lady on a bus. He'd wasted half the distance before finally finishing his stipulations: "Remember, this isn't sex therapy."

"Okay," she'd answered meekly.

So the ground rules were set. And as if following the guidelines, the counselor—fiftyish, gray hair falling out of a bun, rumpled pedal pushers with hairy ankles showing, men's leather sandals, horny toenails sticking out—asked them to tell her a little about their marriage in the early days.

He telegraphed silently to Fanny, *Please don't look at me.* She was staring at her thumbs, pressing them together, end to end. She looked like when she used to sew by hand in the afternoons as they watched TV, hardly ever looking at the screen, just sitting there curled up over the pinned-up material, making pillows out of old clothes.

"Everything was new," she said slowly. "First time living with someone, first time out of school, first place to redecorate and develop my style."

"So it was the newness that made you happy—nothing else?"

"It's not that simple."

How many pillows was it? It *seemed* she'd worked on them—pincushions on the coffee table, bags of stuffing sitting around, ironing board blocking the way to the bedroom—for *months.* Now those pillows, what was left of them, were faded to the color of dust, flat and frayed. Like all the other old rummage and remnants still sitting around the house.

"But it does seem," Fanny was saying, "that with everything new, it *was* more fun."

"Like a game," the lady said sweetly. "But you can't play the same game forever, right?"

"Not without getting somewhere."

"Do you think Morgan kept you from getting somewhere?"

"No. I just ran out of gas and didn't notice, coasted for a while but finally stopped, and maybe for a while didn't even notice I'd stopped."

I'll call this style Crate-Art, she'd said. There were old tomato crates on the walls and the floor, holding everything from records to plants. She described things she hadn't done yet but planned for the future: She would paint an old trunk, using a watercolor paintbrush to go around each tarnished brass stud, and she would polish the brass. The can of Brasso and a package of Q-tips actually sat on the trunk in the living room for about a month. She'd opened the can once and started working on one of the corner braces, but he'd told her he was being asphyxiated, so the stuff sat there and sat there— and was one of the things that disappeared in the robbery. She'd laughed weirdly about that.

"Why do you think you had so much more energy and ambition when you were first together?" the lady asked in a practiced tone.

"I don't know. I felt good. I'd never even had a boyfriend before Morgan."

"Does that have something to do with feeling good about your life?"

Fanny didn't answer. Morgan glanced at her quickly and saw that her cheeks were blotchy pink, the way he'd heard women were supposed to look when sexually aroused. But for Fanny, it was only a sign she was about to start bawling. Not that she actually cried a lot. Just that quiet pacing, room to room, into the yard, back into the kitchen. A few years ago, getting the dog had seemed to improve things for her.

"Do you think," the counselor pressed, "that you need to have someone love you in order to see any value in yourself?"

"You have to love your work in order to want to do it, right?" Fanny's voice was surprisingly strong.

"Think about what you're saying, Fanny. Did someone have to love you in order for you to love your work—is that what you're saying?"

She would lie on the floor with the puppy crawling all over her, chewing her hair, digging under her neck, licking her eyes and nose and ears and mouth, while Fanny pretended to kick and fight, giggling, *Lacy loves her mommy!* The dog hadn't been there but a week or two before there wasn't much in the house without teeth marks. With a short burst of energy, Fanny had built the dog run outside and fenced off the garden beds. She'd tried to have the puppy sleep in bed with them, but the dog hadn't even bothered to get off the bed to pee on the floor. Fanny stumbled to the bathroom for a towel to put over the spot. "I've always heard about couples having to avoid the wet spot in the middle of the bed," she'd said, which had frozen them both into silence.

"Maybe I should've put it differently," Fanny said. "It was the first time everything seemed possible."

"Because you were in love?"

"I don't know . . . if that's what you think I'm saying . . . if that's what you're hearing me say."

"You must've had some ambition before you met Morgan. You must've liked your life when you were planning this fascinating career for yourself."

"I can hardly remember anything I may've felt before I knew him, about myself or anything else."

Morgan let a breath out heavily. Once he'd told her a story about something he'd seen or done in high school—he couldn't remember the story but recalled telling her as they sat wrapped together in a blanket on the sofa. She'd murmured sleepily that she couldn't imagine who he'd been before she knew him, and hearing about him, even in stories he told about himself, was like hearing about another person altogether. He stared at his legs in their out-of-style, worn shiny corduroy jeans. It *was* another person in those stories. Where had *he* disappeared to? The boy who spent his Saturdays willingly in ballet classes held upstairs above the music store, who had to beg his parents to skip the Bing Crosby Christmas special so he could watch *The Nutcracker* on PBS, who went to New York by bus when he was seventeen and spent five years' worth of summer savings seeing every dance performance he could, sleeping at the youth hostel with German and Italian kids who were biking or backpacking up and down the East coast . . . had *that* boy really ceased to exist—drugged, poisoned, gelded, lost, sacrificed—and was that why he'd been a chorus dancer in a struggling backwater company for ten years, spending his free time on a broken chair watching shadowy black-and-white movies, without ever asking himself if *this* was all he'd planned for himself?

"Here's what I hear you saying, Fanny," the lady switched to an instructional voice. "You were happy and energetic, building a life, fueled by your dreams to be a designer but also fueled by having your first lover, which made you like *yourself* for maybe the first time." She scratched her hairy ankle. "But all that went away as the novelty wore off. A vague depression has been sapping your strength. Maybe a basic place for us to start is: Do you love Morgan? Do you feel he loves you? What's changed about *that?*"

"This isn't accomplishing anything," Morgan said abruptly.

"Why do you think so, Morgan?"

"Because I don't want to do this. I've wasted so much time already. I'm losing *my* career because the fucking management can't see beyond the wallets they're sitting on with their fat asses, and we're lolling here talking about a career *she's* never had the gumption to have in the first place."

"Maybe we'd better talk about how each of you feels about the other's career frustrations and disappointments and how you can support each other."

"No. I've already wasted half of my adult life. I don't know how it happened, I'm not blaming anyone, but for me, time's already running out, and it's not fair—by the time I'm forty, it'll be over, I'll be an inept *ex*-dancer the rest of my life. Doing *this* is pointless. I don't want it. I just . . . I don't want to be married anymore."

The lady sat as though stumped, as though no one had ever bailed *during* a marriage counseling session before. She crossed her legs, sat back, and looked at him, and he noticed how thick her glasses were, making her eyes huge and blurry. Beside him, Fanny cried silently. He heard her wet sniffle, felt her wiping her eyes. Without breaking his glare at the counselor, he put an arm around Fanny.

We were in a different park because the husky needed to work in unfamiliar places to make her concentrate, despite the stimulation of new territory to explore. In the parking lot, three or four guys were playing hockey on Rollerblades. Across a service street, on another patch of grass, a group of people in white pajamas were practicing kung fu, shouting together with each kick. We monopolized one whole piece of grass with Scott's agility equipment set up into a complete course. Afterward, I sat in the shade with Fanny, who lay on the grass, and Scott in his beach chair. I decided Jack had come far enough in his training to be truly bonded to me, so I allowed him to run a while with the other dogs after working. He was circling the two bitches as they played their towel game, yipping a high rhythmic cadence, staying about five feet from them.

"He's trying to join the pack," I said. "They're the alpha bitches right now, and he's the adolescent male who has to prove himself." Then, stupidly, I added, "Like us, right?"

Fanny smiled at the ground, from which she was picking blades of grass.

"Can a pack really have more than one alpha bitch?" Scott asked.

"They'll fight a lot," I told him. As long as he kept bringing his equipment, I tolerated this little communal thing afterward. It was better than leaving the two of them there talking and whispering while I continued working with Jack. "Did you know only one bitch is allowed to have puppies?"

"You mean when the others come into season, *none* of the males will breed them?" Fanny asked.

"What are the other types in a pack?" Scott asked.

I explained the hierarchy: They all have a place and know where they stand, but every social pack has different personalities, so each combination will have different dynamics. But some things are always the same: Some individuals are the ones who get hurt and have all the scars, some rise above. To some, survival is a greater driving force; some give up too quickly. Some get all the food; some—in extreme cases—get none. Depends on how fierce their drives are and what *kind* of drive is the fiercest. If their flight drive is their strongest, they'll spend their whole life running away. The real dynamics involve the puppies growing up—they're subordinate, of course, but as their personalities and drives mature, some aren't going to be satisfied staying on the bottom rung. If they're born alpha—true alpha, with all the keen drives—they'll fight for top spots. But usually they'll go away for a while first and fight their way into another pack. The others can tell which young males are going to be alpha, and they kick them out of the pack before they really start to assert themselves.

"There's a good example," Scott said, pointing to the six men in white in two rows of three, kicking, grunting, punching, shouting. "They've been expelled from their family units and are out developing their drives before attempting to assert their domination over a new pack."

"Must be why everyone hates teenage boys," I laughed. "We can sense their rise in testosterone and kick them out of our packs!"

"Or they just leave on their own," Fanny said softly, "regardless of their testosterone."

"Yeah," I continued, "and the *old* males who can't hold a place anymore—they'll go off too, but they can't survive long without a pack."

"They'll find a pack of renegades who'll feel sorry for them," she said.

I saw Scott touch Fanny's shoulder. So she must've told him, too, about her husband leaving. I shot a look at him, and he took his hand away from her shoulder.

"It's okay," Fanny looked up. "Don't act like it's taboo. In a way, it's a big relief."

"Yeah," I pointed out, "and *luckily* he didn't ask for partial custody of your dog."

"The dog's the last thing on his mind."

"At least he could've decided *before* you went to marriage counseling."

"If we hadn't gone, he might've *never* decided and just stayed rotting in the house forever."

"But then wouldn't *you* have left—eventually?" Scott asked.

"What'd you do after the session—help him pack?" I interrupted before she could answer, thank god. "Didn't you just want to snap your fingers and have him be gone instead of having to drive home together and watch him get his stuff and go?"

"Lacy took me on a walk," Fanny smiled. "She showed me all her favorite bushes and holes in the ground. When we got back, I went to take a nap, and she jumped right on the bed, uninvited, and slept beside me."

"She feels like the alpha who got rid of her main rival," I laughed again. God, I was being stupid. *My* mistake was that I didn't just stay out of it and *train*. I had my dog, I didn't need Fanny. But I said, "She'll probably protect you if he comes back. Some dogs can be unbelievable that way." I told them about this guy who got killed falling off the Torry Pines cliffs. They found him *and* his dog dead at the bottom. There were different stories from different witnesses. Nobody could tell if the guy fell trying to save his dog or if the guy was slipping first and the dog fell because it was trying to save the guy.

The three dogs came back, Lacy still holding the tattered, wet towel. Fanny and Scott both reached their arms out and held their dogs, and I saw them exchange a strange intense glance. "Maybe the dog wasn't trying to *save* the guy, exactly," Scott said, "but, you know, some dogs want to go wherever their person goes, no matter what."

"*Either* would be a pack drive," I heard myself lecturing, instead of, as I'd intended, ignoring his stupid two cents. "But one's more assertive, the other more submissive. Either way . . . the dog's dead." Jack had his front feet on my shoulder and stood above me, panting, his tongue hanging almost to my face as I looked up at him, scratching his chest. "He feels like a big man today, joining the girls."

"And they don't even know he exists," Scott said.

I moved my hand to Jack's belly, tickling him with two fingers, gazing across the park at a jogger approaching us. I should've had some *instinct*. The husky and spaniel were wrestling, husky on top, one of the spaniel's ears drenched with spit. I tried to ignore the sound of Fanny's voice giggling as Scott did a mock play-by-play of the wrestling match. A roar suddenly covered all other sounds, until it was joined by a scream, shouts, even my own voice, *"No, no, no, no."* The jogger was on the ground grasping his thigh, yelling, "Hold your damn dog, I'll call the police!" I had Jack's collar, was mashing his face to the ground, but he was bracing his hind feet, attempting to stay standing. Fanny was on the ground lying half over her dog. Scott on his feet with his dog between his legs. The men in white pajamas were running toward us. "What the hell do you think you're doing out here, isn't that a wolf?" the jogger was still shouting.

"It's a hybrid," Fanny said in a tiny voice. Probably only I heard her. The guys in Rollerblades were plowing across the grass with their hockey sticks.

Jack was still growling, still resisting my efforts to get him all the way down. I couldn't let go of him, looked again at Fanny and Scott.

I couldn't leave him, and no one would help me. The husky was struggling underneath Fanny. Scott told his dog to sit and stay, then approached the jogger. As Scott got close, the man uncovered his thigh. I couldn't see. I screamed *"Down,"* then one last growl burst out of Jack as I finally forced him to the ground. "We'll pay for a doctor," Scott was saying.

"Damn straight. I should sue your ass off."

"We'll pay all your expenses," he repeated calmly. "Suing isn't going to get you any *more*—she doesn't own anything. It's just a couple of puncture wounds."

"Is it bad?" I called, still kneeling over Jack, keeping his head down on the grass.

"Not good," Scott answered. "He didn't get all four teeth in. But it'll be a big bruise."

"Vicious dogs should be against the law," one of the hockey players said.

"Get your damn dogs on leashes," one of the kung fu guys said.

"Assholes like *you* should be against the law," I snapped back. God, what did *they* know?

Fanny left her dog in a down-stay and finally came to me with a leash. The jogger was shouting for someone to call the police. Scott kept talking to him in a low voice, but the guy didn't seem to be listening. The hockey players and judo choppers were all talking too, each chipping in a story about a dog bite they'd seen or heard of, of dogs being trained to kill and fight, or wild packs roaming the streets and threatening the lives of children. Fanny had Jack on a leash, so I got up, letting Fanny hold him back away from the crowd. He was wagging his tail and looking at the spaniel. I went to the jogger, standing now, his thigh turning blue, two darker holes with big blue rings appearing around them. "Fucking vicious dog oughtta be killed right now, if I had a gun—"

"Listen a minute," I said, reigning myself to keep from talking too fast, my voice shaking. "The reason some dogs are vicious is bad temperament—fear biters. They've been mistreated and poorly bred, it's not a healthy fight defense—"

"What the hell are you talking about?" the guy said. "I hope someone went and called the police." The hockey players and kung fu guys were starting to leave.

"What I mean," I went on, closing my eyes in an effort for more patience, "is that some dogs *are* dangerous because they have poor temperaments. When they get stressed by an intrusion of their space, because they lack natural confidence, it's a reaction they have, to bite—just sort of a response to invasion stress in dogs with bad temperaments. But *this* dog was carefully bred, carefully socialized and trained, he's not a fear biter!" My voice rose and actually broke. I sounded like *Fanny.*

"Look," Scott said, "I'll take you to a doctor right now. They'll have to send a report to the police. So let's just leave it at that. The dog is registered, and she's a professional trainer."

"My ass," the guy said, but turned to go with Scott, who turned and gave Fanny a look.

"We'll pack up the equipment and lock it in your trailer," Fanny said. "I'll take your dog home if you're not back by then."

"No, wait—" I yelled as Scott and the jogger began walking away, but they didn't stop. I turned to Fanny. "He already has one bite. If this goes on his record, he'll officially be labeled a dangerous dog. One more time, and they'll— Can't they take him to some doctor who won't report it? Why'd your boyfriend have to butt in anyway?"

Fanny just looked at me with faded eyes. *Her* lack of gumption ruined everything.

When he'd shown up at her door with a suitcase and a couple of grocery bags stuffed with clothes and said he had nowhere else to go, Renee's first words had been "Except a motel." Then his slumped shoulders shook a little. She couldn't see his face very well through the screen, his mouth blocked by one of the aluminum brace bars, but his eyes didn't blink. She hated that wounded-puppy look, but she opened the screen and said, "C'mon, camp out a while."

He didn't tell her anything, and she didn't ask. But after a few days, Renee suggested, "Maybe I should go see Fanny for a little while?"

"No, she's probably fucking some guy who trains dogs with her by now."

"*Fanny?*"

"I don't care. This isn't about her. It's about me. It's about all the work I never did—all the exercises and lessons and auditions I skipped. All the choreography I never studied. All the everything I let go by without noticing. All the nights I didn't go out to funky clubs, all the people I didn't get to know, all the feelings I never had."

That first night, they'd stretched her futon into a bed and she'd made it up with sheets. Then she'd gotten all her candles, thin ones stuck in wine bottles or thick ones sitting on coasters and plates, set them all around the room on the floor. She sat on the floor and Morgan lay on the futon and they hardly spoke. Renee thought of the nightly routine she wasn't doing, wondered if it would come back to haunt her when she went for her audition in Baltimore. She put on a tape of harp and flute playing Irish folk songs and visualized each of the movements she should be repeating. Morgan lay like a corpse, hands folded on his chest. His eyes looked like two dark holes in his face. "Maybe I'll tell my mom," Renee had said, "it'll make her happy to hear I've got a guy here." She saw his dark smile. "The only way I ever thought I'd be living with a man was if we were sharing a cute little bi."

His black eye holes turned toward her, and she smiled back.

Daytimes she didn't know what he did. She spent most of the day at the theater, using the stage to work. She had to check in with someone in the office before using the stage and again when she was finished, just so they'd know how long the lights had been on and to make sure it was locked up. That meant they also knew how long she'd worked, and a few people always wandered through or took coffee breaks sitting in the third row, too dark for her to see who it was except that she knew Dani never came in and was never the one in the office when she checked in or out. Sometimes she ate dinner downtown before going home or stayed for a while in the gay reading room to watch the news or read a few magazines.

Morgan seemed to be getting worse. At least he wasn't changing much. After offering him a glass of wine one night, she noticed he always had one nearby, but he wasn't getting drunk, and the wine wasn't disappearing quickly.

The futon and stereo were set up against one wall; another wall was interrupted by the door, so her work table was against that short one. The other two walls and more than half the floor space were empty, barres installed and one wall mirrored. She pushed the candles away so they were all around the futon and did her exercises at night. He wouldn't speak until she was between repetitions, wiping her face on a towel or sagging against the barre, facing herself in the mirror. He would ask where she learned certain moves, which primas she admired most, had she ever gotten personally involved with anyone she worked with, what was wrong with their lawyer, and why hadn't they heard anything about negotiations. He didn't even put his foot on the barre until she finally invited him, then she took almost twice as long with her evening routine because she showed him each set of movements and corrected his flaws. After they were finished, he said, "If I asked you to coach me, would you say no because I'm a lost cause, do it *only* for the money even though I'm a lost cause, or do you think I still have something?"

She said, "No one should ever give up. Unless they're obviously injured."

That night when they went to bed, she'd put on a tape of musically enhanced nature, a pond at night with frogs and crickets, an owl, wolves in the distance, rushing water, wind through leaves, a light rainfall. Not long after the tape clicked off, Morgan appeared in her doorway and whispered, "You asleep?"

"I always wake up when the cassette player clicks off."

"Renee, I . . ." He came toward her, his arms and legs and head almost invisible in the dark, his body a whitish blur in undershirt and underwear. His voice was strange, not a sob, not cracking, not hoarse, but thick and weary. "I just— Please . . . just hold me . . ."

She didn't move for a second, then pushed herself over to make room on the bed. He lay on the outside of the covers, facing away from her. She didn't touch him at first. "I'm scared," he murmured.

"Of what?"

"That I'll never have what I want."

"You're a professional dancer, Morgan. Most never make it as far as you have."

"I don't just mean that." He struggled with several breaths, the bed shook, then he seemed to sag heavily, and the shaking of the bed changed to a tiny vibration. "I can't have you—" She could hear the wet sound of him trying to swallow his sobs.

She almost said, *No, Morgan, I think you want to* BE *me.* But she stopped herself. After a second, she rolled to face away from him, and he turned swiftly, clutching her around the waist, burying his face between her shoulder blades. "I'm sorry, please, I'm sorry. Don't go."

"It's okay, Morgan, I just had a kink in my neck and had to move." She was holding the edge of the mattress in one fist, as if Morgan was trying to pull her across the bed. "Morgan, I do need you to talk to. There are things *I* need to let out too. Something happened a few weeks ago, maybe more like a month, it's been bothering me, I can't get it out of my mind. I need to talk to you."

"Tell me," he said, his voice steady, but he didn't let go of her.

"I had a date at that Thai place on Park, you know the one. Well, while we were eating, Dani—you know, from the office—she came in. The room got so full of vibrations. I sort of completely ditched my date, in my mind . . . I mean, just blotted her out. I couldn't help it, there was so much . . ."

"Sexual tension?"

"I guess. I could hardly breathe, hardly hold my chopsticks, and I think Dani felt the same. But maybe she was scared . . ."

"Because she doesn't know she's gay?"

"Of course she *knows.* No, because of *me,* because I'm, sort of, you know, the new star with the company and she's just . . . whatever her job is, it's not very significant. I think we ought to get to know her, Morgan. But she's so scared of me, I mean . . . *you're* probably not as scary, you're easy to talk to."

"Why would she want me?"

"I think she's bi."

He had calmed down, but she could still feel his pulse, she wasn't sure from where, and there was a warm damp place where he was breathing on her nightshirt.

"I think maybe she has some personal hang-ups or confusion about her sexuality and needs supportive friends. We can find out what's bothering her. You know, there might be a strike."

"I know, I'm dreading it, I'll vote against it."

"I mean, that's something that I think is *also* confusing to Dani. She's really one of *us,* but she doesn't know it, she needs to realize her *real* friends are on *our* side. Dykes should stick together."

"Are you including me in this *us?*"

"You can be an honorary dyke."

His arm tightened and his face moved, probably wiping his eyes against her back.

"Morgan, you *have* been the best friend I've had since I moved here. I can admit to you how hot I was sitting in that restaurant with her across the room. But I'm not just asking you to go out and get me a woman. I think it's . . . a good way to . . . if you want to . . . really *know* me . . ."

Neither of them said anything more that night. Long after he fell asleep and had crawled under the covers, turning and putting his spine up against hers, she lay there trying to decide whether or not to go sleep on the futon. Every time she dozed off, she twitched, her muscles jumped, as though waiting until she was asleep to jerk away from him. Her hands were fists and her legs felt as if they might kick out involuntarily any second. She told him in the morning that she needed eight solid hours of sleep in order to concentrate on her work. He agreed the bed was pretty small and didn't mind the futon at all.

"But imagine *three* people in that bed," he said, almost offhandedly.

"I've imagined it," she said, turning to show him a smile.

He returned to Fanny's house the next day, Sadie on the front seat, grinning out the window.

After waiting at the urgent care facility with the jogger the previous day, then going back to the park to pick up his trailer, Scott hadn't gotten to Fanny's house until almost eight. Then it had become eight-thirty, and then almost nine, and the ticking clock in his head had drowned out the thunder of his pulse. What a fool he must've looked, hard-on still making a bump in his pants as he'd backed out the door with his dog's leash tangled around one leg. He knew he would be back the next day, and she must've known too.

"Notice anything?" She stood in her kitchen, smiling with a pursed mouth, hair swept off her face with several combs, a green scrub suit shirt and the same swim trunks, bare feet in canvas loafers, one brown ankle with a thin chain. "Lookit the stove!"

The stove, in slanting light coming through the smeared kitchen windows, was streaked with circular sponge marks. He wanted to take the combs out of her hair, kiss her throat as each fell, then take off the scrub suit and shorts, leaving her with only the ankle bracelet, but he felt like a paralyzed plaster cast version of himself, afraid to move.

Yesterday as he'd filled her in on the jogger's condition, his eyes had swept around the kitchen and living room, which he'd only imagined before. Suzanne had been grumbling lately that the house was too much for her to take care of alone. For Fanny, he knew there were more important things to occupy her energy—she'd never complain about something so trivial. But he hadn't been able to help noticing the array: a blue rug filmed with dog hair in front of the TV, whose screen was so dusty that colors must be muted when the set was on; dirty coffee cups on a piece of furniture that seemed to be made out of grocery boxes; faded, rumpled sofa and chair; kitchen floor smudged with muddy dog prints, some smeared as the dog skid around a corner. He'd been confused by his reaction: *comfortable.* She'd noticed him looking around. "I'm not much of a hausfrau, I admit."

"I wouldn't want you to be a hausfrau."

"Yeah, I'm a waitress." She'd rubbed her finger on the stove and tested the stickiness against her thumb. "I don't know what happened. I just stopped caring."

"Don't you think it's time to start again?"

"About what?"

"Your eyes are so pretty."

She'd laughed, but looked away. "I should start using makeup."

"Why?"

"To cover my raccoon rings. I wear sunglasses too much."

The two dogs had been playing in the yard, chasing each other back and forth, pretending to fight over one of Fanny's gardening gloves. "Sounds like a real war out there," she'd said with another laugh, and went to the window. He followed, stood behind her, suddenly saw his own two feet on either side of hers, his arms around her waist, her body leaning back against his. His hands had moved slowly up her body, felt her ribs under the thin material of her shirt, the tiny breasts that seemed to just fit the shape of his palm, the points of the nipples like little buttons. He wondered if she could feel his erection against her back or feel his heartbeat between her shoulder blades. Then she'd groaned softly, and his breath stuck in his chest. He dropped his face to her neck, opened his mouth against her skin, which smelled faintly of eucalyptus, moved his lips up behind her ear, and she actually writhed under his hands, squirmed and turned to face him, and they'd stood staring for a moment, panting gently in each other's face before kissing. He thought his cock might be squeezing out the top of his jeans when she stuck her tongue in his mouth, he thought he might come in his pants if she accidentally touched him there, or he might have a heart attack before coming and die with this hard-on. They'd stood clutching each other as though keeping each other from blowing away in a hurricane. But he knew every breath was a second, and the seconds were flying, and it was already late. "I have to go," he'd whispered.

"Why?"

"It's much later than I usually get home after training."

"Didn't you get your own apartment? Or did you move back in with your wife?"

"No, no," he'd held her hair off her face with both hands, like holding a doll's head that came barely to his throat, "don't worry about that *ever* happening."

"Then . . . I don't understand."

"She knows what time I get home from work, or how late I'll be if it's a day I'm training."

"How does she know what days you train?"

"She could easily check the apartment parking lot to see if the trailer's there."

Fanny had a hand on each of his hips, trying to straighten her arms to push herself back, but he was pulling her closer. She'd said, "Aren't you allowed to get home whenever you want? Is she keeping watch over you? Let her, if that's what she wants."

"No, I don't want her to think I left her *just* so I could . . . you know . . . I don't want her to think . . . that I ruined her life just so I could . . . When I left, I told her I wasn't having an affair. I don't want her to start thinking I lied."

Fanny had stopped pushing back against him, and for a second she was crushed up next to his body again, then he'd heard her muffled voice say, "Okay," and she broke away, went to the door, and called his dog inside.

He'd paused before going out the front door—his hand through Sadie's collar, the dog already outside on the front step, the screen closed across his arm. "Maybe I'll see you tomorrow."

"I'm probably not training tomorrow. I'm going to call Doreen and cancel."

"Okay." He'd paused again, but she didn't move, had a funny crooked smile and was looking down at his shoes, so he said good-bye and slipped out the door.

So he was back—it had seemed like last night was a week and the day at work a month. Fanny was standing with a hand on either side of her stove, looking down at it, saying, "I haven't even used this thing for months. I don't think I've cooked since coming home from Tahoe. Maybe I'll just leave it and see if it gets dirty all by itself."

"Want to go get something to eat?"

"Not really," she said. "Unless you want to."

"Let's sit down."

On the sofa, he sat leaning back with his hands behind his head. Fanny kneeled facing him, her bare feet tucked under her butt. "It would be nice to go have dinner sometime, though," he'd said, "without *us* being the ones serving it!"

"Yeah." Her voice was soft, almost shy.

"Turn off the lights, okay?" He was afraid it didn't sound like himself, more like a twenty-year-old virgin.

As she turned away to reach for the lamp on her side of the sofa, she said, "You won't be able to see your watch."

"No deadline," he said. "I had to stop by the house this morning to trim a bush that's swallowing the mailbox—she'd told me the mailman complained—and she was just leaving for work. I mentioned I was doing a dinner tonight and wouldn't be home, I told her that's why I had Sadie with me."

"I thought you didn't want to lie to her."

"I just don't want to hurt her any more than I already have."

Although the room was now dark, he could see a little tint of light from her eyes. He reached for her, and she took his hand in both of hers.

"You poor thing," Fanny said, "you leave her for your sake, but then, for *her* sake, you sacrifice having *your* own life."

"She just doesn't have to know what I do."

Fanny opened her hands, but he left his hand lying there in her palms. His eyes had adjusted to the darkness and he could see her looking down at his upturned hand as if it was a baby bird she'd captured. "Well," she said, nearly a whisper, lifted his hand, and held his palm against her face. "Are we really going to do this?"

"I think so . . . but . . . sorry I'm acting weird, I'm, uh . . . a little rusty."

She smiled. "You've been a good friend, and I haven't been a lot of fun."

"Me neither."

"I'm glad you came back today."

"There was no question."

Fanny stood beside the sofa and shed her clothes quickly. He took off his shirt and undershirt, but before he got any farther, she was kneeling between his feet, her fingers on his belt, undoing the buckle, slowly releasing the button, digging for the zipper, easing it down. He heard a little piece of his voice in every breath. For most of his adult life, until everything dwindled to nothing several years ago, he wouldn't have dared exhibit any appetite before the lights were off and they were in bed, both silent, as though preparing to sleep. Even then, it was always *his* need, and someone else putting off her night's rest for his sake. More and more often it hadn't gotten any farther than his careful whisper, "You tired?" and her slow answer, "Yes, very." And not even that much said for over two years, maybe three. He lifted his hips as Fanny slipped her hands around behind him and began pulling his pants off. He knew he should be touching her, kissing her, doing the things that had made her writhe yesterday as they stood in the kitchen, but she was out of reach. He could touch her hair with his fingers but was afraid he'd involuntarily grab a handful the same way he was grasping the back of the sofa, holding two fistfuls of the loose upholstery, as she ran her fingers up the backs of his calves, ticked the backs of his knees while she kissed the insides of his thighs. "My god . . . ," his voice finally escaped, "nobody's ever . . ."

"Ever what?" Her fingers were dipping inside the elastic leg holes of his underwear. He couldn't answer. She was freeing his hard-on from his underwear, cupping it in front of her face and slowly kissing up the shaft. She circled the tip with her tongue several times before taking him all the way into her mouth. He could see her eyes close as her head lowered, her lips circled around him, sucking gently. He wanted to shut his eyes too, didn't want her to catch him watching himself get his first blow job at age forty-three, watching a woman's lips pull him into her warm mouth, her fingertips fondling his balls, grazing the insides of his thighs, wanting him, wanting him.

She stood, put a knee on either side of his legs on the sofa, straddling him, while simultaneously he reached and fumbled in his cast-aside shirt for the rubber he'd put in his pocket that morning. Then she guided him into herself and lowered her body over his, bending at the same time to kiss his forehead, his cheek, his temple, his neck. "I've always had a fantasy," he whispered in her ear, "of a woman seducing me, wanting me so badly I just sit there and she . . . does everything to me."

She put her forehead against his, continued moving her body over him, said seriously, "No, I'm *not* part of some fantasy world, never again."

"I'm sorry, I didn't mean . . . I just meant . . ."

"Tell me this is your real life."

"It is. I can hardly believe it, but it is." He lifted her without separating their bodies and laid her on the sofa. Instead of just lying there, she had her legs wrapped around his waist, moving her hips to meet him. And when he finished, she didn't immediately squirm to get up from underneath him. She stroked the sides of his face with her fingertips. "Were you afraid?" she whispered.

"A little. Not enough to make me want to stop."

"Me too." Her voice hoarse and breathless.

CHAPTER 7

A fetal position was out of the question. Not only did his knee demand that he lie straight, the ice packs alone would've made curling up impossible. The tape Renee had put on for him when she left had long ago clicked off. He could probably hobble to the stereo, but why bother? "I sure am a piece of shit," he'd told her as she prepared to leave, but should've kicked himself with his remaining good leg for saying it. She'd looked annoyed and said, "Cut it out. Aren't there more important things to worry about right now?"

She meant the negotiations. Management's stall tactics were obvious but seemingly impenetrable. He and Renee had just discussed the little notice in the paper that morning announcing that the Moscow Ballet was returning to San Diego next fall, booked into *their* theater by *their* company. No mention in the article of how the company hadn't yet bothered to schedule a season for its own performers. No season announced, a month late now, no negotiations planned, so why had Renee been so anxious to rehearse a pas de deux? "I might as well put you to use," she'd said, and quickly taught him moves she needed from a male partner, but he'd never even gotten his arms around her—a 180-degree turn then directly into a lunge, something popped in his knee, and their scene was over. And maybe what was left of his career as well. Renee said it was just a strain, filled her ice packs, and left him on the futon. She'd said, "Don't worry, you'll still be able to handle your parts."

The chorus, a male kick line, wannabes and has-beens, square dance partners, human props. Fifteen years ago, he could've called it breaking into the business. Now it was a pathetic parody, a farce that was supposed to fool him into believing the dream that started when he was ten or eleven had not already run its course. Maybe a person could live comfortably, even with only this much to show for his ambition, if he knew he'd gone full tilt the whole time allotted to his body by the business, by the competition, by reality. "If you want a long career, go be an opera singer," they'd said in master classes. "The hours you'll put in for the next ten or fifteen years will be the same as the average person's entire adult working life." So what the hell had managed to occupy his time the past fifteen years? It wasn't even as if he'd wasted it all on fast living, exotic travel, interesting friends, or love.

And yesterday he'd had ten minutes to experience what his life should've been all this time. The dance with Renee, even as short as it was, had actually made him feel the warm elastic tautness in his body again, the squeeze of joy in his gut, the feeling that the next day, the next hour, the next minute was always a hole to burst through into a bigger, more potent, energetic world.

But there was still a dance he could do with Renee. If he was ever going to feel alive again, if he was ever going to know a form of euphoria, it would be by making love to Renee. And not just once. Passion in the night, sweet pleasure in the morning, lazy hunger in midafternoon, a warm-up routine that heated into raw sensuality. That was the way she danced, and the way she talked about dance, and the way she read with her eyes devouring the pages, and the way she ate spaghetti—sucking in the last three inches and licking the sauce from her chin—the way she did everything. He could still have a life.

She was still talking about Dani. Not all the time. But whenever their conversations—about the company and negotiations or dance competitions she had won or friends from her past or plans for her future—lagged, when Renee's eyes rose slowly like the moon, glowing darkly, he wondered if she were thinking of Dani. He felt a dull ache in his chest, wanting to hold her and tell her he understood.

"I want to get someone to choreograph a dance for me for three people," Renee had said last night. "God, why is it always pas de deux? I want a dance to show an equal triangle. Three women, or even two women and a man."

"But not two men and a woman?"

She'd wrinkled her nose and shook her head. "Not for me, at least."

He knew he was the one she was turning to for that choreography, telling him that without Dani, he wouldn't ever have her.

Rolling carefully to his side, he took Renee's address book from the floor beside the futon and looked up Dani's number, realized, while moving, that he had half a hard-on. He punched the numbers quickly, hoping just to leave a message on her answering machine at home, but someone answered after only two rings, a familiar voice—it was Fanny! He hung up, sweating, even panting a little.

The next time, he pushed the buttons slowly, looking at the number written in Renee's address book after each one, and sure enough, Dani had an answering machine.

It wasn't really a warm evening, but they'd worked several hours in a steamy kitchen and overly heated banquet hall, so he suggested sitting outside when they got to Fanny's house. She had no patio furniture, but there was a plot of earth surrounded by park benches built on railroad ties in the middle of the yard. The dogs played, rustling in the darkness, trying to catch each other's ears, then flashing past on the lawn.

"Sadie likes staying here during a job," he said. "I'm sure she's feeling pent up in that apartment most of the time."

"Well, you'll be getting a place with a yard, won't you?"

"Eventually." He picked up one of her legs and draped it over his. She was wearing her short black waitress skirt but had taken off the athletic shoes and socks. "But not until we decide what to do about the house. Which probably won't be until we get the divorce." He ran his hand up the back of her leg, feeling the shape of her calf. "Which I haven't even brought up yet."

"Why?"

"I don't know . . . the thought *has* to have occurred to her by *now.*"

"Are you waiting for *her* to suggest it?"

"Not really . . . just taking things one step at a time. I don't want to give her more than she can handle right now." He was looking at her leg, one hand on her thigh, the other feeling the arched shape of the bottom of her foot.

"That feels great," she said. "My feet hurt after a job." She put her fingers in his hair, touched lightly around his ear and down his neck. "I must be out of my mind." She pulled her leg from his lap and put her foot behind him in the garden dirt. His heart lurched. She was straddling the bench, facing him. So he turned toward her, also straddling the bench. Then she smiled, "I mean, I shouldn't trust men, right? I should vow no more *relationships*. What an icky word."

"Well . . . you don't like *mistress*, do you?" He tucked her hair behind her ears. "If so, maybe instead of making dog equipment, you'd want me to buy you clothes and jewelry, then take you to Paris or Monaco."

"Ha! I'll do all that myself when I make a million as a freelance waitress."

"How about when you make a million from your own interior design business?"

"What a laugh."

"I could help you get started, if you want. I think it would be exciting."

The dogs came to them, the husky with one of Fanny's shoes in her mouth. Sadie flounced into a sit beside Scott's leg, threw her head back toward him, her loose lips hanging in a crazy grin. "Thank you for bringing mommy her shoe, sweetheart," Fanny said to her dog. "You're having a fun time, aren't you?"

"I can tell Sadie's having fun," Scott said. "Her neck and ears are covered with your dog's spit."

"That's a fun time, all right. Maybe I'll cover you with *my* spit."

He let his breath out in half a laugh, more like a gasp, smiling. "What a naughty girl. What're you doing?"

She was unzipping his pants. He put a hand on each of her legs and slowly pushed her skirt up until it was just barely hiding her underwear. When he slid his thumbs up the insides of her thighs and slowly under her skirt, he gasped again, "Nasty girl! You're not wearing any underwear. Were you like this at work tonight?"

"Maybe, maybe not." She smiled down at his crotch. His cock was out of his pants and out of his underwear, standing straight up in her hands. She scooched closer. The dogs were wrestling on the ground beside them, mouths open, trying to catch each other's muzzles, vocalizing from their throats. Fanny imitated the sound as she opened her mouth and bent to put her lips over him. Then, "Lie down," she whispered, so he collapsed backwards onto the bench and felt her recline forward, on her stomach, her mouth still on his cock. He could imagine her skirt still pushed up, her little round white butt exposed to the cool dark air.

After a while, Fanny got up, stood beside the bench with her back to him, stroking both dogs, one with each hand, while he took the silent cue and got the rubber from his shirt pocket. She turned and threw one leg over him, like mounting a horse, looked him in the eye while she lowered herself onto him. "Help, Sadie," he said, smiling, reaching out for the dog who was right beside him, patted her back while she continued her mouth-chasing game with the husky. "I'm being raped."

"I'm actually surprised," Fanny said breathlessly as she rode him, "that they aren't noticing this. You'd think it would arouse their animal instincts."

"Sadie's spayed," he said. "She's never thought about anything like this. And she's sure as heck never *seen* anything like this!"

They stayed lying on the bench, Fanny on top of him, her head on his chest. The dogs had also finished playing and were lying quietly, head to tail beside the bench. "Oh Sadie," he groaned, "Don't ever tell your mommy what you just saw."

"Someday she'll have to know," Fanny said softly into his shirt.

"There's no reason for her to know . . . yet. It's none of her business."

Fanny didn't say anything.

"It hasn't been easy," he said, "but so far I've managed to . . . well, keep her from feeling she's been thrown out like some trash I don't want anymore. I don't want to be married to her, but there's no reason for me to make her feel worthless and . . . abandoned. I told her we'd still be friends and still . . . you know, do things friends do."

"I'm cold." Fanny got up, sat on the bench with her knees drawn to her chest, hugging them. Scott had to go take care of the condom, then came back outside. The husky was sitting on the patio beside Fanny, the dog's cheek pressed against Fanny's legs, panting and gazing into Fanny's face while Fanny fondled her ear.

"I'm not hiding anything from you," he said gently.

"I know."

"I'm leaving her. I just want to do it right. Leave her with some self-respect, let her know she's not just a terrible, awful person that I want to get away from as fast as I can. There's no reason why I shouldn't treat her with the respect she deserves after being the closest person to me for almost twenty-five years."

"I guess you do that by lying to her," Fanny said dully.

He didn't answer right away. He put his hands in his lap like holding a bowl, and his dog slipped her face there. He scratched her cheeks. Something rustled in a bush, and the dog rolled her eyes sideways to look, but didn't take her head away from his hands.

"It's a very difficult time, Fanny. I understand what you're going through. I want to be there for you, and I need your help too. I feel like it's you and me against . . . all this."

She looked at him, her eyes luminous for a second, then she bent to kiss her dog between the eyes. She said, with her mouth pressed against the dog's face, "What if I told you I'm just in it for the *sex?*" He was pretty sure she was smiling.

Why *not* Saturday? Suzanne had, for once, let herself press the issue, and he'd had no response to that. It wasn't flirting, it wasn't begging, she didn't like the gardener he'd tried to hire, she *did* need those bushes trimmed, and it would take several hours. He'd offered to come by on a weekday morning when he didn't have to go into his business so early. She didn't remember him *ever* not wanting to get to the office early. She pointed out she'd like to be there too, to bundle the branches and bag the leaves while he trimmed, so she wouldn't have to come home and find a mess to clean up by herself. "What's wrong with Saturday, Scott, did you have other plans?"

"Not really. No."

Then he showed up with a chain saw he'd borrowed from somewhere, and in a half hour the job was done, might've even been done faster if he hadn't turned the damn motor off two or three different times to check his watch. She stood below holding the ladder. It was impossible to say anything.

But he'd cut so fast, she couldn't keep up with the bagging, especially since she'd eventually let go of the ladder and gone inside to make lemonade, so there was plenty of work remaining when he finally killed the motor for good.

She tied a kerchief over her hair and put on sunscreen, then pulled her gloves onto her hands, feeling them tug against her engagement diamond, which she usually removed before doing yard work.

"Come on," he urged, "we can get this done in no time."

"Want some lemonade?"

"No thanks. Let's finish this." He began raking leaves into piles for her to bag.

"Scott, I finally solved the problem of that bare corner in the foyer." He didn't respond; a sudden hot flush began to spread over her body. She went on quickly, "I found a cute little white-and-gold antiqued whatnot that fit perfectly. You know, a corner shelf—you'll have to come in and see it. It's perfect for little knickknacks that haven't seemed to belong anywhere before."

"That's good."

"If you don't like it, I'll take it back. I saved the receipt."

"If you like it, keep it."

Suzanne stood abruptly with an armful of leaves, then threw them down toward his legs, completely covering one of his feet. "Since when do you not care what's done to this house?"

He turned and looked at her, lifting his foot from the leaves. It might've been the first time that day that he actually stood still and met her eyes. But he didn't say anything. She kicked an open bag, half spilling it, then went and sat on a lawn chair with her back to him. She heard the scrape of the rake continue, the rustle of the bag, the crunch of the leaves, and the snapping of twigs. He was breathing hard. Under the patio table was a fresh bowl of water she'd put there that morning before Scott arrived, but he hadn't brought the dog. She let the tears come, then went back to him. The job was almost finished. He was tying up the bags. "I wish you'd brought Sadie," she said softly. "I miss her sometimes."

"She might've been scared of the chain saw."

"Scott . . . would you like to take a shower, cool off, then get some lunch?"

"I . . . I can't leave Sadie cooped up this long." He took a white washcloth from his back pocket and wiped his face.

"Scott . . ." Her voice fluttered. "My friends say we, you and I, won't really stay . . . friends. They say . . . but I said they don't know you, you're different. They said that you'll . . . but I always stick up for you when they start saying how men only have brains in their pants, how men aren't capable of considering another person's feelings, how men don't even see their signature on a piece of paper in the same way a woman does. I never let them talk that way about you. I . . ."

"This is hard for both of us, Suzanne."

"Yes, and I tell them I know you better than anyone . . . so why couldn't we . . . why shouldn't we still . . . plan things together, and still . . . well, they'll see for themselves."

"It doesn't matter what other people think, does it?" He picked up two bags and went through the garage to place them on the sidewalk for the trash pickup. Suzanne followed with two more bags, smiled and waved to a neighbor.

On the way back through the garage, she said, feeling easier, "I'll tell you what else they say, Scott, they say you'll start to see other women and won't want anything more to do with me, just toss me away like I'm . . . branches you trimmed off a tree." By the time she finished, her voice was hard to control again, she could see how it made him wince and look rigidly forward as he walked beside her, picked up the chain saw, and began winding the cord. He looked at his watch *again,* but then sat in one of the lawn chairs.

"Don't worry about stuff like that right now, Suzanne, okay? Let's just . . . don't think up things to worry about, okay?"

"You're right." She sat beside him. "I shouldn't listen to them, they don't understand, they don't know you. Are you ready for that lemonade now?"

"I . . . okay, I guess."

When she came back with a tray, pitcher, bowl of ice, chilled glasses, and some oatmeal cookies, he had his head back, eyes staring into the sky. He didn't pour much lemonade into his glass. "Is it half full or half empty?" she smiled. He looked at her as though waiting for a punch line he wasn't even interested in. Once again, her heart suddenly hammered a gush of hot blood into her face. "You know, I . . . I still have those weeks off work . . . you know, the Greenland trip. There's still time to . . ."

"I can't leave the business that long." In the same motion, he drained his glass, put it on the tray, and stood up.

"You said we'd still be friends!" She bent over forward, her face in her hands. "They said you'd make a million excuses . . . they said you'd only promise things to make getting away from me easier—how can you *do* this to me?"

She knew he wasn't moving, just standing there—he would stare at the bushes he'd just trimmed, or at the opaque windows of the house, the weather vane sitting silently on the garage roof. He hated that weather vane, a rooster with one foot raised. The day their offer on the house was accepted, he'd said he was going to rip the weather vane off the roof. She lowered her hands from her face, gripped the front edge of the lawn chair, body still bent over, rocking slightly, her face hovering over her legs. "Scott? Why didn't you ever take down the weather vane?"

"I don't know." He sounded exhausted. "Out of sight, out of mind, I guess."

"Like me?" She looked up as her voice flared between them. She had to shield her eyes from the glare on the patio.

"What's that supposed to mean?"

"You don't have to think about what you're doing to me as long as you never see me. Is that why you've been avoiding me?"

"Avoiding you?"

"Yes, Scott, avoiding anything to do with me, our home, our vacation."

"That trip is the least important thing right now, with everything else we're going through. There'll be other trips."

"When? When will we have another twenty years to plan for a trip of a lifetime? But you don't mind taking that away from me. Taking away more than twenty years of working together so we can have nice things and wonderful trips. *I* wasn't having a midlife crisis, *I* was happy with my life, but you're so selfish—what did I do to deserve this?"

He bent and pulled a foxtail from his sock. "I would think," he mumbled, "with the way you obviously feel right now, that you wouldn't *want* to go on that trip."

"Why wouldn't I? You said we'd still be able to do things together. You said we'd always . . . but I guess I shouldn't put too much faith in what you've *said*. I guess I know now how much it means."

A breeze had come up. A neighbor's wind chime tinkled. A leaf skipped across the patio. Finally the weather vane groaned and moved. "I can't afford a big trip right now," Scott said slowly. "But maybe we could do something else. Maybe we could . . . I don't know . . . tour the national parks. Maybe the western parks, or the southwestern parks."

"Cut my slice smaller and smaller. Is that supposed to take the place of *Greenland?*" She looked at the cookies he hadn't touched. Her eyes stung. Patches of bright color floated in her vision. She fumbled in her skirt pocket for her sunglasses, then picked up the tray. "Let me put these cookies in a bag for you."

She washed her face at the kitchen sink, waiting to hear him follow her into the house, but he stayed on the patio, came to the door to take the sack from her. "I'll be okay, Scott," she said, smiling.

————————

It had been too good a day to go home yet and face Morgan's eyes. He'd only been laid up a few days, hopping on one foot to the bathroom and back, continuing to stay on the futon most of the day. She'd gathered all of the magazines out of the greenroom at the theater, and he usually had four or five things he wanted to read to her when she got home. He'd begged her not to tell anyone in management or anyone she saw while at the theater about his knee. As if he would actually come up as a topic of conversation, as if anything that happened to an aging corps dancer who'd been mediocre at best in the first place would ever be considered news. But she simply assured him she hardly ever spoke to anyone at the theater.

"But you were right," he'd said, "we can trust Dani."

She knew he'd been talking to Dani on the phone at least once a day and had told her about his knee, about camping out on Renee's futon, that he had night terrors about losing his job and having nothing to fall back on, maybe having to spend the rest of his life in a gas station cashier's booth until someone shot him for forty dollars. Renee knew exactly what he'd told Dani because those were also the things he said to her.

"You didn't tell her *I'd* encouraged you to call, did you?"

"No. I think you were right about her, she seems lonely, I don't think she has any friends in the office."

"Did she say anything about herself?"

"No, I guess I did most of the talking, but she really listens."

But now, by sheer dumb luck, Renee knew something about Dani that Morgan probably wouldn't find out until he quit whining about himself. Renee usually went to the gay reading room after her workout to give herself a chance to slow down and think. Who could think clearly with Morgan hopping around behind her, following her from tiny room to tiny room, reading aloud about some crazy old lady who kept thousands of bats as pets in her house, or an editorial about the baby boomers easing into their forties and fifties?

Today, by chance, Renee was wearing a dance company t-shirt, one that they sold in the lobby to patrons, and a man about Morgan's age with close-cropped beard, round wire-rimmed glasses, Dockers, and loafers, said, "Do you work for the dance company downtown? I know someone who works there."

"I'm a solo prima," Renee had said, glancing up only briefly, until the fag said, "Oh, really? Dani's been telling me I should go to a show, maybe I'll see you."

"Oh, Dani's a good friend of mine," Renee had the presence of mind to say quickly. "You know her?"

"We sometimes rave together."

Renee had heard rumors about gay raves before she moved here, couldn't believe anyone in the nineties would do anything as stupid as group sex and drugs. Most people doing the more publicized hetero raves were in their teens or early twenties, but she supposed there were a number of others like this guy, thirties and forties, lost after the bathhouse era ended. She'd heard it described as a combination scavenger hunt and mass orgy. The participants had to get a word-of-mouth invitation from someone in the chain, were told only what door to knock on and what password to give to find the address of the vacant warehouse where the rave was taking place. People who raved didn't usually advertise it. But Renee had found there was a strange openness in a gay reading room, as though anyone who walked in and sat down had nothing to hide, and people said things to strangers they normally might not even admit to a friend or colleague.

So Dani raved. Renee knew it was useful information but hadn't decided *how*. She didn't just want to have dirt on Dani, she was going to break the bitch, show Dani that she *could've* gotten what she wanted by going *through* her as easily as she already had by going *around* her. Hopefully Dani wouldn't know about the private negotiations Renee had finished during her midday break in working out. No one was supposed to know, but Renee had specifically told the general manager and artistic director that some of the office girls were pretty friendly with performers, and if any of this got through to the other dancers, she would consider the agreement void.

They hadn't told her what they were planning for the rest of the company, whether or not they were trying to clean house and start over by canceling another entire season. But for her promise to not seek work elsewhere, they had—in addition to agreeing to continue her salary through any type of work stoppage—given her a written agreement that her requests would be clauses in her next contract. She would have an equal voice in artistic decisions, including who danced backup and other lead parts in productions that featured her.

A girl came into the reading room, backlit in the doorway, just a silhouette, frail looking in baggy jeans, tank top, short straight hair—too neatly combed to be Fanny's hair, but Renee felt a jolt just the same. Her fingertips, resting on the arm of her soft chair, throbbed. The girl went into another room.

I was working harder than I'd ever worked, including my two-month career as a dental assistant, the only job I ever had, and I don't *entirely* regret it—I use the dental tools I lifted to scale the dogs' teeth once a month. My mother's life insurance, invested by my uncle, was enough to live on. But sometimes extras were difficult to budget, like the agitator I was going to have to hire soon for protection work. The husky was ready too. I wasn't sure about Fanny's finances, but her boyfriend had money, so I figured maybe he could finally be useful to the husky's development as a Schutzhund dog instead of either a constant distraction or emotional downer.

Whenever we trained with him there, Fanny only wanted to lie on the lawn with him sitting beside her, tickling her with a leaf or making twig huts. And when we trained without him, mornings,

Fanny would show up, set up her equipment, then kneel on the grass as though tired already, sigh, and say, *I don't know* or *I can't think about this today.*

I probably should've said, *Fine,* changed parks, and forgotten her. But I told her, "See, this is what I mean about relationships. First this Tahoe guy blows you out of the water, then your husband dumps you, now Scott's playing the *same* games, why do you bother with this shit? Without this crap, you might have your Schutzhund I title by now."

"Why does Lacy have to get that title?"

The hundredth time I'd explained it: Both Jack's parents are supposed to be titled in order to ever compete in Europe, which I have to do to establish my new line. I obviously couldn't title the wolf and was going to have to seek some kind of exemption as it was.

It was as good a time as any to talk to her about showing, about the aggressive instinct you have to have: a focused mind-set, a confident and unemotional determination, no wavering—god, you can't even be *close* to timid. I said, "You know, maybe when you show, you should register as Fran or Frances. It'll make you seem more of a contender."

"I don't know about that. It's not . . . me." The dog was sitting beside Fanny, but the husky's slit eyes stayed fixed on me. "Why can't we just get an agility title?" Fanny asked. "Scott's almost ready to go for his."

"Yeah, because it's so simple. Schutzhund isn't some Mickey Mouse game for yuppies and their retrievers that they got as standard equipment with a Range Rover."

"Why don't you like Scott?"

"Let's just get to work, okay?"

The answer should've been obvious—she'd actually admitted that she and Scott had to go places in *her* car because he didn't want to take the chance that his wife might see them together in *his.* Some crap about how the D-word hadn't even come up yet, and he didn't know when it would. *When she can handle it,* was what he'd told Fanny. I didn't care what he did or didn't do with his wife—it's not that I could give a flying fuck if he lied or manipulated—but Fanny was less and less able to function as any kind of dog trainer. One day, she'd sort of folded to the ground after doing just two retrieves with the husky, held the dumbbell in two hands against her chest, and said, "I don't know, Doreen, is it happening again? Am I really this stupid? How long will he protect her from knowing he wants to be with me, how long will he live some sort of alternate reality with her, even going on goddamn vacations to Mt. Rushmore and Yellowstone?"

"He's going on a *vacation* with her?" I couldn't help it.

"Yeah. He told me he didn't see any way out of it."

"How about saying *no?*"

"He said he doesn't want to be mean. But I should say *Fuck this shit,* right?"

"Yeah," I said, "you've got your dog. Don't let her go to waste. I'll take her and work her if you want."

"No." Fanny put an arm around the husky.

"Then *train* her. God, not everybody gets a dog like this out of just dumb luck."

"But she's so wild—"

Wild. God, but I tried to be patient and explain everything again, that the dog has a lot of energy, but the reason she's so good is that she's got just the right *balance* of drives—mostly prey drive but also enough defense mood to give her intensity and raw power in times of greatest need, like true protection situations. That's why we needed to hire an agitator. Her prey drive would keep her attacking the sleeve all day, because that's what it was to her—*prey.* But she has to have a defense mood that will turn on when *she's* attacked, just enough sharpness to react out of *some* fear, but with the courage to fight back in deadly circumstances.

"How in the world does a domestic dog know what deadly circumstances are?" Fanny asked. "Even your wolf has only known a cushy life—"

"Instinct," I interrupted her inane babbling. "Do you think only a demoniacally savage dog can do this stuff? No, *too* much sharpness means the dog is always suspicious, it has a low tolerance for sensation and overreacts. A dog like that can barely function. Only an animal with a steady, confident, reliable nature can tell the difference between a time when aggressive defense is necessary and a time when there's just a lot of noise and confusion but no threat."

"She knows what crying is," Fanny said, holding her dog's head, talking nose to nose with the bitch. "She acts crazy and silly to make her mommy happy again."

I think it was that night, around there, that I was scaling teeth, and Jack whimpered when I hit a little bit of gum. His newly developing pain sensitivity could've been because he was nearing adolescence. I'd been reading a lot, trying to find out if anyone had done research on how to maintain a stable temperament through a time when hormone levels were five times normal, when a dog might get an overblown sense of himself as an alpha stud or else lose his self-esteem entirely, neither attitude necessarily born out of anything more than surging teenage chemicals.

God, I had hated teenagers since I was one myself—boys bashing open the doors to the girls' locker room for a peek before running away, howling like baboons, snickering when the coach used the word *sanitary* in a lecture on first aid, marking territory with globs of their own spit. I left school as soon as I had enough credits, foregoing graduation and proms and yearbooks, buying myself a shepherd puppy as a graduation present.

I'd never had any trouble keeping my dominant male dogs down on their backs, but Fanny told me that she needed help to cut her dog's nails because the husky fought so hard, especially didn't like being held down on her back. "Because she's alpha," I said. I *should've* told Fanny the husky didn't need to ever be part of a real canine pack in order to recognize that her owner was the submissive bitch who pressed her ears flat and kept her head low, kept her body in a curving slinking crawl, her lips stretched back and smiling, creeping to each of her superiors to lick at their mouths, lying down in front of them to expose her underside, letting them sniff at her, letting them snarl at her, letting them take her food, letting them rip patches of her coat away, then coming back to lick their mouths again. I should've told her, *You know that dog with the perfect temperament we're looking for to be a top competitor—its life is based on its OWN drives, its OWN abilities, its own courage and motivations and desires, never on whether or not another animal loves it. That's why it WINS.*

Alone, when it seemed all he did was think about her, he marveled that he never would've believed a girl like Fanny—with her loose clothing and shaggy hair, her thin boyish shape and unsophisticated body language—could be right for him. Yet here she was in the passenger seat, smiling slyly as she reached for his belt buckle with one hand and played with his ear with the other. And this girl who, a few years ago, never would've been the kind he would've thought he could want, could consistently make him at once both rigid and liquid with excitement, appetite, and tenderness.

She slipped a finger between the buttons of his jeans. "I'm still just so psyched, I don't know what to do with myself. God—what a *place.*"

After discovering she'd never been there, he'd taken her to the design center in Los Angeles. She seemed to know that the design business wasn't just a person going furniture shopping with someone else's money; that the custom decorating end of the business alone was far bigger and more complicated—involving business and reception areas, hotels, any conceivable kind of indoor space. She also obviously already knew that there was another side to the business involving the design of furnishings from chairs, tables, and sofas to bath and light fixtures and linens and ornamental decorations. But she'd been like a kid in a petting zoo when she saw the huge wholesale mall of showrooms, each manufacturer displaying its current styles, exclusive designs purchased from a particular artist. Some manufacturers specialized in certain materials, like leather or metal or Plexiglas. The people working in the showrooms weren't just salespeople, they'd studied design or had some experience in design, they knew the trends in fabrics, accessories, new materials, and colors.

Several times since they'd been seeing each other regularly, she'd called herself an ex-designer, and he'd finally had to say, "You didn't even try." For a second, he'd seen anger flare in her eyes, but when he'd asked *Did you try to sell your designs to a manufacturer? Did you try to work for a manufacturer? Did you try to work for a large interior decorating company? Were you familiar with some of the custom manufacturers?* the answers were *No—no—no—no,* until she'd stopped answering and just sulked.

She still had two fingers in his pants, her head against his shoulder, looking down into his lap. "You could've had a job there," he said, "instead of being a waitress." He lifted the arm she was leaning on so her head nestled underneath, against his ribs.

She undid one of the buttons so her fingers could go farther into his jeans. "How could I not know that place was up there?"

"Yeah, what'd they teach you in school, anyway?"

"Oh, color and shape and space and texture. Abstractions."

Another button released. He wanted to reach into his pants and straighten his erection, wanted even more for *her* to do it, and the anticipation was also delicious. "I'd love to help set you up in business."

"Thanks," she said softly, "I'll think about it." She took him out of his pants, then for a moment her touch was gone. He glanced down; she was reaching into her purse. When he felt her fingers again, it was with something cold and smooth, and an herbal scent filled the car. She said, "Keep your eyes open, okay?"

"I'll try." But it was more difficult than he'd ever thought, those times he'd dared imagine someone touching him like this while he was engaged in a business call, or working on his computer, or driving. The trip to the southwestern national parks in a few weeks would mean long stretches of driving. He'd been picturing doing it with Fanny, seeing her hair whip around in the wind, her hands in a now familiar position clasped in front of her throat as she waited for a gusher in Yellowstone, then reaching out with her palms to catch a few drops of water. Or stopping in the Badlands to get out and kneel together to look for arrowheads or fossils. Being the only two people in a meadow at Yosemite, where they could hear the roar of the falls, making love with two-foot-high grasses standing up around them. Silly dreams. As much as he hated planned tours, he'd tried to talk Suzanne into doing the trip with a group, just to avoid all those hours alone in a car with her. But Suzanne had looked at him acutely and said, "You hate bus tours."

"But think how simple it would be—we wouldn't have to make decisions or arrangements."

"You love making all the arrangements," she'd said in the same chanting voice.

So they'd had to sit down together with a map. Suzanne's long fingernail had made a dry scraping sound that made the back of his throat itch as she traced highways and prospective routes. The first time he'd said "I don't care" to one of her suggestions, a long arid silence had followed, both of them facing the map on the tabletop as though studying it, but neither moving, until he'd finally forced himself to say, "I always wanted to see Capitol Reef," mustering some enthusiasm, and her fingernail had returned to the map.

"We got the trip planned," he said to Fanny, immediately regretted opening his mouth. Her hand slowed on his cock. "I tried to fix it so we'd have to make phony small talk to strangers on a bus instead of me having to think of what to say to her."

Fanny was still holding him, not moving. "There are things you *should* say to her."

"I know, but I can't. Yet. I don't want her to know how quickly you and I . . . started. You know that this trip doesn't change anything about you and me, don't you?"

"You've said so." Her voice was dull, muffled against his shirt. Then she let go of him and sat up, looked away from him out the window on her side.

He yanked his shirt out of his pants and covered his cock, which was too stupid to stop being erect. "I won't go on feeling guilty forever," he said quietly. "But right now, this is the only way I can feel comfortable about leaving her. I don't want to be with her, you know that. But . . . look what I've done to her. A day or two before we planned the trip, she called me out of the blue, asking *why* again, *why* was I so unhappy—she said she had to know what was so awful about her that made me have to get away from her."

Fanny was moving slightly. He glanced over and saw she was rubbing her hands together to get rid of the extra lotion, her forehead leaning against the window glass.

"Rationally I know she's trying to be a martyr and feel sorry for herself—"

"Martyrs don't feel sorry for themselves," Fanny interrupted woodenly.

"You know what I mean, though—she's trying to blame it all on herself but feeling sorry for herself, which is really blaming me. Then when I said I didn't have an easy time making the decision to leave but I knew it wasn't the way I wanted to live the rest of my life, her voice got this really nasty tone and she said, *You decided what was best for YOU, not for me.*" He touched Fanny's shoulder with a fingertip for a second. "I just want to do this right. I want her to realize it's best for both of us. She won't if she thinks she was thrown out and replaced with someone else. Oh, shit, why can't she just realize she'll be happier without me? Then you and I could do whatever we want."

Fanny sat up and glanced at him. He turned his head toward her five or six times, in between watching the traffic, which wasn't light, and finally she smiled sourly. "You are a pathetic *thing*, look at you, coming out of your pants, all untucked and rumpled. Like some old coot on a park bench."

"I *am* an old coot. But my cock hasn't lived as long as I have. I think it's still nineteen."

"I shouldn't've stopped doing you," she said, "I could've bitten your thing right off." The car drifted toward the next lane, a stake bed truck honked, and Scott swerved back into his own lane. Fanny laughed, grasping a fistful of his jeans with one hand.

Daylight savings time made it feel as if she was driving home in the middle of the afternoon, even after a few hours having coffee at a sidewalk café near the theater. Renee hadn't seen Dani come out, but that was a long shot anyway, because there was a big parking structure on the other side of the building where most of the employees left their cars. All the day jobbers were out in the park as she drove past—jogging, playing softball and volleyball, throwing things for dogs.

A dog ran to the edge of the grass to grab a Frisbee. Renee recognized Fanny's husky.

There were three people across the lawn, near a parking area, and Fanny, when she stood up, was unmistakably one of them, brushing grass off her jeans, then pushing her hair from her face with both hands. Renee slowed her car and pulled to the curb. There were several large pieces of equipment. A tall redhead was sending a gawky dog over an A-frame. She was the one Renee had seen at Fanny's house messing with the puppies, the one Morgan had complained about—how she sang and shrieked and babbled to the puppies for hours. And the man—no mistaking who *he* must be. Fanny was on the ground again, with her husky's front feet standing on her stomach. Then she rolled over and looked like a corpse the dog was eating until the man reached a hand down and helped Fanny to her feet.

For a wild moment, Renee imagined striding across the grass, taking Fanny by the hand, pulling her aside to tell her, in a firm undertone, that what she really needed was to get her life out of town, anywhere away from here, and don't even take her dog along.

The same thought had come to her last night with Morgan lying on his back across the foot of her bed, his arm across her ankles.

She'd been reading in bed when he'd come in, softly sliding his bare feet on the shag carpet. At first he just sat on the foot of the bed and told her about going with Dani to an afternoon film at one of the art galleries. Ever since he'd been able to limp with a cane, he and Dani had met for lunches, gone to galleries and bookstores, and he'd spent a few Saturday afternoons at Dani's apartment listening to her collection of New Age jazz. He hadn't been able to tell if she had other plans in the evenings, just that the signals had been obvious enough that he should leave. So far, he'd said, the subject of the dance company had not come up, nor had Dani's sexual preference been a direct topic, although she had referred to a former lover with female pronouns and once to an ex-husband, in passing. The former lover was neither valuable nor a revelation to Renee, the ex-husband neither surprising nor uncommon nor particularly useful information. She hadn't any idea if anything would come of Morgan's friendship with Dani or if she should continue to try to connect with Dani on her own. Then, last night Morgan had said, "I do talk about you a lot. But not, you know, sounding like I'd rather be with you than with her."

"How do you know it doesn't sound like that?" Renee asked.

"Because I told her that *she* was the first person who came to mind when you and I were discussing how I need a new circle of friends. And I told her that even though you and I were talking about *me,* that I thought *you* also felt the need to have a new circle of people you can relate to, artistically as well as personally or emotionally or . . . whatever."

"What did she say?"

"I'm not sure she said much right then. I also said that I thought it was difficult for you to make friends because people are intimidated by you, don't see you as a real person who needs friends just like everyone does. And I told her I thought you might like to do something with us, that you seemed lonely and reclusive."

"What did she say to *that?*"

"Actually, I'm not sure. She didn't say no, I know that much, but . . . what *did* she say? . . . I was concentrating so hard on what *I* said, you know, not wanting to sound like . . . you know . . . like . . . you were lusting after her or something."

Renee had laughed. "Maybe I am."

"I think what happened," Morgan said, after a moment of silence, "is that I hit a nerve. I think *she's* intimidated by you a little, and when I said that, it gave her something to think about."

"Does she always just want to do those quiet artsy things?" Renee asked, after another pause.

"I guess those are the things you do when you don't want it to seem like a *date*. The only other thing she's ever talked about doing has been an eventual someday thing—living in Vienna." That's when Morgan had fallen slowly backwards across her bed, his feet still on the floor. She couldn't see him anymore. He'd said, "Wouldn't that be cool, the three of us living in Vienna."

Renee had put her hands under her head on the pillow. At the same time his arm settled on the bed across her ankles. She wanted to move her feet away, but with him on top of the covers, it would be a major adjustment. She'd started to talk, imagining her voice as a cloud of thin vapor coming out of her mouth and floating up, across the one band of light from her reading lamp, spreading out along the ceiling. "Moving and starting over isn't something everyone can do, but probably everyone thinks about it at least once in their life. I mean really moving. Packing just a few suitcases and going. Leaving lovers you've just broken up with, relationships that've been strained by your success or talent, people you've *almost* made love with and now can't look in the eye at a party. Or leaving a room with a wall you've stared at for too many heartbroken hours, a radio station that babbled about sunny weather as you cried into a pillow. I guess that sounds too romantic or something, but you know what I mean. I did it. Sometimes it almost feels like it's time to do it again." For a minute, neither of them moved.

"No one should have to do that alone more than once," he'd said, getting up. He'd held onto the bed, reaching for the door, then paused in the doorway. "Goodnight."

Renee pulled away from the curb and continued slowly on the road around the park, but none of the three people noticed her.

Right behind Scott's apartment was an underground aqueduct that looked like a dirt path in a tiny valley, flanked by two short hillsides of ice plant ground cover, running lengthwise between the backsides of two streets of apartments. He'd told Fanny this was the selling point of this apartment: he could let the spaniel go out his back slider, and she could do her business in the aqueduct area, even roam for a few minutes while he stood and watched. He had let his dog out and showed Fanny the aqueduct when she'd first arrived, just hours before she would have to use it herself.

Fanny hadn't been too careful about avoiding dog shit when she'd slid down there to hide, but she was lucky. The pipes were underground, with access places every hundred yards or so—circular platforms of cement about two feet high with locked metal doors in the tops. Fanny sat on one a few yards down from Scott's apartment. She could still see his bedroom window, which he'd shut behind her after she'd jumped out. But if anyone looked out the slider, they wouldn't be able to see her.

They'd had sex already, so she was dressed by the time she'd suddenly had to leave. She inspected a few long white scratches on her bare shins, took off her sandals so the moisture from squishing through the ice plant would dry. She looked at the sandals beside her on the aqueduct cover. The leather straps were cracked, almost broken in a few spots.

When they had been getting dressed, deciding where to go for dinner, she'd said, "How about shrimp? But wait, I didn't wear anything good and didn't bring makeup."

"What does that have to do with *shrimp?*"

"Well, we can't go to a *nice* place. Hey, do you think I need a makeover—should I go to a makeover salon?"

"Why? If that's what you want, you could probably do it yourself."

"But . . . want a nice party, hire a caterer. Right? Want an integrated design in home furnishings, hire an interior designer. Want a new face, use an expert. Want a pleasant vacation . . . get a travel agent. But you didn't. Isn't doing it yourself unfair to a fellow professional?"

She hadn't intended to bring up his vacation, which was getting nearer every day. She *wouldn't* be another woman crying when he turned his back the way he'd said he could hear his ex-wife's voice after he left the house, sometimes wailing, sometimes hysterical, as if she might choke to death. In fact, just yesterday, he'd told Fanny, after he'd been there making final plans for the trip—and she'd seemed so normal—as he walked down the front walk to his car parked in the street, he could hear her moaning.

"What did you do?" Fanny had asked.

"Got in my car and drove away. What else could I do? I'm trying to act like this isn't a catastrophe. From her point of view, I took away everything she's lived her life for. I want to show her she's still got a life."

Fanny hadn't answered right away; then the phone rang. "I'm not getting it," he'd said. "It might be her." The phone rang ten or twelve times before it stopped.

"Do you ever call me, then hang up?" Fanny had asked, turning to the mirror but looking at a snapshot of Sadie stuck in the frame rather than at her reflection.

"No—but I've done it to Suzanne a few times, when I need to go over to get something but want to do it when she's not home."

"Well, someone's done it a few times to me."

"Morgan?"

"No. He knows he can talk to me . . . if he wants to."

Scott was getting something from a drawer. "I want you to have a copy of our trip itinerary."

"Why?"

"I'd like to feel that you know where I am. Even though I won't be able to call you, I'll be thinking of you." He was still holding the paper. She hadn't reached to take it.

"I could baby-sit Sadie at my house. Then you could call me to check on her."

"No. Here, we're starting at Yellowstone, then Badlands, Arches and Canyonlands, Bryce, Zion, then the Grand Canyon."

"Why wouldn't you want me to take care of your dog? She knows me. She knows my house. She's friends with my dog. It would be unnatural *not* to leave her with me."

"I can't tell Suzanne *you're* taking care of our dog."

"*Our* dog?"

"Well, she *was* our dog, Suzanne still wants to be able to visit her, Sadie's always crazy to see her."

"Would it be so unusual to have a friend take care of your dog while you're gone?"

"We've always used the same kennel—how could I explain that all of a sudden I'm giving Sadie to a waitress who works for me? Suzanne's already suspicious of my dog friends. I don't want her to think she's out of the picture for a few months and I'm already boarding my dog at someone else's house—for all she'll know, *I'm* living there to."

"God knows you'd never want to do *that*," Fanny had muttered. She'd gone around the bed and sat looking out the little window she would soon be crawling through.

"Fanny, please," he'd said, "Suzanne's suspicious and jealous. Why should I do anything that would exacerbate those feelings?"

"You don't have to feel guilty, Scott, if you're honest. Tell her the truth. Get it over with quickly. That's less painful."

"I can't. I'm trying to avoid an even worse situation. I know how she would react—she would feel thrown away and completely worthless. I would be the selfish horrible person who destroyed not only her life but her self-respect."

The dog jumped on the bed and stretched out behind Fanny. Then the mattress began an almost imperceptible rocking as Scott scratched the dog's belly. She could hear his fingers on her skin.

"My relationship with you *is* the most important thing in my life," he'd said. "You have to know that."

She'd laughed—more like a grunt in her stomach. "Yes, I'm wonderful at changing men's lives. Their lives—which belong to somebody else."

"That's not fair. I *left* my wife."

"Did you?" She hadn't turned to him until the silence was several minutes long. Then he'd looked up from rubbing the dog when she did turn. His nose was red. His eyes were wet. "If she had to have an arm amputated," Fanny said, "would you want it done quickly, or would you want to cut very slowly so she could say a nice long good-bye to her hand while the knife saws slightly deeper each week?"

"I have to do what I think is right."

She hadn't touched him, wasn't sure he'd want his tears acknowledged. When he turned his head to dry his face on his sleeve, the dog jumped to her feet, barking.

"Was that the doorbell? I couldn't hear!" He and the baying dog rushed together out the door, down the hall. She could hear Scott bump into the wall a few times, probably jostling for space, tripping over the dog. But he came running lightly, silently back into the room. "Suzanne's at the door, you've got to get out of here. Go down in the aqueduct. I'll get rid of her. Hurry!"

The doorbell rang again, causing a new eruption from the dog. Her toenails scraped as she leapt against the front door. Scott opened the window, unhooked and pushed out the screen. Then Fanny put her head and shoulders through, climbed to the sill on her knees, landed palms first on the piece of lawn surrounding the building, scrambled to her feet, and slid down the embankment.

She was lying on the cement platform on her stomach, her knees bent and feet kicking slowly back and forth in the air over her back, looking down at the dirt, where she was scratching pictures with a stick. First the spaniel came crashing through the ice plant, grinned at Fanny before charging down the trail to hunt during whatever precious amount of time she would be free. By the time Fanny kneeled upright, Scott was already down the embankment and coming toward her. He whistled for Sadie, then sat down beside Fanny. "She was dropping off my bag from her new set of carry-on luggage."

"So you'll match," Fanny smiled. "How cute."

"And they're light blue." He grimaced, then returned her smile.

Renee had a wonderful look on her face when he told her about Dani's predicament. Her eyes bulged gently, staring at the pencil she was tapping against her wine glass, her lips pursed slightly and smiling, her cheeks and ears red. "We have to help her," Renee said. "We have to show her that not everybody will think she's a deviate, that we accept her for who she is. Then, not only will you have been a good friend, you'll have gained an ally against management—she'll see she's more like *us* than them. You can't turn your back on people who know and accept you . . . intimately."

He'd just come in from seeing three Bogart movies with Dani at a film festival downtown, then they'd had an early supper, and Dani, apologizing for being weepy after the films, explained it wasn't Bogart and Bacall affecting her but the constant secrecy she had to maintain for the sake of her shared custody of her child. She and her ex took turns having the boy every other month. Her turn was coming up in less than a week. Her hands had been shaking, sipping nervously at her mixed drink, and Morgan had waited quietly. "It's not Karl, I always look forward to having him," Dani said. "But it's getting harder to maintain my . . . front. See, if my ex finds out I've had women lovers, the joint custody is off, I'll probably never be able to see Karl at all."

"That's not *certain,* is it?" Morgan had asked. "I mean, gay people are given custody or partial custody."

"In a stable environment, yes. But . . . I didn't want to tell you this . . ."

"Tell me, it's okay."

"Sometimes . . . most times . . . actually, lately, *all* the time, I don't know my lovers. Sometimes I don't even know their names. Some judges won't let a parent like that keep a child. And it's very difficult during the month I have him. I love the kid, Morgan, but maybe I really *am* an unfit mother. I get baby-sitters so I can go out and get my rocks off." Then it was as if something in her neck had snapped, and her head hung over the table, her shoulders shook with sobbing. Morgan took her hand, stroked her arm with his fingertips, smiled at her when she finally looked up again. "Thanks for listening. I'm really sorry," she'd said, wiping her face with a napkin.

"Absolutely nothing to apologize for."

He'd kept a tight arm around her as they went to her car. It felt as if she was made of tiny cat bones, so unlike the strength of Renee's muscled body. Less and less often he pictured himself fucking Renee while she and Dani kissed and fingered each other—perhaps that would be *part* of it, perhaps not—but it would be enough for him just to have them making love to each other on top of him

. . . to hear Renee's fulfilled cries, her nails digging into *his* flesh while finally knowing the love of the woman she'd longed for; to stroke the back of Dani's hair and see her shy, half-closed eyelids as her tongue flicked at Renee's clit; to see two different hands cupping Renee's round breasts, Dani's slender fingers caressing one nipple and his own on the other.

"Probably some screwed-up thing in her mind only allows her to satisfy her desire for women in an anonymous way," Renee said slowly, running her finger around the rim of her wine glass, still focusing her eyes there. "So she goes to these parties where you might not even see the face of the woman you're eating or the one eating you." She looked up, her radiant face illuminated by a street-light that leaked into the dark room through a crack in the curtains. It was all he could do not to lean over and kiss her. "She needs our support, Morgan, to show her she can find all the sensual things she craves, *plus* commitment, love, friendship, devotion, all that stuff. To show her the fallacy in her choice of a life where friends are never lovers and lovers are merely a source of physical gratification during a faceless orgy followed by shame. To show her that a family isn't just mommy, daddy, and baby-makes-three."

"There are other families where three's just right," he said, grinning.

Renee blinked her eyes, then got up and walked to the stereo. "We need to think, Morgan, we need a plan."

A car went by and he listened to find out if the street was wet—perhaps soon rain would be pattering from the eaves into the ferns in the planter boxes outside. Why was he waiting for rain in the summer? "The three of us could go to dinner. I've already sort of hinted . . ."

With one finger in the dent on her upper lip, Renee studied a row of compact discs. "No . . . not quite right . . ." She selected a disc and put it into the stereo. Handel's *Water Music*. Maybe next she would get out her candles and place them around the room. "You're her friend now, and she trusts you, we can tell that from what happened tonight. Why can't you get yourself invited to go with her to a rave?"

"But if the point of this rave is anonymity, why would she want to take me along?"

"I don't think that'll be a problem. I think she's ready to have a nonanonymous relationship; that's why she opened up to you. Taking you along will be like a transitional gesture. Then I'll meet you in the parking lot and we'll appeal to her emotional needs and bring her back here for our own evening of . . . closeness. We'll try to get to her when she's balanced on the fence: Inside it's faceless, feelingless flesh. Outside it's . . . sincerity, loyalty, affection, concern, blah-blah-blah. She'll choose us, don't worry." She returned to the table for her wine but didn't sit. She held the glass up against her forehead, then against one cheek. The room wasn't warm, but Renee looked flushed. "You won't know where it is until you're on your way, so I'll follow you. How soon do you think you can do it? We have to get this thing going because I'm going to Baltimore in a few weeks."

"What's in Baltimore?"

"Oh . . . a lesson. A master class with Androv. He's almost retired, but maybe if he likes me, he'd want to do a program with me . . . I mean here, next season."

A shot of adrenaline cut through his guts. "Is there going to *be* a next season? Have you heard anything?"

"No. But we might find out something from Dani."

He'd put his forehead down on his hand, then pushed his fingers through his hair. No rain had started. Of course not. The only sound outside was someone going past with a boom box, bouncing a basketball. "Have you ever thought about starting a dance school, Renee? Isn't that what dancers do when the end of the line is visible up ahead?" He bit his lower lip to stop his jaw from quivering. "I never thought about doing it by myself, but it might be fun in a partnership, wouldn't it?"

"Let's talk about this some other time, I need to do my routine." She stopped *Water Music* in the middle and put on one of the tapes she normally exercised to. Morgan finished his wine, watching her, then finished another glass, closing his eyes, feeling how his body would fit next to hers as she went through her positions, finding each one with the same grace and power, matching her perfectly.

My mood wasn't good to start with. The police dog training facility was on the same property as the firing range. I had no idea the popping of pistols would make a difference to Jack—he'd been entirely sound-proofed as a puppy—but it took me fifteen minutes to get him to stop trying to back out of his collar. I got his burlap sleeve and encouraged him to play an aggressive tug-of-war so that the adrenaline of his prey drive would overcome the stress, but he was still rolling his eyes toward the firing range. Someday he would have to function with courage and stability when a gun was fired during his Schutzhund tests. My voice was happy and full of encouragement, but I wanted to kick him in the balls for being afraid.

The agitator wouldn't be available until noon, but I wanted Fanny there an hour early and felt myself tighten even more when Fanny's car was followed into the lot by that old man boyfriend of hers. I just turned my back, resumed the tug-of-war contest with Jack, but *he* kept letting go of the sleeve and looking around. At least when I shook the sleeve and dragged it on the ground, he did focus again and attack it. But maybe Jack was sensing my impatience—my anxiety *could* heighten his, a dog can smell human chemical changes—so I stopped and scratched his chest, waiting for Fanny's husky to come panting and huffing across the grass, choking herself on her collar and dragging Fanny along. When I finally looked up again, Scott was setting up a beach chair on the edge of the training field. Fanny was still over there, holding her husky's lead with both hands, her body braced to keep the dog from jerking her off balance. At least *one* of them wanted to work.

At last Fanny left the old man and headed toward me, dropping the lead so her dog could run full tilt. The husky sped past me, made a wide turn, streaked past again, made a circle around Scott's beach chair, then returned to leap first against Fanny's back, knocking her to her knees, then bounced into my face. "She knows she's gonna have some fun today," I said.

Fanny looked up from where she was still kneeling. "Maybe today's not a good day for this."

"*Why?*" I grabbed her dog's lead and put her into a sit beside Jack. One of the dogs was making a high squeaky sound, but it wasn't the husky. She sat panting with smiling eyes. The husky was so stable, I think *she* was pissing me off even more. "Look, I've got enough on my hands with him in adolescence and getting sound sensitive. I

can't take another of your emotional, whiny days. Let's get to work."
Jack was sitting with one foot raised, the sound coming from *his*
throat, and he looked toward the firing range. The gun noise was
really no more than balloons popping at a birthday party across the
park. I grabbed his head with both hands, holding the skin on his
cheeks, jerked his face back around, and gave him a sharp *"No."*

"Was that the right thing to do?" Fanny asked.

"Probably not."

"Then maybe neither of us should be doing this today."

Maybe I shouldn't've let her have it like I did. "And when *would*
be the right day? As far as I can tell, you'll *always* be moping over
that asshole for one reason or another."

The fronds in a row of palm trees began to rattle as a breeze
passed through. So Jack turned in *that* direction. I stomped my foot
to make him look at *me*. I was all he was supposed to be concerned
about. His ears were slicked back on his head. A group of men in
police T-shirts began jogging around the training field.

"Scott's leaving day after tomorrow." Fanny's voice was thin and
high.

"God, this is pathetic."

"I know. I'm sorry. Okay, what'm I supposed to do?"

"I don't know," I said, "maybe I'm too mad to work now."

Someone was growling. I glared at Jack—his ears up again, his
mouth pursed, his eyes following the jogging policemen rounding
the near end of the field. Then his eyes caught and focused on
another figure walking toward us. The husky's fox brush tail was
waving. I stopped Jack's growl with a hand around his muzzle,
quick jerk of his head, and *"Quiet."*

A spray of accelerated popping erupted from the shooting range.
Scott stopped beside Fanny, reached past her to scratch the grinning
husky under her chin, and asked, "When's this show gonna start?
The crowd's getting restless."

Fanny laughed. The jogging policemen's footsteps began crunching as they hit a stretch of gravel.

"Why?" By that time I couldn't stop myself—he was ruining
*every*thing. "In a hurry to be off to see America with the little *wife?*"

"Doreen!" It *almost* sounded like Fanny was still laughing. She
took his hand, but he pried her fingers off with his thumb.

"Not that I'm required to explain anything to you," he said, "but Fanny and I have talked this all out—"

God, he was so *egocentric!* "Bullshit. She's a goddamn zombie, we can't accomplish *anything* because of you—just what're you *doing*, is it more *exciting* to stay married and have Fanny on the side, is *that* it?"

"This is really none of your business. I guess I shouldn't've come here today."

"You shouldn't've come around this year." I heard Jack start to growl again, his eyes rolling toward the popcorn sound of the firing range. Then his head twisted to follow the joggers. "Hold them," I said, and Fanny moved between the dogs, slipped her hands into their collars.

"Look," he said, "not that it'll make any difference to you, but sometimes you can't just barge ahead and do things exactly the way you want. Fanny understands what I'm doing—"

"Oh, *please.*" I crossed my arms. "Just shit or get off the pot, I can't believe your gall—can't do things the way you *want?* Bullshit, you've got *everything* you could want. A wife on one side, a good lay on the other. Do you ever think about *anyone* else?"

"Doreen." When Fanny spoke, her voice low, I could tell that my voice had nearly been a screech. I didn't care.

"God, Fanny, it's *time* to scream, isn't it? Why aren't *you* screaming and running away from *him* as fast as you can?"

"Just butt out, okay?" He stepped forward. *Stupid.*

"I wish I could. I'd give anything to not have to deal with this shit. But here we are, trying to put some titles on this dog, and *you* come along—lying, lying, lying—and she can't concentrate for five stinking minutes."

"I haven't lied to her."

I whirled toward Fanny. "How do you know he *hasn't?*" Both dogs were standing up. Jack's ears level with his eyes, sticking out on either side of his head. I saw him, but lost it—she made me *blind.* "I'm sick of this, I'm just going to work my dog, just get *out* of here, you make me sick!" I was still screaming.

"Wait, calm down."

"I don't want to calm down, I just want you to stop this bullshit, leave us alone, leave *me* alone!" I caught a glimpse of him reaching for my arm, so I jerked out of range and raised my fist up as though to hit him. He flinched back. Brainless Fanny said, "Hey, you two," stepped forward to get between us—*letting go of the dogs.* One of the jogging policemen was wearing a radio that popped, crackled, then a metallic voice and garbled clanging words. Then chaos. I screamed *"No"* as Jack lunged. Fanny was holding Scott's arm. Jack went right past her toward his head. At the same time the husky, who'd circled around and was behind Scott, leapt at Fanny and pushed her back into me. It seemed thousands of people were screeching *"No, no, no."* But it wasn't me, I was gasping for air on the ground after Fanny's elbow had pushed into my gut. It sounded like a hurricane had begun roaring. Then I could hear Fanny yelling *"Help, help,"* and gravel spraying, footsteps approaching, the continuing sound of guns firing in the distance.

I opened my eyes, still on my back, flailed one arm out and grabbed one of Jack's hind legs. Or it might've been the husky's. One dog was on top of the other and Fanny tangled somehow with them. Scott was there, too, but I couldn't see *any* of him, just suddenly, clearly, as though the confusion and thunder was abruptly silent and the whirlwind of motion had frozen, I saw Fanny's arm snaking out, her hand grabbing onto Jack's testicles. It seemed her hand was there forever, the tendons in her wrist standing out, her arm beginning to tremble. Then the loud scream, and Fanny panting "I got him, I got him." On her knees, still holding his balls, pushing him from behind as he whipped his head back and forth, shrieking, until she and Jack were eight or ten feet away from the crowd of men around Scott. I got to my feet, caught the husky, but before I could get over to take Jack's collar, one of the policemen was there slapping a leather muzzle over his head. Fanny was standing up, just letting him take my dog, leaving to break back into the crowd around her pathetic boyfriend. I heard her say, "Oh, my god." But I was already heading the opposite direction, toward my dog.

"I'll take him." My voice was hoarse.

"Sorry, ma'am, we're going to have to confiscate this animal."

I said, "He's *mine,* I can take him. I'm a trainer."

"Nobody's taking him. He'll be brought to animal control. Could I have your name, please? Is this animal registered?"

It finally dawned on me what the bastard was saying. "Wait! You can't! It wasn't his fault!"

Suddenly Fanny was back beside me. I glanced over my shoulder. Scott was walking toward a police car with a T-shirt wadded up against his head. A bare-chested cop in shorts was helping to hold the T-shirt, another was opening the car door. Fanny said, "His ear's torn and his shoulder's all bit up." There was a streak of blood on the front of Fanny's shirt.

I grabbed her elbow. "Did you get a close look—was it a full bite? Dogs that bite full aren't doing it out of stress or fear, so they're *not* dangerous. We must've given Jack some kind of pursuit signal by *mistake—*"

Another cop had come over wearing huge leather gloves up to his elbows. He took Jack's lead and started to leave. Stupid Jack followed like a docile pony.

Did they expect me to go along with it calmly too? "*Wait, no!*"

The cop with the radio stepped in front of me. "We'll need your name, ma'am."

I don't know why I caved. "*No, no, NO.*" I turned—I don't remember the last time I'd cried. Hot tears coming from my eyes felt like they might be blood staining *my* shirt too. I took about two steps, stumbled, dropped to the ground, plugged my ears, but the silence was still a roar. I knew they'd get my name from spineless Fanny. I knew I should be fighting, should be using my fingernails and teeth to get Jack away from the cop who was leading him away, should be slapping a hand over Fanny's feeble traitorous mouth, should be doing *something.* So now who should be kicked in the balls for lack of heart? How long had I been coaxing and half carrying *her* through each training session—just who was it visualizing a mission, conceiving a strategy, designing the method, *keeping my head uncluttered by this kind of hysterical shit?* Then one huge lapse— all because you're forced to deal with someone *else's* freakish weakness . . . and *I* lost *everything.*

In the next breeze that rattled the palm fronds, I could actually hear a wind chime attached to the building beside the firing range. I could hear car doors slamming. I could hear the slow deep breathing of a resting animal.

By the time I felt Fanny's hand on my back, raised my head, and sat up, everyone was gone. The husky was stretched out like a lioness in the sun about six feet away, head up but eyes closed. The sound of the popping guns came back, as though it had stopped for a while. Fanny said, "Are you okay now? I've got to get to the hospital for Scott."

"What?" I stared. Wasn't she *un*believable? "Oh, of *course* that would be the first thing out of your mouth. I've just lost *everything*, and you're worried about some man."

"Scott almost lost most of his ear."

"*Shut up!* Scott Scott Scott . . . I've lost everything, it's all falling apart, all because *you* can't survive without some husband or boyfriend you can moan about after he shits all over you."

Fanny's face was purplish. She stepped backwards as I got to my feet. "What's the matter with you?"

Jeez, like everything only happened to *her*. "God, Fanny, you gave them my *name*, all they have to do is look in their computer and see Jack has two other bites—they'll kill him, I've been set back an entire year. All because you're dragging some married guy around everywhere you go. Why do *I* have to pay for *your* stupidity?"

"He's not—" Fanny's voice broke and she turned, went to her dog, squatted, holding the dog's ears, one in each hand, rubbing the insides with her thumbs. She looked back at me.

I'd thought I was completely drained, but I guess not. "Oh, god," my voice rose almost to a scream again, "*stop it*, just *stop* it."

"You can use Lacy for another breeding," Fanny choked, her chest starting to jerk, her nose running.

"That won't make up for my lost time. I should sue you, both of you—Jack was the foundation of my kennel. I can't believe I just let them take my dog away."

"What else could you do?"

"That's *your* typically feeble way of handling anything." I crossed my arms and stared at the firing range, my eyes burning but now dry, my pulse heavy but not in my stomach. Fanny crouched, clutching her guts, wiping her eyes on her sleeves. What a jellyfish. "I don't let anything stand in my way," I said. I don't know where it came from, or came *back* from, but finally I kept my voice cold and steady. "Especially not emotional shit. I can sue you *and* your idiotic boyfriend. What was he doing here? He showed up where he didn't belong and then didn't stay put where he should've. I'll sue him for loss of future income, and it doesn't matter to me how *you* feel or if it sends him right back to his wife—I don't care."

Fanny rocked forward, let her knees hit the ground, held the husky around the neck and spoke, sobbing, into her fur, "Just leave him alone. Maybe he should sue *you.*"

"What'll he get from me? I just lost everything. Let him try. *I* deserve some kind of compensation. You can't just come out here, get my dog killed, and then go on with your goddamn affair as though nothing happened."

"What do you want me to do?" Fanny wailed. The husky licked her ear, got up, and stretched.

I took a deep breath. I didn't know I would say it, but I had a weird feeling of control. "Give me your dog and I'll be glad to be rid of both of you forever."

"For how long? She's not due in season again until—"

I stayed rational and level. "I don't want to *borrow* her. I don't want to have to deal with you or him or this kind of emotional mess again. Give me the dog, and we'll forget everything."

"How can I give away my dog?"

"You gave away *mine* easy enough." Fair's fair, right?

Fanny's fists were holding handfuls of her dog's skin and fur, but the bitch just sat there, panting gently, her eyes on a few blackbirds grazing in the grass several yards away. Her ears didn't even swivel in the direction of the firing range. Fanny looked like she had a wrinkled-up monkey face, huddled over her magnificent dog, shaking, wheezing, sniffling.

"It's your choice," I said. "The dog or . . ." The palm fronds rattled again, and the husky lifted her nose into the new breeze for a taste. "What's it going to be, Fanny, d'you want me to sue your boyfriend? D'you want it in writing, that I promise I won't seek legal compensation in exchange for you giving me the dog?"

Fanny lifted her head, tears streaming on her cheeks, heaving like she couldn't breathe, her lips dark and swollen as though she'd been beat up. "Let me have her tonight to say good-bye," she finally managed to say.

"I didn't get to say good-bye to Jack." I took the lead, and she didn't fight it. Her arms tightened around the dog, her face went back down into the dog's fur. I waited a second, then began to walk away, still holding the lead. The husky followed, disentangling herself from Fanny's arms. Fanny just sort of disintegrated. As the dog stepped free of Fanny's body, I took one glance over my shoulder— saw Fanny collapse on the grass where the dog had been supporting her weight.

The hospital smell was making him light headed. He knew he hadn't lost enough blood to be dizzy. Maybe it was the painkiller. The table he was lying on was narrow, with wheels and crinkly tissue paper. They'd taken away his shirt and put a sheet over him. The whole left side of his upper body still throbbed dully in the background of the painkiller. "It must feel like you've been beaten with a baseball bat," the doctor had said. The left side of his head, where his ear was sewn back together, was numb. A large padded dressing, like half a headset, was taped to the side of his head. The bloody shirt with the police insignia on the front was still wadded underneath the gurney.

Even with one ear, the noise around him was clearly specific. Through the quiet din—the hum of a nurse's voice speaking to another patient on the other side of the curtain, the single intercom bell before someone was paged, the distant tinkle of phones, water splashing in a sink, clink of glass containers on a cart rolling past, static of the paramedic band radio—he was listening for either the sound of heels on the hard floor or the patter of sneakers and the light squeak of rubber on linoleum. Every time the automatic doors in the hall burst apart and rolled open, his breath stuck, his ears pricked, but his heartbeat drowned out any noise at all for a few hot seconds.

But instead of footsteps, he heard Fanny saying his name out in the hall. She barely moved the curtain, slipped inside, touched his forehead with her fingertips, and his whole body jumped. "Hi," she whispered, "they sure fixed you up fast."

"Seems like forever since I got here. I've lost track of time."

"A lot more happened . . . since you got here."

One of her hands was still gently touching his hair, the other, he noticed, was rigidly holding a handful of the sheet that was covering him. "Tell me later," he said.

"It's important. Can't you listen for a second? Did they give you something?"

"Yeah. The doctor needs to talk to you. He has to make a report when he treats a dog bite. I didn't know Doreen's last name."

"I already told the cops."

"But the doctor needs to know. Then you can go on home, and I'll call you later."

"How'll you get home? What about your car?"

A nurse ripped and wadded the tissue from the empty gurney on his other side. Someone was stacking metal charts. In a moment of relative quiet, he smiled, "Look at you—grass in your hair, bloody shirt, dirt on your nose." Her face as pale as he'd ever seen it, except for the streak of mud alongside her nose. Her lips almost white. "People will think a cute little homeless waif has come to see me," he said, still smiling. "Please, don't wait for me. I'll call when I get home."

She stared at him. Took her fingers out of his hair and wiped at the side of her nose with the back of her wrist, but the dirt was on the other side. Her other hand was still holding the sheet, tangled tight in a fist. "Don't you want me to take you home?" she asked. "I need to tell you what *happened* . . ."

He put his hand on her arm, ran his fingers down to her fist, and loosened it. "Your arms are so strong, must be from training that big dog of yours." Her eyes seemed to darken. She grabbed his hand with both of hers, her nails cutting into his skin, took a breath, and opened her mouth to say something, but he said, "Fanny, you've got to go. They called Suzanne when I first got here, and she's on her way. Her name's still on my insurance card. I don't want her to find you here."

Before Fanny dropped his hand, somebody's heels clicked all the way down the hall toward the emergency room. The sheet was suddenly clammy with sweat, his wounds all throbbing quicker, but the heels went on past the ER. Then Fanny turned and left, once again ducking around the curtain without moving it.

"I'll call you," he said after her. He couldn't hear footsteps. The automatic door opened and shut.

But he couldn't call that night because Suzanne insisted on taking him to the house instead of his apartment, stopping on the way to pick up Sadie. The next day, they went together to get his car from the police facility and deliver Sadie to the kennel. The rest of the afternoon and into the night he stayed in his apartment, taking pills for the searing pain in his ear and the bruises that were locking his upper body into a stiffness like rigor mortis, trying Fanny's number every fifteen minutes. But he only got her answering machine. At first he left messages. Imagining her in the room listening to his call, he spoke to the machine, asking her to please pick up the phone. The last several dozen calls, he hung up when the machine clicked on.

He tried again at six-thirty in the morning, but the phone rang and rang; no machine ever answered.

He had to drive with one hand. At least the arm that shifted gears was not on the side of his body that felt as if it had been hit by a train. At seven, he arrived at the house to pick up Suzanne, packed her suitcases into the car, and headed northeast toward Yellowstone.

CHAPTER **8**

Alpha Bitch

She'd shortened her black waitress skirt several inches and found three-inch black heels at a discount shoe store. From a sweater outlet, she'd bought a short loose knit top with a wide neck so the sweater rode off one shoulder. It was white, so she was still in correct uniform for the jobs Scott's business would do while he was away. They were mostly small-convention cocktail buffet parties where there would always be those men—pausing in the doorway to attach their name tag, then fixing a plate and getting a drink— who stood alone, eating while they surveyed the room full of old acquaintances, watching the others in loud knots of three or four who were laughing and gesturing and calling out first names to other old pals they'd met here a year ago. Once Fanny had pointed out one of these men to Scott. "Poor guy, he probably got all excited about coming to this convention—he probably read in a brochure about the big welcome party and the dinner reception and the farewell bash where everyone is everyone else's best friend, but when he gets here and comes to the first party, he doesn't know anyone and no one talks to him."

Scott had said, "He probably has a boss who forced him to come and he's just here getting a free meal."

"No, look, I think he bought a new suit just for this, it's so sad!"

"Okay," Scott had smiled and raised an eyebrow. "So why don't you go over and personally offer him a refill and make his day?"

Since she'd left Scott in the chilly glaring light of the hospital emergency room—driving with her teeth clenched and eyes fixed, expecting at any minute that a siren would erupt from her head, blaring out her plugged ears—she'd made their day for at least three guys to whom no one had spoken a word or offered a handshake at three or more identical banquets.

Her ears had never popped, tightening daily as though from altitude, her voice sounding as if it was coming from another direction. The feel of nylons unrolling up her legs, the stroke of makeup brush on her face, the touch of a hand on her skin actually felt like it was happening on some layer of gristle three feet away from where she actually was.

She put on black eye shadow with some red highlight up near her eyebrows, black mascara, lightened her hair with lemon juice, and used a hair drier to form a windblown style, back from her ears and up off her face, but with enough gel that no breeze could change it. It would get changed later, though, in a hotel room, either when the lonely guy put his hands in her hair to pull her head faster and harder onto his cock, or afterwards in the shower.

She slept all afternoon with the phone turned off, although she'd given none of them her phone number.

While Suzanne read aloud from tour books, Scott did all the driving. He'd wanted to see the fossil forest on Specimen Ridge but said nothing when Suzanne directed him to follow the rest of the traffic toward the Geyser Basins. Scott had brought a case of cassettes and would push one in as soon as she finished reading whatever passage she was on. Before leaving, he'd removed any tapes he'd gotten from Fanny. Once, during the middle of a song, Suzanne put her hand on his arm and exclaimed, "I forgot we had this one!" He turned to stare at her, and she took her hand away. She'd brought a few paperback novels with flowery covers and raised gilt letters that kept her occupied for fairly long stretches. His bandaged ear was on the far side of his head from her, so he couldn't say *Don't bother trying to have a conversation because I can't hear you.* Not once but *twice* she'd closed her book, looked up, and started a sentence with, "When we get back we ought to—" The first time, the car had careened slightly in its lane for a split second. The rest of the sentence had been something like "—reorganize the garage," or "—get the car's windows tinted." The other time it had been, "—invite the Drakes over to see the videotape."

She'd borrowed a video camera from a neighbor. She kept offering it to him, but he didn't want to use it. He kept seeing men his age with legs scraped free of hair by years of elastic socks, big bellies in pink-and-yellow plaid sport shirts or t-shirts from Disneyland or Sea World, sweatpants with the name of some college they'd never gone to written on the leg, baseball caps and a little tail of gray hair hanging down their necks, wives with big earrings in sunglasses and scarves, on their first vacation alone since the kids had left, as one had announced to a gift shop cashier. And all of them had video cameras. Whenever Suzanne turned on her camera, Scott moved away. But worse than the idea of himself standing in a crowd behind a rail with a video camera, worse than the possibility of a shaky tape showing him in *his* plaid sport shirt reading the brass inscription on some monument . . . worse yet was the prospect of receiving guests in his house for a homey evening of vacation videos. It wasn't the first time the vision had occurred to him—he'd packed, then *un*packed, his own 35-mm camera. So he was able to appreciate the hilarity at Old Faithful as the geyser began its appearance with a roar of water like a river turned upright—the natural sounds of spray and hiss, jays complaining in nearby trees, rustle of squirrels, overpowered by the clicking of hundreds of cameras, like the sounds in a Swiss clock store. He'd turned to share his smile of disgust, but it wasn't Fanny in her wrinkled boy's swim trunks and surgeon's shirt and tumbleweed hair beside him.

That's why he was at the pay phone by the ice machine at the Old Faithful Inn, dialing her number. Was there a graceful way to insert into a hasty conversation—with the ice machine rumbling in the background—that so far the motel rooms always had two beds and without exception he was automatically selecting one and Suzanne the other? But it was too much to say into an answering machine, so after her low, fuzzy voice finished the instructions, after the long beep, he quietly replaced the receiver.

When Morgan was in college, before he met Fanny, he and two friends had driven twenty-four hours to Denver, slept for two hours at dawn in the car behind a Denny's, went into the restaurant for coffee—all they could afford—changed into leotards in the restroom, then bluffed their way past the security guard to spend an entire morning rehearsal backstage among the dancers of Joffrey's touring troupe. The cramped sleep in the car had been the sweetest, deepest he could remember. The coffee that morning pungently mellow. His body felt quick and sharp, tightly strung yet lithe. The fall air tingled, smelled faintly of smoke, car horns in front of the theater were productive and optimistic. He probably could've flapped his arms and flown.

In almost two decades, he had never again approached anything like that feeling, and it had taken almost two decades to realize it. But it was close—reachable, touchable—as he stepped up to Dani's apartment building, seeing Renee's headlights blink off behind him down the block. The evening air was fresh and quenching on his face and neck. His new jeans felt snug. A jasmine vine was blooming on a trellis above the mailboxes. Even the dull ache in his knee was almost nostalgic.

Dani came out immediately, and they got into her car. "I didn't know what to wear," she said, bending to start the engine.

"You're the one who's gone to these things before!"

"But alone. And for a different reason. I mean . . . I never heard of anyone going on a kind-of *date*. Usually I . . . I want to meet someone there, so I might . . . I don't know, wear really wild make-up that'll light up under black lights or spike my hair with glitter in the gel, put on fake fluorescent tattoos . . . this is embarrassing." Dani's jeans had big holes in both knees, a thick white fray of threads around each hole. Her blouse was a purple peasant style with puffed sleeves and an elastic neck, hanging like a smock.

He said, "Do you . . . are you supposed to have clothes that . . . well, that you can get rid of easily?"

Dani laughed. "I hate this blouse. My mother gave me this for Christmas. I didn't want to wear anything too dykey, didn't want to call attention to myself that way tonight. See, usually you let out another part of yourself. It's a real part of you, but not what even *you* would recognize as yourself. It's like everything is anonymous, the old-fashioned masked ball where no one is supposed to know who they're dancing with. It's kind of strange that you would encourage me to go . . . or *not* encourage me *not* to."

"I'm not standing in judgment of your life." He checked quickly over his shoulder to see if Renee was still following, but he couldn't pick out her headlights from the string of cars behind them on the city street. "But it seems," he went on, "you're looking for an excuse to stop going, or for someone to talk you out of it."

"Maybe I am." She looked at him, her dark hair in smooth bangs across her brow, her face lit by street lights, her eyes soft but clear. "I really appreciate this, Morgan."

She parked in front of a vegetarian restaurant with sidewalk tables. "Just a sec."

While Dani was inside, Morgan looked again for Renee, saw her car double-parked at the end of the block. She eased forward, pulled off the street into a bus stop, still idling. She was going to say that she'd received an anonymous invitation and pretend it was pure fluke to run into them at the rave; she would say she was scared once she got there, but was relieved—to the point of crying—that she'd found people she knew. Then the three of them would go have dinner together somewhere, later coffee at Renee's place. Renee had promised to set all the candles out around the living room.

"It's the same place as last time." Dani jumped in and slammed her door in one motion. As she pulled out into traffic, Renee's car slipped out of the bus stop, several cars between them. "Hope you're not expecting a lot," Dani said. "It's mostly dancing. It's *all* dancing, actually. It's dark, just a lot of flashing black lights. No one asks anyone to dance, you just get out there and move. You can't see anyone unless they've got things that light up in the dark. You may start to hook up with someone, without saying anything. I've heard rumors about orgies, couples screwing all around the edge of the dance floor, even fucking upright while they dance, but I've never seen anything like that. I'm talking so much. I must be nervous."

They got on the freeway. Morgan had to force himself to *not* keep checking for Renee's car behind them. Within a couple of minutes they were getting off again, driving on a new road between the dark, empty buildings of an unoccupied industrial park. Abruptly they came to one parking lot that was full. Dani drove along the back edge of the lot and stopped in a far corner, choosing the farthest possible space. Morgan couldn't tell which, among the few cars that came into the lot after Dani, was Renee's. When he got out of the car, he could hear crickets in the empty lot behind him, then slowly became aware of the low pulsating thud coming from the warehouse attached to the parking lot. He could see people moving among the cars, going toward the warehouse, but they were all too far away to look like anything more than dark shapes, head and body and legs.

Morgan and Dani shoved their hands in their pockets as they began walking through the parking lot, around cars, toward the warehouse. Sometimes they went on either side of a car, winding on separate paths in the same direction.

"Oh, my god." Dani stopped. Morgan squeezed between two cars and came up behind her, but Dani didn't turn around. "What's *she* doing here?"

"Who?"

"Who do you *think*. She must've *followed* us! Morgan—did you tell her?"

Over Dani's shoulder, Morgan could see Renee locking her car. If she hadn't been under a light post, she might've been invisible—she was wearing a black leotard and black tights, a dark green sleeveless miniskirt dress, and black men's work shoes. Her hair was slicked to her head like Fred Astaire's.

Dani whipped around to face him. "You bastard, Morgan, why—"

"I— Maybe she got her own invitation."

"Yeah, what a *coincidence*. I'm not stupid. You've been talking about her like she's your guru. You *had* to have her along, didn't you, you can't do anything without her watching over you. She must have you so bamboozled—"

"Hi, you two, small world." Renee was approaching from the side, as though she'd walked away from the building instead of toward it, then circled back.

"You absolute bitch," Dani said, her voice losing all inflection.

Renee's simple buoyant expression didn't melt away, it snapped, as though a switch was thrown. Her smile, her big glowing eyes were gone in a split second.

"Dani." He put a hand on her arm, but Dani shook him off so violently her ring scratched his inner elbow, drawing blood.

"God, I could've expected it of *her*. But you, Morgan? She can hardly keep her two faces a secret, but you must *really* be sly to've made this much of a sucker of me."

"What're you talking about?" He caught his breath, glancing at Renee. Her arms were folded, her weight all on one leg, her lip curled, but it wasn't a smile.

"What else can you expect," Renee said. "She has a kid, but here she is at some warehouse to sniff out her next tongue-fuck. Suppose your ex finds out about this?"

"You're not going to get anything by fucking with my life, bitch," Dani sneered. "It won't get you any *more* under-the-table special treatment than you've already slithered in and demanded. What is this, punishment because I wouldn't lick between your toes like everyone else?"

"Wait," Morgan begged, "what're you talking about? Dani, I swear, we wanted to help you, Renee said—"

"Is *that* what she said?"

"Don't be so sappy, Morgan." Renee's tone was acid. "Shit, some people—"

"God, *Morgan,*" Dani's mouth showed her teeth as though grinning, but there was no smile in her voice, "you either deserve an Academy Award or you're the world's biggest dumb shit. I had good reason for loathing her, just out of support for the rest of you dumb fucks—I could never understand why *you* thought her shit didn't stink."

"I don't know what you're talking about." His throat hurt as though he'd been screaming.

Someone's headlights flashed before they killed their engine. A car alarm sounded, then was snuffed out quickly. Renee was muttering, "God, what am I doing, wasting my time with these people?" while Dani said, "Well, I sure want to thank you for all your understanding and kindness, Morgan, you're a great pal."

He looked back and forth. Dani had spit in the corner of her mouth. Renee's eyes bulged more than usual, her nostrils flared. Dani's jaw flexed. Then Renee glanced at him. "Don't even bother listening."

"*Sit up, fido,*" Dani chanted, "*roll over, play dead.* She trained you pretty well. Were you equipped with a two-way radio in your collar or did you just remember everything I said and bring it back to her with your tail wagging? What was your reward gonna be—did she promise you her little chicken ass?"

"She's full of delusionary bullshit," Renee said. "She probably takes god-knows-what before coming to these things and is already out-of-her-mind high—"

"You *wish*—you'd've sucked me dry every night for the rest of my life if I'd've agreed to help you get a contract when no one else is going to get one. You'd've grown a dick and fucked my ass if I—"

"*What?*" his voice cracked, he had one hand over his mouth because it felt as if instead of words coming out, he might puke. "Jesus Christ, Dani, what're you talking about?"

"She's crazy," Renee said, "she thinks she's some big shit insider, but she's a minimum wage clerk, what can *she* know?"

"I know a slimeball when I see one!" Dani swung an arm as she spoke, but Morgan caught her wrist before she hit anything. Renee flinched, her hands in front of her eyes, turned to leave, but he grabbed her arm too. Her wad of keys clanged onto the pavement.

Dani's laugh sounded like startled geese. "I don't care what she says, her pathetic attempt at extorting me couldn't have gotten her anything she hasn't *already* weaseled out of *them.*"

He raised both hands, still shackling their wrists, shook their arms, shouted, "What's with you two!"

The two women were talking at the same time. "I don't need this," Renee's voice rose. "Why should I waste time with an office gofer and a washed-up wannabe?"

"Yeah?" Dani's voice pushed through. "And she *also* isn't going to waste time striking with the rest of you—she made sure *her* inflated paycheck will keep rolling on in. Even when the company disbands and reorganizes under a different name, who d'you think will be their first contracted star, who d'you think will be deciding when and with whom she performs, long after your picket line peters out and you're all flipping hamburgers?—"

"And you're above working to make your life better and protecting yourself?" Renee's voice by this time nearly a scream.

"Not above protecting myself from *you*, that's for sure."

Morgan released their arms, felt himself sway. Then found his back braced against a parked car. The thumping warehouse and other people's faraway chattering laughter seemed louder than the voices and panting and sounds of scuffling right in front of him. As if he was a doll with a broken neck, he felt his head tip back and his helpless, painted-open eyes stare at the stars while Renee grabbed a handful of Dani's shirt, Dani a handful of Renee's hair, and Renee's open palm batted at Dani's face. The hard soles of Renee's shoes scraped on the sandy parking lot. Dani said *Fuck you,* crying. The peasant blouse made a harsh ripping sound. Renee spit at Dani and turned to leave. Dani pushed her. Renee cried out once when her knees and palms hit the pavement. Dani kicked at her but missed. Her shoe boomed against a car. Then she was gone, and Renee was gone soon after, muttering, *Have a nice life* and picking up her keys, which jangled like a musician dropping a cymbal during a delicate frozen passage on stage. Morgan had his hands over his ears, his back slid down the car he was leaning against, his butt hit the ground.

––––––––––

It started with the very first one. When the guy came back from getting rid of his rubber in the bathroom, Fanny was still in bed, covered in the blankets and curled on her side. She said, "Aren't you going to offer me money, don't I seem like a whore to you?"

"Not for a second," the guy said.

"Why not?" she'd asked.

"I think whores usually want to leave right away."

"Maybe they have to get home to their dogs."

"I don't think whores have dogs."

"I don't either."

"So what made you think of dogs?"

"Well, for a second I thought I should get going because she would need to be let outside or fed, because if she's cooped up too long she'll chew something to a pulp. But . . . then I remembered . . ." She realized she was speaking in a monotone. She hadn't done that when she'd offered to freshen his drink in the banquet room. "Actually, I never *forgot* that Lacy's not there anymore, but, you know, I had to say it somehow."

"I'll buy you a puppy if you want," the guy had said.

Fanny laughed. "I wonder how many people will say that if I tell them I miss my dog. If I tell you I lost my boyfriend, would you offer to buy me a baby?"

"Did she die or is she just lost? Maybe she'll come back."

"She's not lost. She's not dead." She lay on her stomach and bit a fingernail. "Neither is he."

She'd thought, *What am I doing?* But she hadn't answered the question by the time she got ready to go out to the next job the next night. She could've asked herself again, that second night, when *she* supplied the condom, when she ripped open the foil package, deftly pressed her thumbnail into the center to put an invisible slice in the stretched rubber before unfurling it onto the erect guy.

None of them ever seemed to notice they wore a split condom. But every time she said she missed her dog, the guy offered to buy her a puppy.

Down the street from Renee's apartment, at a twenty-four-hour coffee shop, Morgan waited through the rest of the night with sleepless old people, taxi drivers, policemen, and students; then through the morning rush—moving from his booth to a stool at the counter when two men in suits needed a table for their briefcases while they soaked up syrup with pancakes. Through the mini blinds and the lunch specials painted on the window, he saw Renee's car head down the street away from her place, so he paid for the donuts, pie, soup, bran muffin, and bottomless coffee that he'd stretched through the night and went back to her living room where his clothes still lay piled in one corner, the sheets on the futon untouched since he'd risen yesterday morning.

He clutched the doorknob, stumbling—as his toe caught on the doorjamb, a hot needle pushed into his knee and out the other side. He paused, eyes squeezed shut, blotched colors swimming in his head, until the needle was long gone. When he moved the knee gingerly, eyes still shut, there was no pain, no feeling at all, just gristle.

The sweet ache in his knee while he'd lived here had been *his* contribution to the fantasy loft where a dancer lived with her hundreds of eclectic tapes scattered and stacked on the floor in front of the stereo, candles, pillows, exercise mats, barres on the empty walls, juice and fresh vegetables always in the refrigerator. He stared at the splotch of sun that hit the floor in front of the mirror, where Renee stretched and warmed up in the mornings in a glare of backlighting, muting the colors of her leotard and leg warmers. This is where the pain in his knee had meant he was a living dancer. But the stale smell of sweaty clothes, the last lingering steam from Renee's morning shower were now the lavish but terminal atmosphere of a tomb. If he knew he couldn't stay here a minute longer, then his brief life as a dancer must also be over, so it seemed appropriately macabre that he should return to where he had been steadily decaying for so many years, with the person who had been slowly but certainly killing him.

A dancer with no time left could do nothing to bring it back. But the end must be far easier to face for someone who knew he'd used every heartbeat of the good fifteen or twenty years a dancer has to immerse himself, not only pushing for physical improvement, but the mental endurance as well, the esthetics, all the ethereal crap that had been swept further and further to the corners of the house he'd shared with Fanny.

He got off the bus with his pillowcase of clothes and started limping the two blocks to the house, closing his eyes and seeing the living room, the bedroom, hardly changed in fifteen years, a time capsule of college student housing in the 1970s. And its mummified decorator. The day after they'd moved in, he'd had a rehearsal, and when he'd returned to the house, the stacked boxes and bags and piles of junk in empty rooms had been transformed. She had been breathless and laughing, cheeks flushed, hair sweaty and slicked in a cowlick in front where she'd pressed a hand. And as he came in the door she leapt at him, throwing her arms around his neck. She'd gone back to a regular schedule of waitressing the next day, for a while still planning future designs for the house in her spare time, several different makeovers that she showed him, slowly flipping pages of a sketchbook, and probably as many others that she hadn't showed him, but he'd seen them once when he went into her study for a pencil. And he'd realized that not only had the house's floor plan changed in her drawings, but—since the one day she'd arranged the house with all their junk—her designing career had existed only in the flat air of her cramped office, on paper in a sketchbook, and behind her often expressionless eyes. That was after the break-in, after the weeks and weeks it seemed it took for her simply to put the bricks and boards back where they'd been. He didn't care how the rooms were arranged, how much clutter he had to wade through, if she had only filled the house with the vigor she'd had for just that one first day . . . god, what might've happened instead of this?

Perhaps it would've been a miracle more superhuman than Renee was capable of to pull his remains from Fanny's tar pit and breathe life into him. He'd realized Renee wasn't divine but, in fact, was fantastically alive. Even superior life forms could not help others escape extinction. Her own survival instinct, burning so ardently, couldn't help but consume his husk as fuel. She couldn't risk her future waiting for him. And his future was buried, like silt and ashes in the dust covering Fanny's unread books and brown plants and furniture made of old fruit crates in a house where the air never moved anymore.

He unlocked the door and stepped inside. It was a little after nine-thirty in the morning. The dog wasn't barking. No water was running. No radio playing. The room seemed larger. The curtains were gone; simple roll-down shades covered the glass. The stereo speakers sat side by side on the floor with the receiver and tape deck stacked on top. All the dead plants were gone. The sofa no longer piled with the old, worn, limp pillows. No bricks, no boards, no books, no magazines, no newspaper, no pencils, no glasses, no plates, no knickknacks, and nowhere to put them if there had been, except the coffee table—bare and empty, but dusty. He found the TV on the floor beside the bed, but that's all there was in the bedroom. The coatrack gone, the dresser shoved into the closet, the chair in the corner gone, likewise the curtains replaced by the simple white blinds of a flophouse. The oak bookcase headboard was empty except for a clock. The books and pottery figures and pencils and box of tissues and discarded earrings and water glasses gone from there as well. The bed was unmade. The other room, his exercise room, was totally empty, not even anything on the walls, just the barres still attached. As he went through the kitchen—the sink piled with dirty dishes, but the counter free of the appliances that used to live there—the front door opened and shut quietly, and he heard her footsteps, in heels, tap into the bedroom.

She was taking off her blouse, her back to him. He paused in the doorway. "Uh," he started, but said nothing more as she quickly pulled her blouse closed and turned to face him, holding the blouse like a robe to cover herself.

Her eyes leveled at him. "What're you doing here?"

"Where've *you* been all night?"

"Probably doing what you wish you'd been doing."

He felt his head jerk back involuntarily, as though she'd thrown water at him. "What's that supposed to mean?"

"That I gather you're here because you finally gave up trying to get Renee to let you boink her."

"You don't know anything. I went to stay with a friend, a colleague, but you wouldn't understand that. But I decided why should *I* move out and inconvenience myself? *You're* the one who went on a fucking spree in Tahoe . . . which, I see, obviously hasn't ended."

"If you want to reduce what happened to us to that, be my guest. I have to get some sleep before work today." She started to shut the door, but he lifted his bad leg and kept the door from closing with his foot. "Oh," her voice iced even more, "did you expect a warmer homecoming greeting?"

"I've *expected* nothing from you for years, since that's exactly what you've given."

"Fine. I'm going to bed."

"So'm I." He pushed past her and sat on the far side of the bed, kicked off his shoes, and got under the covers. The sheets had a familiar clammy feel, a familiar salty smell. He heard her undressing. Shoes clattered into the closet. She was breathing hard, maybe crying, or else muttering under her breath. Maybe whispering to the dog.

"Where's Lacy?" he said, without moving his head from the pillow or turning his face from the wall.

"I don't have her anymore."

He searched her voice for an emotion, but her words came flat and without pause. She hadn't been crying. He felt her ease herself onto her side of the bed, slowly push her legs under the covers, gently arrange the sheet and blanket around her shoulder.

"Good, no barking to wake me up," he said abruptly.

Hiking single file was obviously preferable to sitting side by side in the car, where the atmosphere of being sequestered in an air-conditioned bubble as you traveled through scenery might too strongly suggest they should be having some kind of conversation. Rain had kept them in their motel room near the Jackson Hole Airport until after noon. He'd taken a long bath, gone out to retrieve sweet rolls for breakfast, and made three separate trips to the motel office—picking up different brochures each time—to call Fanny. He wanted her to know where he was. He had to tell her he'd canceled the Badlands because it was too far—a whole day's drive out there, he couldn't go through with it—and that maybe the whole trip could be shortened if he could slice a little here, a little there. He wanted to feel himself be able to laugh and tell her it would've been *bad* driving that distance through the middle of nowhere trying to say god-knows-what to you-know-who, *bad,* and hear Fanny groan at the pun. But Fanny's machine wasn't even on. Somehow, if Fanny didn't know where he was—if she couldn't possibly know—he felt cut adrift to fend for himself. He knew he'd told her the itinerary more than once, but now that he thought about it, it was always one of those times when she had curled up close to him with her chin tucked so that all he could see was the top of her head. He'd also tried to give her a detailed written itinerary, but she'd put it into her back pocket without looking at it.

When the rain finally stopped and he suggested a hike to Lupine Meadows, Suzanne had changed into a pair of leather Swiss shorts with suspenders over a tight T-shirt, kneesocks with tasseled garters, and brand-new hiking boots. She looked as if she wouldn't be able to bend her waist in the leather shorts, which came up too far.

"Where'd you get those?" he asked carefully as she was getting into the car.

"I got them for you for Christmas three years ago, don't you remember?" she smiled. "I forgot—you don't remember anything. I'm lucky you remember my birthday . . . and our anniversary." Her car door thumped. Sudden silence seemed to boom up around them as the motel sounds of kids shouting, engines warming, housekeepers' carts, and the ice machine were snuffed by the insulated car.

Driving toward the trailhead, he could see the Tetons conveniently ahead and on his left. Sightseeing had been confined to straight ahead and out the window on his side of the car, as though a stiff neck or back brace had prevented him from turning his face past the midline to look out Suzanne's side of the car. But throughout the trip he had felt her sitting there, her spine against the back of the seat, feet on the floor, seat belt in place. This time he could even hear her breathing.

It still looked like spring in Lupine Meadows. With the late start, the drive, stops at the visitor's center and a historic site, then the hike into the meadow, it was almost four o'clock, but the clouds had broken apart. The meadow with its lake of wildflowers was more yellow than green. The Teton peaks in the background, the emerald sides of the hills rising from the meadow, the clumps of evergreens and exposed boulders in an ancient glacier's moraine were all magnified by the perfect crystalline light that only comes just before dusk after a storm.

"The dogs would love it," he said out loud, without thinking. Then his stomach flopped. But Suzanne was still twenty yards down the trail, taking a picture with her Instamatic. So he turned back to the view to imagine Sadie, crisply black and white, bounding reindeer-style through the grasses and flowers. When she would return to him, her huge feet would be sloppy muddy, her loose lips stretched in a crazy grin, panting puffs of hot fogged dog breath into his face as she stood against him, her stump a blur of wagging. If Fanny were there, she'd be wanting to sit in the flowers. Soon the two dogs would bolt away and resume a frenzied style of hunting and racing and wrestling at the same time. No other tourists on the trail this late in the day. He would kneel over Fanny and kiss the sunburn on her nose, then move to her eager mouth, unbutton her shirt, and feel the springlike chill of the lucid dusk harden her nipples. At some point the dogs would return, at first keen to join what they perceived to be a game, but quickly settling, panting drowsy-eyed into the sunset, so close he could feel the rhythm of their heaving rib cages, feel their fur against his leg as he slid into Fanny. The dogs would prick their ears and stop panting when she moaned.

"I don't think we should be out here after dark," Suzanne said. "I think we better start back."

It was dark by the time they were in the car. Neither had spoken since leaving the meadow. He found a Salt Lake City radio station that could be picked up at night.

"Something wrong, Scott?" She sounded as if she'd wanted to ask for days and had rehearsed the words in her mind too often.

"No. I guess I miss Sadie."

Without looking, he could feel Suzanne fold her arms across her chest and stare out the front windshield.

It was easier to do most of his sleeping when she wasn't home, but it was becoming more and more difficult to tell when that was going to be. He hadn't really spoken to Fanny since coming home, except a grunt as they passed going in and out of the bathroom. She didn't cook meals and didn't shop for groceries. He was careful not to eat anything he hadn't bought. He went out every day, walking not to the closest or the second-closest grocery store, forcing himself to use the knee, trying to feel the pain, killing up to three or four hours a day.

His mail, which still arrived with Fanny's through the slot, brought the announcement of the dancers' meeting at a community room in a shopping center close enough to walk to, so he wouldn't even have to ask Fanny for use of the car. He did pass three bus stops on the way to the meeting. A man at a bus stop had a suitcase and duffel bag. That bus might go downtown to the Greyhound terminal, to the train station, or out to the airport. Morgan wasn't carrying anything. If he hung a suitcase from the end of each arm, what would he want to put inside them? Was there anything he wanted to keep? Or was his disinterest only a side effect of living in empty or nearly empty rooms at home? But could a man move away, leave an old life behind, empty-handed?

He stood in the doorway of the meeting room. Most of the heads, facing forward, had close-cropped hair and shaved necks, or else hair piled up with the thin white necks exposed. But the back of Renee's neck wasn't among them. He didn't answer when his name was called, but they might've marked him present, if they saw him. When they called Renee's name, someone said they thought she was out of town.

"Rats deserting the sinking ship," someone in the back row said to a friend.

Morgan left without voting, after he heard that the committee was recommending a strike, even though they knew that as soon as they announced a work stoppage management would announce cancellation of the entire season, which hadn't been booked anyway.

Fanny was lying on the love seat, dressed for work, her feet up on the armrest, causing her skirt to fall back toward her crotch, bunched up as though a guy had just had his hand there. She opened her eyes. "Were you asleep?" he asked.

She didn't move, looking at him, then sat up and swung her legs to the floor, moving awkwardly as though drunk. "No," she finally said. "Thanks for asking."

"Well, I guess they don't need my letter of resignation." He waited, but she didn't ask what he was talking about. "There's nothing to resign from," he finished.

"But resigning from something *would* feel good, wouldn't it." It seemed her thin voice wasn't really coming out of the still figure sitting with hands in her lap.

"What's that supposed to mean?"

"It means nothing."

"It means nothing. God, you sound like some sort of affected faggot choreographer."

"I thought you had a newfound love for choreographers . . . not to mention faggots. Or is it just female faggots?"

"Being gay doesn't have anything to do with Renee fighting and working and looking out for Number One." He crumpled backwards into the chair, slouching so that he was barely bent at the waist.

"I know. I guess she and I are about as opposite as you can get," Fanny said.

"She'll get paid through the strike. No one else knows."

"Are you going to tell anyone?"

"I don't think I'll see anyone again. I'm quitting. They don't know that either."

"What're you going to do?" Her voice was soft, but somehow deep and real.

Footsteps tapped outside, then the mail thumped in the chute. But no dog barked or ran to leap and crash, front feet first, into the door. Fanny's eyes were closed, her lashes wet.

"I wonder if it even matters what I do," he said.

"Then you're more like me than you are like her. Maybe you can get a job as a waiter."

"Maybe *you* can get a job as a whore." The force of the words coming from a slouched position made his stomach hurt.

She didn't say anything. She let out a short quick breath but didn't even open her eyes. Then she smiled weirdly. "But would I really make any *more* money? My hand jobs are so damn slow."

One of the neighborhood cats who wore a bell ran across the front yard. A car with a thumping stereo went past, and across the street a motorcycle began warming up, revved impatiently by its driver. The engine cut out, the cat bell tinkled, the motorcycle grumbled again, buzzed, popped like an automatic weapon, ripped like a chain saw. Morgan smiled, then laughed. "God, what a wonderful neighborhood. The only ones who're safe are the fucking birds."

"Safe from what?"

"Wanna get outta here? Let's just take off and go until we find someplace that says, *You two losers belong here.* Let's just do it."

She stood, again with a drunklike awkwardness. "You're crazy. Why would I want to do that, especially with you? I may be a miserable quitter, but sometimes, in some situations, even *quitting* is better."

The motorcycle's voice rose like a mosquito's hum then dwindled down the street, leaving a familiar silence. The dog used to go berserk every day when that motorcycle warmed up, scrambling through the house, roaring like a tortured bear, digging under the front door, scattering rugs, loose pieces of mail or other papers from the coffee table flying in her wake.

"God, I'm glad that fucking dog is gone," he said. Fanny had already left the room.

With Suzanne in the car just thirty feet away, he dialed Fanny's number. Calls from Arches, Capitol Reef, and Bryce had all gone unanswered. Sometimes her machine was on, sometimes it wasn't. He couldn't stand the thought of her being there, listening to his voice leave the message but refusing to pick up the receiver, so he never spoke after the beep.

He'd told Suzanne he had to call in to the office to check on how things were going, to see if the man he'd left in charge was having any problems. And he had to check his machine at home, he said, because he'd told the guy to leave messages there if he had any questions. He'd also told the kennel to call his home number and leave a message if they needed him to contact them, if Sadie was sick or not eating or in any way seemed unwell. The first few days of the trip, Scott had only called in to retrieve messages once a day, usually in the morning while Suzanne was showering. There hadn't been any. He called the office once a day, as close to 5:00 P.M. as possible, for a daily report. Now he was calling his home phone four, five, six times a day, whenever they passed a clump of rest rooms or a mounted map beside a pay phone. And the last few nights he'd been asking his manager to run down the list of waitresses and bartenders he'd used for the previous day's jobs. Her name was always there.

On short hikes into scenic areas, he'd found his mind no longer had to flip a channel changer on a frantic search for something to say because he'd simply started vocalizing thoughts about Sadie: the squirrels she'd be hunting, how gloriously dirty she'd be getting, the wild scents she'd go crazy over. Somewhere along the line, Suzanne had stopped responding, had slipped into a taut reticence. And in the car, long brittle silences grew under the squall of the air conditioner and the radio playing country music, the only stations he could find. He also listened to long farm reports, community event calendars, lists of funerals, and rodeo recaps.

At the Court of the Patriarchs, he said Sadie would probably try to use her agility training to go into the end of a hollow log lying just off the trail, thinking she'd find an animal there to flush and chase. At Weeping Rock, he mentioned that the dog would probably want to dash into the shower of water falling from the rock ceiling over the trail, leaping to snap at sparkling droplets the same way she played with the garden hose. At the scenic viewpoint for the Great White Throne, he just said that by now she'd be so happy-tired, her tongue would be flying like a flag. Silently, he followed the train of thought farther—to Fanny, climbing over the tourist fences and kneeling to creep as far toward the edge of the lookout bluffs as possible, the dogs sitting on either side of her, raising their noses and leaning into the wind. She might try for echoes at every outlook over every majestic gorge. In his mind, she shouted, *Hey Scott, where are you!* He searched the turnouts and picnic areas for telephones.

After giving a urine sample, Fanny lay back on the crackling tissue and let her legs dangle over the end of the table. She still had her moccasins on. It wasn't her regular doctor. This one had given her his card at one of the catered lunches this week and said to call if she ever needed help, especially a work-related injury. This information gathered between their exchanged laughter over doctor jokes.

He came into the examining room, reading the forms she'd filled out, looked up, and his face broke into an undoctorly expression: wide grin, squinty eyes. "I honestly didn't expect to see you again so quickly."

She smiled before answering. "I didn't want to be one of those people who meets a doctor and immediately wants medical advice. Besides, I was working."

"Very hard, as I recall. You made that dour luncheon a lot more fun, I'll have to commend you to your boss."

"You do that." She shut her eyes and held onto either side of the narrow table.

Since he'd come back, Morgan had been lying on the very edge of the mattress, like a corpse turned face down, his crossed arms underneath himself, and as soon as he fell asleep, his muscles twitched. Drifting to sleep last night, despite his spasms she could feel through the mattress, Fanny had heard her husky's toenails click on the floor. Suddenly wide awake, heart thudding, there was nothing but the house settling, the wooden skeleton making ticking sounds as the night air cooled the sun-warmed walls. Then the refrigerator had clicked on and begun humming. Fanny had gotten out of bed and started out on a walk but didn't go far. Put her hands in her jacket pocket and found an old leash there.

"Slide up to the very edge of the table."

She put her feet in the stirrups. Nearly the same position she'd held Lacy in while Doreen had artificially inseminated her. As Doreen had bent over Lacy's crotch, Fanny unable to see anything but Doreen's thick straight red hair falling forward, Doreen had said, "I guess your pack would've been extinct if you'd been wild, girl, you may be dominant but you don't want to accept the responsibilities of being the alpha bitch, do you?" As the semen drained into the husky, Doreen had sat up. "You know that, don't you? A wild pack doesn't just have a dominant male, there's always an alpha bitch too. All the other bitches and subordinate males are all low and slinky around her, tails tucked, ears slicked back. She'll stand there with her hackles puffed, neck arched. The others lick her ears and mouth. A pack's alpha bitch gets whatever she wants, just like the male, and she'll fight for her position if she's challenged. And only the alpha bitch is allowed to have puppies, so she's the only one who breeds. Whatever males are strong enough, dominant enough to get her to allow the breeding—one of *them'll* be the father. That's how wild canines breed for stronger and stronger temperaments. The weaklings don't reproduce."

She knew where Lacy probably was this very minute, just after eleven in the morning on a summer day. Crashing over a nearly vertical A-frame, soaring over the high jump, pursuing a fleeing tennis ball, and loping back with the soggy ball wedged in her mouth—then some feral scent might snap her head sideways, the ball forgotten as she foraged for the source. Until Doreen came and got her by the collar once again.

She didn't know where Scott was, and even though Morgan had spread a U.S. road map out on the coffee table yesterday, she hadn't let herself look.

"It's probably too early to be sure," the doctor said.

———————

Tomorrow, on a mule, on a path a half a foot wide, on a switchback trail that would take eight miles to go a mile down, there would be no phone. He might as well be free-falling into a bottomless pit if he had to zigzag into the canyon, spend the night, and come back up without getting Fanny on the phone first. Suzanne was moving at exactly his pace as he browsed gift stores—slowing down to look when he paused to pick up moccasins or a rattlesnake head, continuing to travel in his wake as he moved on, like a pair of cowlike animals at the zoo pacing their enclosure, heads bobbing, in some sort of wordless but implicitly understood dance of captivity. As the afternoon got longer and she showed no sign of heading for the rest room, he felt an increasing rashness, a willing to risk recklessness. In their fourth or fifth gift shop, after the once-around tour of the aisles, as they neared the exit, Suzanne finally paused to twirl the postcard rack. Scott sped up. Just outside the door was an exposed pay phone. After three rings, he knew the machine wasn't on. After the fourth ring, sweat broke everywhere from his neck to his crotch. After the fifth ring, he squeezed the phone in his fist, his face wincing. And then she answered.

"Hey, I finally caught you." He plugged his other ear and leaned forward until his brow rested against the coin slot.

"Whadda you mean?"

"I've been calling. Every day. Several times."

"You have?"

He couldn't tell from her voice whether she'd be smiling or not. "Yeah, sometimes your machine's on, sometimes it's not."

"I've been out a lot," she said. "I don't know why Morgan doesn't answer. But there haven't been any messages. Unless he didn't tell me."

"What's *he* doing there?"

"He came back."

Scott increased the pressure on his free ear. He watched his breath fog the chrome on the phone, even though the day's temperature was well over 100 degrees. "So . . . what's it mean?"

"It means he's here and I have to deal with it. I can't throw him out, and if *I* left, I'd have nowhere to go."

The entire back of his shirt was wet even though he was in the shade of the building. But hot flashes of adrenaline seemed to make sweat actually spurt from his brow and temples. "Maybe you could stay with Doreen?"

"Yeah, right," her tone flattened, then snapped. "Why should *I* go sleep on someone's floor while you're off on your second honeymoon?"

"We've been in separate beds the whole time."

"Sorry, I don't have that luxury."

His heart clogged his throat as Suzanne stepped out of the store. She glanced at him, then walked toward the other end of the building where there was a bench. Scott turned so he had his back toward her. His eyes stung and he was afraid his voice would crack. "Please, Fanny, don't be mad. This isn't easy."

"I know." Her voice kissed his ear softly.

"I miss you," he said, "I miss my dog. I even miss your dog."

Fanny didn't answer.

"Hello?" he whispered. "You still there?"

"I miss my dog too," she said.

"What? Why?"

"She's Doreen's now. They took Doreen's puppy and destroyed him."

"That wasn't your fault. You didn't have to give her your dog!" His voice was louder than he'd intended. He took a quick glance at Suzanne. She had her arms folded and her legs crossed, tapping her upper foot in the air.

"You didn't *let* me tell you. She was going to sue you for causing the attack that caused her to lose her dog."

"That's crazy."

"Her dog was an investment in future earnings. He was going to build her reputation so she could become a nationally known clinician, write dog-training books, make videos . . ."

"Fanny, legally a dog is just personal property. Even if I *shot* her dog, all she could sue me for would be the dollar value of a dog in a pet shop window."

She was silent for a moment, then said, as though she hadn't heard him, "She said she knew a lawyer. So I gave her my dog." She must've been crying.

"Fanny, I just didn't know."

"How could you know," probably still crying, but her voice was dark, "you were too worried about making sure the little Mrs. got her holiday."

He stood dumbly. He could hear Fanny sniffle and sigh. Suzanne's shoes scraped on the pavement as she got up, checked her watch, and started coming back toward him. Not a thread of his shirt was dry. "I'm gonna hafta go," he murmured.

––––––––––––

When the car finally rolled to a crunching stop on the shoulder, he threw his head back against the seat and said, "Happy birthday, sweet sixteen."

Fanny snorted, "I wish. What's wrong?"

"I think the gas gauge is broken. It didn't move when I filled up this morning. We must be out of gas."

"Morgan, we're thirty miles from anywhere!"

"Yeah, typical us, huh?"

"God, as long as I was going forward, I could stand it. I'll *explode* if I have to wait around here for hours and hours."

"Relax, enjoy your birthday, have you ever had a party in a peaceful nature setting?"

"There's no shade, it's gotta be a hundred degrees, and it's not my birthday."

"There's shade beside the car."

"Piece of junk. I hope it melts."

Morgan laughed. "Yesterday it was your only hope for reaching lover boy's arms."

Fanny got out of the car and slammed the door. She disappeared, so he figured she was sitting with her back against the fender. He propped his chin on his arm on the open window. Vehicles passing on the interstate sent gusts of hot air against his face. He could hitch a ride to El Centro in a matter of minutes, so no one was *stuck* here. Probably yesterday he hadn't really believed they would go all the way to Arizona anyway.

He'd taken a nap from one or two o'clock until almost five, then had come out to the living room and found her packing a duffel bag. The map he'd spread on the coffee table three or four days ago was still there. He'd asked, "What're you doing?"

"Going to Arizona."

"Why?"

"Why not?" She pulled the drawstrings of the bag. "I'll pretend it's my birthday. A present from me to me."

"What kind of present is Arizona in the summertime?"

"A hot one." She went into the kitchen, where a picnic cooler was sitting on the shelf.

"Well, hey," he followed her. "You're not running off with our only car."

"Oh? You waiting for me to invite you along?" She threw the blue ice into the cooler. "Or you afraid I'll go off and sell it, then live like a queen off the profits?" A bag of carrots and two apples thudded against the bottom of the cooler. She was still looking into the open refrigerator.

"Hey, *I'm* the one who wanted to take off, get out of here, but you were little Miss Responsibility. Now what if *I* want to pack and get the hell out—I won't have a car."

"So pack and get in, I don't care." She laughed, looking at a bottle of cocktail olives that'd been in the refrigerator for more than three years. "Yeah, why *shouldn't* I show up with my *husband?*"

"Does this have anything to do with that Tahoe asshole?"

She shut the refrigerator door softly and stood looking at him. "No. But thank you for calling him an asshole. He really was."

"I thought you were lovesick over him."

She'd stepped forward. If the kitchen counter hadn't been directly behind him, he would've moved back. He flinched, then boosted himself up and sat on the counter. She said, "I don't know if you can understand this, Morgan," with either mock patience or the real thing, "but I *was* sick—sick over being duped by sex. I know that *now.* But now I'm afraid it happened again, almost the same damn thing, only this time I'm not sick. I'm *mad.* Maybe I've never been mad like this before. I've *never* felt like this. All I know is, I have to *do* something. *This* time I have to *do* something. *Why* didn't I love my dog enough? If I did, I'd still have her. I don't have a plan or anything, I just know I have to do *something.*" She'd turned to look in the pantry cupboard, pulled out a box of crackers, held it in the crook of her arm, and continued staring into the shelves of canned soup and cereal boxes. The open cupboard door blocked most of her. He could see only the back of her head. "I don't even know if I'm ready to fight something or fight *for* something." Then she'd shut the cupboard and was looking directly at him. "Maybe you felt this way when you went to go stay with Renee . . . or maybe not until you *left* Renee, I don't know, I'm not asking, I don't really care."

The next morning when she'd put the cooler and her bag in the backseat of the car, he'd locked the house and got into the passenger seat. "Suit yourself," she'd shrugged.

The car radio had finally broken. Going up over the mountains between San Diego and El Centro, she'd punctuated the sound of the straining, wheezing little engine with statements he wasn't even sure were directed at him. "I might've given my dog away for *nothing.* That alone should piss me off royally." Ten miles and fifteen minutes later, "He's upset 'cause you came home, and he's off on vacation with his *wife*—and refuses to even *tell* her she's about to become his *ex*-wife."

She'd pulled over twice on the mildly twisty freeway to open her door and vomit. When she'd stopped just outside El Centro—said she had a headache, and they'd switched places—she'd said, "You haven't even wished me a happy birthday."

He'd begun suspecting the gas gauge five miles into the desert past El Centro, but didn't say anything.

After they'd been motionless and silent for twenty minutes, he heard Fanny open the back door. She slid the cooler out and closed the door again. Sweat was already gathering in rivulets between his shoulder blades, behind his ears, down his temples. He got out and went around to where she was sitting on the ground in a strip of shade made by the car. "Here." She handed him an apple. "They're not very good." He sat down and took a few small nibbles, then forgot he was even holding it—pulled his feet toward his butt, tucked his hands in the space between his thighs and chest, leaned forward to put his brow on his knees, closed his eyes.

———————

His first impulse was to cancel the rest of the trip and go home. But Suzanne had talked about riding a mule into the Grand Canyon for years, even before they'd planned more extravagant trips. How could he bail out now without some kind of explanation? What kind of explanation could he give? "Fanny's dog was taken from her." But he knew it couldn't, mercifully, *end* there. *Who's Fanny?* And then what? "The girl I—" What? What next . . . *love? fuck? am dating? can't stop thinking about?*

He couldn't imagine ending the sentence, let alone how the conversation would get him quickly packed and onto the westbound freeway. Despite her having been so woodenly silent the past several days, Suzanne had already commented several times on their incredible luck in getting onto this mule trip from the waiting list. "Ironic, as you would say," she'd added. "For the high point of the whole trip, we go a mile down."

His head and stomach hurt in unison, or maybe in dissonance. He felt he had to squint, even in the dark motel room, to protect his eyes from a glare coming from inside his head. Maybe he could help Fanny get her dog back by making a few calls. Were there lawyers who specialized in pet owners' rights?

"Maybe there's a little public library somewhere around here," he said. "We have nothing planned this evening."

Suzanne stopped looking through her suitcase. She stood up straight. To her full height. Had she been slouching all these years? What was she, six feet? "What's the matter with you, Scott?" She flung the suitcase lid down.

He was holding his hand up to his forehead as though shielding his eyes. Then he sat, facing away from her. "I don't feel so well. Maybe I shouldn't go tomorrow."

"We're here. We miraculously got onto the mule trip. When's the next time you'll have this chance? You're going to pass it up because of a headache? But you'd rather go to the *library?*"

"I wanted to look something up . . . for work. Which anniversary is emerald."

"Can't they look it up themselves? Can't the ones having the party tell your people if it's an emerald anniversary or not? You're on vacation, Scott." She slammed emphasis on the first word of each of the three sentences, and again on his name at the end.

"I feel weird. I miss my dog." A stab of guilt into his throbbing head and simultaneously through his gut. Not just for whining like a six-year-old child actor, but . . . *his* dog would still be there for him when he returned—what about Fanny's dog? "I guess I've also been feeling guilty about . . . leaving the business this long. Things at home need my attention. One of my waitresses . . . has . . . legal problems."

"There are thousands of waitresses." Her flat volume faded a little, the last word changing to the snuffed and hollow tone of the bathroom.

"This one is important. She knows . . . the business."

Suzanne didn't answer. The water was running in the bathtub, and he was still facing the opposite direction, not speaking very loud. It was like a dress rehearsal to prepare Suzanne for hearing about his new life, so she could accept each piece as it was given to her, no piece so big that it would hurt. He'd thought about and planned and decided each stage he would gradually lead her through, a natural progression, no one abandoned for anyone else, no one left crying. But maybe Fanny was crying now, with no strong, sturdy dog to hold and muffle her anxiety against, having foolishly given the husky up for *his* sake. The past several weeks, he'd felt energy gurgle away at the thought of the course that still lay ahead of him with Suzanne, but now it was a kick in his already tight, burning stomach to imagine going through those steps without Fanny.

He'd tried to sneak out to call Fanny during the night, but just as he slipped from his sheets, Suzanne also stirred and said, "What're you doing?"

"Getting aspirin." He lay still for a long time trying to tell if she was sleeping or not. He could hear the travel alarm ticking on her nightstand. Once he thought he would have to get up and puke, but he held it back, no longer wanting to cancel the mule trek because he had decided the twenty minutes it took to drive to the corrals were the best time to say something. Once at the mule station, they'd be with a group, then single file, each with a private view of the canyon walls opposite and the crevice below. Not a place for a discussion.

Scott thought he would feel clearer, more prepared in the morning, but he was sandy eyed, his gut still twisted, his head like a swollen thumb that had been hit with a hammer. Since last night— like a song verse stuck in his mind, endlessly repeating—he kept picturing a game Fanny had played with him and her dog. She called it *dangerous kisses*. She stood stradling Lacy and holding her by the scruff of the neck, getting the dog all riled and excited, then the dog was released and told to go give a kiss. He was to kneel, without flinching, eyes open, and accept the kiss, a sloppy lick of mouth and nose that might also bash his head backwards or throw him entirely off balance. That's why he'd wanted to call Fanny last night, to tell her: "Give me a dangerous kiss."

He'd already wasted over half of the drive by the time he finally said, "I've, uh, realized we need to be honest . . ."

As he paused to dig for words, Suzanne sighed and turned to him, smiling gently. "That's the best thing you've said in two months. If we're going to work this out . . ."

Finding a spurt of strength, he was talking again and hardly heard her. "I've been seeing a girl. We—" Already a sign warned that he was nearing the mule station. He turned up the air conditioner.

"What do you mean?" Her words came out separately, robotically, hardly a question.

Scott quickly glanced at her three times; each time her face, staring at him, seemed bigger. "You know what I mean. I've been seeing a girl—"

"Since when?"

"Before this trip. A few weeks. We're . . . you know . . . dating, I guess you call it."

"Dating." Again no question mark. Then gravel popped on the little road into the mule corrals. His eyes were flicking from the dashboard to the corral area to Suzanne's rigid jaw and set lips. A couple of dusty dogs barked behind him as though guiding him into a parking space, then trotted off to meet the next car. Suzanne muttered tightly, "I can't believe you've done this." A cluster of people in sunglasses and every conceivable type of hat waited on a little platform. "Dating," she repeated.

In a paddock, two hands were saddling mules and hitching them together. A shorter string of mules were already prepared without saddles. A hand was loading them with small duffel bags and knapsacks taken from a pile at the end of the platform. The instructions in the literature had said to bring personal clothes and items in a small soft bag. "Did we remember to pack our little bags?" he asked, getting out of the car. Opening the car door was like opening an oven, even at eight in the morning.

Suzanne was out of the car too. "You're married, Scott," her voice rang out, the words clear and enunciated. "Is that such a difficult concept to remember? What do you do, store your memory in your dong?" A few people at the end of the platform turned in their direction. One of the hands laughed. The barking dogs were herding a minivan into the last parking space.

———————

What the fuck was he doing out in the desert in the hottest part of the summer, cringing beside the car in a shrinking band of shade? He'd taken off his undershirt and rolled the end into the car window. By holding a sleeve in each hand, he could stretch the shirt out like an awning over his head, but his arms got tired quickly, so the awning had to wait while he rested. Fanny was sideways against the car, like a monkey cowering in a corner of its cage. One of her hands was cupped up around the side of her face.

"We could lie *under* the car," she said.

Morgan held his awning up for a few seconds, then dropped it over his face and let his throbbing arms fall across his stomach. His legs were flat on the ground, mostly in the sun. He was pink from the knees down. "I hafta pee," he said through the rank odor of the shirt.

"Go out there. You're lucky you can."

"I could do it right here on the tire like a dog."

"It'll stink." She was scratching in the dirt with a stick. "I still think we should lie under the car. Or else one of us could hitch back to El Centro for gas."

He stretched his awning out again but could only hold it for a few seconds. "God, my body's like ninety years old," he muttered.

"That's what you get for quitting."

He squeezed the sleeves of the T-shirt in two fists. The material stretched suffocatingly across his face.

"Whereas for *my* punishment," she continued after a few minutes of smothering silence, "my boyfriend's probably in an air-conditioned shop choosing gifts for his in-laws."

Morgan sucked the T-shirt into his mouth then bit down and ground the wad of cotton in his teeth.

"For all he knows," Fanny drawled, her stick still scratching the ground, "I've lost my senses in the desert heat, no water, eating rotten apples, warping my rationality."

Suddenly flinging the T-shirt away from his face, Morgan gasped for air, choked, coughed, then said, "Certainly explains why you're sitting in the middle of nowhere talking about lying under the car and buying souvenirs."

"Then what's *your* excuse?"

"It's probably contagious." He jerked his feet toward himself and turned sharply into the same position as Fanny, with his back to her, his cheek on his knees, looking out, away from the car.

"Yeah," she said slowly. "Like when someone's pregnant, and their husband gets morning sickness." Two or three huge semis roared past on the freeway, each one shooting a boom of air against the other side of the car. "We, for example," she continued in the silence that followed, "are even in a fetal position together."

"I'm just trying not to pee in my pants."

"You have a whole entire desert to pee in."

"You wouldn't care if your *dog* peed on the tire."

Fanny's stick started scratching the dirt again. The sound made his skin prickle. "She's a bitch," Fanny said. "She wouldn't pee on a tire. She may be alpha, but she still squats to pee." The stick stopped, then a handful of pebbles flew and spattered into a bush. "But, you're right, if she was here, I wouldn't care if she peed right next to me."

Another handful of rocks rattled the bush.

"I know what your plan can be," he said.

"What plan."

"To get back at this guy you're mad at. Kill his dog."

"What?"

"He's got a dog and now *you* don't, right? *He's* to blame? So kill his dog."

"God, Morgan, what did Renee teach you, anyway?"

"Number One, baby, Number One."

Another convoy of trucks blasted past, this time in the lane closest to them. Morgan found himself ducking farther and holding his head in his hands.

"Are you going to go for gas or am I?" Fanny said. "Decide, because if it's me, I'll get going."

He stood, but had to do so slowly. His legs were tight, his knees felt nearly locked. "I'll go."

Had he been staring at the gray bristle on the back of his mule's neck instead of soaking up the breathless view of vivid pink, red, and orange veins in the opposite canyon wall, instead of leaning out from the trail carved into an almost vertical bluff to see the thin trickle of the river a mile away straight down? Scott was the only one on the mule train without a hat. When the switchback trail went east, the ten o'clock sun flared into his face. Going west, it drilled into the back of his head. He couldn't see how far down they would have to go to be in shadows. Maybe he'd find out what it felt like just before a person blacks out. Then the mule could pack his crumpled body to the bottom and back, and no one would notice his slumped shoulders and head bobbing crazily down against his chest. Especially with the safety strap attached to the saddle and buckled around his waist, like a child on a ride at Disneyland.

Suzanne was on the mule ahead of him. A wide-brimmed hat hid her head and neck. The strap of her binoculars was diagonal across her back. His head swam as he glanced up. The front of the mule train had turned the corner of a switchback and was going east again on a trail so narrow he couldn't see it only ten or fifteen yards below. As Suzanne's mule made the turn, he could see the side of her face for a few seconds before his mule was also on the corner, and he ducked his head against the sun as he came around.

Suzanne turned slightly and said something. He didn't hear her but didn't call out for her to repeat it. Then her hand came around and braced on the back of her saddle so she could turn farther. "Are you listening or just daydreaming about one of your dates?"

He suddenly noticed the jarring of his spine with each step the mule took. The trail was becoming steeper. She said, "There must be something wrong with you."

The clop of the mules' feet became crisp in the silence of the canyon. He could even hear a faint roar from the white water in the river far below. The sun was higher, no longer glaring in his eyes, but now like bricks on his head. Lizards disappeared like flashes of light into cracks in rocks.

"You never wanted to have an adult's mind," she said, "an adult's point of view. You know what's wrong with you? You have a defect, you don't know what it means to honor something substantial and wholesome."

The motion of the mule probably made it look like he was nodding. He held the saddle horn in both hands, stared at his mule's ears, which were swiveled forward and alert. He could hear cameras clicking behind him.

Suzanne faced forward again, but in another minute she reached around to brace herself with her other hand, this time turning toward the side where the canyon dropped straight down beside them. "*Values,* Scott." Her voice was thinner but spreading farther, like rocks that were kicked off the trail but could still be heard clattering and rolling minutes later, far below. "What do you think people mean by values? Is this defect just in *you,* or do all men let their cocks decide their values?"

His head jerked around and it seemed the guy on the mule behind his had a long zoom lens pointed directly at him.

"Can't you even look at me?" Suzanne said, finally loud enough, harsh enough for a little echo. He noticed she was wearing the leather hiking shorts again, and one of his shirts.

"Can we talk about it later?" he murmured.

"What's going to be different later?" she shrieked. "Will your dick shrivel up and make all of this unnecessary?"

Sweat dripped into his eyes. He tipped his head and looked up toward the rim where they'd started, but neither the zigzag trail nor a distinct crest was discernible.

"People say women are materialistic, but women know how to honor the important things. *You're* the materialistic one. What's twenty years anyway, it's obviously not part of your materialistic value system."

The guy behind him coughed quietly. The others on the mule train seemed to have fallen into a church service aura, a hushed reverie. His face still skyward, Scott tried to be part of it. A small tour plane came into view. Scott kept his eyes on it, waiting to hear the drone of its engine. A plane like that had crashed here recently.

"You've *always* been materialistic—the biggest lawn mower, the most powerful satellite dish—*she's* just another possession, another trendy toy. Why can't you grow up? What'd you do, put off being a teenager till now? Got any pimple medicine in your bathroom cabinet? Posters of the Rolling Stones on your bedroom walls? Pictures of sluts under the mattress? Did you bring her a corsage for your first date? Did you ask her to go steady? Did your armpits get all sweaty while you asked her to go miniature golfing?"

A couple of big birds were circling. He couldn't see the west-bound switchback where they'd just been, thirty yards up the side of the canyon, but he could see the heads of hikers bobbing along the trail up there, following the mule train, staring down at him.

"Don't you have anything to say for yourself?" Suzanne was practically sitting backwards on her mule. "Didn't it even once occur to you while you were asking this little princess on a *date,* that over twenty years ago you made a vow, an *oath*—remember?" Her voice switched to a singsong mimic, "Let's see, what was that all about, anyway, something like honor and cherish for the rest of your life? Sound familiar at *all?*"

"Suzanne . . . ," he tried, but saying anything was like poking her with a stick.

She screamed, "Why does something as wonderful and natural and noble as *that* either scare you to death or mean less than shit to you? What *is* your value system, Scott—if you can stick your *penis* into it, then it's valuable?"

Far down in the canyon a mule brayed. As if in answer, Scott's mule shook its head, spraying the froth forming on its lips in several directions. Some splotched on Scott's shirt.

She told Morgan they still had an old gas can somewhere. When he went to the rear of the car and opened the trunk, Fanny opened both doors on the passenger side. The gas can made a hollow metal boom when he hit it against his hip or the car's bumper. The trunk lid didn't want to close. He slammed it down three times.

When Morgan turned toward the road, Fanny turned toward the desert and took off her jeans, sitting down again to finish pulling them over her legs. Even hitting warm, motionless air, her skin almost sighed in relief to be out of the denim. Morgan would have to go to the other side of the freeway to hitch a ride back west to El Centro, but there were easily enough breaks in the sound of cars and trucks ripping past for him to get across. Just one hundred fifty miles from home, but the clichéd desert, the bleached sky and dunes of rippling sand split by the freeway like a river of gusting wind, made the place feel like another continent, another planet.

She got a map from the passenger seat and folded a paper hat, but there was no brim to block the sun. So with a rag made from an old T-shirt, kept behind the seat for checking the oil, she tried to make the map into a baseball cap by tying it to her head, making a knot with the two ends of the T-shirt under her chin. But the map was too old and the creases where it had been folded were more than just dog-eared—the long brim of paper came flopping down in front of her face. A footstep crunched sand up near the headlights. Fanny's whole body twitched—bounced nearly an inch off the ground—she pushed the map up off her face, her heartbeat punching her rib cage and her guts, then moving like a throb of radar into her suddenly liquid and weak arms and legs.

Morgan was standing beside the fender looking at her through the window of the open passenger-side door.

"God, Morgan, you scared me."

"I have a birthday present for you."

"Oh, yeah? There was gas already in the gas can?"

"No." His hair matted with sweat, his eye sockets and gaunt cheeks blackened by their own shadows, he looked old, sickly.

"Then what is it?"

"Me!" He came around the door, naked from the waist down. With a solid and unfamiliar dark red hard-on.

"Morgan!" She'd thought his name would come out with a laugh, but it was as though her voice was torn away by a truck going past too fast, nearly careening out of control, sounding its air horn. Then silence again, and she was struggling to get her feet underneath herself, to stand up, still holding the limp map off her face with one hand. But Morgan, landing with a grunt on his knees between her feet, pushed her back down. Her head hit the bottom of the car's doorway.

"We're going to get this right for once. Aren't you going to get rid of the underwear?"

"Morgan!" She almost had no breath to get any sound out.

"What are you laughing at?"

"I'm not!"

He jabbed a finger into the crotch of her underwear then jerked his hand back, pulling the underwear halfway down her thighs. "Okay, let's go."

"Wait."

"*I'm* ready, you're not ready?" He crammed his palm into her crotch, scouring as though trying to start a fire. She could only see the top of his head, his dank hair, then the map fell back over her face as she felt his teeth close over a breast, grinding slightly, not quite enough to break skin—not searing pain, it was the slow crunch of a bruise. But no sound from her, no scream, no shout, no curses. Her jaw clenched, her body knotted. Rocks ground into the skin on the back of her head. She was holding a handful of sand in each fist. She waited for rage to create that mysterious explosion of rebellion and strength when a victim finally says *No more.* She could've thrown dirt in his eyes, smacked her palms against his ears, scratched parallel stripes down his face. She could've dragged herself under the car, scrambled out the other side, and run in her underwear westward along the freeway shoulder. Or roll the car over onto him, squish him like a bug. Stranger feats of power from an unknown source had been recorded.

Nothing came. She couldn't even take a deep breath. But she could swallow. Once, and slowly. Any further word or sound was snuffed, her toes uncurled, the sand poured from between her fingers. Every muscle went slack. She stared, without any hope of being able to see, at the blurry, faded roads and rivers and towns printed on the map lying directly against her eyes.

When his head pulled away, he still had her shirt in his teeth, then he let go and his penis began its stabbing search. His breath heaved, he panted, "I'll get it, I'll get it . . ." His finger found the way, his penis followed, pushed slowly instead of ramming in, scraping against her dry skin, a feeling like the sound of raw brakes before a collision. The only collision was his body hitting hers as he began to thrust, and he said, "I've owed you this . . . for a long time." Each plunge pushed her lax body backwards until her head was halfway under the car, her eyes suddenly in shadows, the inappropriate relief adding another degree of inertia to her joints.

But Morgan, without withdrawing, yanked her back out into the sun. Her shirt slid up and her bare back scraped the hard sand on the freeway's shoulder. She'd probably become like play dough, rocks or sticks or fingers or a penis digging into her without resistance, becoming embedded or tearing away soft little pieces, pulling her out of shape or squeezing her down again. Not even the old clenched reluctance—spontaneous and unwelcome—that *used* to be part of her body opposed him.

With three or four spasmodic jerks, he got her turned parallel to the car. He held her arms on the ground above her head, and, because of their height difference, her face was buried and crushed against the hard bones of his chest and shoulder. So she heard his voice in stereo, from his chest and—farther away—from his mouth, buzzing, hoarse, "You always looked at me like . . . you acted like . . ." He paused, lay completely still for a second, but she could feel his whole body inhaling. He withdrew almost completely, hovered, hung there, as though dangling her or both of them together over a cliff . . . then pounded into her, pushing air out of her with an involuntary grunt from her throat, although her mouth never opened. She could see the tendons strain in his neck, the words squeezing out of him, pausing, each time he slammed into her: ". . . acted . . . like it . . . was all . . . my fault . . . limp prick . . . limp spine . . . failure . . . but I . . . it was like living . . . with a . . . hypnotized goldfish who just . . . all day just . . . glided back and forth . . . back and forth . . . never doing anything, just . . . going up to the glass . . . but not even looking *out* . . . how the hell was I . . . supposed to . . . how could I . . . *damn it to fucking hell* . . . what else did you . . . *expect?* . . . You thought I *couldn't* . . . you thought it was something . . . wrong with me . . . but it was *you* . . ."

Sweat, either his or her own, stung her eyes. Her fingers and toes numb, her hands, her feet, a stupor moving up her legs and down her arms. Wasn't he right? A throb in her nose felt black and purple, marking her: *Pathetic.* Yeah, what would Doreen call it? The *Submissive Subordinate,* the one with the tucked tail, slinky posture, ears pressed flat. No permanent scars because there was never enough of a fight. The gutlessness just part of who she was. Giving up. Caving in. Where was her justifiable fury? Defunct, just because it was only Morgan heaving on top of her. Moaning as though in fevered delirium. Unhealthy fatigue slowing him down before anything was done. The same Morgan, after all, who'd sagged beside her on the sofa the night of the robbery, crossing his arms on his gut and rocking forward and back, looking at her with glossy child's eyes, then gazing back at the tangled pile of junk that was all they owned. The same Morgan who'd slumped around in the picket lines for five or ten minutes, then handed his sign to someone else and returned home to take his rumpled place on the sofa beside the stack of newspapers folded to unfinished crossword puzzles; or to follow her from room to room, reading aloud the day's article or press release or letter to the editor about the lock-out, then the comics, then Dear Abby and Ann Landers; to stare at the wall above the flickering TV as she unloaded government surplus food from boxes, turning to meet her with such an imploring gaze as she came into the room, that *she'd* been the one to say, as though reading a script in his liquid eyes, "What're we going to do?" But his face had hardened, his eyes abruptly the flat color of rusted steel—he'd turned away without a word. It was *that* same Morgan fucking her on the hot sand of the freeway's shoulder, so why shouldn't she feel the familiar helplessness, the hopelessness, the unremitting impotence to stop or change, fix or regenerate, improve or ascend? Was that what he'd been waiting for, expecting, *asking* of her? Looking with fear to someone he thought was stronger, who only looked back with paralyzing disillusionment? They were the epitome of what Doreen had said about domestic canines: the domestic pack dysfunctional and diseased by unnatural emotions they got from people: jealousy, embarrassment, low self-esteem, and fear.

Fanny had tried to argue: "But wild animals are afraid, it's part of survival."

Doreen had shook her head with a patient smile. "That's natural *caution*. Fear is different. Fear is crazy, unpredictable, irrational, destructive. No member of the pack should be afraid. Either alpha or not, but *not* afraid to be what you *are*. Domestication just confuses everything. There's the alpha being told to be subordinate. If we joined a dog pack, instead of the other way around, all those crazy emotions would be gone, and with them most of our problems."

Sand was sticking to the damp undersides of her legs. Morgan's cock collected it as he pulled out, so the sand scoured her inside with each thrust. He was breathing harder, panting unintelligible words, louder, until his raw voice rose above the whisper, "Fucked, fucked, fucked," becoming a shout, *"We're fucked, I'm fucked, you're fucked, everybody and everything is fucked!"* And he finally collapsed.

Probably his searing headache was a double whammy—the sun shooting into his skull from above and the mule nailing his spine into his brain from below. Suzanne's voice flared like sun glare.

Like the swimming colors and black holes and blaring pyrotechnic strobe that he saw looking directly into the sun, her voice faded in and out, words lost in the quake of the mule's back, in the thundering that was either blood in his ears or wind somewhere in the canyon, in the staccato of his pulse, so that only every third or fourth word came through. "Values . . . sanctity . . . immediately . . . honorable . . . game . . . midlife crisis . . . therapy . . . superficial . . . twat . . ." Like listening to a rap song while you quickly plug and unplug your ears, an uncoordinated rhythm you couldn't possibly even walk to.

Or maybe the whole canyon undulated, writhed in dizzy confusion at its own polarity: a constant flash of contradictory ingredients crashing together—a mile of land that didn't go forward but *straight up or down,* from the fiercely bright, bone white summer sky to the bottomless shadows and quick cold water below. Bungee jumping from one extreme to the other—flying down, hitting the black shade like a convulsion and bouncing back up, the churn of jostled guts, teary blindness of eyes that couldn't focus fast enough on the smear of detail spinning into view from every angle—wouldn't be any different from this string of mules inching its way downward, back and forth along the sheer limestone wall.

Sounds that had been far away crowded up close to him. Children or women farther ahead on the trail, farther down in the canyon, singing *I'm happy when I'm hiking.* Twitter of tiny birds that flitted from bush to bush. Someone on the mule train blowing his nose. Drone of a single bee. Reverberation of a person on the rim calling for an echo to answer their long hello. Groan of saddle leather.

"You can answer me, Scott," Suzanne said, "I'd like to hear what you have to say."

He watched a fly ride on his saddle horn for three or four steps.

"Nothing more to say, nothing at all? You're just going to tell your wife of over twenty years that you're trading her in for someone new—nothing *else?* You don't have *anything* else to say to me? How about at least how old she is. What color hair and eyes? What does she do?" Suzanne spoke faster, gulping for air. "Is she beautiful, glamorous? Is she rich, interesting?" As her pitch became higher, thinner, the mule seemed to stumble a few times. A hawk screamed suddenly. "Does she enrich your intellectual or cultural life, collect art, discuss foreign movies . . . or is she a *dirty little girl?*" Suzanne's screech ripped like wind past his ears. "I knew it, I knew it, I knew it, oh, it's *easy* to honor your commitment, your promises, your vows right up *until* you find a slut who'll grab your whizzer more often than hold your hand . . . and you go blank, like a sixteen-year-old, like a pimple-faced *geek,* and have no memory whatsoever about the future, the past, plans . . . just throw away everything that was wholesome and solid—"

Something like a rock crashed into his cheek and jaw, Suzanne's voice replaced by the bray of a mule—*his* mule. As he jerked and fell sideways, then forward, the animal tossed its neck, bashed the back of its head between Scott's eyes, snapping him upright again. The mule was hopping or dancing somehow without going forward. Suzanne was turned completely around, her own mule stopped dead still, so close its butt was tucked into Scott's mule's chest. It almost seemed his mule was going to mount hers. She was holding her binoculars by the strap, her arm cocked—she swung and hit him again. He could almost hear the crack when the binoculars bashed into the top of his head. His mule continued shrieking, turned almost sideways on the trail, its back feet on the crumbly edge. Scott was gripping the saddle horn with both hands, but he couldn't find the stirrups with his feet. The mule's back was thumping, jolting against his ribs, Scott's legs flailed, feeling nothing but the empty canyon beneath, attached to the mule by just the safety strap like a lopsided pack. The binoculars hit him square in the face. A blast of darkness and silence. Then Scott's mule reared up before lunging forward. In a moment of frozen clarity, he could see the mule's neck stretched, ears flat, lips drawn back, big yellow teeth flashing. Suzanne's mule bolted, trotted ahead on the trail. Scott was still clinging to the saddle, both legs hanging off one side, a chorus of mules braying up and down the line, his own answering, louder than all the rest, scrambling for balance, trying to keep up while trying to kick him, to get rid of him, to send *him* over the edge before they *both* fell into the canyon.

As soon as he pulled out and got up, Fanny moved—silently, like a snake, sideways, without getting up off her back—so she was lying under the car. He could only see part of one shoulder, her side, the edge of one hip. Seated in the passenger seat, his feet outside, Morgan put on his underwear and pants. He lifted the jug of water from the backseat, filled his mouth, stood, then shot the mouthful out onto the dirt. Fanny didn't move.

He yawned loudly, then stretched, groaning. "Okay," he said, "time to go get help." He walked out away from the car where he could see a little more of Fanny, but still not her face. "Yessirree, time to go get help." He drew a line in the sand with one foot, running parallel to the freeway, then drew an arrow on both ends of the line. "Which way should I go?"

About six or eight huge motorcycles buzzed like chain saws going east on the freeway. But not one of the riders had long hair, a beard, or leather jacket. They all sat very erect behind their big windshields. All had helmets—blue and maroon and purple—that matched the color of their bikes and the luggage compartments built onto the sides.

"We could've told our grandchildren," he said, "how we were lost in the desert and survived by our wits." He went around the car to get the gas can from where he'd left it beside a signpost. The sign said SOFT SHOULDER. Then he went back to the car and put the can down close enough so she could've reached it from where she was lying. "That is," he said, "if you consider a time when you know exactly where you are as *being lost.*" He looked at her jeans hanging over the open passenger door. "So, I guess this is good-bye."

"What'll you do?"

"Gee, I think I'll walk to New York and audition for the Rockettes. By the time I get there, I'll have the legs for it."

A dog barked at them from a rusty pickup going slowly, loaded with old furniture. The dog was riding loose on top of a sofa. Morgan could see Fanny's hand picking up a little pile of fine sand, emptying it and scooping it up again.

"Why do you ask—do you care or just morbidly curious?" he said.

"I don't know."

"Well, hey, what happened to all the fight that was in you yesterday?"

"Do you care or just morbidly curious?"

"Touché, baby." He did a little softshoe step, bowed, then turned and left the roadside campsite behind him.

Things were cleaner and clearer, progress more consistent, goals simpler, motivation more logical without having to deal with some other person and her soft *human* temperament. I had gotten farther with the husky bitch in a month than Fanny would've in the dog's lifetime. I was nearly ready to bring her out at a trial, but there was another pressing matter. You see, biology is as rational as a charted training plan when it's not encumbered by sniveling or moping: The bitch had come into season again and was ready to be bred.

She was restrained in a tracking harness, tethered on both sides by leashes nailed to the ground. Her head was kept still with a wire muzzle and training collar fastened to a post pounded into the lawn that prevented her from moving her neck more than an inch or two. Her tail was bound to one hind leg with a spiral of masking tape. Whatever was right with this bitch's working and natural canine temperament, the glitch in her nature was that she still refused to stand for a stud. Maybe it had been the artificial insemination that had made her so disinterested in her puppies last time. Maybe some chemical reaction during the natural tie—a period of fifteen to twenty minutes long that prevents sperm from coming out until there's been enough time for the most viable cells to reach the eggs—spurred a bitch's instinct so that the maternal drive would kick in.

I got the stud from his pen. Not even full grown yet, his ribs hadn't sprung, bone still hadn't fully developed, adult coat maybe two or three years away, but already capable of producing sperm. I'd contacted all of the people who'd bought male pups from the last litter, tested all of them several times, and selected the one with enough of the prey drives and keenness, but not too aloof, not a loner.

The young male knew immediately how ripe the husky was. When he licked at her vulva, his lower jaw chattered. He poked at her butt, above her tail, with his nose—testing to see what her response to the mount would be. The first time he put one front paw on her back, the growling bitch sat, so I held her in a stand, my hands keeping her knees locked. The male dog was practically dancing on his toenails. His body was humping air. Unfortunately the courtship, however necessary it might have been to stimulating the right hormones, had to be bypassed. In two sessions with the husky loose in the yard, she'd lashed out at the stud in a snarling fury, chasing him off, keeping him out of range. He had to satisfy his urges by lifting his leg on the fence. He must've remembered that experience, because he was obviously hesitant to mount.

Keeping one arm rigid and extended under the bitch's loin so she couldn't sit, I patted the bitch's back and encouraged the male to get up there. He hopped in place, continued to burrow his nose in the fur just above her tail, then finally, with a bigger hop, locked around her loin with his front feet and began to thrust. With my free hand, I felt underneath, found the jabbing penis, and guided it to its target.

The bitch's snarl grew to a savage pitch, but penetration had already been achieved, and the tie was beginning. The two dogs would have to stay attached until the knot in the stud's penis went down. Much of the time, he would continue pumping sperm and other fluids. I carefully helped the stud put his front feet on the ground beside the bitch, then lifted one hind leg and had him step over the spot where their bodies were joined. His penis swiveled in place, then he was on all fours, attached tail to tail with his mother in the natural tie position. I squatted beside the two, keeping one hand on each dog's stomach, so I'd feel if they started to struggle or move too soon. The husky's low growl grew softer, then stopped. I reached up and unsnapped her collar from the post.

Isn't a canine pack a much less complicated world, unfettered by how any member *feels* about their place? The bitch now seemed totally unaware of her son standing rigidly behind her, attached to him not by an umbilical cord but by his penis. Pretty soon she was just looking around, panting, her keen eyes catching the slightest movement in the bushes, her nose twitching as she scented, obviously simply looking for something exciting to do when this business was finished. I lay my cheek against the warm, stiff fur on the bitch's back.

It would be admirable—or maybe just more dramatic, Renee admitted—to leave with less baggage than she'd arrived with. She had her career, her first agent, and all the opportunity and possibility the East Coast promised . . . maybe even, someday, choreography. Why bother to spend this petty time packing and shipping?

The walls in the living room were bare except for the big holes where the barres had been bolted. The futon folded and covered in its plastic bag, the stereo wrapped in towels and tucked into pillowcases. She filled shoe boxes with her tapes and compact discs, then started to wrap beer and wine bottle candleholders in tissue, but paused, looking at the green glass spattered with wax. Who the hell would drag this garbage across the country as though it meant anything? She got a trash bag, filled it, and left it on the curb.

In the bedroom, she made a quick survey. Sell this bed, the dresser, and nightstand—they weren't worth the trouble of hiring a mover. She'd already moved them from her girlhood bedroom in her parent's house to her college apartment, to Kay's house, back out of Kay's house, then here. No need to go any farther. Each place had been its own kind of nightmare, its own kind of necessary phase, but the furniture had played no part, had no nostalgic nicks or wistful stains. Once again, she was taking no one with her.

Through it all she wouldn't acknowledge the hot wire of pain in her knee.

She opened two suitcases on the floor beside the dresser and began loading sweatsuits, leotards, and t-shirts into one. At the bottom of the drawer, Renee found the little white box. She kneeled slowly, wincing, then caught herself. *Ignore it.* The neighborhood had been extraordinarily quiet this morning. No arguments coming from open windows, no thumping car stereos, no sirens. Far up the street the repeated beep of the trash truck's backup warning. She opened the box and held the ear cuff in two fingers. She'd never noticed that each fingernail on the tiny hand was painted red. What was the date—the end of July? The gift would only be seven months late. She got up and sat on the bed, still holding the ear cuff in two fingers, reached for the phone, heard the dial tone as she lifted the receiver. The trash truck was getting closer, the neighborhood no longer very quiet, dogs barking, and metal cans clanking on the sidewalk. Why was it two minutes ago she probably could've dialed the number in the dark, pushed the buttons without the numbers even vocalizing in her mind? But now her hand didn't even know where to start. The trash truck hovered right outside, using its mechanism to push the collected rubbish up out of the way. She put the phone down and used both hands to fix the ear cuff onto her own ear.

CHAPTER **9**
In Hand

Finally there was a moment when he wasn't woozy with painkillers, dead asleep, being bathed or fed or helped to the bathroom. They'd said don't try to talk. A ridiculous suggestion. They'd helped him dress and left him perched here upright on the bed while they went for a wheelchair to take him outside to a taxi that would take him to the airport. Left him in easy reach of the telephone.

But after one ring, there was a series of clicks, the sound of an open line, then a beep. "Hello? Fanny? Is your machine on?" The words had to slide out of him like each was written on a piece of paper and slipped through a crack under a closed door. "Something happened . . . is this working? I don't know, so I'll just go ahead. I had a little accident." Talking not only required the jaw to move, it meant breathing a little deeper, a little quicker. He stopped to let the shooting needles in his taped rib cage subside. The phone beeped again then clicked off.

He redialed. The same clicks, the same dead air, the first beep. "Fanny—I hope you can understand this. I think I sound like someone's pressing a gun to my face. I'm kind of banged up. I just want to get home and get my dog and—" The second beep.

On the third call, he tried speaking faster, but it only seemed to make him slower. "I'll tell you what happened in the Grand Canyon when I get home. Luckily there was a safety strap on the saddle—"

He was breathing hard, making a little sound in his chest, holding himself around his broken ribs. He closed his eyes while the fourth call was connected, while the phone rang, while the machine clicked. "It's me, again . . . continued . . . anyway, I still can hardly believe this—I knew it would be hard to tell her, but never imagined anything like this—"

He redialed so fast he got a busy signal. He closed his eyes—the only part of his body that didn't ache. Then dialed again. "Hi again. I don't even know whether it was yesterday or the day before . . . it's so unbelievable. I tried so hard to . . . I don't know . . . make everything come out right. It's weird how much I miss my dog. I wish I'd left her with you after all. She would've loved this trip . . . far more than I did, believe me . . . but then she'd be going home with Suzanne now, so it's a good thing I didn't—"

Tears stung in his eyes. "Dammit, Fanny, I knew it would hurt her to go through this breakup, but . . . I wanted to ease her through it. I tried to do what would make the people around me at least content, if not happy. I just didn't want anyone to be . . . I tried to fix it for everyone. Instead, now *nobody's* content. Sadie's in a *cage.* And you—I don't know what you're doing. But I hope, at least, that you'll understand, eventually . . ." He was speaking in the kind of loud voice someone would use at an outdoor pay phone, as though having to be heard over the singing pain. But the machine wasn't giving the second beep. "I don't know if you're getting this, Fanny, I just . . . I was just trying to do what I thought was right. Do you realize how *easy* it is to make our dogs happy? Is that why we want our dogs and miss our dogs when we're without them, because it's so easy to make them happy?" There was a string of clicks, then, instead of a beep, the connection fell off into a dial tone. Scott didn't hang up. "But I didn't only miss Sadie," he murmured, "I . . . thought about you."

A cheerful nurse arrived with the wheelchair, took the phone from him, and hung it up. "You haven't been talking, have you? Just pretending, I hope."

Every clock in the house was flashing a time that made no sense. One blinked exactly noon or midnight and never changed. The others strobed at her hysterically, asking how long had it taken her to hitch into El Centro and take a bus home? Three hours or thirteen? Three days or three weeks? Was the sun coming up or going down? Had her puking nausea on the bus actually been time changing speeds? Does queasy vision spin to rush *ahead* a day, or warp and blur to paddle backwards? The old VCR flashed ERROR in its neon green letters. The phone machine pulsated PF. None of the machines were changed or corrected as Fanny passed through the rooms. She drank sour milk from a carton in the refrigerator, rushed to the sink to vomit again.

She loaded the bathroom shelf with cosmetics—including some stage makeup she'd borrowed in college for a Halloween party. She had no memory of what she'd masqueraded as. And she hadn't even thought of this makeup the day the three of them talked about how they would dress up with their dogs for a costume parade at one of the local dog shows. Scott said he'd come as an English hunter, but his dog was already prepared the way she was. Likewise, he'd said, if Doreen came as Little Red Riding Hood and came with her wolf, the dog was already dressed. Fanny had bought a clown suit made for a dog, so Scott decided *she* should dress as a high-wire acrobat, a glittery body suit and stiff tutu, ballet slippers, hair slicked back as though in a bun, bright red dot on each cheek.

But today the necessary disguise was suburban housewife.

The skin tone base was like thin, creamy mud between her fingers. Immediately reminiscent of the color and consistency of very early puppy diarrhea when they'd been overfed. She stopped to retch silently, neck bent, then raised her eyes, continued to smear the slippery brown liquid on her face. Not watching her fingers. Looking into her own eyes. Seeing herself another day in the park when—Doreen telling a story of a dog dying in a fall from a cliff in an attempt to save his human partner—they'd each clutched their pets silently for a moment, pulling the dogs' panting faces close to their own, then looking at each other in a weirdly solemn exchange before the impatient dogs broke free and bounded away, teeth bared in play masks as they wrestled and ran. "So much for *our* dogs' devotion if we're ever in trouble." Someone had said that. But *who*?

There were still freckles lightly visible. The dark spots under her eyes and the surrounding white circles caused by sunglasses were also not successfully covered by the base makeup. Blemishes. A small scar on her chin. All still showed. She opened the stage pancake and applied a layer. It provided a clean surface for the blusher. Plumberry, it was called. For winter complexions. Wasn't it July yet? The blinking clocks didn't know. There were probably thousands of people at the beach getting their blush from the sun. She'd never used liquid eyeliner. Her hand wasn't steady, the black line jumped away from the edge of her lid, so she drew thicker lines to cover the mistakes. The brush touched her eyeball, only a momentary sting, no tears. In the palette of eye shadow shades, she scrubbed the applicator in Ultramarine Blue, coated both eyelids, swept a wing of color out to meet the tip of her brow. Then added Sunset Violet above the blue to the rim of her brows. Cherry Jubilee or Frosted Fruit Punch lipstick. Blended, they made a color like beets—or a beating heart red—but there was no taste, of fruit or beets or blood, when she touched her tongue to her lips, although her stomach roiled again. She closed her eyes and shuddered. Had she never looked like a *wife* before?

Lacy had worn her clown suit once. Fanny had lain on the sofa and watched Scott dress the husky. Lacy's gray-and-white masked face smiled snidely at her from under the pink-and-yellow clown hat, her front paws danced in the silly pantaloon leggings with pom-poms on the feet that she immediately ate off. Then the dog had used her feet to wipe the hat off her head, and shook it as though killing a rabbit.

Her hair was still a problem. She wet it, added gel, made two slick pointed sideburns beside each ear, plastered a fringe of bangs on her forehead, combed the rest straight back behind her ears, fitting it to the shape of her head and neck. If she couldn't look like somebody's wife, maybe she'd pass as a busy businessman's secretary.

She had some jeans hanging on a hook for several weeks now with two of Lacy's muddy paw prints still on the leg. After putting on the jeans, she stopped dressing, got out a phone book, and began listing addresses of kennels. Just before she left the house, she replaced the jeans with black silk evening pants she'd bought long ago to wear to the dance company productions, put her feet into the new black heels, and finished the outfit with a white blouse with a gathered lace collar that she used for catering assignments.

It was apparently around midday, and traffic got steadily heavier as she went one by one to boarding kennels, her path like radar radiating in bigger and bigger circles around the area of Scott's apartment. After the fourth or fifth try, she found his spaniel. A handwritten and signed letter on his business letterhead easily sprung the spaniel from the cage into Fanny's custody. Leaving the kennel's front desk, hearing the sound of her heels, like the toenails of the dog, the clerk singing "Bye-bye, Sadie," Fanny thought she might be fainting and floating gently to the ground. But she must've kept moving through the spell of vertigo and gotten the key into the lock of the rental car on one try.

The barely discernible trail led precariously down from the cliffs to the isolated nude beach. There was also a groomed, maintained nature trail along the top of the cliffs, with fenced-off lookout points. A sign warned that the path *down* the cliffs had not been put there by the parks department, was at-your-own-risk and not even advisable. She didn't use a leash, instead held the spaniel by her collar as they stood on the cliffs, the sun leaning toward the west, with anywhere from one to three hours of daylight remaining. The afternoon wind was already stiff and pungent. Ordinarily her hair would've been lashing back and forth, becoming matted with the damp salty air. But the gel held fast. The spaniel braced and leaned into the wind, her nose up, nostrils twitching. Her ears flew back. Barefoot, Fanny stepped onto the little path, keeping the spaniel close beside her.

At first the trail seemed barely to go downhill at all. But the grade must've been steeper than it felt, because not too far along, she already couldn't easily be seen by anyone up on top, where the sign was. A rock jutted out on the side of the path, a perfect diving platform if the ocean had come right up to splash against the bottom of the cliffs, but it didn't—the nude beach was between the bottom of the cliffs and the water. Fanny could see waves breaking on the sand, postage stamp blankets, finger-sized people, but she couldn't see the bottoms of the cliffs straight down below as she sat straddling the protruding rock.

The splash of briny air soothed her spinning head. Her right arm was crooked around the spaniel's neck, her left hand holding the spaniel's collar. The dog's head held tight against Fanny's ribs, the rest of her standing behind Fanny on the rock. The dog wasn't panting hard, but when her normal breathing shifted to scenting, Fanny could feel the pulse of air in the animal's ribs. An updraft brought the putrid odor of gulls' nests from the edges of the cliffs just below where she sat. Her stomach rolled. The dog's ears were quivering and alert, her body tensed and poised, her eyes steady and trained on the gulls floating on air currents, rising on the updrafts without beating a wing. As they glided past, their heads turned or cocked to look at Fanny and the dog. The same way Lacy had turned to look as Doreen guided her away, but Lacy's weird light eyes had held no panic.

The spaniel stepped forward, onto Fanny's leg. "So, you're not *scared?*" Fanny could hardly hear her own words. It seemed so quiet here, but the surf far below was like the roar of a freeway. And up on the ridge behind her, wind rattled the eucalyptus, whispered and moaned in the centuries-old gnarled pines. Between gusts, fragments of voices flickered, like stars glinting through a passing broken storm. The dog made high-pitched whistling sounds, then poked at Fanny's cheek with her nose.

"Is something wrong with us, Sadie?" When she spoke, she could feel how the dog's wagging stump tail made her whole back wiggle.

Under all the high and wild noise of the surf, wind, and gulls, which one of them was listening to hear Scott's footstep crunch on the path behind her? Which one of them *imagined* his return? If he was suddenly warm and tight against her back, straddling the rock with his legs outside hers, fingers laced together on her belly, under her breasts—then *she'd* be the one held tight, turning to press her nose and mouth against *his* cheek, quivering with some sort of sheer energy, unaware that with every breath she was sighing a little whine—her body *howling.* But wouldn't it be just an animal instinct, surging *not* because of ambition or betrayal, or even love?

Fanny grabbed the dog's upper forelegs with both hands, digging underneath the animal's elbows. Trusting, Sadie leaped voluntarily as Fanny pulled her up and yanked her forward. "Which did you miss most, Sadie, chasing, sniffing, digging, or *him?*" With the momentum of the dog's oblivious leap, Fanny swung the dog out over the cliff. Then the dangling dog's toenails clawed frantically at the slanting underside of the rock, her head strained toward Fanny's face. Most of the spaniel's body was out of sight, suspended over the edge. Fanny screamed, *"Why're we so easy to leave?"* The dog's kicking hind legs braced suddenly against the side of the rock, and she stopped flailing but stayed quivering in Fanny's hands.

"C'mon, Sadie. *Get mad!*" As Fanny shook the dog by her upper forelegs, the dog just strained farther forward, stretching the loose skin on her throat. "He left you in jail—why aren't you *furious?* Because you knew he'd finally show up to get you out?" The dog's eyes bulged, showing white almost all the way around. Her lips stretched back toward her ears. Her rear legs ran a treadmill in the air, rasping against the rock, then her feet braced there again. "Don't you want to make him *sorry* he didn't keep you with him wherever he went? To make him think twice next time? Or maybe you just don't want to *have* to be someone's best friend anymore? Don't you ever wonder *why* you don't want anything more than *that?*" The spaniel began puffing short breaths out the sides of her lips. Her body was vibrating. Her front legs, still held at the elbows by Fanny's fists, were rigid as though splinted. The birds were all gone, the wind eased, someone's portable stereo throbbed way down on the beach. A Frisbee glinted in the setting sun, and a black dog charged into the surf to get it. Suddenly Sadie heaved a sigh and rested her chin on the tip of the rock. Her bulging, staunch eyes softened, never left Fanny's face.

The grass was high, so she asked the neighbor to start the lawn mower for her. After mowing, she edged with hand clippers then swept the bricks and patio all the way around the lawn. Scott probably wouldn't be able to do much yard work for a while, but she didn't want him to have to face a jungle of overgrown bushes and weeds when he was well again. The hedges needed trimming, the azaleas needed to be fed and have their old blossoms removed, the roses needed spraying. She sat on the patio with a soda. The pottery wind chime she'd bought in Zion would be pretty here, and she'd always remember to take it inside in the winter to keep the shiny yellow-and-orange coyote-shaped plates from breaking in a high wind. But she would wait to put it up, like all the other things she'd bought on the trip—the authentic kachina doll in a Plexiglas display case, the hand-woven shawl, the big rattlesnake skull she had purchased after seeing Scott pick it up two or three times as he perused a gift shop in Canyonlands, and a picture of red rock buttes made of colored sand sandwiched between two pieces of glass. They were all set out carefully on the dining room table. There was no hurry. Scott would know how he wanted to display them in the house.

The restraining order had been delivered to her that morning. She'd answered the doorbell, thinking, *it COULD be—*

Soon the lawn furniture where she was sitting would be in full sunshine. Her legs could use the color, but, on the other hand, the furniture needed new upholstery because direct sun had faded and rotted the material last year. She could probably re-cover the frames herself. It would be a good project for the next few weeks. Last year Scott had talked about building a gazebo in the backyard on the patio, as sun protection, as a pleasant place for her to read or crochet. It would have flower boxes all around the outside for pansies and marigolds. The new wind chime would be perfect hanging from an edge of the gazebo. A nice place for supper during the hottest months. The dog would appreciate the shade too, instead of having to come in the house from noon to two every afternoon on weekends and staying in the garage all day during the week. In a few weeks, Suzanne's legs would be tanned, the furniture re-upholstered, the garden brought back under control, and Scott would probably start building the gazebo when he came home.

Exhausted by some sort of empty thing that wasn't exactly sorrow and not exactly fear, he sat in his car in front of the apartment building, waiting for anything—wretched tears or his own voice howling or his fist splintering the glass. But he just sat there. He closed his eyes to embellish the most glorious self-pitying thoughts he could imagine: how he'd been attacked by his wife and now abandoned by everyone and everything, even his dog, *gone,* and despite his restraining order against her, he would have to face Suzanne again to get the dog back. But he didn't have the balls, not now—maybe *that* was actually the vacant thing keeping his numb ass in the car seat instead of . . . *what?* What else should he be doing? Going to Fanny to lay his face in her lap, to cry through his aching clenched teeth, *My dog is gone and I'm afraid to try to get her back?* Would she touch his hair with her fingertips, cradle his head, caress the new scar where the dog bite stitches had been removed, bend to lay her cheek against his wired jaw? Or spit in his ear and stand, let his head fall like a rock?

His head rolled against the back of the seat, then he opened his eyes, staring out the passenger window, almost a relief finally to be able to turn his neck to the right without Suzanne's profile against the window. And even if he'd ever tried to look out the window on her side, what Suzanne's head had been blocking for three weeks was visible to him now: smeared, dried nose prints on the glass. Fanny used to call it Sadie's sketchbook. Hadn't they one time fondled each other in the front seats while Sadie lay sleeping in the backseat after a workout, Fanny's husky likewise quiet for once in her car parked in an adjacent spot? Fanny had said they should add their own prints to Sadie's nose smear art on the window glass. Had she gone ahead and smeared his semen on the window? If he'd had Sadie's nose, he would've caught a faint scent of it and intuitively smiled. If *Suzanne* had been a dog, she could've smelled it too, and would've known for herself instead of having to be told. But he'd always washed the car once a week, so if Fanny had finger painted on the glass, it was long gone. Sadie always added new prints after every washing, so these were from her last trip—to the boarding kennel.

It wasn't even as if he should be *mourning* the dog. They'd said at the kennel that a woman had picked her up. It had to be Suzanne. But even the words he'd planned to comfort Fanny when he saw her were of no use to him: *Think how horribly awful you'd feel if Lacy had died in a fight with that wolf. At least it isn't that bad, at least you know where she is.* Sadie wasn't dead, she was back in her own yard. He knew where Fanny's dog was too. In fact, he probably knew where she was this very second. He checked his watch. Almost 1:00 P.M. A time the parks were still empty of kids, plenty of room on the big stretches of grass for dogs and pens and equipment.

He hadn't spoken since talking to Fanny's phone machine from the hospital. So he practiced while driving to the park, starting with saying the alphabet. First his voice cracked and gurgled from disuse. He cleared his throat, hummed the alphabet tune, then spoke the letters through the wiring on his jaw. Doreen might assume the wire, as well as his stiff movement from the taped ribs, were the result of the dog attack. Let her.

He saw the A-frame on the grass from a block away. Naturally his brightly painted equipment wasn't there with it. He saw the blur of a gray dog climb the A-frame, pause at the top, then bolt down the other side. He heard the shrieks of praise, a sharp command to drop. He parked so that his car was almost concealed behind the rest room building, but he could still see the setup, and when he rolled his window down, he could easily hear the patter of talk as the husky heeled beside Doreen.

Then he saw Fanny in a rental car. It was parked alongside the curb where the grass met the sidewalk, far enough down the street that an absorbed Doreen appeared to be unaware. His hand habitually reached for the binoculars that had been wedged between his seat and Suzanne's. At the same time, his jaw remembered the last time he'd seen them, and obviously they hadn't been returned to the car. The only thing he could find was a glossy brochure for Arches National Park. He rolled it and looked through it to augment his vision. There was someone sitting in the car with Fanny.

He left his car, closing the door softly, then began walking away from Doreen along the sidewalk, going clockwise around the park, a circle that would bring him around to Fanny's car, approaching from the rear. He had to walk slowly. Each step jarred his jaw, which felt as if it was made of cast iron and might crunch the rest of his skull if he stumbled or brought his foot down too heavily. He began breathing hard very quickly, even at the slow, careful pace, because the tape on his ribs was tight. He panted shallowly.

The layers of dirt on the rear window made it impossible to see who was in the car with Fanny after he came around the far end of the park, turned right, and began to get nearer. He didn't know until he was beside the car, and by that time the spaniel was already standing on Fanny's lap, pressing her nose to the cracked open window, singing her tuneless dog melody, the same continuous whine of joy he'd always been greeted with, whether he'd been away two hours or two weeks. Behind the quivering, sputtering, anxious head of his dog, Fanny's face looked gravely out the window.

He put the tips of his fingers into the cracked window for Sadie to lick. A gush of relief washing over him, all his tensed muscles suddenly breathing easier, his exhaustion turning into sweet drowsi-

ness, as though he'd found Fanny and his dog nestled in a soft feath-
erbed and he was being invited to crawl in, curl up, and doze in
complete solace.

But Fanny's face was smutty, streaks of dirt on both cheeks, her
eyes heavy and half closed. A twinge of chill came back over him.
He said, "Hi," or at least tried to. It came out of his clenched teeth
fuzzy and indistinct. It wasn't until he went around to the other side
of the car and got in to sit beside her that he saw the putty color of
her skin, the beads of mascara on her lashes, slashed lines of black
outlining each eye, powdery color under the dirt on her cheeks, lipstick mostly scraped away by her teeth.

"I got your dog back for you," she said.

"So I see. Thanks." The spaniel was on his lap now, but it hurt to
have to jerk his head back and forth, trying to avoid being smashed
in the face by her muzzle or a paw. "Here, Sadie." He took her collar and encouraged her to jump into the backseat. "I don't suppose
it means you got my message?"

She shook her head, examining her fingernails, her face bent over
her lap. "You're banged up."

"Yeah, a little. I'll tell you about it."

"Later. Okay?" She glanced up into the rearview mirror, biting a
nail. "What a goofball your dog is. She didn't even know she missed
you till she saw you just now."

Scott reached over the seat and caressed his dog's ear. He saw
Fanny take her eyes off his dog in the mirror and settle her gaze on
her husky, out on the lawn, scaling a wall jump with a dumbbell in
her mouth. "*She* misses you," he said softly.

"No, she doesn't know she misses me yet."

"I missed you."

"Yeah," she echoed.

"Look at you." He said it smiling, as best he could. He took out
a handkerchief. With a hand on the back of her head, he wiped at
her face with the dry handkerchief. "What is this shit—it doesn't
come off."

"Ouch, you're scouring my skin away." Her voice lost its ghosty
dullness.

"Well, if you'd cry, I'd have some wetness to help wash you."

"I'm not going to cry. What I'm going to do is start designing again. I have to. *Fantasy Designs.* How's that? I'll accept your offer. For a start-up loan—you can be a ground floor investor."

"Can't I be anything else . . . too?"

She was scraping mascara off her lashes with her thumbnail, stopped, and looked at him. "I should've trusted you'd be back. But not *needed* you to come back. Not in order to do my work. Lacy obviously doesn't need *me* to make her love to do what she does."

"Don't start sounding like Doreen."

"You mean, like, *Why can't people be like dogs—THEIR drives aren't complicated, frustrated, thwarted, warped, or perverted by relationships with the other members of their pack?* It's true, and, unfortunately, we're *not* dogs. But no, I don't want to be like Doreen. She goes too far. I think it's probably okay to *like* being with someone."

"Things will be different this time, Fanny."

"I *know.*" She got out of the car.

———————

As she crossed the sidewalk, Scott called, "Hey," and she turned. He'd unrolled the window, his spaniel was on his lap again, and both their heads were leaning out of the car, both gently jousting for position to see around each other. "Want me to come with you?"

"No, wait a minute."

She went across the grass, up to the unmarked perimeter of what would be a show ring, and stood as if a spectator outside the fluttering ring ropes. The husky, dumbbell in her mouth, had her back to Fanny. Doreen was invisible on the other side of the A-frame, but her voice chirped "Climb," and the husky pushed off her powerful hind legs and up the nearly vertical side of the A-frame. A vocal celebration of praise erupted on the other side of the A-frame, then Doreen came around holding the husky by her collar. Doreen stopped abruptly. The husky, seeing Fanny, leapt forward but was restrained by the collar Doreen still held, so her lunge was broken off, frozen—the dog stayed standing on hind legs, leaning forward against the collar, straining and wheezing. Doreen had to take two jerky steps to keep her balance. Then the dog started hopping on her hind legs like a circus horse, pulling Doreen along with her, until Doreen let her go. The husky landed once on all four feet before leaving the ground again, this time crashing into Fanny, who fell on her butt and rolled to her back, covering her face with both arms, the dog frantically circling her, digging at her shoulders and ribs with her front feet, growling and singing and barking all at once. Finally Fanny was able to gasp, "Okay, okay, okay, okay!" The husky sat beside her, one paw still waving, digging at air, as though to pull Fanny closer. Fanny got up.

"I've come for Lacy," Fanny said.

"I expected you to eventually . . . was wondering what was taking you so long."

The dog put a paw on Fanny's knee, then, like climbing a ladder, rose on her hind legs, put her other front foot on Fanny's waist. When her feet slid back to the ground, the husky buried her face against Fanny's stomach. Fanny cupped an ear in each hand, softly running her thumbs up and down the insides of the ear leather.

"Know why your bitch is so good?" Doreen said. "Know what we forgot about when picking the best puppy?"

"*We?*"

Doreen laughed. "Anyway, she has the courage, the drive, and desire, but I *can* keep her in hand. Maybe sometimes she's on the verge of not being there, but she's still *aware* she's part of a team— she *doesn't* just follow her urges and forget all else."

From the car on the street, Scott's spaniel began baying out the window. Lacy stood at attention, charged halfway across the grass toward the car, stood at attention again, ears pricked forward. Scott opened the door and the spaniel blasted out, running like a lure across the grass past Lacy. In a second, the husky was also at top speed. The two dogs ran parallel as though harnessed, making sharp turns and zigzags. Scott stood on the sidewalk leaning against the car. Doreen said, "Okay, make a liar outta me, Lacy."

Together they turned slowly in place, Fanny's vertigo wafting, watching the dogs play in a wide circumference, never going farther away than fifty yards in any direction. One of them turned wrong and their bodies crashed. The husky landed on her side, the spaniel on top.

"Oh, god," Doreen muttered, then said, "be careful with her for a while. She should be pregnant."

For a second, there was only the sound of high-pitched yapping, purring growls, and their feet running full tilt across the grass.

"Damn," Fanny said softly. "I might be too."

Doreen was holding her hair out of her face with both hands. "So . . . you ended up alpha, huh?"

Fanny laughed, "God, if only alpha could mean never being *able* to be so stupid again."

The bitches wrestled, then untangled to run again, snapping at the air around each other's heads. Scott left the car and began approaching. Doreen picked up a dumbbell, tossed it from one hand to the other. Fanny smiled, tilted her face to the sun, nausea dwindling into simple equilibrium. The two dogs raced huge parallel circles around the three people.